THE VINYL DETECTIVE

FLIP BACK

ANDREW CARTMEL

TITAN BOOKS

The Vinyl Detective: Flip Back
Print edition ISBN: 9781785658983
E-book edition ISBN: 9781785658990

Published by Titan Books
A division of Titan Publishing Group Ltd
144 Southwark Street, London SE1 0UP

First edition: May 2019
10 9 8 7 6 5 4 3 2 1

A CIP catalogue record for this title is available from the British Library.

Printed and bound by CPI Group (UK) Ltd, Croydon, CR0 4YY

Did you enjoy this book? We love to hear from our readers.
Please email us at readerfeedback@titanemail.com or write to us at
Reader Feedback at the above address.

To receive advance information, news, competitions, and exclusive offers online,
please sign up for the Titan newsletter on our website:

www.titanbooks.com

For Scott Cochrane, with thanks for a lifetime of friendship.

1. WHITE MULE, BLACK DOG

I've been shot at before.

I had hoped it would never happen again.

The way it came about this time was, like so many misadventures in my life, largely thanks to the intervention of one Jordon Tinkler.

"How long have we been friends?" said Tinkler.

"Here it comes," said Nevada, from the kitchen. My sweetheart tends towards the cynical.

"Am I not your *best* friend?" continued Tinkler, ignoring her and giving me his finest beseeching look. It made him look like a cute little puppy who just at that very instant has contracted rabies. You can sort of see the mad force of the virus swimming up in those big, moist eyes.

I sighed. "What do you want?"

"Yes, what are you after this time, Tinkler?" said Nevada. She came in from the kitchen carrying a bottle of wine by the neck in one hand and in the other three glasses, held by their stems in an untidy but somehow elegant cluster. She set the glasses deftly down on the table without so much as a clink and then proceeded to pour the wine in a precise steady stream from a considerable height, standing over the first glass with the bottle neatly aimed. The wine poured in a graceful golden flow and she didn't spill a drop.

"What is this?" said Tinkler. "White wine?"

"Don't try and change the subject," said Nevada. She finished filling the glass and started on the next.

"But you only ever drink *red* wine!" exclaimed Tinkler, all innocence.

Nevada corrected him, frowning with concentration as she poured. "I only ever drink *Rhône* wine. Or Rhône style. And this is from one of my favourite Rhône producers."

"But it's white."

"Yes it is. In fact, it's called the White Mule." She finished filling the second glass and moved the bottle over to the third. The pale golden wine glugged softly into the Riedel crystal. "But stop milking it, Tinkler. What kind of favour are you sniffing around for?" As she said the word 'sniffing' she picked up a glass and held it happily to her nose.

"A favour?" said Tinkler. "You wrong me. I just want to hire your boyfriend here to do what he does best."

"Find a record?" All of a sudden I was interested.

"Yes. I can't believe I'm saying this, but I want to hire the Vinyl Detective. You do realise it was me who first thought up that name?"

"No it wasn't," I said. I remembered getting the idea, standing in front of the machine that printed the business cards. Late at night, in an airport, during the grinding, endless red-eye wait between planes.

In many ways it had been a bad idea and had led me to bad places.

On the other hand, it had led me to Nevada…

Now she stopped sniffing the bouquet of the wine and smiled at me. She knew I was thinking of her, the little minx. She handed me a glass.

It was cool in my hand. I gave the honey-coloured liquid a tentative sniff. It smelled good. That was about the extent of my expertise. "What about me?" demanded Tinkler, and she handed him a glass. I took a sip from mine.

It was creamy and complex and some other adjectives I had learned from Nevada.

"So," she said, turning to Tinkler. "How much are you going to pay him, to find this record that you want so badly?"

"Jesus, you're so *mercenary*."

"I'm his business manager," said Nevada. "It's my job."

"Don't worry. I'll pay you. You'll get paid."

"You'd better. We'd better. How much?"

"A fair amount."

Nevada sighed. "That doesn't sound very promising, Tinkler. Suddenly I'm not sure we can even fit you in. As a matter of fact, we were thinking of taking a holiday. A nice, long holiday."

"You can't go on holiday. Your cats are too neurotic to be safely left on their own."

"We have friends who will look after them. Proper friends. Not like you."

Tinkler turned to me imploringly with his big, but slightly

crazed, puppy eyes. "Oh, come on. Find my record. For *me*."

"How much are you going to pay us?" Nevada was remorseless.

A look of glum resignation came over Tinkler's face. He realised despite all his attempts at evasion he was going to have to talk turkey. "Depends on the condition. Obviously. But let's say…" His forehead furrowed with simian calculation. "Fifty per cent of the median *Record Collector* guide price."

"Seventy-five per cent," said Nevada instantly, despite not having any idea what the median *Record Collector* guide price might be.

"Oh, for Christ's sake," said Tinkler. "Don't I get the friends and family rate? Don't I rate it? Don't I rate the rate?"

"What is it?" I said. They could thrash out the gory financial details later. They both looked at me blankly. "What are you after?" I said, patiently. "What is the record?"

Of course, nothing can ever be straightforward.

And it all began to get a lot more complicated on the very first day I started working for Tinkler. It was a bright winter morning with a cold bite in the air. I caught the bus across Hammersmith Bridge in the low, streaming sunlight and then took the Tube to Shepherd's Bush. From here I worked the charity shops eastwards towards Holland Park.

It is still possible to find astonishingly rare records at bargain prices in charity shops. Of course most of these shops have resident 'experts' to sift through their stock and pull out any choice items for premium pricing. In practice this means anything by the Beatles or Elvis being assigned astronomical price tags regardless of their scarcity or collectability. But the same chump who thinks a digitally remastered reissue of the King's greatest hits on wafer-thin late 1980s vinyl is worth a small fortune might well let a British Vogue yellow label release of a Sonny Rollins Contemporary slip through for a pittance.

And these treasures do turn up, going for a song, to be seized on by someone like yours truly, with trembling hands and a corresponding song of gratitude in their heart.

Today, however, the god of charity shops didn't smile and my search had yielded nothing—or rather, it had yielded a nice early Stan Getz on a French Verve reissue. But no trace of what Tinkler was after.

I wasn't worried. It was early days yet. And checking the charity shops was just part of my strategy. I was also going to be visiting the record dealers.

I started with Lenny at the Vinyl Vault. I endured his questions about Nevada, questions that were transparently designed to run a health check on our relationship. Lenny was smitten with Nevada and was just waiting for the first sign of trouble between us, at which point he planned to swoop. In so far as someone like Lenny is capable of swooping.

But while he was picking my brains about Nevada, I was picking his brains about a record label called Hex-a-Gone.

"Hexagon?" said Lenny.

"Hex-a-Gone. Like they once had a hex but now it's gone."

"Oh, yeah, they had a picture of a hexagon on their label, didn't they?"

"Yes. It was a multi-layered piece of wordplay."

But Lenny wasn't listening to me. I had pushed his buttons and now he was like a computer helplessly and automatically disgorging facts. "Late 1960s folk label, which was absorbed by one of the majors. Was it Atlantic? Anyway, their stuff is very rare. Very collectable. Expensive."

This last bit was just the boilerplate, so to speak, and Lenny would have added it in response to any enquiry, in an attempt to soften his customer up for whatever price outrage he was planning to perpetrate. Now he went on for a while about how costly and sought-after Hex-a-Gone records were. Which was useful to me, because I soon learned that he had no idea what constituted the most desirable artists or rarest albums.

This was just what I'd been hoping. It confirmed that, in addition to finding gems in charity shops, it was still also possible to get terrific records from dealers at bargain prices, providing they didn't know what they were doing.

Which, as in most forms of human endeavour, was about ninety per cent of the time.

I left Lenny's, buoyant and optimistic about my prospects of finding Tinkler's record. I was making my way along the winding back streets of Notting Hill when suddenly I had the oddest feeling.

It was a quiet street and I'd been on my own for the last couple of minutes, walking through this peaceful backwater in the pearly light of a winter's day. Everyone had gone into work and no one was coming out yet for lunch.

But now, alone in the cobbled street, I had the sudden intense feeling that I was being watched.

I stopped and, despite myself, looked behind me. There was no one there.

I scanned the street. Blank white walls, black iron gates, windows with elegant curtains drawn tightly shut. Apart from some windowsill knickknacks—three beige pottery dogs and a benignly smiling brass Buddha—I was entirely alone.

I started walking again. But I couldn't throw off the sensation that I was being followed.

I've begun to regard paranoia as an inevitable consequence of what I do for a living. Or at the very least an occupational hazard. And I've also begun to listen to my instincts. I'm not mystically inclined or a believer in the sixth sense or anything similar—I leave all that to Nevada—but better safe than sorry is my motto. And right now my instincts were telling me to walk more quickly, get the hell away from this lonely back street and out in the open, among other people.

To find a crowd and lose myself in it.

I began walking as fast as I could, across Pembridge Road. Then I turned into Pembridge Gardens and hurried towards Notting Hill Gate. I kept up the pace even though I couldn't see anyone following me. At least there were other people around now. I began to relax, but as I was crossing the street towards the Tube station a big black cab came rumbling out of nowhere, loudly blaring its horn. The noise spooked me and I turned, angry, ready to curse the driver.

But behind the steering wheel of the taxi, smiling at me, was Agatha DuBois-Kanes.

* * *

Better known to her friends as Clean Head, Agatha must be London's most stylish black cab driver. "Careful how you parse that sentence," was her standard comment at this observation. Because she is, if not black then at least mixed race, the sort of beautiful blend of esoteric genes which argues for the total enthusiastic mongrelisation of the human race, and the sooner the better.

She also has a shaved head, which is why we call her Clean Head.

It was warm and snug sitting behind her, on the big comfortable leather seat in the back of her taxi as we drove along the A402 towards Bayswater.

And safe.

The sense of being watched had abated as soon as I climbed into the cab.

"Thanks for giving me a lift," I said. Clean Head didn't reply. The intercom was on, but she was concentrating on the traffic and wouldn't speak until she deemed it safe to relinquish her full attention from the task at hand. It was a reassuring trait in a driver.

Despite everything London's world-class vehicular congestion was throwing at her, we were rapidly approaching the corner of Queensway. This would be a good place for me to catch the Tube.

The thing was, I couldn't at the moment afford a cab ride all the way into the West End, particularly in the slow-motion traffic currently on display. Any spare funds I had were earmarked for our supper, the cats' supper, and—naturally—records.

Of course, Clean Head wouldn't necessarily charge

me for the ride, but I didn't feel I could deprive her of a paying customer, of which there were plenty, judging by the number of people leaning out to hail our taxi, then seeing the dimmed TAXI sign and subsiding in disappointment.

"Anywhere up here would be good," I said, reaching for the door. "I can hop out."

"Just sit back and chill," Clean Head said, in a relaxed, droll voice that told me the traffic pattern no longer required her undivided attention. "You're not hopping anywhere."

"But you could get a paying fare."

"You *are* a paying fare." She glanced back in response to my startled silence. Her eyes were amused. "It wasn't just a coincidence that I picked you up. I was looking for you."

"Looking for me?"

"Your tootsie sent me. She said you'd be around here."

"My tootsie?"

"Nevada," said Clean Head in exasperation. Then, by way of explanation, "I've been reading Damon Runyon." We were safely stopped at a light so she slid open the panel between us and handed me a paperback. I inspected it. The collected short stories of Damon Runyon.

"It's not a Penguin Modern Classic," I said.

"No, but you can't have everything." She took the book back from me, making sure that I hadn't mauled it. Clean Head was a bit of a stickler about her paperbacks. She collected them, and god help you if you bent the cover of a book or, the ultimate crime, broke its spine. "So anyway," she said, "sit back and relax. And don't worry, it's on the tab."

"Now we're running a tab with you?"

"Only if you're working. And Nevada told me you're working. You have a new assignment."

"Yes, hilariously enough I've been hired by Tinkler."

"Is he still porking that teen kleptomaniac?" asked Clean Head casually. I repressed the urge to ask if 'porking' was a term used by Damon Runyon.

There was what you might call history between Tinkler and Clean Head. It was a history that mostly consisted of him hopelessly longing to get into her—no doubt stylish and skimpy—knickers. It had persisted thus until a pretty but predatory young woman called Opal had fallen into our orbit. And, to the astonishment of us all, including Tinkler, Tinkler had had a brief and passionate fling with her. Opal had parlayed this encounter into a well-received university dissertation and, potentially, a thriving career in the media. Tinkler, characteristically, had parlayed it into a broken heart and guilt.

Guilt because he felt, in some obscure way, that he had betrayed Clean Head and ruined his chances with her. Which was weird. Especially since Clean Head did indeed behave exactly as if this is what had happened.

"In fairness," I said, "the teenage kleptomaniac never actually stole anything."

"We're not interested in fairness around here," said Clean Head.

After the Vinyl Vault, the next record dealer I was visiting was Styli, which is located north of Oxford Street in London's

West End. It had once been run by a nice guy called Jerry. Unfortunately Jerry had been murdered, brutally beaten to death. To the police this was still an unsolved case, and the perpetrators remained unknown.

But I knew who they were and I knew they were dead. A fact that still gave me a primitive stab of satisfaction whenever I thought about it. They deserved it for what they did to him.

I had liked Jerry.

He'd certainly known how to run a record store.

Which was more than I could say for Glenallen and Kempton, his two former stooges who were in charge now. It wasn't that Styli had become a bad place, it was just that it had somehow lost its soul and whatever had once made it special. It had turned into a strictly commercial venture like so many others.

It had also been recently redecorated, giving the whole operation the usual soulless glass and chrome look that the corporate mindset deems modern. And they had added racks of CDs and DVDs, embracing these digital formats just in time for their extinction.

The kid whose name I could never remember but who was my enemy for life because I'd once given him hell for selling a record to someone else when it had been reserved for me—well-deserved hell, I still thought—was behind the till in the downstairs section where they sell rock and pop and current chart music.

Gilbert, I thought. *That's his name.* I nodded at him as I came in and he ignored me. I went up the stairs.

This was where they kept the jazz, blues and folk. There

was also a newly added display of brightly coloured T-shirts and other garments behind the till, all featuring the Styli logo. And a range of matching DJ accessories, which to me clearly signalled the dismal new world we were in.

Kempton and Glenallen were standing behind the counter against this polychromatic backdrop of branded merchandise, both leaning intently forward, talking to Nevada, who had her back to me. The two men had identical rapt expressions on their faces, gazing at her. They were Nevada's willing slaves.

They looked up as I came in.

They both looked unhappy to see me.

On the other hand, Nevada turned around and her face lit up. And she's the only one who matters. She gave me a kiss, brief by her standards but too long for the comfort of the two chumps behind the counter who gloomily resumed their appointed tasks.

Kempton went back to hand-lettering some plastic dividers, which would be used to separate the bins of records into some kind of coherent sequence. Glenallen picked up a digital stock scanner and cursed as he fiddled with it. But it wasn't entirely feigned bustle. They seemed legitimately busy—and there certainly had been a healthy number of customers downstairs. So evidently the tacky new tactics were working and business was booming. They were going to have to take on a fourth staff member soon.

Glenallen hurried out with his scanner and Kempton grunted and abandoned the section dividers on the counter, disappearing into the stock room. Nevada released me. We were all alone. "I suppose you'll be wanting to look through the records now," she said.

"You know me so well."

She followed me into the Folk section and took out her smartphone to peruse while I flipped through the racks of vinyl. It was peaceful up here, just Nevada and me, with all these records to look through. Presumably Glenallen and Kempton had made themselves scarce in case we started kissing again.

It was too good to last, though. A young guy hurried in, clad in a regulation Styli hoodie. He had the hood up over his head, and he was wearing a pair of enormous retro sunglasses—indoors in the middle of winter, mind you.

He mistakenly seemed to believe he was being hip. But the dark lenses merely rendered his pale face anonymous, hovering unconvincingly above his weak mouth and lack of chin.

This hooded apparition saw the pile of section dividers Kempton had left on the counter and immediately picked them up, turning to the record racks where he began industriously looking for the correct places to insert them.

I stood corrected. Apparently Styli had already hired its fourth employee.

As the hoodie minion distributed the alphabetical dividers in the Blues section I looked for the letter *B* in Folk, and started flipping through the albums.

"What is this record?" said Nevada. "I mean I know it's called Black Dog," she continued, "and that it's folk music. But why does Tinkler want it so badly?"

"Black Dog is the name of the band," I said. "The album is called *Wisht*. With a 't'."

"Extraordinary title."

"It apparently means eerie or haunted. It was their difficult fourth album."

"Why was it so difficult?" said Nevada.

I finished looking through *B* and started on *D*, just in case someone at Styli—possibly the very hoodie minion now labouring opposite us—thought there was a musician called Mr Dog, first name Black. That would presuppose, however, that he understood how alphabetic order by surname operated. An increasingly lost skill. "They were a great British folk group," I said. "But they wanted to become a great British *rock* group. And this album was their transition point."

The hoodie minion was getting closer to us, working his way down the racks of Blues LPs. I noticed he was listening to something on his phone, the headphone cable emerging from the neck of his hoodie. He was nodding his head in time to whatever the music was, blissfully oblivious to our presence.

"Did they become a great British rock group?" said Nevada. "If I sound sceptical it's because I've never heard of them. Perhaps they should have called themselves Black Cat, and then I would have."

"No, they never made it. This was their last album." I gave up on looking under *D*—a long shot, in any case—and started on New Arrivals. "Black Dog was basically a volatile mixture of wild talents who were always on the verge of flying apart. It was only thanks to the genius of their manager that they stayed together as long as they did. And once they lost him, that was the end of them."

"One always needs a good manager," said Nevada. "I'm yours. In case you hadn't noticed."

"I had."

"But you're not just looking for this album *per se*, are you? I mean, there's some special version of it that you're after. That *Tinkler* is after." She glanced up at the hoodie minion who drifted past us. At least he had his music turned down low enough not to bother the customers. He continued putting alphabetic dividers in the rows of records behind us.

"That's right," I said. "*Wisht* was released in two different versions. The first one is the rare one."

"Of course."

"It was recalled to the factory and destroyed."

"Of course it was. Why?"

"Contractual dispute within the group. One member of Black Dog wasn't happy with it, and legally he had control. So all the LPs were destroyed, and so were the master tapes."

"That would tend to make it scarce," said Nevada.

"A few copies survived, but just a few. All this would make them hard enough to find. But what complicates the picture even further is the second release of the album."

"The second release?"

"Yes, when the unhappy band member left, the other members of the band—"

"The happy members of the band."

"I suppose so. Anyway, they were happy to stay

together. And they promptly went back into the studio and re-recorded the album. They released it again with exactly the same songs and exactly the same cover art. Even the same catalogue number. Which makes it difficult to tell from the rare original issue."

"The rare and *valuable* original issue."

"That's right."

"But *you* can," said Nevada, taking my arm. "You can identify it, can't you?"

I nodded. "The two versions are almost identical, but there are some subtle differences. For one thing, you can tell them apart by the covers. The first version has a flip back."

"And what is that?"

I showed her, illustrating the point with a copy of a John Mayall album from the Blues section. "It's got this laminated cover, you see, and at the back it's got these sort of..."

"Flips? At the back?"

"Yes, I guess so."

"But surely the word is *flaps*?"

I shrugged, returning the Blues Breakers to their appointed section. The hooded minion had finished distributing the alphabetic dividers—rather haphazardly, I thought. Perhaps he was indeed fashionably postliterate. Now he was crouching down to get new stock off the bottom shelf and replenish the racks, head bobbing in time to the imperceptible music on his phone. "In any case, if you find a cover like that, then you've got the unreleased original version. And instead of being worth a few hundred, it's worth many thousands."

"Many thousands," said Nevada, savouring the phrase. "That's the kind of thousands I like."

"And, more importantly, you can listen to the original versions of all the songs. The ones recorded when Shearwater was still in the band."

"Is that a person?"

"More or less. Max Shearwater."

"And he was the true genius amongst that lot?"

"He was one of them," I said. "Black Dog was the great British folk band."

"Only they wanted to be the great British *rock* band."

"Correct. And that is what caused them to fly apart like a… detonating hand grenade." I made exploding gestures with my hands. Glenallen came back up the stairs and into the room. He was grasping his stock control scanner. He still seemed to be trying to work out how to operate it.

The hoodie minion went out the door and back down the stairs as soon as Glenallen came in, as though there was a strict store policy that no more than one member of staff could be on duty in the same place at any one time. Because that would be too helpful. You don't want to spoil the customers.

Glenallen smiled warmly at Nevada and then looked at me vaguely, as if trying to remember who I was.

Kempton came in from the back room, in strict violation of store policy. He stared at the counter and frowned. "Where are my section dividers?"

I said, "The new guy put them out."

"What new guy?" said Glenallen, not looking up from his scanner.

He did look up though—his face very surprised—when I ran past him, down the stairs. On the ground floor I saw Gilbert working behind the till and some customers flipping through the racks. The hoodie minion was gone. I checked the door to the street. It was still drifting shut on its hydraulic hinge. I pushed through it into the cold, deepening gloom of a winter's afternoon.

There was a vehicle parked just up the street.

A mud-spattered Land Rover.

The kid in the hoodie was getting into it. He slammed the door shut as I watched and the vehicle shot away, moving at speed, with a shriek of rubber. I watched them go and the uneasiness I'd been feeling all day drained away to be replaced by a chill, sick feeling of certainty.

I had been playing catch-up. I'd been missing vital clues and failing to read the signs.

And I felt a cold premonition that I was going to pay for it.

I heard the door of the shop open behind me and turned to see that Nevada had followed me out into the street. "He doesn't work here," she said. "And when he was skulking around up there, skulking around us, he wasn't listening to his phone."

"No," I said. "He was listening to us."

A black taxi eased out of the traffic stream and pulled in beside us. It was Clean Head. She opened the window and looked at me. "We were being followed. I should have spotted them sooner, but I only noticed them when I was circling the block waiting for you, and I realised they were circling too."

"In a muddy Land Rover," I said.

"You've seen them?"

I nodded. Nevada took my arm. "Someone's got a lot of questions to answer," she said.

We got into the taxi and Clean Head accelerated away. We searched for the Land Rover but there was no sign. It was long gone. And night was falling rapidly, plunging London into winter darkness. I was thinking about the figure who had gone scrambling into that mud-spattered vehicle. The hoodie minion.

There was something familiar about him. His posture. The way he moved.

Once again I had the unpleasant sensation that I was missing something important. And it was going to come back to bite us.

We crossed the river at Battersea Bridge, heading towards Putney. Nevada sat close beside me, peering at her phone. She grunted softly with satisfaction. "I looked up the dictionary definition," she said, switching it off.

"Of what?"

"A word I'd never heard before. Wisht." She looked at me, her face glowing in the passing streetlights. "It means to invoke evil upon. To bewitch."

We drove across the dark glittering river, heading south.

2. LOVE OR MONEY

"Tinkler, what have you got us into?" Nevada jabbed her finger at him and Tinkler flinched. We'd collected him at his house in Putney and now we were sitting either side of him in the back of Clean Head's cab as she drove us along the Upper Richmond Road, as swiftly and smoothly as the savage and chaotic evening traffic would permit.

Tinkler thought we were on our way to supper, which we were. But en route we intended to interrogate him about what the hell was going on.

"Got you into?" he said, looking back and forth at us. "Nothing. What are you talking about? What have I done now?"

We told him about being followed. He stared at us, a convincing picture of innocence—or at least bafflement—and shrugged.

"So you have no idea why anyone would be keenly interested in our business?" I said.

"No."

"And you don't know of anyone else, perhaps someone rather dangerous, who is currently looking for this very same record?"

He shrugged again. "No."

I said, "Why are *you* after it?"

"What do you mean?"

"Yes, what do you mean?" said Nevada, looking at me. "He's a record nut. Why *wouldn't* he be looking for a record?"

I indicated Tinkler. "He doesn't listen to folk music."

"Yes, I do. Or at least I listen to rock. And Black Dog are folk-rock. So I listen to the rock part."

Nevada frowned at him, eyebrows pensively angled. "No, you don't. You're being shifty. You're up to something."

I leaned towards Tinkler. "What haven't you told us?" The back of a taxi is a good place for getting intimidatingly close to someone.

Tinkler sighed. "Okay, I'll tell you." He looked at us, then leaned forward conspiratorially. "Is the intercom off?"

"Yes, it is."

"So Clean Head can't hear me?"

"No, she can't."

He relaxed. "You see, it's about Opal."

Nevada shot me a quick glance. This disclosure was evidently an unexpected bonus. "What about her?"

"Well, you remember Opal was into folk music?"

"This record is for *her*?"

"Well, she's a huge fan of Black Dog, and she's never heard the lost original version of *Wisht*. I thought if I got a copy, it might, you know, win me a way back into her heart."

"Back into her knickers, you mean," said Nevada.

I said, "Wait, if I find a copy of the record you're going to give it to Opal?"

Tinkler snorted. "Of course not. No, I'll make her a sacrilegious digital copy, which will be more than adequate for whatever pitiful MP3 device she's using, and the lovely, lovely analogue original vinyl I will keep for myself. In my own collection. Forever. Or at least until I can sell it for a thumping and obscene profit."

"That sounds more like it," I said.

"But that's all I'm guilty of. Being pathetic and grovelling and trying to get my ex-girlfriend back. I don't know anything about weird people following you around and eavesdropping on your conversations."

Nevada nodded. "Okay, we believe you. But why didn't you tell us this in the first place?"

"Because I was embarrassed. It was humiliating." He looked at me. "But you're still going to find the record for me?"

I nodded. "Of course," said Nevada. "We have a business agreement."

"Good."

"But just so we're clear," she said, "we're doing this because you're sad and lonely and a sexually desperate loser."

"Yes. Okay. All right."

"On an ill-fated quest, an obviously doomed bid to reawaken the affections of a frankly unsuitable girlfriend who is gone for good."

"How many times do I have to say yes?"

"Okay. That's settled," said Nevada. "But still, you

should have been totally on the level with us. Up front."

"You're saying I wasn't up front? Or on the level?"

"No. Not sufficiently so. You have transgressed and so you deserve mild punishment."

"What kind of punishment? How mild?"

Nevada leaned towards him. "You know when I said the intercom was off and Clean Head couldn't hear you?"

"Oh, shit," said Tinkler.

Tinkler had the good grace to offer to pay for dinner at Albert's, our local gastro-pub. Clean Head dropped us off by the railway crossing because the pub was in a narrow little alley where she couldn't drive the taxi. I asked her to join us but she said she had to work. Tinkler was bereft. We hurried down the winding Dickensian alley to Albert's, braving the winter wind until we were gratefully pushing through the stained-glass door.

It was warm and cosy in the pub and smelled of good cooking and beer. Albert himself wasn't immediately in evidence behind the bar, which in many ways was a bonus. He was probably in the kitchen second-guessing whatever new expert chef he'd hired. They were always new because they were always leaving. Because Albert was always second-guessing them. He fancied himself a gifted cook. Which indeed he was. But far too lazy to run a busy kitchen in even this tiny pub. So he had to hire someone else to do the cooking for him, while he constantly looked over their shoulder.

We found our favourite table. Albert took a brief break from chef-bothering and came out of the miniature galley kitchen at the back of the pub to tell us about today's specials. We ordered food and—after a microscopic examination of the wine list by Nevada—drinks.

Albert returned to the kitchen, and harassing his new chef.

The Australian girl behind the bar was also new, which explained why soon after we arrived she checked her watch and went to the radio at the back of the bar and switched it on. An annoying and all-too-familiar piece of theme music started up, followed by an unctuous announcer's voice declaring, "And now for *Stinky's Stellar Stars*."

Nevada winced. "Stellar stars," she said. "Jesus Christ."

"The series in which Stinky Stanmer profiles the music stars of past, present and future," continued the announcer smoothly. Or with what passed for smoothness in the realm of Stanmer.

Tinkler was looking at me as though he expected me to explode. I didn't feel like exploding. I just felt weary. But I got to my feet and started for the bar.

Before I could get there, Albert came hurrying out of the back of the pub. "Janine," he said.

"Yes?" said the Australian barmaid.

"Could you turn the radio off, please?"

"But we always play the Stinky Stanmer show," said Janine. Her willingness to argue with him suggested that Albert had once again fallen into the trap of sleeping with the help. Or maybe it was just because she was Australian.

"This week, a half-forgotten legend of the British

music scene..." continued the announcer.

"We don't play the radio," said Albert, "when *he* is in here." He nodded at me. "Not the Stinky Stanmer show, anyway."

"Why not?" said the barmaid pugnaciously. I decided it was both because she was Australian *and* she was sleeping with him.

He gestured vaguely towards me. "We have an agreement."

"What kind of agreement? Why?"

During this Socratic dialogue, the radio kept right on playing. And now the oleaginous tones of the announcer had yielded to something even more awful. "Good evening, space cadets," chirped Stinky. Even though he was safely many miles away and only a digital transmission, it was horribly as if he were in the room with us.

Albert gave me a helpless glance and then turned back to Janine, who was standing, slim suntanned arms determinedly folded, right in front of the radio. Nobody was getting past her. Evidently a Stanmer fan.

But I had once helped Albert out of a rather tricky situation, and in return he had promised a moratorium on playing the radio whenever I was in his establishment. With special reference to Stinky Stanmer.

Albert moved closer to Janine and lowered his voice. I was nonetheless able to make out the words. "At university together... based his whole career on imitating him... Stinky is rich and famous... always steals his ideas... gets more rich and more famous... while *he* hasn't got a pot to piss in." An anxious glance in my direction to make sure I couldn't hear any of this. But I could. All of it, quite clearly.

I think Albert's hearing had been damaged by years of standing behind the bar with his head beside the radio.

Stinky was still running through his repertoire of wooden catchphrases and stilted patter. The Australian girl's face was darkly angry in a way that suggested trouble for Albert later, and possibly also sooner. But he leaned past her and switched off the radio. As he did so, Stinky was saying:

"The great lost British folk band—"

The radio went off and there was suddenly silence in the pub. I was on my way back towards the table where Tinkler and Nevada were sitting when suddenly I spun around on my heel and went back to the bar, my heart thumping.

"Could you turn it on again, please?"

Janine looked at me truculently. Albert with astonishment. "Turn what back on?"

"The radio. Please."

Janine turned to look at Albert. "You said…"

"*Please*," I said.

I guess the note of urgency in my voice cut through all the usual crap, because Albert turned the radio back on. Stinky was saying, "A legendary British folk group— some would say folk-rock group—Black Dog was basically a volatile mixture of wild talents who were always on the verge of flying apart, like a detonating hand grenade. It was only thanks to the genius of their manager that they stayed together as long as they did. And once they lost him, that was the end of them."

I remembered, with glum vividness, a hooded figure scrambling into a muddy Land Rover.

"Their last album, *Wisht*, was released in two different versions. The first one is the rare one. It was recalled to the factory and destroyed because of a contractual dispute within the group. The band's co-leader and accordion player, Max Shearwater, wasn't happy with the record, and legally he had control. So all the LPs were destroyed, and so were the master tapes. A few copies survived, but just a few. That would make them hard enough to find…"

I remembered the same figure crouching over the record racks, virtually at our elbow, while I'd talked to Nevada.

"But what complicates the picture even more," continued Stinky, "is the second release of the album. When the unhappy Max Shearwater left, the other members of the band went back into the studio and re-recorded the album. They released it again."

Now I knew why he'd looked so familiar.

"With exactly the same songs, the same cover art. Which makes it difficult to tell from the rare and valuable original issue. The two versions are almost identical. But there are some subtle differences. You can tell them apart by the covers. The first version has a flip back…"

"Okay, you can turn it off now," I said.

Once again, there must have been something in my voice, because Janine turned it off without an argument. Albert took one look at me, then fled back into the kitchen. I returned to our table. I looked at Nevada and Tinkler. I wondered if my face was as pale as theirs.

Probably.

"That evil fucking little shit," said Nevada.

"How did he know…?" said Tinkler.

"The fucking fucker eavesdropped on us."

Tinkler shook his head. He looked like he'd been hit with a baseball bat. "Now he's told everyone."

"At least it wasn't a TV show," I said. "Only radio."

"He doesn't have a single original idea in his head, does he?" said Nevada.

"He's told everyone about the flip back version," said Tinkler. I thought he was going to cry. I knew how he felt. "If there are any copies out there, prices will go through the roof."

"There are copies out there," I said. "I know there are." I could feel it, but I didn't add that, because I'm supposed to be the rational one.

"Maybe," said Tinkler. "Maybe. But now we won't be able to get one for love or money."

Our drinks came and we proceeded to all get drunk.

Once again Stinky had fucked things up for us.

Little did I realise, this was going to be the least of our problems.

3. THE HOUSE WITH THE MOAT

Nevada was curled up in one of our armchairs, reading a Patricia Highsmith novel—in French, of course. She looked up at me with those disquieting blue eyes and said, "Honestly, what's wrong with you?"

I was sitting on the sofa, hunched over the laptop. I sighed. She could read me as easily as that book. I said, "I wasn't aware I was radiating disquiet."

"Stroppiness," she corrected me.

"Or that."

"It's perfectly obvious, from the way you're ignoring poor Turk."

It was true. Our cat Turk—short for Turquoise—was standing on the coffee table, peering over the computer screen at me. I hadn't even noticed that she was there.

As soon as I looked at her, she extended her paw.

"Sorry, Turk," I said. I knuckle-bumped her, which is what she had been waiting for. She then subsided contentedly into a sprawled heap on the coffee table and resumed licking herself shamelessly. I looked at Nevada.

"I'm preoccupied," I said.

"I know. I noticed." She put a bookmark into her Patricia Highsmith and came over and sat beside me on the sofa. "I like a man who takes his work seriously." She kissed me. "But you shouldn't let it *gnaw* at you."

"I can't help it. When I started this project, a first pressing of *Wisht* by Black Dog—a presumptive first pressing, that is—"

"I love the use of the word 'presumptive'."

"Because in theory the original version has been completely suppressed—"

"In theory."

I sighed. "You see, when we started looking for that record, copies were cheap. And any one of those copies might have turned out to be a true original." Despite the theoretical complete suppression, several hundred of the originals had escaped into the wild.

So to speak.

"Because most people didn't know about the flip back, right?" said Nevada. "I still want to call it a *flap* back, you know. I think that would be a much better name. Anyway, most people didn't know about it."

"That's right," I said. "Unless you really knew what you were looking for, a rare original could easily be mistaken for one of the common ones."

"And pass unnoticed, by whatever fool was selling it."

"Yes," I said.

"And we, by which I mean *you,* but actually of course

I mean both of us, and the cats, would have scooped it up."

"Yes."

"For a bargain sum. And then we could have sold it to Tinkler at a hugely inflated price."

"The friends-and-family hugely inflated price," I said.

"And everyone would have been happy. In Tinkler's case, 'happy' meaning miserably and hopelessly pursing a sexual lost cause."

"Yes," I said. It was a pretty fair summary.

"But then Stinky went on the radio."

"Yes. And he got everybody stirred up. By everybody, I mean his small audience of listeners."

Nevada shook her head. "In fact, almost a million—I checked. Unimaginable, I know, but that must also include all the radios that are on all over the country playing in the background, unheard, while people are doing better things."

"No doubt," I said. "Anyway, now suddenly everyone is interested in the original version of *Wisht* and on the lookout for it."

"So prices are soaring."

"Yes. Copies are selling for about ten times what they cost just a week ago." I'd just been on Discogs and I was still trying to get my blood pressure back down.

Nevada winced. "Ouch."

"And Stinky has also got everybody confused about what the hell a flip back version is."

"In other words," said Nevada, "people don't know if they've got an original copy or not. Everybody is mixed up now."

"Everybody was mixed up before," I said. "But back then it was to our advantage. It gave us the chance of finding a rare version of *Wisht* being sold as a common one."

"And getting a bargain," said Nevada avidly. She really liked the idea of a bargain. So did I, for that matter.

I shrugged. We could forget about that now. "Unfortunately, now it's all flipped around with even the cheap version being mistakenly priced into the stratosphere."

"All thanks to flipping Stinky," said Nevada. I thought she was being a model of restraint.

I said, "I've begun to resign myself to the fact that we're never going to find this record."

"I understand your despair, but it's still no justification for ignoring Turk."

"True." The cat watched us from the coffee table with her strange, pale eyes. She looked from one of us to the other. She might have been aware that we were talking about her and closely following our conversation. Or she might equally have been thinking about that satisfying crunching sound a mouse skull makes when you sink your teeth in.

"What I'm really dreading is telling Tinkler."

"Tell him what? That you're going to quit? You're not going to quit, are you?"

I shrugged. "It isn't fair to go on charging him expenses if we're never going to find the bloody record for him." I looked at the computer. "Anyway, he knows something's up. He's been trying to reach me all evening." I indicated an annoying little flashing icon on the corner of the screen. "No point postponing it. I'll tell him now."

"But he's paid us until the end of the month."

"We'll give him his money back."

"The hell we will. We'll think of something. *You'll* think of something." Nevada put her arm around me. "You'll find it."

"I have a feeling I'm being wheedled."

"I am a world-class wheedler."

I clicked the icon and Tinkler's petulant, chubby face appeared on the screen. "Where have you *been*? I've been trying to—"

Suddenly the image froze and the sound went dead. This wasn't unusual. For some reason, we'd been having trouble with the broadband lately. Digital technology at its finest.

The frozen image of Tinkler's face had caught him looming at the camera in a grotesque mid-expression. "My god, he looks ugly," said Nevada. "And that livid illumination doesn't help. He seems to be in a shoestring production of Dante's *Inferno*."

"He's using his lava lamp," I said. "And no doubt destroying his brain by smoking pot."

The image suddenly unfroze and Tinkler leered at us. "I heard all that," he said. "But I'll give you hell later. Why haven't you been answering? I've been trying to reach you all evening. Where have you been?"

"Avoiding you," I said.

"Avoiding you and *brooding*," added Nevada. "You should see him brood. He's even been ignoring the cats."

"My god," said Tinkler. He tut-tutted while his stoned brain tried to remember the reason for his call.

While he was doing that, I got on with business. "Tinkler, look, I don't think we're going to be able to find this record of yours."

"Because of fucking Stinky and his fucking shenanigans."

"Yes."

"Well fuck fucking Stinky and fuck his fucking shenanigans," said Tinkler. "I have a great idea. That's what I wanted tell you. I've thought of something."

What he had thought of was Erik Make Loud, the rock guitarist and now Tinkler's bosom buddy.

It still seemed odd to think of him as that. Erik (formerly Eric) had enjoyed semi-legendary status in the 1960s as a member of the psychedelic band Valerian. He was the only famous person Tinkler knew—unless you wanted to count Stinky, and nobody wanted to do that. Anyway, Erik was quite an anomaly in Tinkler's life.

But the two seemed to have become genuinely friendly. Of course, they had cannabis in common.

And, to be fair, a genuine love of music.

I arrived at Erik Make Loud's house by the river in Barnes promptly at eleven o'clock on a bright winter's morning. I was alone on the pavement. I'd got here before Tinkler.

Or to put it differently, Tinkler was late.

Late for our carefully arranged and painstakingly negotiated meeting.

When you have three or more parties involved in agreeing a common time for anything, it becomes almost impossible.

And when one of the parties is convinced he is a rock god, as was Erik, that impossibility is greatly magnified. So it wasn't as if Tinkler was unaware of the exact day and time we'd agreed. It had, god knows, taken us long enough to negotiate it. I sighed, breathing in an exasperated lungful of cold London air. Then I tried phoning Tinkler. No answer.

I waited outside Erik's large white house in the freezing morning as long as I could, pacing up and down the footpath by the river. My temper wasn't improved by the fact that one of Erik's near neighbours was having extensive renovations—basically their whole house was being gutted—and the noise of hammers, drills and indeed hammer drills was so loud that I felt my hearing was imperilled. So finally I decided I'd had enough. It was time to go in on my own.

There was an intercom on the locked iron gate outside Erik's. I pushed the button and in response there came an immediate buzz and the lock clicked open. The gate creaked complainingly as I pushed it inwards and stepped through onto the short section of iron footbridge that led to the front door.

Erik called this his drawbridge, although it didn't draw. I suppose the name made some kind of sense, because it ran above what he called the moat. This was a kind of deep rectangular trench in the concrete around the house. Big enough to stroll about in, it surrounded the house at basement level.

This basement contained Erik's guitar room. His pride and joy. Indeed, Erik had the moat built in event of flooding, because he thought it would protect his guitars. It had been pointed out to him that, to do any good in terms of sparing his house from the attentions of an angry River Thames, the moat would need to be about ten thousand times its current size.

Tinkler had told me his only response to this was to say that, in event of any such watery catastrophe, Bong Cha had firm orders to carry all the guitars upstairs to the attic.

When asked why he hadn't built the guitar room upstairs in the attic in the first place, Erik's only response had been angry laughter. He might well laugh. His basement was the most vulnerable place he could have chosen for his precious collection. Apparently he only realised this after he'd already installed the elaborate setup down there—the guitar room had everything including controlled humidity—and by then of course it was too late.

Because Erik's pride was at stake.

So, rather than admit he was wrong, rather than move the guitars to the top of the house, he'd had the 'moat' dug.

As I crossed the footbridge my footsteps echoed in the concrete canyon of this folly. Ahead of me, the front door suddenly sprang open. Surprisingly, standing there peering out was none other than Erik Make Loud himself. His middle-aged female housekeeper Bong Cha, Korean by way of Birmingham, was nowhere in evidence. This was odd. Bong Cha usually looked after the tedious details of ordinary life for Erik. Like opening doors.

Erik's abundant Viking beard flowed into the hirsute chest revealed by his loose green silk Hawaiian shirt. A number of gold and silver necklaces hung around his neck, with matching bracelets on his wrists. His long hair, profusely streaked with grey, was secured by a black scrunchie. His chest and shoulders were powerful but his legs looked absurdly long and skinny in tight black drainpipe jeans.

He was wearing a pair of rose-tinted granny glasses and was grinning broadly.

The grin faded as soon as he saw me, or rather as soon as he realised that I wasn't Tinkler.

For a moment I thought he was going to shut the door again.

But instead he opened it just wide enough to allow me grudging entrance. Things would have been different if I'd been with Nevada. Erik closed the door behind us and we stood in the entrance hall, pale and clean in the calm winter daylight that came through the window.

There were big black and white tiles on the floor, brightly coloured vintage rock posters framed on the wall and a gleaming antique mahogany bookshelf full of titles about military history. It was a pleasant, warm, well-lighted space and I could have quite enjoyed the peaceful order of it if Erik Make Loud—born Eric McCloud—hadn't been looming over me.

He removed his tinted glasses, perhaps so as to loom more effectively. He examined me with thorough and varied disapproval, and in so doing revealed his extravagantly dilated pupils. They were the big dark gaping bullet-hole eyes of someone who has smoked lots of weed. Suddenly I was aware of the sharp tang of cannabis, detectable despite the musky and no doubt expensive aftershave he was wearing.

Evidently, Erik had been smoking dope all morning. When Tinkler arrived, the two of them would probably smoke dope all afternoon. It began to look to me like a very long and very tedious day.

My only drug is coffee. And I probably wouldn't even get a decent cup of that. Once again I wished Nevada was with me.

As if by some stoned telepathy, Erik said, "Where's your girlfriend?"

"She can't make it today."

"Pity."

It was, but Nevada had found a whole new string of charity shops just south of Wimbledon. The most recent hiccup in our economy had slain any number of struggling small businesses and, as these premises were abandoned, the charity shops moved in. "It's an ill wind that blows no good," Nevada had said. "Have I got that right?" I knew what she meant.

She meant that there were new opportunities for high fashion acquisitions at low, low prices. And she needed fresh stock.

Nevada had discovered charity shops through hanging out with me and she'd begun by snapping up bargains for her own wardrobe, and then had expanded to selling fashion items to others. Now, thanks to a combination of her own innate good taste and cut-throat business sense, she was in danger of becoming a thriving business.

And of course the Internet had helped.

There was a sound on the staircase and Erik and I looked up to see Bong Cha peering down at us. She was standing on the floor above and looking over the banister rail. Only a segment of her face was visible, but it was enough to show she was unhappy to see me.

If she'd been a cat she would have hissed.

She withdrew.

"Come on downstairs," said Erik, raising his hand as though he was about to slap me on the shoulder, but thought better of it and ended up instead gesturing vaguely in mid-air. These gestures indicated a door in the wall, which might have led into a closet. I knew instead it led to the basement. And the guitar room.

We opened it and walked down a concrete stairwell. The walls here were smooth white plaster and there was a high oblong window with black iron bars set in the long wall above us, the outside wall of the house. It provided enough thin winter daylight for us to see by. At the bottom of the stairs another tall, barred window peered outwards. But here it was dimmer because the window faced out into the moat.

We turned to the left and down the corridor to the guitar room. It was a large room, which must have occupied fully half of the basement. Again, high barred windows provided as much daylight as the moat outside allowed. Enough illumination for Erik to save on his electricity bills. At least I assumed that was his reason for ignoring the light switch.

The guitars gleamed in the cold, pearly light of day. I didn't know anything about guitars but I recognised some Fenders. They all looked like rare and valuable vintage instruments.

Erik gestured towards a long black leather sofa. "Have a seat. Don't touch the guitars. Or the chord books. Or the sheet music. In fact, just don't touch anything. To be on the safe side."

I sat down on the sofa. He looked at me for a moment then went out. I expected him to return momentarily, but I gradually came to realise that I'd been parked in here.

I didn't touch the guitars, chord books or sheet music.

I didn't even look at them.

I just sat there being mindlessly bored. It was peaceful and quiet in this room but I was too much on edge to enjoy it. I didn't feel comfortable here. Erik might come back at any minute. Or on the other hand he might have slipped out the back door and got a taxi into town.

But he wouldn't do that to Tinkler, I told myself.

So I sat there listening to the subtle, distant whisper of sophisticated air conditioning. I wondered if the ideal humidity for guitars was the same as for human beings. I certainly didn't feel that I was being best served by my environment. The air was dry and caused my throat to itch.

Erik strolled in again about a quarter of an hour after he had first withdrawn and briefly stared at me. He looked disappointed that I hadn't undergone an interesting transformation during his absence.

I thought I heard a sigh as he withdrew again.

I leaned back on the sofa, trying to adopt a Zen-like acceptance of the wave of boredom that I expected to wash over me. I anticipated it being a long, long day.

I didn't know that in less than an hour someone was going to try and kill me.

And not just me.

4. MONEY TO BURN

I settled in for the long haul on the sofa in the guitar room. In fact, I started wondering if I could put my legs up on one of the nice chocolate-coloured cushions—made of expensive, butter-soft leather—and maybe snatch a nap. I'd take my shoes off first, of course.

Almost at the same moment I conceived this scheme, and in what some soft-minded souls would take to be a verification of telepathy, Erik stepped through the door and gave me a suspicious look over his ridiculous pink glasses. His pupils were still dark, huge, stoned.

Perhaps he was trying to work out if I had stolen one or more of his guitars, having used some kind of miniaturising ray, and then concealed them in my pocket.

But in fairness to my host, he was also carrying a tray. He set it down on a table beside the sofa, and sat down in a chair nearby.

On the white tray were two black cups with gold rims set either side of a chunky black ceramic pot with a contorted spout. From the spout came a warm, perfumed fragrance.

Tea.

Didn't he know I was a coffee drinker? Surely Bong Cha, whom I assumed was the only one who was capable of making a pot of tea in this household, would at least have remembered that? Was this intended as a deliberate insult?

I decided not to be paranoid, and politely accepted a cup of the insipid stuff. Maybe I was wrong about Erik not being able to make a pot of tea. He certainly succeeded in pouring out the two cups expertly, despite the fact that the spout on the pot was as convoluted as a model of the human digestive system.

Thankfully I was spared the necessity of pretending to drink the tea because, as soon as he'd finished filling the cups, Erik got up again and walked across the room. He looked at the guitars there. Some of these were standing upright on the floor on special mounts, while others hung on the wall. Some particularly notable specimens were in display cases. He selected one of the guitars from the wall, an acoustic model of beautiful polished wood, and brought it back with him.

He sat down in his chair with it cradled in his lap. Since he made no move to touch his cup of tea, I felt at liberty to also ignore mine. We sat there while Erik endlessly tuned the guitar and the tea gradually got cold. We didn't speak until finally he said, "So, Tinkler wants to meet Tom."

Tom was Thomas Pyewell, one of the members of Black Dog, co-leader of the band, in fact. And along with Max Shearwater was—I suppose—its other bona fide star. It turned out that Pyewell, sorry, *Tom*, and Erik were friends. So Erik was in a position to arrange an introduction. Anyway, that was Tinkler's big plan.

I said, "Tinkler only wants to meet this guy because he thinks he might have a copy of that record, you know. The guy, I mean. Tom Pyewell. Tinkler thinks he might have a copy of *Wisht*."

"*Wisht*?" said Erik, strumming slowly and softly on the guitar. "Great album. Fucking great album."

"Tinkler wants the original version."

"Even better." Erik strummed away happily. "Even better."

"The one with the flip back cover."

"That's right." He nodded as he played softly, at the edge of hearing.

"He thinks your mate Tom has got a copy."

"If anybody's got a copy, Tom has."

"You do realise that if he does have one, Tinkler will pester you until he gets his hands on it."

Erik, head bent over his guitar, didn't answer me directly. Instead, he said, "What do you know about Black Dog?"

I started to outline what I'd gleaned about the band, from books and magazines and of course the Internet, but he interrupted me almost immediately. "Do you know why they were called Black Dog?"

"No idea."

The music he was playing became a little louder. It was now just audible, a slow, mournful folk air. "They named themselves after the *barghest*, a ghostly black dog in folk legends that is said to haunt wild places, prey on lonely travellers and foretell deaths."

"Busy dog."

He continued to strum the guitar. I was amazed at the way he just seemed to conjure music from the strings with the most trifling of movements. He didn't appear to be doing anything, but he was doing everything. He played more loudly, and eerie chords filled the room. The sun went behind a cloud and the basement was suddenly flooded with darkness. "He *was* a busy dog," said Erik. "Also known as a wisht hound." He took off his glasses and looked at me bleakly. Somehow he managed to do this without interrupting his playing.

The folk strain he'd been strumming had transformed to a blues, haunting and mournful and repetitive. He said, "I thought I saw some weird shit when I was with Valerian. I mean, John Blacklock and all his Aleister Crowley crap and all that. Everybody was mucking about with the dark arts in those days. It was very much the done thing."

The daylight seemed to have been completely extinguished, as though the apocalypse had silently arrived and was politely waiting to announce itself. I wondered why my host didn't turn some lights on. Maybe it was Bong Cha's job. "But Black Dog," he said, "they really got into it. All kinds of really weird shit. There's even a story they tried to manifest the devil."

He seemed to expect a response from me. When none was forthcoming, he just kept playing his tremulous, eerie blues. "That's right," he said, as if agreeing with me, although I hadn't said anything. "They tried to summon him up on stage one night while they were playing."

"Why?"

"Why? To join them, I suppose. To join in."

"To join in the concert?"

"Yes."

I thought, *Opening Act: Satan*. I said, "Did he bring a pick-up band?"

"The old gentleman didn't show. But at least they tried." He played thoughtfully, the guitar giving voice to an endless cascade of chill, rolling chords. It was starting to get a bit repetitive. That's the trouble with the blues, if you ask me. "A black dog is also called a wisht hound," he said, for the second time. Then, perhaps sensing that I was losing interest in his performance, and his monologue, he added, "The Hound of the Baskervilles was one."

"Only he wasn't real, was he?" I said. "I mean, even in the *story* the evil dog wasn't real. Sherlock Holmes unmasked him. One of the few occasions when anybody's had the opportunity to unmask a dog."

He shook his head. "Joke if you like, but some people take this sort of thing very seriously. Ever so seriously."

I was saved from having to reply by the doorbell.

My host's face lit up. "Tinkler!" He was overjoyed. I knew how he felt. Erik stared up at the ceiling. "Bong Cha will let him in." Indeed, there came a rattle of impatient footsteps descending a staircase, then a pause, and then the sound of a door opening. Indistinct voices echoed, just about identifiable as Tinkler and the reluctant housekeeper. More descending footsteps, then the door of the guitar room opened and Tinkler came in, beaming.

Bong Cha glanced in over his shoulder, shooting a poisonous look at her employer. That seemed to be the sole purpose of her visit, to let him know she was pissed off, because when she finished glaring she withdrew again.

Tinkler shook hands with Erik, who had set his guitar aside and risen enthusiastically from his chair, and then shook hands with me. I should have known better, but I was glad to see old Tinkler. I even forgave him for being late. "I see you've brought the sunshine with you," I said.

He glanced towards the window and the inky darkness beyond. "Yes, it's black as night out there," he said. "I even had the headlights on."

"You drove?" I said. "You could have got here quicker if you'd walked." He only lived in Putney.

"That's London traffic for you," said Tinkler. "I blame all those other drivers."

Erik leaned over and slapped him on the shoulder. "Well, you're here now, mate, and that's what counts."

"So, where is he?" said Tinkler, looking around the room. "Tom. Tom Pyewell. Mr Pyewell." He grimaced anxiously. "Should I call him Mister?"

"Yes, that's right, mate," Erik twinkled. "Call him Mr Bastard. Mr Bastard Knob Head. That's about right." He chuckled and Tinkler chuckled too, but much more uncertainly. He glanced at me with his big, worried brown eyes.

I said, "I can't believe you're so nervous about meeting this guy, Tinkler."

Erik swivelled a disapproving gaze my way. "Why shouldn't he be nervous?"

"Yeah, why shouldn't I be nervous?" said Tinkler.

"Tom Pyewell is a major figure in British music," said Erik. "Him and old Max Shearwater were like our answer to Simon and Garfunkel."

"Well, that's sort of my point," I said. "As half of a partnership, Pyewell was someone all right. But without Max Shearwater he hasn't exactly had a glittering career." I was being generous. Shearwater had been the presiding genius of Black Dog. After he decided to split with the band, it had been pretty much downhill to oblivion for all the others.

Erik pretended he hadn't heard me. He turned to Tinkler. "Anyway, how you been keeping, mate?"

But Tinkler wouldn't let it go. I'd got him worried. "No talk about creative decline when Mr Pyewell arrives, all right? No suggestion that he is any less of a rock god than he used to be." He eyed me nervously.

"Folk god," I said.

"Whatever. Folk-rock god."

Erik deigned to join the conversation. "And whatever you do, don't mention Max Shearwater when he gets here. He'll go spare if you do." I didn't point out that he was the only one who'd brought up Shearwater's name so far.

"Still bad blood between them?" said Tinkler.

"There always will be, mate. Always will be."

"Because Max Shearwater broke up the band?" said Tinkler.

Erik shook his head. "Tom hated Shearwater's guts long before that. Everyone in the band did. Come to think of it, people all over the world who didn't even know him hated his guts."

Tinkler nodded sagely. "Because of what he did with the money."

"That's right, mate. Because of what he did with the fucking money." Erik suddenly took his phone out of his pocket and squinted at it. "Excuse me. Got to take this. It's him." He walked out of the room with the phone to his ear.

I turned to look at Tinkler. "It's him," he said excitedly. "Tom. Mr Pyewell. I think I'll definitely go with Mister."

"What was this about the money?" I said.

"What?"

"You said people hated Shearwater, 'Because of what he did with the money.' What did you mean?"

Tinkler stared at me. "You mean you've never heard about that?"

"I'm hoping to hear about it now," I said.

"Well, you know how there were all kinds of 'artistic differences' in the band?" Tinkler made heavy quotation-mark gestures in the air. "Which is what ultimately led to them breaking up? Well, these differences were because Shearwater was totally avant-garde." Nevada would have picked him up on his pronunciation. "In fact, that's a polite name for what he was. But it wasn't just a matter of Max making weird sound recordings. At the same time he abandoned conventional music he began a series of other goofy art projects and conceptual 'happenings', as they used to say in the 1960s. Each one stranger and more far out than the last." I thought of the alleged attempt to raise the devil on stage, and wondered if this had been one of those. But I didn't want to interrupt Tinkler. He looked at me. "These came to their—you'll excuse the expression—climax when one day he announced he was going to burn a million dollars."

"Jesus," I said. "*Burn?*"

"Yes, burn, baby, burn. Make a big pile of banknotes and just set fire to them. Whoosh."

"You mean in a kind of anarchistic gesture?"

"In an *artistic* gesture," Tinkler corrected me.

"In other words, basically just for the hell of it."

"Yes. Basically just for the hell of it."

"Jesus," I said. "You see what happens if you smoke too much dope? You lose your mind."

"More importantly, you lose your money," said Tinkler. "But reportedly he pulled this particular stunt during one of his lucid intervals. Drugs had nothing to do with it."

"Nevertheless... still... Jesus."

"Yes. And don't forget a million dollars was a lot of money in those days."

I said, "Why was it dollars and not pounds?"

"He converted the pounds to dollars before he burned them. I imagine he took a loss on the exchange rate. But I expect that didn't matter too much, since he planned to burn them anyway."

"That doesn't answer my question, Tinkler."

"Why was it dollars not pounds? Because a million dollars sounds cool. A million pounds just sounds kind of..."

"Parochial?"

"*Uncool.*" Tinkler smiled at me. "Anyway, a million

dollars was a shitload of money in those days."

"I know," I said. In fact, I was trying to do the arithmetic in my head. However you chose to compensate for inflation and calculate it in the years since then, it represented a staggering sum.

Tinkler started chuckling.

"What's so funny?"

"You never having heard about Max Shearwater burning a million bucks. Everyone's heard about that." He pointed a chubby finger at me. "You live in such a shell. You're such a hermit. Such a shut-in. You're a shut-in hermit."

Despite myself, I was nettled. I said, "Look, what's this really all about?"

"What do you mean?"

"Why am I here?"

Tinkler was all injured innocence. "Because I want the record. Your old friend wants the record. And Tom Pyewell has got a copy. He's definitely got one. I'm pretty sure he's got one." He looked at me. "I'm almost positive he's got one. At least, I suspect he's got one. And I need you to negotiate for it."

"No, you don't. You can negotiate for it yourself." Nevada would have been horrified. Here I was talking myself out of a job. But the thought of just leaving Tinkler and his mad musicians to it, just walking away from this riverside house into the quiet winter's afternoon darkness, was suddenly enormously appealing.

I had a tremendous impulse to simply get the hell out of there.

5. LOOPY GROUPIE

Nevada would later say, when I told her about how I felt that day, wanting to flee the place, that it had been some kind of atavistic psychic survival instinct kicking in, trying to warn me of what was about to happen.

But I think I was just bored.

"No, I couldn't possibly do that," said Tinkler. "I couldn't possibly negotiate for the record myself. I've got to have you. You're my buffer zone. My firewall. I couldn't possibly *haggle* about money with Erik's friend. With a friend of my friend. It would be totally not cool."

"Well, we couldn't have that," I said.

"Thank god we've got that straightened out," said Tinkler. He leaned forward and examined the teapot. "Is this tea?" He put his hand on it. "Still warm." He looked at the cups. "Have both of those been used? I don't want anybody else's saliva in my tea. I'm old-fashioned that way."

"You don't really want it," I said.

He looked up at me from the pot. "Is it that bad?"

"Not the tea," I said. "The record. You don't really want it."

"Don't I?"

"It's just a grand gesture to try and win back your ex-girlfriend."

"My supremely hot ex-girlfriend."

"She *was* fairly hot," I conceded. There had been one terrible moment when quite involuntarily on my part—if such a thing is possible—Opal and I had almost got involved. Fortunately sanity had prevailed. My sanity.

Tinkler sighed and moved away from the teapot. "No. It may have started off like that, with me going after the record just because of Opal. But now I've been bitten by the bug." He looked at me helplessly. "I really want it. I want to get this fucking record. I want to *hear* it. The music is said to be phenomenal. Don't tell me that you're not interested in hearing it."

I paused. He had me there. "I wouldn't mind," I said. Of course, we could have located and listened to the music, or a debased copy of it, in some corner of the Internet. No doubt there were dodgy MP3s and YouTube renderings of it. But no one in their right mind would settle for those when the original, on vinyl, was out there somewhere.

"You're *dying* to hear it," said Tinkler confidently. "And you will, you will. I can feel that we're on the verge of getting hold of a copy." He rubbed his hands together.

"If you say so," I said, trying to sound sceptical. But, in fact, I'd begun to have a similar feeling.

"And don't think I haven't filed away your embarrassing

ignorance concerning Shearwater and the money. Not knowing that he put the flames to a million bucks. A million buckaroos. Up in smoke on a remote island off the coast of England. Wait until I tell Nevada."

"What island?" I said.

"Halig. Halig Island. It's near Durham, or somewhere like that. There is a place called Durham, isn't there?" Geography was one of Tinkler's many weak points.

"How do we know he really did it?" I said.

"Really burned the money, you mean?"

"That's right," I said. "Maybe he faked it. If it had been me, I would have faked it."

"Me too. But there was official verification. Of the conflagration. There was conflagration verification."

I still wasn't convinced. "What form did this official verification take?"

"Whole bunch of reporters invited out to the island to witness the burning."

"Maybe it wasn't real money; maybe it was counterfeit."

"No." Tinkler shook his head. "They examined the money before it was put on the pyre. The reporters. They passed the money around to everyone so they could check it. And when they got the money back to the pyre they found that about ten thousand bucks had gone missing. That's how real it was."

"By missing, you mean stolen?"

"Yup."

"By the reporters?"

"By *some* of the reporters. But they didn't know which

ones. And it was too embarrassing to search everybody. There were maybe a hundred journalists there from all over the world."

I said, "The cream of the global media."

"Don't be so hard on them. They only stole about ten grand. That averages out to just a hundred dollars a head. That's getting off lightly where journalists are concerned. That's a journalistic cheap date. So, anyway... Max Shearwater went ahead and burned the remaining nine hundred and ninety thousand dollars."

"Not quite as impressive as a round million."

"True. But the press agreed to tell everybody it was a million."

"Further high-calibre honesty from the fourth estate."

"I don't see how you could have missed this colourful anecdote during your scrupulous research." Tinkler put air quotation marks around these last words. I could see this turning into an annoying habit. To add to an already generous inventory.

Erik came back into the room and sat down on the edge of his chair. "He should be here any minute." He suddenly seemed charmingly nervous. He looked at the tea things on the table, scowled at them in disapproval and picked them up and took them away upstairs. Apparently such was not good enough for the likes of Mr Pyewell. Erik came back and sat down on the edge of his chair again.

Then the doorbell rang, and for some reason we all jumped, despite knowing that our guest of honour was due to arrive imminently. Something about the dark, muffled winter day had cast an eerie mood on us.

My nerves were shot, and I hadn't even had any coffee. Perhaps that was why they were shot.

There was no long delay with Bong Cha this time. We heard her answer the door immediately. Perhaps she had been briefed on the importance of this visitor. Erik certainly surged to his feet and stood there expectantly, like a dog waiting to be taken for a walk. There were distant voices, then the confident clunking of male feet coming down the stairs. Erik hurried to the doorway just as a man came down the corridor.

"Tom," he cried, full of good cheer. "Are you all on your own? Where's that good-for-nothing housekeeper of mine?"

"Don't you say a word against that daughter of paradise," said the newcomer. "She is even now preparing some divine snacks to bring down to us. To bring down from the heavens."

"Good to see you again, mate." The two men embraced tightly in a clatter of male jewellery. They pounded each other on the back, then shoved each other apart, gazing fondly into one another's face.

"Good to see you," said Thomas Pyewell. He was very pale, tall and rake thin, wearing what at first looked like a chunky black silk suit. But from the way it creaked when he moved I realised it must be leather. Under it he wore a lacy white shirt and a thin black tie, also leather. On his wrists a variety of bracelets jangled. Draped over his shoulders was a tasselled black and white Middle Eastern scarf more suitable to the desert than our English winter.

His Ray-Ban sunglasses were equally inappropriate, given that the day outside remained as black as a coal sack. No rays to be banned.

If he'd been wearing those while he was driving, it was no wonder he'd found the traffic a challenge.

The dark glasses gave him a distinctly sinister look, amplified by his smooth shaven skull. I assumed he was one of those men who'd begun to lose his hair and decided to hell with it and had done away with the lot.

It was a look that was a lot more flattering on Clean Head than it was on him. Especially since Tom Pyewell had left a little shark fin of hair—I almost called it fur—at the back of his head, dyed chestnut brown.

He took off his sunglasses to reveal a pair of bloodshot and cynical blue eyes.

"Sit down, mate, sit down." Erik indicated the armchair beside his, where a moment earlier Tinkler had been sitting. Tinkler was standing up now, having sprung to his feet when our new visitor arrived. Tom Pyewell sat down in the chair he had vacated and Erik sat in the other one.

Tinkler accepted this demotion in status with good grace, coming to sit beside me on the sofa. There was a sudden and slightly awkward silence in the room.

"You know who I was just thinking about?" said Erik, anxious to fill it. "The other day? Norrie."

Tom Pyewell nodded thoughtfully. "That's funny. *I* was just thinking about him on the drive up here. Thinking how different everything would have been if he hadn't got himself killed."

"He was murdered, wasn't he?" I said.

Tom Pyewell looked at me. Erik glowered over his shoulder. I hadn't been given permission to speak. Bad me. But Pyewell nodded and said, "That's right. Shot dead by one of our groupies."

"At least he *had* groupies," said Tinkler. For a moment I thought he'd horribly overstepped the mark. But Erik started laughing and, taking his cue from his host, Pyewell allowed himself a thin smile.

"Some of our groupies were lovely girls," he said. "*Most* of them were lovely girls. But not this one." He frowned, a man being submerged in memory. "I mean she was beautiful. Gorgeous. But, you know, *troubled*."

Erik nodded. "I remember her. She was what, Swedish?"

"Norwegian, I think. Scandinavian, anyway."

Erik chuckled. "Norwegian Wood. The dark and hairy forest. I never ventured in there, personally."

"I did," said Pyewell. "And I can tell you, it was like Bonfire Night. You know, flame and fireworks. In all the good ways. But also in some very bad ways."

"What does that mean?" said Tinkler, leaning forward. "If you don't tell me what that means, the question will torment me to my grave."

Tom Pyewell smiled a little wider this time, almost like a real smile. Was Tinkler actually getting through his defences? Could he succeed in befriending two rock stars? Or one rock star and one folk star? I held my breath.

"It means she was unstable, mate. A total nutcase. Loopy. That's what we called her. The Loopy Groupie."

Erik laughed. "Yeah, that's right. I remember now."

Pyewell was looking directly at Tinkler. "I mean, she was insane, mate. You didn't realise it at first. No, at first it was great. She was great. You're with this girl and you're thinking, she's amazing. You can't believe your luck. But then some of the things she did. Some of the things she *said*." He shook his head. "It was like biting into this beautiful piece of fruit and finding it's all rotten inside." He feigned a shudder and Erik leaned forward and slapped him on the knee in a comradely fashion.

"What sort of things did she say?" said Tinkler. "What sort of things did she do?"

"Oh, she was a complete nutcase. I mean she *believed* in all that stuff about the *barghest*."

"The what?" said Tinkler.

"Black dog," I said. "It's an old word for a supernatural black dog."

Pyewell shot me a surprised look. Apparently I'd scored some points. "A dog that foretells death," he said.

"And that's what you named your band after?" said Tinkler. He'd acquired a kind of smarmy smoothness. He might have been interviewing the guy for a magazine.

"I suppose so. Sort of. It seemed like a good idea at the time." Pyewell nodded reminiscently. "We were probably in the pub, all pissed as farts."

"Why didn't you call the band Barghest?" said Tinkler.

"We didn't think anybody would be able to spell it." He glanced at Tinkler, looking directly and squarely at him for the first time—even making eye contact. Then he did the same with me. He was warily including us in the conversation, as if we were of equal status. If he wasn't careful, we'd soon be like a bunch of normal people having a chat.

It was a relief that he was dropping his guard, but why was his guard up in the first place? I suppose it was a standard reaction by famous people. Of course, Tom Pyewell wasn't really famous anymore. But maybe it wouldn't be such a great idea to point this out to him.

"Where's Bong Cha with the bloody refreshments?" said Erik suddenly. Apparently he'd just remembered he was supposed to be our host.

"You can't hurry perfection," said Pyewell. "What were we talking about before? Oh, yeah, *Norrie*," he said. "Mr Nelson. What a man. That man was a genius of a manager."

"That's what I was thinking," said Erik. "The other day."

"We didn't appreciate it at the time. But once he was gone, we really felt the difference." Pyewell caught my eye. "People argue about whether the true genius in the band was me or Max Shearwater…"

Actually, I thought, *nobody argues about that. Everybody thinks it's Shearwater.* But I continued to listen politely.

"But they're all wrong," said Pyewell. "Both sides are wrong. The true genius in the band was Norrie Nelson. If he'd still been around, we might never have split up. We were all hotheads, but Norrie had a way of calming us down."

Erik suddenly got to his feet and left the room. He'd evidently had enough of waiting for Bong Cha. Tom Pyewell didn't even notice this departure. He seemed to be submerging himself in memories again. Or maybe they were rising around him, inexorably, like floodwater.

Pyewell's gaze grew distant. He shook his head. "It was all that bitch's fault," he said softly. "She did for him."

"The Loopy Groupie?" said Tinkler. I could tell he just wanted to say the name.

"That's right. Her real name was Berit Barsness. We used to call her Merit Mare's Nest, because she was always so bloody mixed up. But it turns out she was organised enough to do for poor Norrie." Pyewell shook his head.

"What happened?" I said.

Pyewell shrugged. He suddenly seemed morose and withdrawn. "Oh. Well. You know." There was a long pause and I wondered if that was all we were getting. Then he said, "She got hold of a gun from somewhere. Shot him and shot herself." It was as though he was sending a message by telegram, and paying by the word.

"Why?" I said.

Pyewell gave a long sigh and then fell so profoundly silent that I thought this time we really weren't going to get an answer. I looked at Tinkler and he stared worriedly back at me. Had I overstepped the mark and somehow offended the man?

But then, as if some kind of blockage had abruptly melted away, Pyewell started talking again. And he spoke now in a detached, matter-of-fact way, like he was dispassionately discussing someone he hardly knew. "She left a note, written after she killed him and just before she killed herself. You should have seen her handwriting. Her English was pretty good, but every time she wrote a letter 'i' she drew a little flower over it instead of a dot. Like a daisy. Funny, the things you remember. Must have slowed down her penmanship like a motherfucker, that."

"What was in the note?" I said.

"She said that she did it because a black dog had been howling outside her window at night." Tom Pyewell paused and then made a sound that was supposed to be a chuckle, but came out more like a snarl. "As if that explained everything." He shook his head. "As if that explained *anything*."

"A black dog?" said Tinkler. "You mean, like…"

Pyewell nodded. "Yeah. Like the *barghest*. Like the name of the band."

6. BONFIRE NIGHT

Now we were all silent. I imagine we were thinking similar thoughts. That somehow through naming their group after a messenger of death, they'd brought death into their circle.

But maybe we were thinking very different thoughts, because Tom Pyewell suddenly chuckled again, except this time it sounded like genuine laughter. "Max almost shat himself when he found out. He said it could so easily have been him, instead of Norrie, because he was shagging her at the same time Norrie was. She was clearly off her crust, and she'd just decided to kill someone, and it could just as easily have been him." He suddenly hunched his shoulders and rubbed his hands up and down his arms. He was shivering. "Is it me, or did it suddenly get cold in here?"

I didn't know about suddenly, but he was right. It *was* cold in the guitar room. Maybe our host had decided to economise on the central heating as well as the lighting, so he could channel his funds into more important areas. Like recreational drugs, and guitars. Or maybe it was just the power of suggestion. Anyway, now I was shivering, too. The sensation was so sudden, and strong and unaccountable, that I thought of the old expression 'someone walking over my grave'.

I looked over at Tinkler. He was briskly rubbing his hands, so evidently he was feeling the cold as well. "You know what would really warm us up?" he said. He gave Tom Pyewell a look of wide-eyed innocence. "*Burning a million dollars.*"

I felt my heart contract. In a long and eventful history of Tinkler saying inappropriate things, this really took the cake. What in god's name was he thinking? That this would break the ice or something? And what had become of the shy and nervous Tinkler who had been looking for the most respectful way to address Mr Pyewell?

Right now Mr Pyewell was staring at us in disbelief. He looked at me as if for a cue on how to respond—if that was indeed what he was looking for, then he was out of luck—and then back at Tinkler. And then his shoulders started to heave.

It took me an understandable second or two to realise that he was laughing.

Tom Pyewell raised his chin and let his head fall back, and laughed and laughed and laughed.

Tinkler stared at me, then he started too. And then, after a moment, I found myself joining in, largely out of a giddy sense of relief.

There was the sound of rock star footsteps on the stairs and Erik Make Loud came hurrying in. It reminded me of one of our cats rushing in whenever she suspected her sister might be getting a treat. They didn't like the possibility of missing out on something, and neither did Erik.

He stared at us. The expression on his face just made us laugh harder.

"What's going on?" he said, when he could finally make himself heard.

Tom Pyewell wiped the tears from his eyes and pointed to Tinkler and said, "This bastard here is a funny bastard, isn't he?"

"I told you you'd like him," said Erik mildly. He sat back down in his armchair and folded his hands on his chest.

"Did you really?" said Tinkler. "Did you really tell him that?" Erik nodded. Tinkler grinned. He was pleased as Punch. I could see that getting away with this would make him insufferable. Or more insufferable.

"This bastard was talking about the money," said Tom Pyewell.

Erik swivelled his head to Tinkler and gave him a look that was somewhere between horror and admiration. "*The* money? You mean…"

"Burning the money," said Pyewell unequivocally.

"I told them not to bring that up," said Erik.

"No you didn't," I said.

"Well, I meant to."

Pyewell was shaking his head. "It doesn't matter. I mean, it mattered at the time. You can bet it bloody well mattered. Fucking Max fucking Shearwater. We'd all worked so hard for that money. And we didn't have as much of it as *he* did."

Max Shearwater had written most of the band's material,

so most of the composing royalties went to him, making him the richest member of the group. I said, "Does that mean he contributed more to the…"

"Bonfire?" said Pyewell, thoughtfully helping me out with the word. "Nope. We all donated equal shares. It just meant that he was better able to absorb the loss afterwards."

"Equal shares," said Erik. He shook his head.

"Yeah," said Pyewell. He was grinning wryly. He seemed perversely proud.

"Why did you do it?" I said.

He shrugged. "It seemed like a good idea at the time."

"Did you regret it?" I said.

"Oh, yeah. Right away." Pyewell twisted around in his chair, the better to look me in the eye. "It was *bad*. It was bad in the way that you'd expect—we'd just burned a million fucking dollars. Gone from our wallets, right? But it was also bad in a way you wouldn't expect. Or at least in a way that *we* didn't expect. People just hated us. Just. Hated. Us. They took it personally. I mean, it was like we'd burned their money instead of our own. I guess it was because people worked so hard all their lives and never earned a fraction of what we did." I was impressed with this level of empathy coming from a wealthy musician. Or a formerly wealthy musician. Maybe that was what made the difference.

"So when we burned it, it was as if we were saying that none of it meant anything. None of it mattered. They slaved their guts out and could hardly make ends meet and there we were burning a million dollars with gay abandon. It was like a…"

"A big fuck off," said Erik.

"Yeah, exactly. Which I suppose is exactly what Max intended. He was always the big provocateur. And it was Max's idea. But we went along with it, I must admit that. We were all willing participants. Except for Norrie. It drove Norrie nuts. But in the end when he saw that Max was serious about doing it, and so were we, he went along with it, too. He organised the press coverage and everything." Pyewell grinned. "He used to like to say he got ten million dollars' worth of publicity out of it."

I said, "So according to Norrie, the band made a handsome profit from Max's bonfire."

Pyewell shook his head, frowning. "It certainly didn't feel that way at the time." Then he smiled and turned to Tinkler. "Have you got anything else controversial you want to talk about?"

Tinkler nodded happily. "Yes. Is it true that you and Max Shearwater are both broke?"

Erik's eyes widened and he flushed bright red. *Tinkler's done it now*, I thought. But Tom Pyewell didn't miss a beat. He just shrugged affably and said, "Nope, I'm doing quite well, thank you. Thank goodness. And old Max is rolling in it. But he always was rich. Comes from a wealthy family, don't you know. Bugger never had to do a day's honest work in his life."

"So I guess that means the band isn't getting back together," said Tinkler. "Since you're not hurting for money."

Pyewell shrugged again. "Well, never say never, as they say. And we're all still talking to each other. But we're not talking about *that*. Not at the moment." He smiled. He seemed entirely at ease now, in fact genuinely friendly.

As if sensing the profound change of mood, Bong Cha chose this exact moment to join us. She came into the guitar room carrying a white oval tray, which looked like a miniature surfboard. It was almost as long as she was tall and she carried it with her widely spaced hands palms up on the underside. It was a masterpiece of finely judged balancing.

The contents of the tray suggested that she'd recently organised a ram raid on a seafood wholesaler. There were blinis piled with curls of reddish smoked salmon and tiny wedges of bright yellow lemon, all sitting on clusters of green rocket leaves. Dark brown triangular slices of rye bread had formations of fat pink prawns resting on them, embedded in some kind of pale green sauce and decorated with crescents of lime. Arrayed on a large circular black plate with a gold rim was a radiating formation of creamy-green halved avocadoes, their hollows filled with what looked like sour cream and alternating dollops of red and black fish roe. In a silver ice bucket there was the traditional bottle of blueberry vodka nestling in a white jacket of frosted chips. Plus plates, glasses, cutlery, napkins. Besides being an impressive balancing act, carrying all this stuff was a considerable feat of strength.

Tom Pyewell's face lit up at the sight of Bong Cha. "Oh, celestial princess!" he cried.

"Don't any of you buggers bother helping me," snarled Bong Cha in her best Brummie accent. Cue four grown men scrambling to their feet like frightened children. The low glass and chrome coffee table was in front of the sofa where Tinkler and I had been sitting, and now a path was cleared to it by a swift rearrangement of chairs, and the table itself was cleared of clutter.

Bong Cha lowered the tray onto the table while Erik displayed a rare example of making himself useful by dragging over another armchair so Bong Cha could join us. There was clearly no question of her disappearing back upstairs without partaking of the food and drink. In this respect at least, the Make Loud household was commendably egalitarian. And Erik garnered some extra brownie points, from me at least, by pouring drinks for everyone.

We began to eat and drink, and the mood in the room became even more relaxed. I decided now was the time. I leaned forward, and I guess my whole manner suggested getting down to business, because Tinkler immediately realised what was afoot and he took it so seriously he even set down his plate of food, watching me with his big, eager eyes. I tried not to let them put me off.

I cleared my throat and said, "Tom…" I'd decided to take a chance on first names. *Mr Pyewell* sounded both ridiculously formal and like someone in a nursery rhyme. He looked at me.

"I was wondering," I said, "if you might have a copy of one of your old records. Which you might be willing to part with."

"Part with?" he said, thoughtfully gnawing at a salmon blini.

"To sell to us. We're looking for an original pressing of the first release—"

"With the flip back cover," added Tinkler, who despite extensive assertions of how he couldn't be involved in the negotiations, now couldn't resist sticking his nose in.

"Ah," said Tom Pyewell. "*Wisht*."

And, at that very moment, as if to accompany the name of the album, there was a loud metallic cracking, which changed instantly into a sort of crystalline spattering, transmuting just as quickly into a thick, low thud of impact.

I turned my head and saw that a dark hole had appeared in the white wall on the far side of the room. I looked the other way and saw that one of the tall, barred windows now had a small, irregular hole in its glass surrounded by a milky halo with a complex web of cracks spraying outwards from it.

It was a bullet hole.

7. RED AND GREEN

I was the first to realise what was happening, because I was the only one who'd been in a situation like this before. "Someone's shooting at us," I said. Everybody was busy either looking with puzzlement at the hole in the wall or at the hole in the window.

Now they all turned to look at me.

My voice had been calm, matter of fact, even conversational. But now it cracked with tension. "*Get down*," I said.

I slid off the sofa and dragged Tinkler onto the floor with me.

The others didn't move, just stared at the two us, lying there face down in the dusty carpet. Tom Pyewell looked puzzled, Erik irritated, Bong Cha thoughtful. "Get down," I repeated. "Someone is shooting at us."

"Don't be bloody silly," said Erik. And, instead of getting down he stood up.

Immediately there was the metallic report of the gun,

the crystalline rupture of the window glass and another thud as—thank god—a bullet again dug into the wall instead of flesh. But it must have passed so close to Erik that he heard its flight, because he lifted his hand protectively to his ear, like a man who'd been buzzed by a wasp.

"You fucking fool," said Bong Cha. "Get down!" I realised she was on the floor now beside Tinkler and me. She lunged across the carpet in a sort of slithering, high-speed crawl and grabbed Erik around the legs, toppling him with a low rugby tackle.

He collapsed among us, narrowly missing both the coffee table and Tom Pyewell, who had joined us on the floor a fraction of a second after Bong Cha.

We all lay there, or crouched, staring at each other through a tangle of disarrayed limbs and the legs of the coffee table. "Someone's shooting at us," said Erik. He sounded both puzzled and pissed off, but at least now he was up to speed.

"*There he is*," said Tinkler in a voice so altered by fear that I hardly recognised it.

We all turned and saw, standing outside the window, beyond the black iron bars, something from a nightmare.

It was a tall, forbidding figure. He wore a red ski mask but otherwise was dressed all in black. And he had a gun in his hand, which he was just now pointing rather carefully towards us.

"Get out," I shouted. I headed for the door in a scrambling motion, which was half running and half crawling, keeping hunched as low as I could. Tinkler was right behind me and so were the others.

I heard another shot behind us and then we were out of the guitar room and in the hallway.

As I was to learn, most of Erik's basement was given over to the guitar room and the laundry room. They were divided by a long white corridor, which ran the entire width of the house, and that was where we emerged now in a frightened cluster. Without any need for discussion we all turned to our left and ran towards the staircase that was set in the far rear corner of the basement. Directly in front of us as we ran was the barred window placed to the left of the staircase, which let a cold grey light into the corridor. That light was abruptly interrupted as a shape reared up outside the window.

It was another tall figure, also dressed all in black. But the ski mask on this one was bright green, and he had a tiny dandified flash of scarlet emerging from a pocket on his chest—a coloured handkerchief.

He was holding a gun, which he now lifted and aimed.

We all turned and ran the other way. "The laundry room," yelled Bong Cha. "In here!" She dodged through a doorway to her left. We all followed.

Because I'd been the first out of the guitar room, closely followed by Tinkler, and because we had reversed the direction in which we'd been fleeing, I was now the last in our short line of terrified fugitives. I was acutely aware I had a maniac with a gun at my back, so I crouched low, leaning forward as I ran.

Which was just as well. Because there was a sudden cracking noise behind me and then the sickeningly familiar sound of a window being broken by gunshot. I thought I heard something hum over my head, and I definitely heard something smack into the wall at the far end of the corridor. But then I was through the door on the left and in the laundry room with the others.

We all stood there, panting, looking at each other.

The laundry room was a long rectangular space. To my left, at the far end, was a wall with a door in it, which led to what looked like a small toilet area. In front of us, the long back wall of the room had a built-in drying rack for clothes and a counter with a sink running along it. More to the point, this wall was blank and windowless—a very welcome sight.

It must have been the rear of the property and presumably the structure behind it cut off any light, so windows were a waste of time from the point of view of daylight. Though of course they would still have allowed a scenic view of the concrete moat that extended around all four sides of the building to more than head height.

To my right was the other short wall of the room. This did look out onto the moat, with a single barred window set into it.

That was one window too many for me.

Immediately to my right were the large white metallic cubes of a clothes washer and matching dryer. The washing machine was likely plumbed into the wall but the dryer would only be connected to it by an electrical cable. And, luckily for us, it was nearer the door than the washer. I grabbed the rear corner of it and began to shove it away from the wall. "Give me a hand," I said. I didn't say please. Good manners had gone by the board.

Tinkler, very much to his credit, immediately leapt to

my assistance. He got on the other side of the dryer and managed to rock it forward.

"What are you doing?" said Bong Cha.

"Leave that alone," said Erik, the scandalised property owner.

We ignored both of them. There was now enough space between the back of the dryer and the wall that I could step between them. I insinuated myself into the gap, unplugged the red rubberised power cable and threw it clanking on the top of the machine. Then I wedged myself against the dryer and pushed. Tinkler was instantly at my side helping me, and both Bong Cha and Tom Pyewell were grabbing the dryer at the front and manhandling it towards them. Erik was still watching with a petulant look on his face. "What are you all *doing*?" he said.

"Protection," said Bong Cha, and with no further explanation assisted us in shunting the dryer forward. It moved with a complaining screech of its metal underside as we dragged it across the concrete floor. As the rear of the dryer drew level with the front of its companion washing machine, I said, "Okay. Stop. Now the other way."

I came out from behind the dryer and threw my weight against the near side of it. Everyone else helped—even Erik, who either by now had worked out what we were doing or was simply following Bong Cha's lead.

With all of us working on it, the dryer lurched sideways with one quick metallic squeal so that it now stood in front of the washer instead of beside it.

I ducked down behind this reassuring improvised wall

of metal and so did the others. I was shaking and it felt as if something bulky and difficult to swallow had lodged in my throat. My heart was pounding so fast and so hard that my blood slammed painfully at the tips of my fingers and the rims of my ears.

That pounding slowed down a little now, but not much.

It was surprisingly comfortable sitting on the floor. The big metal cubes of the washer and dryer were reassuringly solid at our backs, shielding us from the window, and the concrete was warm beneath us, evidently heated by some kind of underfloor system. I found myself thinking that the cats would like it. I wondered if I'd ever see the furry little buggers again. Or Nevada.

But that was not the way to think. Be positive and we'd get out of this in one piece. Nevada... If only I could get in contact with her. If only I could tell her what was happening...

That was when I did the obvious thing and dug out my phone—only to realise that everyone else had beaten me to it and were already staring glumly at their own screens. Except for Bong Cha.

"I've got no signal," said Erik.

"Me neither," said Tinkler.

"Forget it, it's a dead zone in here," said Bong Cha, with the air of a woman who knew. I looked at my own phone. She was right. No signal.

"How do you know that?" said Erik, turning to Bong Cha. "Have you been trying to make phone calls when you're supposed to be doing the laundry?" He seemed genuinely interested.

"Trying is right," she spat.

"Is there a landline?" I said.

"There was," said Erik. He nodded at a pale rectangular mark above the counter opposite us where there had once been a wall-mounted phone. Of course. Nobody had a fucking landline anymore. "We had it taken out," he said unnecessarily. And unhappily. Then he began to move on his hands and knees across the floor, towards the door where we'd entered.

"What are you doing?" hissed Bong Cha.

"The guitars." said Erik. "They could be…"

"You are not going back for the guitars," said Bong Cha in a voice that did not allow for even the possibility of disagreement.

Erik turned and looked at her, staring over his shoulder as he kneeled there on all fours. "Just the Strats," he begged.

"Get back here," said Bong Cha. And Erik crawled back across the floor and huddled with us once again behind our washer-dryer wall.

"Maybe they're gone," he said, after a moment.

"Why would they be gone?" said Bong Cha. "They came here to kill us."

That shut everyone up.

Something bothered me about what they were saying—and not just the obvious thing. I couldn't work out exactly what it was… but something was wrong. I tried to think, but before I could even begin to concentrate on the matter, Tinkler said, "Oh, shit. They're here." He had been peering over the top of the dryer, but now he instantly dropped back to the floor beside us.

"How many of them?" whispered Bong Cha.

"Just one," Tinkler whispered back.

"Is it the one in the red ski mask or the green?" I said. It was absurd, but I was whispering too. Despite the fact that he couldn't possibly hear us, even if we shouted, the mere presence of our attacker just outside the window was so terrifying that it made it impossible to behave in any other way.

"What does it matter?" hissed Erik.

I couldn't have answered that, but somehow I knew it did matter. There was something here that I was missing, that we were all missing—

But any chance of focusing on the problem was destroyed by the sound of a gunshot shattering a window. Then there was a metallic chunking sound and the dryer at our back shuddered with the impact of the bullet. Another gunshot. This time the bullet ricocheted within the metal bowels of the machine, making a complicated and almost musical noise. A third shot. This one caused the drum inside to spin, giving a low, whirring sound. It was as if the dryer was making a muttering growl of disapproval.

"These appliances had better be solid," said Tom Pyewell. He spoke at a normal level—the gunfire had ended any compulsion to whisper—but in a tight, colourless voice.

"They ought to be," said Erik. "They cost enough."

"They're the finest Swedish models," said Bong Cha. "Bought at John Lewis."

Evidently our assailant, at least, was suitably impressed

by them, because he'd stopped shooting for the time being. I stared around the room to reassure myself of what I already knew: that there was no other window that he could get to that would allow him to fire on us in our sheltered hiding place. The long wall didn't have any windows. The short wall at the far end of the room only had the door in it, leading to the washroom. The long wall behind us only had the doorway to the corridor…

My mind raced to a conclusion and Tinkler's converged telepathically at the same point.

"Can he get in the front door?" said Tinkler.

"No," said Bong Cha firmly. "It's locked and it's secure. It's a high-quality door."

I said, "And do all the windows have bars on them?"

"Yes." Bong Cha's rock-solid certainty was very reassuring.

"How did he get in in the first place?" muttered Erik. "That's why I installed the gate."

"He just climbed over the railings," said Bong Cha wearily. "Anybody could climb over those damned railings. I told you that when we had the damned gate installed."

"I thought we were a hundred per cent secure," said Erik wonderingly. Now didn't seem the time to point out that he was the man who'd built his guitar room in a flood zone. And anyway, I'd realised what had been bothering me.

"His handkerchief," I said.

"What?" said Bong Cha.

"The gunman, when we were running towards the stairs. He had a red handkerchief in his breast pocket."

"That's right," said Tinkler.

"I didn't see," said Tom Pyewell. "Because I was behind you."

"And we didn't see," said Bong Cha. "Because we were behind *him*."

"So what?" said Erik.

I was thinking carefully about that flash of red. "It wasn't a handkerchief," I said. "It was the other ski mask."

"What the fuck is he talking about?" demanded Erik. He seemed a lot more angry with me than he was with the mad gunman outside. But then, I was close at hand and not a threat. An ideal candidate for him to vent his anguished fury on. I looked him in the eye and said, "It's just one guy."

Erik gave me a sort of tormented look and said, "I don't understand what you're saying."

"It's just one guy. He just took off the red ski mask and put the green one on, then he stuffed the red mask in his pocket. That's what I saw sticking out."

Erik stared at me. "And he did all this while he was running from the window in the guitar room to the window in the hallway?"

"Yes. He was in a hurry. That's why he didn't do such a great job at concealing the red ski mask. Just jammed it in his pocket."

"So he's running from window to window shooting at us, and changing his ski mask?"

"Yes," I said.

"It was red again just now," said Tinkler helpfully. "The ski mask he was wearing."

"Why? Why would he do that?" demanded Erik, looking

at me. "Why would he change his fucking mask?"

"I have no idea," I said. "But it's just one guy."

Erik gave a little moan of disgust and turned away from me. "You're out of your mind," he said.

"No, no," said Tom Pyewell excitedly. "I think he's right."

"Nonsense," said Erik. "There are two of them. One was shooting at us in the guitar room and the other guy was already waiting for us when we got to the stairs. No one could have got there that quickly from the guitar room."

"*We* got there that quickly," I pointed out.

"You're crazy," said Erik.

"No, he's right!" said Tom Pyewell. "Red and green…" Then he began to hum a tune, gesturing eagerly at Erik as he did so, as if he expected Erik to join in and hum along. Erik didn't. Instead now he was staring at Pyewell like *he* was crazy. Pyewell kept gamely on, though, humming several more bars.

I realised he must be a hell of a singer, because even when making this wordless noise, his voice was effortlessly musical. He kept humming as Erik stared at him blankly, until finally Pyewell faltered and fell silent.

"Don't you recognise that song?" he said, a little forlornly.

"I don't know all your songs," said Erik. He was suddenly defensive.

Pyewell shook his head in disbelief. "It would take too long to explain to you," he said, dismissing Erik. Then he turned to look at me. He smiled, a rather shy smile. "But suffice to say I believe you."

"Good," I said. "Thank you. Why?"

"Because that song I was humming, that was one of our numbers. One that we used to play in the band. It's a traditional song. Very ancient. What they call a murder ballad."

"Oh, great," said Tinkler.

"But the point is, it's about a killer who wears two coats, one red and one green. So people think there are two killers. But there's just one."

The explanation hadn't taken so long, after all. There was silence while it sank in. Pyewell was smiling eagerly. "It's on *Wisht*," he added, as if we might like to go and have a listen to the song right now.

"But these aren't coats," said Erik. "They're ski masks."

"Now isn't the time to be literal, Erik," said Bong Cha.

Erik turned and gazed at me. He looked scared, all right. But also strangely exalted. Maybe it was still the drugs. And he looked scornful, too.

"We're right," I said. "There's just one of them. I'm sure."

He shook his head. "I'm not going to risk my life on you being sure about something."

"I'm sure, too," said Tom Pyewell.

Erik kept on shaking his head. "Or you either. I still don't believe it."

"No, they're right," said Bong Cha. "The men are both using exactly the same gun, in exactly the same manner. It's just one man."

Erik turned to Tinkler, as if he had the deciding vote, and stared at him in mute appeal. Tinkler shrugged apologetically and said, "I think they're right, too. It's just one guy."

"All right, all right," said Erik petulantly. He was outvoted but he didn't have to like it. "So what if it is just one guy? What difference does that make?"

"Well," I said, "it reduces the odds against us by fifty per cent. And I for one feel a hell of a lot better about that." The others nodded solemnly, all except Erik, who eased away from us a little, like a sulky child who wasn't going to get his own way.

But in a sense Erik was right. What difference did it make? It was still the same situation, and it was still a stalemate. Even though there was only one gunman, he could always get to the staircase as quickly as we could. And shoot us if we tried to go up it.

We were trapped here for the foreseeable future.

But perhaps something else Erik had said was also relevant. About it being impossible to get from one window to another that quickly. He wasn't right, of course. It wasn't impossible. But it *was* difficult.

I swivelled around on the floor and turned towards the solid white metal of the dryer, and began to ease up it. "What are you doing?" said Tinkler.

"Just taking a look."

"Don't!"

I didn't bother arguing that Tinkler had done exactly this himself, just minutes ago. I just kept rising slowly behind the dryer, with my hand on top of my head, my fingers skimming its smooth metal. As soon as the metal vanished from under my fingers I knew I'd reached the top and I stuck my head up as quickly as I could.

The man in black was standing at the window, wearing the red ski mask.

Staring straight at me.

Just the sight of him had a sickening impact, like being punched in the stomach.

Then he raised the gun.

I dropped back behind the dryer, expecting him to fire at any instant. He didn't. Even so, I felt my resolve melting away.

I knew I had to act quickly, or I never would.

"I'm going to make a run for it," I said.

All of the others said "*No*" in exactly the same horrified manner at exactly the same time. Four voices in perfect synchronisation. In other circumstances it would have been funny. Now it was… rather touching.

Tinkler seized my arm. "Don't do it," he pleaded.

"I think I can make it," I said. "And once I'm up the stairs…" Actually, once I was up the stairs I wasn't sure exactly what I'd do. Use my phone? What if I still couldn't get a signal? It was patchy at the best of times. "Is there a landline up there?" I said.

"No," said Erik and Bong Cha, just the two of them synchronised this time. "But there's my phone," said Bong Cha. "I think I left it on the counter in the kitchen. And it will work. It's only down here it doesn't. It will definitely work."

I would have preferred her to be a little more definite about leaving it on the counter in the kitchen. This might have showed on my face because she added, "And my tablet is up there. And Erik's laptop. If for any reason you can't phone you can Skype or email, or something." She was right. Once I was up there, a whole world of possibilities would open up for me. For all of us. Possibilities of escape. And dealing with that fucker outside.

I nodded and smiled and Bong Cha smiled at me. Maybe for the first time ever. She had a surprisingly nice smile. She was totally on board with my escape attempt. But not Erik.

"You're out of your mind," he said. I was getting a bit tired of this theme from him.

"Please don't do it," said Tinkler. I looked at Tom Pyewell. Now it was me seeking out a deciding vote. Pyewell just shrugged and made a helpless gesture with his hands. Which rather annoyed me. *Get off the fence, Tom.*

"We're safe here," said Tinkler. "And he hasn't managed to hit any of us yet. But if you try to run…"

"Look," I said. "One of the reasons he's pretending to be two people is because it's easier to control us that way. If we think there's two of them—"

"I still *do* think there's two of them," said Erik in his most snotty voice. *Thank you for the vote of confidence, Erik.*

"If we think there's two of them we're less likely to try and make a dash for it," I said. "I think he's counting on that…" I stopped and looked at their faces. Tinkler aghast, Bong Cha encouraging, Tom Pyewell withdrawn and not meeting my gaze, Erik meeting it but manifestly hostile.

"Oh, fuck it," I said.

I didn't bother arguing anymore. I just got up and, keeping crouched as low as I could, dashed across the room towards the door. I heard Tinkler make a sobbing sound behind me and Erik cursing. Then I was out of the laundry room and into the hallway. I was running as fast as I could, and I was only in that long white corridor for less than a second. But it was enough time to feel a sickening, dreamy wave of déjà vu engulf me. There was the same barred window at the end of the hallway, beside the staircase. The same grey daylight streaming through it.

And, as I reached the end of the hallway, the same black-clad figure appearing at that window.

But this time he was still pulling on the ski mask the green one. While he struggled with it I spun around and raced back towards the laundry room, running for my life. He must have got the mask on—or maybe abandoned the attempt—and raised his gun and fired, because I heard the shot behind me.

But I was already safely disappearing back into the laundry room. I got down on my knees and crawled back towards the others, all of them staring at me and shouting encouragement, the lovely safe white cubes of the washer and dryer bulking large behind them. I skidded across the concrete floor and huddled beside my four dear friends.

There was another gunshot, from the window of this room now. The dryer shuddered with the impact of the bullet.

"Did he leave when I did?" I said.

"Yes, but he's back." Pyewell nodded in the vague direction of the window.

Another bullet hit the dryer.

"No shit," I said.

Another bullet. Our friend outside was angry.

"It's the same bloke. It's all one fucking guy," said Erik, as if he had originated this theory.

"I told you so," snarled Pyewell, as if *he* had.

Erik turned to me. "I told you not to go," he said. But he said it almost tenderly. I could tell by his eyes that he was glad to have me back.

That was when we heard it.

All of us noticed it at the same time.

A siren?

"It's the police," said Tom.

Definitely a siren.

"Of course," said Bong Cha. "Someone heard the gunshots."

"Someone called the police," said Erik.

A siren, getting steadily nearer.

"Thank Christ," said Pyewell.

"Amen," said Tinkler, in a voice evidently devoid of irony.

The siren was getting louder, approaching rapidly. I looked at the others. It seemed too good to be true. Was this really happening? I couldn't believe we were about to get out of here. It felt like we'd been in this room for most of my adult life.

The siren was so loud now it almost hurt to listen to it. But it wasn't so loud that we couldn't hear the gunshot. First the gunshot and then another sound. It was a sound that made us all jump. Funny to think that we'd grown accustomed to the acoustics of being shot at, yet we had.

But this new sound was oddly horrible. It sounded like somebody had dumped a sack of grain outside the window. Or thrown down a large suitcase.

"What the hell was that?" said Tinkler, raising his voice to make it heard over the siren.

The siren was right outside now, at maximum volume. Then it grew quieter. I tried to convince myself that the police had considerately turned it down now that they had arrived. But I knew it wasn't true.

The siren was fading in the distance.

It had passed the house and just kept going.

We were all staring at each other again. But now in horror instead of hope.

"They're not coming here," said Tom Pyewell.

"I don't think it was even the police," said Bong Cha. "I think it was a fire engine."

"Why *wasn't* it the police?" said Erik. "Why *aren't* they coming here?" His was the tormented disappointment of a hurt child, and we all felt it.

But it was the other noise that I was thinking of.

"What was that sound?" I said. "After the gunshot."

Tinkler was staring at me. "Something falling," he said.

"*Someone* falling," I said.

Tom Pyewell was staring at us. "You think he shot someone out there?" he said.

"No," said Bong Cha thoughtfully. "They think he shot *himself*."

"Shot himself," said Erik. He seemed to be having trouble wrapping his head around the concept. I didn't necessarily blame him.

"That's what it sounded like," I said. "First the gunshot, and then, right away—"

"*Thump*," said Tinkler. As he said it he hit the side of the dryer and we all flinched.

"Why would he have shot himself?" said Erik.

"Because the police were coming to get him," I said.

"But they weren't coming to get him. They weren't even the police."

"He didn't know that."

Erik shook his head stubbornly. "No. Nope."

"Yes. He must have thought we called the police."

"But we didn't," said Erik. "We couldn't call anyone."

"He didn't know that. He had no way of knowing that our mobiles wouldn't work or that we didn't have a landline."

Erik thought about this for a while. "So you think he thought the cops were on the way? And what, he…"

"Topped himself," said Tom Pyewell. I nodded. It was odd, but I was absolutely certain that this is what had happened. I couldn't see the window, but I knew that he was gone from it. And not just gone around the corner. He was *gone*.

"I don't believe it," said Erik. "He's just trying to lull us into a false sense of security."

If so, he's obviously not doing a very good job with you, I thought, rage and frustration beginning to rise in me. "I'll go and look," I said.

"No!" said Bong Cha. "You stay here. You went out before. You took a big risk. No more big risks." She began to crawl quickly in the direction of the far wall. "You stay there," she hissed, looking back at me suspiciously.

It seemed to take hours for her to traverse the space of floor between us and the door to the washroom, but it was less than half a minute. Moving along at floor level she shoved the door all the way open, revealing a small lavatory with a sink and a mirror. Bong Cha crawled inside, then shut the door behind her. I wondered if she was going to use the toilet. I wouldn't have blamed her.

But instead of the sound of water, I heard glass shattering. We all nearly jumped out of our skins. Then the door edged open and Bong Cha emerged again. She was crawling more slowly than before, because in one hand she was holding a large, jagged fragment of broken mirror. The milky daylight flared across it in a pearly flash, and I saw my face fleetingly reflected in it as she crawled towards us, and then Erik's, which had a bemused expression on it.

"What's that for?" he said. "A weapon?"

"Reflections," I said.

"That's right," said Bong Cha, grinning. Then she handed it to me. "Don't cut yourself," she said. "Hold it like this." I must have looked surprised because she said, "You wanted to take a look? Use this."

So I crawled out from behind the dryer and across the naked expanse of floor towards the window. I edged forward on my belly, nose so close to the floor I almost rubbed against it. I could smell its sandy concrete odour and a lingering taint of bleach. When I reached the window I held up the fragment of mirror. Daylight—dull, grey daylight, then the window glass, crazed with shatter-lines. Then suddenly a clear slice of the moat outside came into view. I adjusted the angle until I could see something in the depths of the moat. A dark shape.

"He's down," I said. "I think he's dead."

"He could be faking it," said Erik.

"I don't think so."

I lowered the piece of mirror and set it on the floor. I looked back towards the white wall of washer and dryer and saw two sets of eyes peering anxiously over them at me. Tinkler and Bong Cha.

I took a deep breath and stood up. I heard equally deep breaths being taken behind me. Gasps, actually. I leaned towards the window, pockmarked with bullet holes and webbed with cracks, and gazed out.

He was lying on the ground, looking more like a heap of black clothes than anything that constituted a real person. His posture, or utter lack of it, instantly convinced me that he was genuinely dead. There was a dark and slowly growing pool of blood on the concrete around him and, most importantly, the gun lay on the ground some distance away.

In the floor of the moat there was a rusty circular drain with rectangular cross bars, about the size of a soup bowl, set into the concrete. A dark thread of blood was working its way towards this, as if to demonstrate a general principle about the flow of liquid, or perhaps to illustrate the efficacy of the drain's siting.

"He's dead," I said. I straightened up and backed away from the window, never moving my gaze, staring fixedly at the pockmarked glass, as if I expected the bloody and defunct gunman to suddenly rear up grinning—*Just kidding!*—and start firing again.

Only when I reached the others did I dare to turn my back. And then I ran from the room. We all did. Never mind that our assailant was dead and the threat was over. We ran like hell. It was a feral, panicked, unseemly rush, each of us trying to shove past the others and get up the staircase first. Being physically the smallest, Bong Cha might have been crushed in the stampede if she hadn't led the way, loping nimbly up the steps.

8. AT THIS TIME OF THE MORNING

We emerged from the staircase into the front hall of Erik's house. It was like we'd risen from the underworld. The winter daylight was still pale and tentative, but there was a hell of a lot more of it, coming in through windows that suddenly no longer presented a lethal threat. The five of us came to a halt, looking at each other. I suppose we were all a little ashamed of having bolted up the stairs at full speed, but given the chance to do it again I would have run every bit as fast.

Tom Pyewell looked at Erik. "I still can't believe you didn't recognise that tune of ours." He sounded genuinely upset.

"What tune?"

Pyewell gave an exhausted, disgusted little sigh. "Our song about the killer with two coats, one red and one green."

"I'm sorry, mate. I'll be sure to have a listen to it soon."

"So will I," said Tinkler. "What's it called?"

"'The Killer with Two Coats'," said Tom Pyewell.

"That's a lousy title," said Tinkler. "It gives the whole

game away immediately. And it completely spoils the twist at the end." He was grinning now, giddy with relief. I felt the same way.

"We'd better call the police," said Bong Cha, all business.

"No, no, hang on a minute," said Erik.

"We have to call them."

"Yeah, yeah, yeah, but just hang on a minute. Let's get our stories straight first." Erik looked at us. "I always find that, where the filth is concerned, it's best to have your stories straight."

I expected Bong Cha to argue, but instead she was nodding. "The simplest story is always best for the police," she said.

"Right," said Erik. "Madman turns up. Shoots a bunch of holes in the house then finally, fortunately, shoots himself." He nodded at us. "No one else was hurt. No one else was even here. You don't want to sit through a police questioning if you don't have to." I must have looked surprised because he paused and gave me a hard stare. "Unless you *want* to spend the next day or two in the cop shop, giving details of what happened."

Of course I didn't. The temptation now to just go home—to Nevada, our house, our cats—was quite overwhelming. "No," I said, "we'll go. We were never here. That's fine."

Tinkler nodded enthusiastically. So did Tom Pyewell. Bong Cha began handing us our coats—the model hostess at the end of a successful party.

Erik was all business now, too. "I'll call the police, Bong. But first you gather up all the goodies and take them out to the garden. Put them in the fake boulder. They'll never find them there."

Goodies? He meant drugs. Of course he had drugs in the house. He was a rock star. Bong Cha nodded and grinned. "It's just like the old days," she said, helping Tom Pyewell put on a long and elegant black coat.

But Pyewell suddenly froze, then started pulling the coat off again. He shook his head. "Sorry. I forgot. I posted on social media that I was coming to visit you this morning. And these days even the filth reads Facebook. I'd better stay. Could get sticky if they find out I was here and left. Best sit tight." He looked at me. "You didn't post on social media did you? That you were coming here?"

I shook my head, but then I looked at Tinkler. To my relief he was also shaking his, though rather wistfully. "Didn't think of it," he said. "Too late now, I suppose."

I decided to get him out of there before it occurred to him to ask for a selfie.

We all looked at each other awkwardly for a moment, and then we said goodbye. Erik surprised me by lunging forward, grasping my hand firmly and shaking it hard. Bong Cha surprised me even more by giving me a hug, her head tucked under my chin. While she was doing that Tom Pyewell patted me on the shoulder, and Erik gave Tinkler a hug.

Then we were out the door, into November daylight. We crossed the little rattling footbridge, and went out through the black iron gate. It clanged shut behind us. I turned to look back into the moat, to search for the body.

But Tinkler must have realised what I was doing. He grabbed my arm and pulled me away. "No, no, no. You don't want that picture in your head." He was right. And I was glad he'd stopped me.

We walked side by side, with the clean air blowing in at us off the Thames. The sky was grey over the river and it was cold. The streets were almost eerily quiet. "I thought you said the traffic was terrible?"

"It was," said Tinkler. "Look at it now. Everybody's gone. Sod's law."

"Where's your car?"

"I parked it back by Vine Road."

"Christ," I said. "That's miles away."

"Like I said, the traffic was terrible. I parked it and walked the rest of the way."

"Christ," I said again. I was shivering so violently that my teeth were chattering, and it wasn't just the cold.

We walked past the Bull's Head, where we'd listened to many fine hours of live jazz, and then the wine merchants, beloved of Nevada, and the cheese shop, beloved of Tinkler. I was a little surprised that he didn't drop in to make a purchase. But we just kept walking. Past the Sun Inn, where we crossed the road, and past the pond where various elegant waterfowl were wading and swimming as if nothing had happened. I suppose, in their world, nothing had.

We were crossing Barnes Green, heading for the small bridge that spanned Beverley Brook, when suddenly my legs buckled under me. I almost went down onto the grass, like a collapsing structure. A scarecrow, random clothes stuffed with straw, who'd been severed from his supporting pole.

"It's reaction," said Tinkler, putting a hand on my arm to steady me.

"No kidding," I said. My voice was a rusty croak.

"Just reaction setting in," he crooned gently. He lifted my arm and draped it over his shoulders. We kept walking, although maybe in my case walking was not quite the right word. My legs were like rubber springs, but made of rubber that had begun to perish and go spongy and fail in all sorts of chaotic and unpredictable ways. I staggered along, half carried by Tinkler. We walked, in our halting, stumbling way towards Beverley Brook.

We passed a pretty young nanny pushing a double buggy with twin babies in it. She gave us a concise glance of contempt as we staggered past—drunk, and at this time of the morning, too.

Tinkler was a pillar of strength helping me get to his car. But when we arrived and he took his keys out of his pocket, his hands began shaking so badly he couldn't unlock the car door. "I'll be all right in a minute," he said, sounding none too certain.

"Forget it," I said. "Leave the car here. We'll walk back to my place. We're almost there anyway." Tinkler didn't argue. In fact, he gave a sigh of relief. We leaned on his little blue Volvo for a moment, the frosted metal cold at our backs, our breath clouds of steam in the chill air, as we gathered our strength.

Then, as we started walking, I phoned Nevada and told her what had happened—or rather, I got about halfway through telling her what had happened and then she said she was coming to meet us and hung up. She must have run like an Olympic sprinter because she was there waiting on the other side of the second railway crossing when we arrived.

Of course, we hit trains at both crossings today and had to wait for them to pass. We stood there impatiently, waving to each other and I repressed an urge to scramble over the barrier and run across the tracks towards Nevada. It would have been particularly stupid to have survived everything we'd been through today and then get run over by a train.

A train streaked past. Then another one.

Then another one.

"Jesus Christ," I snarled.

"Easy, big fella," said Tinkler.

Then another one.

Then the trains finally stopped coming and the barriers on either side rattled open and I was running towards Nevada and she was running towards me. The impact as she flung her arms around me almost knocked my breath out. A teenage couple and a woman with a bicycle all stared at us.

"No public displays of affection, please," said Tinkler. "We're all British around here."

We walked past Barnes Common, across the South Circular and then we were on Abbey Avenue. We turned off into our housing estate and we were home in a couple of minutes. Nevada's dramatic departure must have cued the cats that something was up, because they surged towards us the instant the door was opened. Even Uncle Tinkler was made a big fuss of.

I poured both of them a large bowl of biscuits, rejoicing in this most prosaic of domestic actions—at the fact that I was still alive and able to do it. And do it without my hands trembling, either, I noticed. Things were returning to normal. Meanwhile, as if to illustrate this point, Nevada pulled a bottle of wine off our rocket-shaped wine rack and opened it. I was touched to see that it was the Paul Jaboulet Aîné Condrieu *Les Cassines*—the most expensive wine in the house.

Tinkler recognised it, too. "Shouldn't you be saving that for a special occasion?" he said. Nevada ignored him, inserted the corkscrew and pulled the cork with a few deft movements and a most satisfying popping sound. She poured us each a glass. We stood there in our little kitchen, the cats busy crunching on their dry food, and the three of us clinked glasses.

"Long life," said Nevada. Then she began to sob. I set my glass down and put my arms around her.

"I knew something was wrong," she said. "I've been on edge all day. I thought it was just my period coming on…"

"'Just'," said Tinkler, sipping his Condrieu.

Nevada wiped her face on her sleeve and gave him a narrow-eyed look. "Do you want to drink that wine or *wear* it, Tinkler?"

"Oh, I'll drink it, I'll drink it."

We polished off the bottle in record time and then another one, this time a lesser Condrieu, then a third one—a good Viognier but not a Condrieu—then rang for a taxi for

Tinkler. He could collect his car another day. He wasn't going to be driving anywhere for a while, even if he didn't have the better part of a bottle of wine in him.

We said our farewells, he tottered drunkenly off and then Nevada and I collapsed on the sofa. Turk jumped up on the coffee table beside us and proceeded to give herself a thorough wash, gnawing and licking at the fur on one elegantly extended leg, while keeping a careful eye on us. Fanny jumped up on the sofa to join us and scrambled up my chest, putting her little pink nose close to my mouth and carefully sniffing at my breath, presumably to make sure that I hadn't been drinking any inferior wine.

Nevada lovingly kneaded the little cat's fur. She said, "This morning... around about the time it all must have been happening to you at Erik's... Fanny ran to the front door and stood there staring and crying out. Such heartfelt little cries. It was the most extraordinary thing."

Personally I suspected that at that moment somebody had been walking past our front door with a roast chicken, but I was too weary to argue the point.

I lay there on the sofa with Nevada and the cats, all in easy stroking distance, for a long timeless while. Then I gradually became aware of the smell of fear on me and my clothes. I went into the bedroom and stripped off while Nevada ran me a hot bath. I lay soaking in the tub with her sitting on the corner of it, chatting idly. It was as if she didn't want to let me out of her sight. The cats kept peering in, too, to check on us.

Nevada handed me a towel as I got out. I dried myself

and walked back towards the bedroom with her. "Don't bother getting dressed," she said, as she began pulling off her clothes.

There was the rhythmic thud of small feet on a hard floor and then our cats were peering around the bedroom door checking that it was safe to come in after the earlier commotion. It was. Nevada and I had sunk back on the bed, gainfully exhausted, our sweat cooling, our heartbeats slowing.

I said, "The near-death experience certainly perks up one's sex life."

"We can find other ways of perking it up," murmured Nevada. "Just don't have any more near-death experiences, all right?" She wrapped her arms around me as the cats jumped up on the bed, each taking their preferred place beside us. Nevada's breathing, and my breathing, settled into a hypnotic rhythm. The cats were already asleep.

We all lay there together, myself at least still hovering on the edge of consciousness in a moment that promised to expand to be timeless, when the phone rang.

The cats jumped off the bed, synchronised and scandalised, and I raised myself up on one elbow, staring towards the bedroom door. The phone continued to ring. It was mine, where I'd left it in the sitting room. The sound had already thoroughly jangled my nerves and I was wide awake again.

"Why didn't I switch it off?" I said.

"As I recall, we were in rather a rush," said Nevada.

I sighed, kissed her and got out of bed, grabbing a dressing gown. As I entered the sitting room Turk was vanishing out the cat flap into the back garden and Fanny was standing on the counter in the kitchen giving me a hopeful look: on the one hand her nap had been interrupted, on the other there was now the possibility of biscuits.

I picked up the phone and looked at it. Tinkler.

Under other circumstances I might have been exasperated or annoyed. But now as I answered I just hoped he was okay. Tinkler didn't seem the type to suffer much from post-traumatic stress, but you never knew…

"Turn the TV on," he said, with no greeting or preamble.

"What?"

"Turn it on. Quick. Now. BBC One."

I hurried back into the bedroom, Nevada giving me a surprised look as I scooped up the remote and sat down on the edge of the bed as the TV screen came to life. I'd lost track of time but it was the London news.

Tom Pyewell was standing on the road near Erik's house with the Thames framed picturesquely in the background. He was dressed the way I'd seen him a few hours ago, including the long black coat. Standing beside him was a big man, somewhat taller than Tom and considerably more bulky. He was expensively, meticulously and eccentrically dressed in black and white checked trousers and a black and gold brocade jacket with a floral pattern on it. He also wore tennis shoes and a yellow and black Rupert the Bear scarf. His long hair and long beard were a wild mess of grey, but both the quality of his clothes and the gleaming intelligence of his eyes cancelled any impression of a drunk, derelict or wild man. As did his voice.

The camera moved in close on him as he said, in mellow and educated tones, "I was in London this morning visiting the Church of St Sepulchre, a regular pilgrimage I make, standing in front of the John Ireland Memorial Window, and I was actually thinking about the band, thinking about Black Dog and Tom—" At this point the man glanced to his side and the camera bobbed back to take in Tom Pyewell standing beside him, just long enough for Pyewell to nod and open his mouth as if he was about to say something, but then the big man started speaking again and the camera closed in on him once more, excluding Pyewell.

And the man said, "So there I was, making a pilgrimage to a shrine—so to speak—of one of our musical heroes, and thinking about the good old days with the band and with Tom and *at that very moment* my phone starts blowing up, with messages about what had happened here." At this point, some lettering and graphics belatedly appeared at the bottom of the screen identifying the speaker as *Max Shearwater, Founder and Lead Singer of Black Dog*. "So of course, I rushed straight over." He turned to look at Pyewell and the camera drew back again to show both men. Shearwater's voice grew husky. "And thank god, he was all right. It really makes you…"

"It really makes you think," said Pyewell.

Shearwater nodded eagerly. "It makes you realise…"

"Realise that all of…"

"Our differences and petty arguments…"

"All of that just, ultimately, doesn't matter," said Pyewell. "What matters is…"

"That you're alive," said Shearwater.

"And you are too. And life is just too…"

"Precious."

"Too short."

"Too precious and too short."

"Too short for any bad blood or differences," said Shearwater.

"For any silly grudges or stupid feuds."

"So we're going to be getting back together," said Shearwater.

"The band is going to get back together," said Pyewell.

"That's right," said Shearwater.

"Black Dog is getting back together," said Tom Pyewell decisively. A caption now appeared under his image. It said, *Tom Piewell, Guitarist in Black Dog.* I didn't think Tom would appreciate either the misspelling of his name or his demotion in comparison to the stature of Max Shearwater, the putative 'founder' of the group. I wondered how long the band's reunion would last after Tom got home and saw this on television. But then I was distracted by the sight of the two men embracing furiously, rocking together tearfully in each other's arms, two burly older blokes standing beside the river. It was actually quite touching, and even the news anchor looked moved as we cut back to her saying it was time for the weather and goodnight.

I switched off the television and put the phone to my ear. "Did you see that?" I said.

"Of course I did," said Tinkler. "I was the one who told you to watch. The band's getting back together. And it's all thanks to us."

"What? We didn't have anything to do with it."

"Oh, come on," said Tinkler. "Pyewell would never even have been there if we hadn't been trying to swindle him out of his record."

"I can't even begin to follow your twisted logic," I said.

"It's all very simple and I'll explain it to you in easy words of very few syllables. But not right now. Right now Maggie's here and I better get back to her." Maggie was Tinkler's sister and I imagine he'd told her what had happened and she'd rushed over to be with him. "Goodnight," he said.

"Goodnight, Tinkler."

I switched off the phone and looked at Nevada, who was sitting up in bed with Fanny cradled in her arms, evidently having abandoned the quest for dried cat treats.

"The band is back together," I said.

"So I understand. It's an ill wind that blows no good."

I said, "That's what you said about the charity shops."

"It applies here, too."

I got back into bed. Nevada switched off the light and repositioned Fanny beside her. Then she rolled over and hugged me, and whispered softly in my ear:

"If anyone ever shoots at you again, and you're running away, run in a zigzag pattern instead of straight. And try and make it an irregular pattern, so they can't predict it."

"Yes, ma'am."

Pillow talk.

9. THE KILLER WITH TWO MASKS THING

In the days following the nightmare at Erik Make Loud's house, details of our attacker began to emerge. His name was Stanley Strangford, from Southcote, Reading. And the now-dead Stanley was rapidly retrofitted into a number of handy media templates, most notably *obsessive fan*, *embittered dropout* (he'd abandoned a law degree at the University of Reading) and *unhinged loner*. Some of his neighbours—there were no signs of friends or family—appeared before cameras and obligingly said how shocked they were and, right on cue, reminisced about how quiet he'd been.

Nevada said, "Just for once I wish that people would say that one of these bastards held non-stop noisy parties."

But I guess bastards who hold non-stop noisy parties have better things to do than end up in news segments. Anyway, add *isolated loser* to those templates.

Stanley Strangford had lived a rich and extensive existence online, however, with a massive presence among Black Dog fan sites and discussion groups. He was utterly fixated on the band, especially poor Tom Pyewell, and Stanley's digital footprint was particularly heavy in the corners of cyberspace where Pyewell was vindictively criticised and blamed for the decline of Black Dog. Stanley had also drilled deep down into the band's supposed occult connections—Black Dog's drummer Pete Loretto featured heavily here—and perused these with an unhealthy appetite and enthusiasm, if his computer's cache was anything to go by.

And then, in his final weeks, Stanley Strangford had spent virtually every waking hour—and there'd been a lot of them; he'd hardly slept—researching Tom's life and routine and movements. So add *Internet fanatic* and *psychotic stalker* and then call it a day…

Having ascertained that Strangford had obtained his gun online—how else?—the police didn't find anything more of interest on his computer, so they did indeed call it a day. And Stanley was forgotten with surprising swiftness. More than fifteen minutes of fame, maybe, but certainly less than fifteen days. Then he was as gone and forgotten as it's possible to be, fading from every human synapse and computer buffer into an oblivion as complete as any being could aspire to.

I felt no regret about this on his behalf, as he disappeared into eternity.

After all, the fucker had tried to kill me.

Christmas came and went, then New Year. The memory of what had happened at Erik's began to fade. I was absorbed back into the everyday business of trying to earn a living looking for records. I wasn't having much luck but my beloved's canny reselling of second-hand fashion items kept us in funds until late spring.

At which point we found ourselves seriously broke. Again.

All this time Tinkler's desire for the flip back copy of *Wisht* had been very much on my mind. To me it was unfinished business. I hated to admit defeat, and I was convinced that I could find a copy, despite Stinky having fucked up our chances by telling the world and his wife how rare and desirable the record was.

I knew I could find it.

What I didn't know was whether Tinkler still wanted to buy a copy, for a very large sum of money. And, more importantly, whether he'd front the funds to provide us with expenses— living and otherwise—while I searched for it again.

He'd gone silent about the subject of the record, and I couldn't blame him for that, or for changing his mind about wanting it, if indeed that is what had happened. And, though we had the sort of friendship where we could talk about virtually anything, including the most sensitive subjects— indeed, try shutting Tinkler up about such things—this was a little bit different.

Neither of us particularly wanted to bring up what had happened to us, or almost happened to us, at Erik's that day. And of course the record was all tied up with this. It was the reason we'd been there, and the reason we'd been in harm's way.

So we avoided the subject.

But we didn't avoid the subject of Black Dog. Or at least Tinkler didn't. He never got tired of claiming that we were responsible for the band getting back together. And there was a modest, but steady and growing excitement about this reformation among fans old and new, fed by a steady string of announcements, rumours and speculations concerning new songs, new albums and a tour, first of the UK and then the world...

All of which came to a screeching halt in mid-May when the sudden death of Black Dog's drummer Pete Loretto was announced. And it wasn't just any old death, so to speak. His wife Sarita had killed him and then killed herself.

I felt a distinct cold chill when I heard this, and not just for any of the usual reasons. I went to Nevada to talk to her about it—she was sitting out in the garden with Fanny—only to find her on her way inside to talk to me about the same thing. She had the newsfeed about the incident on her phone. She held it up.

"Does this remind you of something?" she said.

"Yes," I said, delighted that she was one step ahead. "What happened to Norrie, the manager of the band."

Nevada frowned and shook her head. "No. What almost happened to *you*."

Sarita Loretto had killed her husband and herself using a firearm. Now, in some parts of the world this wouldn't have raised an eyebrow. But in Britain gun crime was still a thankful rarity. Of course, inner-city gangs were known to shoot each other up, but the Lorettos had lived on the idyllic, rural Halig Island.

"Isn't that where the band burned their money?" said Nevada.

I had told her about the million-dollar bonfire and it had made a very deep and vivid impression on her, as well it might. You'd have to sell a lot of second-hand clothes—not to mention records—to have that kind of money in your hands. And then to *burn* it…

"Yes," I said. "That's the place. Apparently all the band members have houses there. Or I suppose, *had* is now the correct tense with Pete Loretto dead."

"Why would they have houses on the island where they burned the money?"

"Good question," I said. "It's supposed to be lovely there, though."

"I would have thought they'd never want to see the place again. I'd never want to see the place again, if it was me. Lovely or not."

The Lorettos had apparently been running a modest pig-breeding business as part of their idyllic, rural, etc. existence on Halig Island. And they'd obtained a handgun, highly illegally, to kill their pigs before butchering them. An odd choice, some might say.

"Poor pigs," said Nevada. "I still want to know why they're all living on the island where they burned a million bucks. The scene of the crime, so to speak."

"I'll ring Tinkler and ask him." Which I proceeded to do. After exchanging comments about how shocking Loretto's death was, I popped the question.

"Well, it's a lovely island," said Tinkler.

"That's what I said, but I don't think Nevada is satisfied with that as an answer."

"Okay. I'll do a bit of digging and find out more and brief you."

"You're being strangely cooperative, Tinkler," I said, suspicion growing in me.

"If you'd let me finish my sentence, it wouldn't seem so strange. I'll brief you, providing you cook supper for me."

"All right." We were about due for a Tinkler visit, anyway.

"Now who's being strangely cooperative? How about making the Ligurian pasta with the avocado pesto?"

"Okay."

"See what I mean? Strangely cooperative."

So I cooked the Ligurian dish—trofie pasta, gently steamed green beans and baby potatoes—and stirred in the pesto, made with a large clove of garlic, a little olive oil, a couple of tablespoons of ground almonds, a large bunch of basil leaves, the flesh of a large ripe avocado and a squeeze of lemon, all blended until smooth. The ground almonds were my own little wrinkle. I substituted them for pine kernels, which I hated because the only ones we could get tasted like cardboard. Rancid cardboard, at that.

"Not bad, not bad at all," said Tinkler as we ate. "The green beans are perhaps a little overcooked…"

"Watch it, Tinkler," said Nevada.

"Did I mention how splendid the wine is?" said Tinkler hastily. We were drinking red with the pasta, of course, a nice M. Chapoutier Côtes-du-Rhône Villages, which Nevada had chosen. Also of course.

"Don't think I don't know you're just buttering me up," said Nevada. "Would you like another glass?"

"Is the pope Catholic? That's a yes, by the way." Tinkler looked at me. "And the pesto is *very* nice. Hard to believe that I like something so much which is vegan. By the way, did you know that was why she killed him?"

"Who killed who?" said Nevada.

"Pete Loretto," I said. "And his wife. Or rather, his wife and him."

"She killed him because he was vegan?"

"Because *she* was vegan," said Tinkler. "And he was insisting on raising these pigs and slaughtering them."

"Poor pigs," said Nevada again.

"And she apparently befriended them, the wife befriended the pigs, during the long process of raising them, you know, from cute little piglets…"

"Poor piglets."

"And in the end she just couldn't stand it. They were supposed to kill the pig and they had this gun ready to shoot it, but she shot him instead. Her husband. And then herself."

"Doesn't that remind you of anything?" I said.

Tinkler nodded as he rubbed the last of the pesto off his plate with a chunk of focaccia. "Yes. What happened to Norrie the manager with the Loopy Groupie."

"No," said Nevada. "What almost happened to both of you with the ski-mask lunatic."

"Oh. Yeah. I guess. Is there any more of this pesto?"

When we were finished eating, and the cats had taken turns coming in and clamouring for attention—read *biscuits*—I said to Tinkler, "Okay, time to sing for your supper."

"Sing for my… oh, I get it. But surely you realise people have to be made to sing *first*. Before their supper. Otherwise what leverage do you have? Plus, who can sing well on a full stomach?"

"Tinkler…"

"Okay, so Halig Island is basically a volcanic cone…"

"You can skip the geology."

"It features a medieval monastery, which was always being raided by Vikings. Oh, those nasty Norsemen. So they built a castle to protect the monastery…"

"And the ancient history."

"Oh, okay. Right, well. So Max Shearwater was the first to buy a place there. And then, not to be outdone, Tom Pyewell got a house on the island, too. And apparently he loved it. Loved the place. In fact, it was Pyewell who suggested they burn the money there."

"He loved it so much that he suggested they burn their money there?" said Nevada.

"That's right. He was the one who chose the spot. For the billion-dollar barbecue."

"It was a million dollars, not a billion."

"I know, but it doesn't alliterate."

"True. Also, it wasn't a barbecue. It was a bonfire."

"Still doesn't alliterate," said Tinkler. "And if you're going to be pernickety pedants…"

"Well, that does alliterate," said Nevada graciously. "So please do go on."

"Thank you. I will. Where was I? Oh, yes, Tom

Pyewell had found a dramatic beauty spot overlooking the ocean—I mean, the whole damned island overlooks the ocean, doesn't it? But apparently this spot particularly. Anyway, Pyewell chose it and Shearwater enthusiastically agreed. Perfect venue for a spot of million-dollar burning. Looked great in the photos anyway. And, after they burned the money, both Jimmy Lynch, the fiddle player, and Pete Loretto, the drummer…"

"The late drummer," I said.

"Ah yes, the late drummer. Poor chap. Never marry a vegan. That's clearly the lesson here. Where was I? Oh, yes, Loretto and Lynch both bought houses there, after they burned the money."

"Why would they do that?" said Nevada. "Why would they want to live there afterwards?"

"Well, it's a beautiful place."

After the death of Pete Loretto, Tinkler shut up about how we'd been responsible for the band getting back together, naturally enough. Because the band could never get back together now. They could have hired a new drummer, I suppose, but it wouldn't have been the same. So all the energy went out of the project, again naturally enough.

This seemed to finally close the door on *Wisht* and Tinkler's desire to obtain a copy. And our desire to make a handsome commission on finding him one. We stopped talking about Black Dog and that was that.

May turned into June and our financial position became

so precarious—no decent charity shop discoveries to flog, in either clothing or vinyl—that Nevada decided to set up a website about our cats. "Might as well see if we can monetise the little darlings," she said.

"You're going to sell your cats?" said Tinkler. "Online?"

"No. We're going to post about their adventures and—"

"Oh, well, that will be a big hit. Remind me to get in on the ground floor. I missed out on Google shares, but this ought to more than make up for that."

This raised Nevada's ire, and the situation wasn't eased when Tinkler said something about "pimping out your cats in cyberspace" and I thought I might have to intervene to prevent bloodshed.

But just then the phone rang.

It was Tom Pyewell.

"I got your number from Erik. I hope that's okay."

"Of course," I said. My voice must have revealed my surprise because in the background Nevada and Tinkler had immediately stopped squabbling.

"I've been meaning to get in touch ever since… ever since… well, you know."

"I do. I do know."

"It was really nice to meet you and your mate…"

"Tinkler," I said, and Tinkler stared at me and touched his chest, eyebrows raised. I shook my head.

"And I meant to keep in touch," said Tom Pyewell. "But you know how it is."

"I do."

"I mean, I sort of felt we'd all become friends during

the… incident… and when it was over I thought we'd formed a bond and that we'd all be in touch. But I haven't even been in touch with Erik. And we're mates. I mean old mates, from way back. What I realised was, although it had formed a bond between us, it also was a bit unpleasant to remember, to think about. So I've tried to avoid thinking about it."

"I understand," I said. "We feel completely the same way."

Nevada was leaning towards me and silently mouthing the words, *Who is it?*

Tom Pyewell, I mouthed back. But Nevada didn't get it. Tinkler did, though, and he whispered in her ear.

"Anyway," said Pyewell. "Today I thought, enough is enough. Grasp the nettle. Like I said, I hadn't even been in touch with Erik since then. So today I rang him up and we had a long chat, and it was great, a real relief. A lovely catch-up. So I was on a roll, and I thought I'd get in touch with you at last. You and Tinkler. Anyway, are you guys still interested in that record?"

"Yes," I said, trying not to actually yell the word.

"The original version of our album *Wisht*?"

"Yes."

"The one with the original version of the songs before Max made us scrap them all?"

"Yes," I said. I wasn't sure my blood pressure could take this conversation-by-instalments. "Absolutely."

"I remember you were asking me about it just when…" *Just when the crazed Stanley Strangford started shooting at us*, I didn't say.

"Yes, that's right," I said.

"Anyway, I didn't think about it for quite a while."

"Entirely understandable," I said.

"But then I remembered. Just before I got back in touch with Erik, I remembered what you said. And I decided to have a look for it."

"That was very good of you."

"Not at all. But I have a lot of records, and they aren't as organised as they might be."

"I know that feeling," I said. And we both laughed politely.

"So I had a good look through my record collection…"

"Yes?"

"And I can't find it."

There then ensued a brief silence during which I had the unworthy fantasy of crawling up the telephone cable to wherever Tom Pyewell was and strangling him with it at the other end.

Perhaps he was waiting for me to say something. But I couldn't think of anything to say. So finally he said, "But I know I've got a copy somewhere."

He sounded very certain, and my hopes began to rise again.

"Or at least I did have one."

My hopes sank.

"I think someone might have borrowed it."

"Oh, well," I began to say.

Tom Pyewell broke in hastily. "But if someone did borrow it, it was only one of the fellows in the band. So if it's not among my records, it will be among theirs. And even if I don't have a copy, I know that one of them does. I'm certain of it. I know I saw one not so long ago." He finished on a triumphant note and I found myself back in the position, despite myself, of believing that we might actually be onto something here.

"So I have a suggestion," said Tom Pyewell.

"Yes?"

"Why don't you come to the Green Ceremony?"

10. THE GREEN CEREMONY

The Green Ceremony was a midsummer folk music festival in Ashington, West Sussex. "The most highly regarded event in the annual folk music calendar." And Jimmy Lynch, one of the surviving members of Black Dog, had a house nearby, in addition to his one on Halig Island. It was Tom Pyewell's opinion that either Jimmy might have a copy of *Wisht* or, rather more likely, that I'd find one at the record fair that took place at the festival. "A huge tent full of records," he told me. "Lots of dealers. It's the biggest folk music record market in Europe. New stuff but also lots of old stuff. Old and rare records. It's the number one event for the folk music collector."

Other than the mention of dealers, I liked the sound of this a lot.

Nevada immediately put the Green Ceremony in our diary.

We set off on the appointed Friday in the teeth of a midsummer heatwave, driving south with the windows cracked open in Tinkler's eccentric little Volvo, known affectionately as Kind of Blue, both in tribute to Miles Davis's great album and to the vehicle's slightly odd paint job. I did the driving, since Tinkler never knowingly missed an opportunity to be a passenger in his own car. Nevada was beside me in the front, peeling oranges and fretting about the cats. "I wonder if Clean Head would mind me just sending her one more text about looking after them?" she mused.

"Won't that spoil the fun of reading all the notes you left for her on the fridge?"

"Yes, I suppose it would," she sighed.

The A24 took us all the way to Ashington where we took the London Road—it was reassuring to know that the way home was so clearly signposted—and then turned onto Rectory Lane. Along here signs began to appear announcing THE GREEN CEREMONY in large green letters on a white background with arrows pointing straight ahead and then, finally, towards our left.

"Why the Green Ceremony?" said Nevada.

"Well," said Tinkler, "Black Dog's first album was called *White Ceremony*. And the second album was called *Scarlet Ceremony*."

"So," I said, "was *Green Ceremony* their third one?"

"Nope. The third album was called *The Hill of Dreams*. The Green Ceremony was just the name of a live music show they did here in 1970, with a load of other bands for support. And it was such a hit that it became an annual festival and has been running ever since."

We joined a long line of cars crawling forward to turn right into a field dedicated to parking. Now that we'd slowed down, the car became oppressively hot even with all the windows wide open.

After we finally parked we walked across the road and joined the long line of people on foot waiting to enter the festival gate. There was a sweet fairground cotton-candy smell of vaping on the air, plus a pungent aroma of weed. Looking around at the crowd, I said, "We're on the guest list. Shall we just jump the queue?"

"I'm not sure I have the temerity," said Nevada. She was looking at her phone with an expression of approval. She showed me what she was watching. It was a video of Fanny crouching in our kitchen sink, lapping at a thin, glinting stream of water running from the tap. This was very much her preferred way of quenching her thirst, though standing in the empty bathtub and drinking from the bath tap was also deemed acceptable.

"Clean Head just sent this," said Nevada. "She is discharging her duties with distinction."

"So I see."

As the line crawled slowly towards the entry point a young woman ambled past us. She wore heavy-duty green rubber boots, a puffy chiffon skirt in a green and brown camouflage pattern and a tie-dyed white and khaki tank top. The tank top revealed that she had a tattoo of a snake rising up the pale skin of her back, circling around her neck and ending in a fork-tongued, beady-eyed and, it has to be said, rather beautifully executed serpent head. The serpent appeared to be whispering in her left ear.

Blonde and green-eyed, she was very pretty. But even

a passing glance at her showed a sense of entitlement—I
suppose a more polite word would be 'composure'—which
was rather repellent. She sailed through the crowd, walked
to the head of the line and simply sauntered past the security
people, utterly ignoring them.

"Who the hell is that?" said Nevada.

I don't think she expected an answer. But Tinkler said,
"The Shearwater daughter."

Ah. Max Shearwater's offspring. That began to explain
things. Daddy's little girl was indeed entitled—to nothing
but the best, it looked like. "What's her name?" I said.

"Max."

"That's confusing."

"It's actually Maxine."

"What kind of demented egotist gives his daughter
virtually his own name?" said Nevada.

"The kind that leads a band," said Tinkler. "It's actually
a combination of his name and his wife's name."

"What's his wife's name?" said Nevada.

"Ottoline."

"Jesus."

"I know, I know."

"All right," said Nevada, watching Maxine Shearwater
disappear into the festival. "*Now* I have the temerity to jump
the queue. Come on."

We strode to the front of the line where the gateway
opened into an area flanked by two tents. Outside the bigger
tent, on our right, there was a poster with the words *The
Goblin Market* on it in rather spidery letters. Underneath was

a painting that I recognised as being by Arthur Rackham, the celebrated illustrator of Victorian children's books. It featured a pretty blonde young woman—not entirely unlike Maxine Shearwater—in a white dress. She was leaning against a gnarled tree with some quite creepy little gremlins fondling her face and offering her pieces of fruit.

The smaller tent on the other side had a placard stuck in the ground outside it which read *Festival Team—Support and Info*. This was our immediate destination.

Standing directly in front of the gate and regulating access were some big and thuggish-looking men. Or at least, they were as thuggish-looking as their bright green and slightly camp high-visibility vests would permit.

The biggest and most thuggish-looking of these approached us. "Tickets, please."

"We're on the guest list," I said.

He looked at us without blinking.

"We were told to go to the organisers' tent and they'd have our names down."

Without saying anything he just lifted his arm in the general direction of the smaller tent. We went inside into the coolness and shade and smell of hot canvas and found that, despite there being a long trestle table with half a dozen chairs behind it, and half a dozen tablet computers on the table, there was only one harassed-looking woman in the tent. She was apparently running the place, simultaneously using one of the tablets and her phone. When eventually we managed to get her attention, or at least a small percentage of it, she denied that we were on any kind of a list.

I was firm, Nevada charming, Tinkler sycophantic, but none of it did any good. Finally she showed us the list—indeed all the various lists: press, guests, hangers-on... And she was right. We weren't on any of them.

We emerged back into the daylight and immediately fell under the mocking gaze of the large thug. He could clearly see that we'd been knocked back.

"Not on the list, then?"

"No. But listen," I gestured towards the big tent. "The Goblin Market. Is that the record fair in there?"

"Yes."

"Is it all right if we just go and have a look?"

"Of course you can." He lifted his arm again in a generous gesture and off we went.

Up close the digital printing of the Rackham image on the poster revealed its myriad deficiencies. But the original artwork was still lovely. "The Goblin Market," I said.

"It's a poem by Christina Rossetti," said Nevada. "It's the ultimate example of volcanic, repressed sexuality."

"No," said Tinkler. "That would be me."

We went into the tent. This was considerably less cool and quiet than the last one. When Tom Pyewell had said there would be dealers here, he hadn't been exaggerating. A quick look around was enough to give me a sinking feeling. The tent was roughly square in shape with an opening in one side. Three walls were lined with tables, as was the fourth wall on either side of the opening. The tables were stacked with LPs in crates, with the sellers sitting and standing behind them. There were plenty of records, all right, but even at a glance I could see that the vast majority of it was new stuff. Recent reissues, still sealed in plastic, with barcoded stickers on them. And as far as I could tell, all of the sellers were professional dealers, including some of the big firms. This was bad news because it precluded the possibility of finding any hidden gems or unexpected treasures. These vultures wouldn't be likely to let anything like the original pressing of *Wisht* slip through their fingers.

How right I was in this assessment became clear as we walked further into the tent, our eyes adjusting again after the glare of daylight outside. At the far end, with the biggest section of table, was a dealer that I recognised. A banner hanging on the wall of the tent behind them announced *Mindy Indie Vinyl—Your Independent Record Seller*.

I knew these clowns all too well, as did Tinkler. We called them Mendacious Mindy, because they were, not to put too fine a point on it, lying bastards. Their stated policy was that they only sold the finest quality, play-graded rare and second-hand vinyl. 'Play-graded' meant that they actually played the records, listened to them carefully, and noted any faults. If so, they were either using the world's lowest fidelity vinyl system or the world's deafest listener. They also claimed that their records were guaranteed and backed by a one hundred per cent no-quibble refund. Tinkler and I had both discovered that there were quibbles aplenty and neither of us had managed to get the entirety of our money back.

That was all on the one hand.

On the other, hanging high above us, attached to the

Mindy banner, was an image of the *Wisht* album cover and a sign that read: *Original pressing flip back version! One copy only! Super rare!*

"Well, that was easy," said Tinkler.

I went up to the guys manning the Mindy stall. They all combined the trick of being simultaneously heavily bearded and very young. The one in charge seemed to be, perhaps naturally enough, the youngest and most heavily bearded. His hair was long and blond, as was his beard. Both hair and beard were knotted with ribbons. The ribbons were green, of course.

I asked the green-ribbon guy if I could see the copy of *Wisht*.

"We're only showing it to serious buyers," he said.

"I am a serious buyer," I said. I didn't bother trying to explain that it was Tinkler, hovering anxiously behind me with a rather excited Nevada beside him, who was the actual buyer. I was the one doing the negotiating. Indeed, that was what I was getting paid for.

Green Ribbon Guy narrowed his eyes. "How serious?"

"I will buy the record here and now, if it's in decent condition."

"All of our records are in 'decent condition'," he said. The sarcastic quotation was heavily implied. "They are all flawless and scrupulously play-graded, otherwise we wouldn't be selling them. And they are fully, one hundred per cent guaranteed." I didn't bother trying to parse these comments for all the plentiful untruths in them.

I just stood there and said, "Show me the record. If it's as good as you say it is, we can close the deal immediately."

I must have sounded on the level, because Green Ribbon turned to one of his colleagues and snapped, "Fenton, where's the van at?" He didn't actually click his fingers at Fenton, but you could tell he wanted to.

Fenton immediately got on his phone, walked a small distance away from us behind the table on a quick and nervous semi-circular course, speaking into his phone, and returned. "They're about ten minutes away. Stuck in traffic."

Green Ribbon turned to me and said, "The record will be here in about ten minutes."

"So you haven't actually got this record," I said.

"The record is in the van. The van is on its way here. It will be here in about ten minutes."

"They're stuck in traffic," added Fenton helpfully. Green Ribbon gave him a nasty look and Fenton fell silent and made himself busy applying—no doubt outrageously inflated—price stickers to the plastic sleeves of LPs which had yet to be put on display.

Speaking of which… "How much are you asking for the record?"

"Two thousand nine hundred and ninety-nine pounds and ninety-five pence," said Green Ribbon.

I looked at him. "Three thousand pounds?"

"Two thousand nine hundred and ninety-nine pounds and ninety-five pence."

I didn't know whether to laugh in his face or simply

punch him. I turned to Tinkler and Nevada and we formed a little huddle. "They're out of their fucking minds," I said.

"Now, now," said Tinkler. "Let's not be hasty."

"Yes, let's not be hasty," said Nevada. Because if Tinkler was willing to accept this outrageous cost, we were on commission.

I said, "Three thousand pounds is a completely insane price." Then I added, "Fucking Stinky." Before Stinky Stanmer had stirred everyone up, the absolute top price anyone would have thought of asking for this album was more like three *hundred* pounds. And it would have been entirely possible to pick up a copy for a fraction of that.

Tinkler was looking at me with a pained expression, shifting from one foot to the other, like a little kid who needed the bathroom. "I really want this record," he said.

"I know, Tinkler. But even so…"

"I really want it. Not just for me, you understand. I want it for Opal, too, of course. And I'd actually budgeted for five grand."

This shocked us all to silence for a moment. Even Tinkler, who'd said it. Maybe it was hearing it said aloud.

"Five grand, Tinkler?" said Nevada. "Jesus."

"I've actually got it here," said Tinkler, and he patted the pocket of his jeans.

"*What?*"

"I've brought the money with me. In cash. Just in case." He patted his pocket again.

"Tinkler!" said Nevada.

"What?"

"You can't carry around money like that," said Nevada. "Give it to me immediately. For safekeeping."

It was a measure of Tinkler's trust in her—and his accurate assessment of which of the two of them was a safer pair of hands—that he did indeed immediately reach into the pocket of his jeans and hand over a fat wad of bills.

"So, you see, three thousand is actually a snip," he said, as Nevada stashed the money in her shoulder bag. I noticed she shifted the position of the bag. Now instead of hanging off her right shoulder she lifted the strap over her head so it rested on her left shoulder, with the bag tight under her right arm. No one was going to get that off her in a hurry.

"A snip," repeated Tinkler. He actually looked relieved not to be carrying the cash anymore.

"Nevertheless," I said, "I'll see if I can haggle them down. I'm sure I can."

"Well, don't lose the record. I mean, we have the fish on the hook but it isn't fully on the hook, so for Christ's sake don't lose the fish."

It was hard to conceive of two men in the United Kingdom for whom a fishing metaphor was less apt, but I said, "Don't worry, I won't lose the fish."

"And, Tinkler, just so we're clear about this," said Nevada. "If we do manage to get the price down for you, then we get, say, fifty per cent of the money we've saved you. As a bonus. Okay?"

"If you get the price down you can have a hundred per cent of the money you've saved me."

"Seriously?"

"Seriously. I just want that record."

I returned to the table where Green Ribbon Guy was waiting and looking anxious, as well he might. He too was afraid of having the fish slip off his line. It was clear to him that I was a serious customer. And it was also clear to him, whatever he might say, that three thousand quid was an insane price to be asking. They'd probably picked up the record for about three pounds. So I began to haggle in earnest.

I lost track of time in the course of these negotiations. When we finally finished haggling I became aware of my surroundings again and I turned to the eagerly waiting Nevada and Tinkler.

"Two thousand pounds," I said.

Nevada grinned and punched the air. Tinkler patted me clumsily on the shoulder. "Really? Seriously? You got him down to two grand?"

"Well, two thousand and five. The five was a face-saving thing so he can pretend he wasn't beaten down a whole thousand quid from his asking price." A thought suddenly occurred to me—I should have suggested two thousand and four pounds and ninety-five pence. Oh, well. Maybe next time.

"There is one complication," I said.

"What?" said Nevada, instantly alert.

"He wants paying right now. And the record hasn't arrived yet."

"When is it going to arrive?" said Nevada.

"Any minute now, they say. It's already overdue."

"So why don't we just wait for it to arrive?"

I glanced back at our ribbon-bedecked friend. "He was very insistent on payment immediately if we want it at that price. I think his street cred is at stake. He has to feel he's imposed a condition."

"Oh, for Christ's sake," said Tinkler. "Give it to him."

"I'm not so sure," said Nevada. She looked at me. "What do you think?"

"Well, they're not going anywhere with the money," I said. "And they genuinely seem to believe that the record will be here at any moment."

Nevada frowned. I could see the conflict. She was healthily wary, but she also didn't want to risk losing our thousand-pound—sorry, nine hundred and ninety-five pound—bonus. Finally she shrugged and unzipped her bag and carefully counted the money off Tinkler's roll of bills.

I went back to the table and handed the cash to Green Ribbon. Fenton was watching and his eyes almost bugged out at the sight of the money. So did Green Ribbon's, which confirmed my theory that they had never expected to sell the record at anything approaching this price. I felt a pang of regret. I wished I'd negotiated a lot harder now. Perhaps I could have got them down to a thousand pounds. Or a thousand and five.

Green Ribbon was busy locking the money in a small metal cashbox—so small that the lock was pointless, since anybody could have just picked up the entire box and run off with it—when Fenton looked up at something behind me and said, "Here it is." I turned to see a big, paunchy man in bulging jeans and a red and grey checked shirt making his way across the tent towards us. He was clean-shaven and almost entirely bald, but despite the lack of hair, and ribbons, I could see a distinct family resemblance between him and the chief negotiator. I suspected this was Green Ribbon's father. Mr Ribbon.

He was holding a large brown cardboard envelope of the kind almost universally used by cheapskate British dealers to send LPs, rather unsafely, through the post.

My heart gave a solid, singular thump when I saw it. *Here we go*, I thought. *At last.*

As the guy joined us I could see he was sweating heavily and in a foul mood. He looked at Green Ribbon and said, "Where is he, Aubrey?" The wonderfully named Aubrey nodded at me.

Aubrey's dad looked at me but made no move to hand over the record. "Has he paid for it?" He was looking at me but speaking to his son.

"Yes."

Aubrey's dad reluctantly handed me the envelope. It had been sealed shut, which I thought was an unnecessary complication, but maybe he felt I wouldn't think I was getting my two thousand pounds' worth if he hadn't made use of the patented adhesive strip.

I tore the envelope open and drew the record out. It was *Wisht*, all right. I turned it over… and it was the flip back sleeve. I began to relax for the first time in what felt like a very long while.

I went to the table where Aubrey and Fenton were

standing and set the now-redundant cardboard envelope down on it. Then I returned my attention to *Wisht*.

I was holding it in my—impressively steady—hands.

At last.

11. PINK COTTAGE

I turned the cover over. This was the first time I'd seen the record in the flesh, so to speak. So I took my time, carefully studying the art on the front. Everyone who was gathered rather tensely around me must have assumed I was scrutinising it to check the condition in a highly professional way. But I was just drinking it in and, to be honest, savouring the moment a little.

The cover of *Wisht* featured a photograph of a young woman of vaguely Pre-Raphaelite appearance with a wild, curly mass of strawberry-coloured hair. She wore an antiquated white dress and equally old-fashioned black button-up shoes. She was standing in a rose garden with a crumbling brick wall visible through the masses of extravagantly blooming rose bushes behind her. In her hand she held a leash, and straining on the end of the leash was a large and distinctly vicious-looking, wait for it, black dog.

The dog's angular head, with its jutting devilish ears,

was pointing towards the viewer, its eyes slits of pure malevolent red. The young woman was also staring at us, her face showing an odd and rather bewildered expression. Of course it could just have been that she was a model hired for the occasion and it was late in the day and she was getting terribly tired of holding that damned dog, pulling defiantly on the end of his lead.

But it felt like there was something much more, and much worse, going on here—although it *did* look like the end of the day. Perhaps the end of all days. The lengthening shadows and soft twilight glow on the scene was positively eerie. It was an impressive piece of photographic art.

Of course, the image had been thoroughly treated and manipulated, including those demonic eyes for Man's Best Friend. This would have been achieved in the dark room in those days, or perhaps during the physical printing process. No computers or Photoshop back then. The colours of the image had also been adjusted so that there was a pale greenish cast to the girl's skin—rather reminiscent of the vampiric chick on the cover of the first Black Sabbath album. And the rose bushes had been tinted a psychedelic, intense, unreal pink which in turn reminded me of Frank Zappa's *Hot Rats*, another piece of cover art featuring a scary-looking woman, come to think of it.

Although the woman on *Wisht* looked as much scared as scary. The way the photographer had caught her, she appeared very pretty, very confused, and utterly lost. I thought again what a great photograph it was.

I turned the record over again to see if there was a photo

credit on the back cover. There was. When I read it, I felt as though I'd been kicked in the stomach.

It was the name of a man who had once tried to kill me and Nevada.

The sweat on my body, from the long wait outside in the sunlight, and then this hot and crowded tent, and the long strain of haggling over the record, suddenly turned icily cold.

I told myself it meant nothing, that it wasn't any kind of an omen. And that I had to get down to business now. I quickly reached inside the flip back cover and drew out the record. It was clad in a cream-coloured paper sleeve, with the Hex-a-Gone label logo on it in rusty red. This logo involved a hexagon, naturally. It was an original inner sleeve, which was a very good sign. The inner sleeve was discoloured with age but otherwise was immaculate, which was another.

I reached carefully inside and drew out the record. I set the outer cover and inner sleeve down on the table and held the record carefully by its edges with the tips of my fingers.

It was heavy, solid and flat. And the vinyl was clean. The light inside the tent wasn't ideal, and I'd have to take it outside and look at it in daylight to be sure, but there was no obvious damage on Side 1. Indeed, the dense pattern of tiny grooves had that intricate, almost hypnotic sheen of something pristine and perhaps never played. I flipped the record over and looked at Side 2.

My heart sank.

The vinyl here was just as fine as on Side 1. Perfect and undamaged.

But that wasn't the point.

Everyone was looking at my face and everyone must have seen my reaction, because I made no attempt to disguise it. And they all began to manifest reactions of their own. "What is it?" said Nevada with concern.

"Ah, shit," sighed Tinkler with resigned disgust. Aubrey's dad was looking at me with truculent readiness, gearing up for an argument. Aubrey himself looked puzzled and Fenton was staring worriedly at Aubrey, as if awaiting a cue.

"It's the wrong record," I said.

"What do you mean it's the wrong record?" said Aubrey's dad. "It's *Wisht*, and it's in the flip back sleeve. It's the first pressing."

"It's the second pressing," I said.

"I think we know what we're doing when it comes to identifying records," said Aubrey's dad. Aubrey was nodding vigorously.

"That's just the problem," I said.

"What is?"

"You think you know what you're doing."

"It's in the flip back sleeve," repeated Aubrey's dad, in case I'd missed that.

"The sleeve is just one way of identifying the original pressing," I said. "There's also the matrix numbers in the dead wax."

"You're saying you checked the matrix number and it's the wrong one?"

"I didn't have to," I said. I tilted the record so that he could see the surface that I'd been looking at; so that they all could. "The first release on vinyl was entirely recalled and destroyed. Except for an unknown but small number of copies. The master tapes themselves were completely destroyed. When they hastily reissued the new version, they had to record all the tracks again, and the length of the tracks were different on the second version. That isn't noticeable on side one. But on side two..." I showed the record to Nevada. "There are three tracks on side two. In the original version there's a narrow track in the middle and a wide one on either side of it."

I went over to Aubrey's dad and showed him the record. An interested crowd had begun to gather around us to hear my dissertation, and I rather wished they hadn't. It was going to be hard enough dealing with this chump even without an audience. "But on the second pressing there's a wide track in the middle and a narrow track on either side of it. As you can see here."

I held out the record to Aubrey's dad, but he didn't take it. I went back to the table and slipped the record back in the inner sleeve, and the inner sleeve back in the cover. I went over and held it out to Aubrey's dad again. He still didn't take it.

"Why is it in the flip back cover then?" said Aubrey, from behind me.

"I don't know," I said. "Maybe somebody had an empty cover, or a cover with a completely trashed record in it, and decided to do a switch."

I kept looking at Aubrey's dad while I said this and his eyes flickered away from mine. He wouldn't meet my gaze.

And he wouldn't take the record. I turned around and went to the table and held the record out to Aubrey. He wouldn't take it either. So I just set it down on the table in front of him.

"I'll take our money back. Please."

Aubrey and Fenton gave me identical frightened looks and then both turned to Aubrey's dad. I sighed and turned around and looked at him, too.

He seemed to be searching for words. When he finally found them, they were, "All sales are final."

"I think not," I said.

But Aubrey was nodding vigorously. "All sales are final," he said, in perfect imitation of his father.

I could feel both Nevada and Tinkler shifting at my back. "On the contrary," I said. "As your website never gets tired of stating, you provide a hundred per cent, no-quibble guarantee."

"This wasn't a website sale."

I pointed up at the sign hanging from their banner over the table, depicting *Wisht*. "And that isn't the record you're advertising."

"It's the flip back copy."

"It's the flip back *cover*. It is not the original pressing."

Aubrey's dad was shaking his head. "All sales are final. No refunds."

"I think you'll find you're wrong about that," I said. I could hear the blood roaring in my ears. "You have tried to sell us goods under false pretences. Now that we have established that, you are going to refund us every penny."

Aubrey was looking at his dad. I could see his dad's face tighten. "You can't just change your mind—"

"I haven't changed my mind. I still want the record you're advertising up on that sign. If you've got it, give it to us and you can keep the money. Otherwise give the money back."

"You've got the record."

"It's the wrong record. And now *you've* got it." I gestured to where it lay on the table. "I've given it back. So give us our money back."

I stepped towards Aubrey's dad. I could feel Nevada right behind me.

"Call security, Aubrey," said Aubrey's dad, his voice as tight as his face.

"No need to do that," said someone.

A man stepped out of the circle of onlookers who were avidly following this little drama. He was big, with grey hair and a grey beard and I knew I should recognise him. He was wearing a white shirt with tiny blue flowers on it, brown corduroy shorts over gnarled pinkish legs and a white linen jacket with a purple flower in the buttonhole. "No need to call security," said the man. He came and stood at my side and gazed at Aubrey's dad, smiling a mild smile. "Although you can if you like. If you do call them, be sure to ask for Trevor and tell him Max would like a word."

Aubrey's dad was staring at the newcomer with a look of almost childlike wonderment. "Mr Shearwater," he said.

Of course, that was who it was. Max Shearwater went over to the table and picked up the copy of *Wisht*. He pulled out the inner sleeve and quickly glanced at the record, then he smiled at me. His eyes gleamed with intelligence—and mischief. "He's right, you know," he said. He ambled over to Aubrey's dad and handed him the record. Aubrey's dad took it. Max pointed at the sign. "It's not the original version, is it?"

Aubrey's dad looked at the record, then looked at me. He was cornered. But instead of frowning—which he was very good at—or breaking down in tears, suddenly his face lit up. He'd had an inspiration.

"I don't suppose you'd autograph it for us, would you, Mr Shearwater? Autograph the album cover?"

Max Shearwater studied him closely. "You do realise that this is the version that I disowned? The one that was released by the chaps, after I left the group, without my permission?"

"Ah," Aubrey's dad's eyes shuttled guiltily towards me. He was about to own up to having lied through his teeth. "Yes…"

"And you still want me to sign it?"

"Ah, yes…"

"Fine." Max Shearwater nodded at me. "Give this man his money back and I'll sign it for you."

Aubrey's dad went over to the table and handed Aubrey the record and gestured impatiently for Fenton to give him the cash box. While Fenton and Aubrey went through a bag of Sharpies and indulged in some swift bickering over which colour would look best for the autograph, Aubrey's dad unlocked the box and took out a roll of bills.

Nevada moved quickly to intercept him, her hand out. He put the roll of bills in it and Nevada counted them with swift and savage precision. "This is two thousand pounds," she said.

"Yes, that's right…"

"And five," said Nevada.

"What?"

"Two thousand and five."

Aubrey's dad quickly handed over another five quid. Evidently he knew what was good for him. While Nevada put the money back in her shoulder bag, Fenton and Aubrey finally settled on a Sharpie—an odd shade of pink, which actually went very well with the colours of the cover. They handed the pen to Max Shearwater along with the album cover and he flipped it over and signed it in the white space on the back with a flourish. Then he handed it to them with a charming smile.

"You'd better change that," he said, pointing up at the sign. "Hadn't you?"

"Yes, Mr Shearwater."

Max Shearwater turned away and walked over to us.

"Thank you," I said.

"Yes, thank you," said Nevada. "I thought we were going to have to give those bastards a hiding."

"No violence at the Green Ceremony, please," said Max Shearwater, smiling. And we walked out of the tent with him.

"Do you know if Tom Pyewell is here?" I said as we emerged gratefully into the weed-smelling heat and the dazzling daylight.

Max Shearwater shrugged. "He's probably around somewhere."

"He invited us to come here," said Nevada bluntly. "He was supposed to leave tickets for us, but he didn't."

"Typical Tom. How is it that you know him?"

"We met under rather… unusual circumstances."

Those intelligent eyes flickered over us again, widening with delight. "At Erik's house? That day when…"

"Yes."

"You're the detective," he said.

"The vinyl detective," I shrugged. "Just vinyl."

"Well, welcome to the Green Ceremony." He looked around, as if proudly surveying his domain. "I just love this thing. I try and make it here every year. Sometimes I even drag the family along."

"We saw your daughter earlier," said Nevada.

"She's gorgeous," said Tinkler.

"She's a handful." Max sounded fond, a little wistful.

Nevada was looking across at the tent where we had tried, and failed, to find our place on the guest list. "I don't suppose you can get us tickets to the festival?" I don't think my darling particularly wanted to attend an in-depth celebration of folk music. I just think Tom Pyewell's failure to come through had rankled her. And I knew how she felt.

"I can do better than that," said Max Shearwater. "Follow me."

Max led us behind the Goblin Market tent to the wire fence that protected the alley where the bands' vehicles and equipment were stationed. There was a pile of black plastic crates forming a kind of improvised set of steps leading to the top of the fence, and a matching pile on the other side.

"Shortcut," said Max Shearwater proudly. He seemed like a man who knew all the shortcuts.

As we walked towards the pile of crates one of the green-vested security guards suddenly appeared and began hurrying towards us. But Max just waved at him and the guard stopped and smiled at us. He waved back and withdrew.

Max went up the staircase of crates with impressive ease for a man of his size and age—and no doubt lifetime drug consumption—and stepped gracefully over the wire fence and started down the other side. We all followed.

On the other side of the fence we had the pleasant feeling of being in a privileged and forbidden zone. We walked past the stacks of sound equipment and the bands' vehicles and a remote recording unit with a BBC logo on the side. Fat cables snaked towards it from various points ahead of us. I realised that one of the stages actually backed onto the fence, or rather a gap in the fence, and that this was where Max was leading us. The music ringing out on the hot, clear air grew steadily louder as we approached.

Max Shearwater looked back at us and, raising his voice to be heard, said, "Jimmy!"

We had reached the scaffolding at the back of the stage and Max led us up the steps, proper steps this time, and we found ourselves standing in the wings in a VIP position where we could see both the audience and the performer.

The performer in question, Jimmy Lynch, was a solo act, a man vigorously playing a fiddle. Deeply tanned, he had a wild bush of curly hair, which had once been black but was now mostly grey. His dark eyes were frequently squeezed shut with pleasure, or concentration, as he played. Those eyes, along with the tan, the hair and a gold ring that glinted in the lobe of his left ear, all combined to give him a gipsy appearance.

He stood rather awkwardly on stage, stiff-legged and leaning forward at the waist. He wore the traditional faded blue jeans, a frilly white shirt open halfway to the navel and, despite the heat, a brown leather jacket and a brightly coloured silk scarf. Even under his leather jacket, the bulk and power of his arms and shoulders was evident.

I wondered if playing fiddle built up the muscles.

The audience erupted ecstatically as the song concluded and Jimmy waved to the crowd and walked off stage, approaching us with a peculiar stiff gait, his scarf swaying from his neck like a pendulum.

"These are my friends," said Max.

"Hello, friends," said Jimmy, but he was preoccupied with putting his fiddle and bow in a case, which stood on top of an amp. It was black and lined with red velvet with picture postcards taped inside the lid. After he'd stowed his instruments he snapped it shut, rubbed his hands vigorously like a man warming them before applying them to bare skin, and said, "Right-o, back to my place, I think." He looked at Max. "Time for a bit of refreshment, wouldn't you say?"

"Are my friends invited?"

Jimmy peered at us, peering in particular at Nevada. "Naturally," he said.

"Actually," said Max, "they're here on a mission."

"Aren't we all?"

"They're looking for an original copy of *Wisht*."

"An original original?"

"Yes."

Jimmy gave him an ironic look. "You mean the one you forced us to destroy."

Max nodded ruefully. "Ah, happy days," he said.

Jimmy Lynch was frowning with thought. "Doesn't Tom have one of those?"

"He thinks he might have lent it to one of you," I said.

"Possible, possible," said Jimmy.

"He might even have lent it to me," said Max. "But all my records are at the house on the island."

Jimmy shrugged. "I've still got some of mine at the cottage here." At these words I felt the old excitement begin again. He looked at me. "Have you got wheels?"

"Yes," I said.

Jimmy turned to Max. "What about you, you old fool?"

"Maxie drove me here. It would be more than my life's worth to take her car."

"Well, then you can ride with me, if you reckon your dentures can take the vibration." He grinned at us, eyes alight with mischief. He had a certain piratical charm, but again it was mostly directed at Nevada.

Jimmy led us to his mud-spattered yellow Saab, which was parked among the band vehicles, and he and Max got into it. We followed them—no easy task, given Jimmy Lynch's high-speed driving—back to Jimmy's house on the far side of Warminghurst.

It was a little cottage with stucco walls of an odd pink

shade and a black tiled roof, tucked back from the main road behind a tangle of ivy hedges that had long since got out of control, and now scraped against the sides of the car as we eased through the gate and up the gravel drive that led to the house. The drive was overgrown, too, with weeds sprouting thickly out of it, high enough to rub against the underside of the car.

We got out and walked to the pink cottage. Its colour made me think of something, and I realised what it was. The cover of *Wisht*. Music was coming from the open front door. As we walked towards it we passed Jimmy's Saab and I noticed that he had some kind of custom set of hand controls fitted to the dashboard.

The house was cool and smelled of patchouli oil. Just inside the front door was a tiled alcove, which had a couple of sheets of yellowing newspaper on the floor on which rested a miscellany of shoes—all women's, I noticed—and some boots…

And Jimmy Lynch's shoes. To which his jean-clad legs were still attached, leaning against the wall.

We all looked at each other.

There was some flesh-coloured plastic protruding from the open waist of the jeans and I realised these were prosthetic limbs.

"Through here," shouted Jimmy. We went into a sitting room with faded art nouveau posters on the wall and big battered floral armchairs and sofas grouped on a thick carpet that had once been white but had long since turned grey. In one corner there was an untidy pile of guitar cases and, on top of these, three or four violin cases.

Jimmy was sitting on the sofa. He had discarded the leather jacket but still wore the silk scarf. From under the tails of his white shirt what was left of his legs protruded. He was wearing black woollen leggings custom-shortened over his stumps, one of which pretty much came down to his knee. The other was considerably shorter.

He grinned at us in greeting. "Do you drink malt whisky?" he said.

"Only when I can get it," said Tinkler, and Jimmy laughed in delight.

Max was standing at a sideboard on which a hi-fi system stood. It consisted of a creditable Rega Planar turntable and some solid-state amps and small speakers. The music coming from them was the Bahamian guitarist Joseph Spence. It was great stuff. Max nodded at me and smiled. He seemed to sense my pleasure in the music, and share it.

Jimmy eased down off the sofa and moved nimbly across the room, walking using his hands. He'd rolled up his shirtsleeves, revealing tanned and heavily muscled arms like the thick branches of an oak tree. He levered himself up onto an armchair, which gave him access to a drinks cabinet with a crowd of bottles on it. He selected one and swung back down off the chair, the bottle gripped in one fist, and moving with the aid of the other.

It clearly wasn't just playing the fiddle that had given him those muscles. "There's glasses on the table over there; help yourselves."

I declined the whisky because I was driving, but he

poured drinks for all the others. I wandered over to the sideboard with the hi-fi on it. The presence of the Rega turntable had made me suddenly hopeful that Jimmy might be serious about his vinyl and have taken care of his records.

"There's some LPs over there," he called. "But most of them are up in the attic. Max, could you go up to the attic with these lads and pull the ladder down for them?"

An hour later Tinkler and I descended from the attic again, empty-handed.

"Oh, you poor things," said Nevada. "You look like miners emerging from… a mine." She kissed me and then wiped a smudge off my face. Then she repeated the procedure with Tinkler, much to his delight.

"No luck?" said Jimmy. He was sitting beside Max on the sofa, his fiddle in his lap.

"Nope, no sign of it."

In a way I was relieved, because keeping records like that—lying flat, in the unpredictable humidity and temperature extremes of an attic—was probably the worst possible way of storing them. And if we had found the flip back *Wisht* it might have been in terrible shape.

Anyway, that was that. So we made our excuses and said we had to be heading off. Jimmy was reluctant to let us go, but we were aided in our escape by Max, who said firmly that he had to be leaving, too.

We waited outside by the car as the two men said their goodbyes. It was thankfully cooler now and the sky was fading from dark blue to black. The smell of honeysuckle in the dark garden was intoxicating, and quite wonderful after the musty air of the attic. "I was glad Max was around," said Nevada. "While you and Tinkler were upstairs…"

"If he hadn't been, I wouldn't have left you alone with him." For all his intermittent likability, and his courage in the face of adversity, Jimmy Lynch struck me as a classic predator.

"No sign of his wife, then?" said Tinkler.

"Jimmy has a wife?" said Nevada.

"Oh, yes."

She shook her head. "He just doesn't seem the type."

"He very much has a wife," said Tinkler. "Valentyna. With a 'y'. I'm not sure if spelling it with a 'y' indicates that she's of Russian extraction, or if it's just more rock and roll."

"Like Erik with a 'k'," said Nevada.

"Exactly like Eric with a 'k'."

"Anyway, if Valentyna with a 'y' had been around he might have chosen a different topic of conversation," said Nevada.

"Why, what did he want to talk about?"

"Pornography," she confided in a low voice. "And masturbation. You would have been right at home, Tinkler."

"Yes, I would have been."

"Anyway, thank god Max was there. He turned the conversation around to music, and he got Jimmy playing. Which was actually rather lovely."

"Yes, we heard. Through the floorboards. It was actually rather lovely even up in the attic."

"And certainly a lot better than the discussion on auto-erotic gratification down below."

Max emerged from the house looking at his phone. He put it away and smiled at us. "If you could drop me off back at the festival site? Maxie will give me a lift home from there." It made perfect sense, just on the basis of the brief glimpse of her I'd gleaned, that the Shearwater Daughter would make her dad come to her instead of picking him up. It was pretty clear which way the dominance flowed in this family, and who had the whip hand.

"Of course," said Nevada.

As we got into Tinkler's little car, Max said, "Thanks. Jimmy offered to give me a lift, but…"

"He's as pissed as a fart and you don't want to die in a fiery wreck."

"Not to put too fine a point on it, yes."

As we drove back along the dark country road I found myself thinking about the eerie photograph on the cover of *Wisht*. More specifically, about the young woman in the picture. It occurred to me that Max might know who she was, so I asked him.

"That's Berit Barsness," he said.

The name was familiar, but for a moment I couldn't think why. And then it clicked, and apparently for Tinkler at the same instant, because he said, "The Loopy Groupie?"

"Yes," said Max.

Nevada twisted around in her seat and looked back at him, or as much of him as she could see in the fading light. "The girl who killed your manager?"

"Yes. Norrie Nelson. She did."

We were all silent for a long moment, with dark fields

flying past on either side of us. Then Nevada said, "Why on earth did you use her photo on the cover after she had killed your manager?"

"Because we were all fucking idiots," said Max. "Including me. Especially me." He turned around in his seat, perhaps so he could get a better look at us, and said, "But it *was* a great cover."

We had reached the Green Ceremony field now. There was a car parked by the side of the road, rather dangerously far out from the verge, with a figure standing beside it. Our headlights picked her out and I saw the serpent tattoo on her neck as she turned to look at us. I pulled in just ahead of her car and Max thanked us and got out while I hit the turn signal.

In the rear view mirror I saw him standing with his daughter in the red flashing light for an instant, then I pulled out into the road and they shrank in the mirror and were gone.

12. FAIRY TALE KINGDOM

"I knew something was wrong. I could tell by your face. But I thought the record had turned out not to be authentic— as indeed was the case." Nevada was lying beside me in bed. After our adventures in Sussex we were back in our little house, in the hot quiet of the summer night, with Turk out prowling on the hunt and Fanny at the foot of the bed working on the difficult quandary of whose feet to sleep on.

I'd finally revealed my discovery to Nevada. I'd been reluctant to do so, but as she said, she'd known something was wrong. So I'd told her who'd done the cover photo for *Wisht*. Our old friend Nic Vardy. I still felt the shock of seeing his name on the back of the album. To be honest, the revelation had really thrown me. "That fucker," Nevada said, whispering in my ear. "Forget about him. He's long and thankfully dead. The fucker is good and fucking dead."

I couldn't have agreed more.

Still...

The fact of the dead fucker's involvement, combined

with the disclosure that the girl on the cover had been Berit Barsness, the murderess who dotted her i's with flowers…

It had inevitably given the album an eerie charge.

I didn't believe that objects held power, or could carry a curse. But there was no denying that this record, or at least the search for it, had already almost got me—and Tinkler—killed.

I thought about how the name of the band signified the *barghest*, the legendary black dog that was said to foretell deaths. And how the title *Wisht* itself meant uncanny or haunted. And the lost expression in Berit's eyes in that photo. The girl who'd killed her lover and then herself, because "a black dog had been howling outside her window at night"…

But I didn't believe any of that stuff.

So I just rolled over and went to sleep, Nevada close at my side, already in the land of nod, quietly breathing, and Fanny having decided to grant me the privilege of using my foot as a pillow, a small and reassuring weight that made her own reedy little breathing sounds.

Like I said, though, it had thrown me.

So I was quietly relieved that the search for the record had come to a dead end. Still, that left us with the question of how to earn a living. The record-breaking hot weather continued without pause and the heat seemed to have an effect on our usual sources of income—vintage records and vintage clothing. Nothing was turning up through the usual channels. Charity shops, boot fairs, the Internet… all were a bust. Maybe everybody was away on their summer holidays.

We could still have got money from Tinkler, for expenses. But I didn't want to do that if I wasn't actively looking for his record, and there weren't any leads for me to pursue.

So things were in a slightly worrying stalemate when we got the phone call from Tom Pyewell.

He started in apologising without any preamble. "I'm so sorry about what happened. Belinda finally told me about it. She was the woman working in the tent that day. At the Green Ceremony. You remember? She told me about how you turned up, expecting to be on the list…"

"Yes," I said. "That's right. We did."

"Oh, mate. What a mess. I am *so* sorry. When I heard, I felt so guilty…"

"It was no problem," I found myself saying. "We ran into Max, and he got us in anyway."

"He did, did he? Old Max? The old bastard got you in, did he? Well, good for him. Good old Max. Which acts did you see?"

Now, ridiculously, the shoe was on the other foot and *I* felt guilty. Because we hadn't bothered seeing any acts. After that brief backstage visit during Jimmy Lynch's set we'd never gone back to the Green Ceremony. It had been off to Jimmy's cottage, or rather up to Jimmy's attic, then back home. We'd seen less than half of one song from the entire music festival.

"Ah, well," I said. "We saw Jimmy Lynch…"

"You saw Jimmy play? Isn't he great? Good old Jimmy. He's amazing. Great bloody fiddler. I've known him forever. Isn't he great?"

"Yes, and we had no idea about…"

"What?"

"The, uh, the fact that…"

"Oh. His *legs*. Yeah. Christ what a bloody mess that was. Smoking, that's what did it. He's knocked the smoking on the head now, of course. Now that it's too late. But he bounced back. Good old Jimmy. You can't keep Jimmy down. You can't keep a good man down. And it hasn't slowed him down at all."

"No, so we gathered."

"So who else did you see?"

"Well," I said, resisting the urge to hastily Google a list of the performers at the festival and lie through my teeth, "as you know, we were primarily there looking for the record. The original pressing of—"

"Of *Wisht*. Oh, yeah. Of course. Of course you were. How did that go? Wasn't that tent amazing? What do they call it? The Troll Stall?"

"The Goblin Market."

"Oh, yeah. Isn't it amazing? Huge selection of vinyl there. Huge."

"Yes, but unfortunately not the one we were looking for."

"You didn't find it, then? *Wisht*?"

"No," I said.

"Well, that's what I was ringing you about. That's primarily what I was ringing you about. I thought, if you hadn't found a copy at the Green Ceremony…" He fell silent for so long that finally I felt I had to say something.

"Yes?"

"Sorry, I was just checking my diary. As I was saying, if you hadn't found a copy of *Wisht* yet, I wanted to invite you to the island."

"To the island?" I said. "Halig Island?"

"Yes. Absolutely. You must come to the island. You're bound to find the record there."

This was the man who'd told me I was bound to find the record at the music festival. And, although it would have been churlish, I very nearly said as much. But it turned out I didn't need to.

"I know I said you'd find a copy at the Green Ceremony, but I *know* you'll be lucky on the island. Do you know why I know that?"

"No."

"Because I asked Valentyna—that's Jimmy Lynch's wife—where he keeps all his old records. And she said their house on the island. And I asked Ottoline, Max's wife, where his records are, and *she* said their house on the island. And I didn't have to ask *my* wife, because the Wicked Witch of the West flew off on her broomstick back to the Marvellous Land of Oz several years ago." He laughed. He sounded genuinely happy, I must say. "And so I didn't need to ask her, because I know that all my vinyl is in my house on the island. And, on top of that, I *know* there is a copy of *Wisht* knocking about. The original first edition. I know because I remember seeing it. I remember playing it. I just don't remember who ended up with it. But, since everybody's record collection is on the island..."

He had me convinced. "Okay," I said. "Maybe you can

provide me with introductions to Valentyna and Ottoline..."

"Oh, I can do better than that, mate, a lot better than that. I can take you around to see them in person. When you come out to the island. And you're going to stay there as my guests. You and Jordon and your girlfriend. Come and stay at my place. There's plenty of room. Plenty of guest rooms. We've got a swimming pool. I'll have to remember to have the pool cleaning bloke come and clean it..."

I could hear him drifting off into pool cleaning logistics, so I quickly said, "We'd love to."

"Eh?"

"We'd love to come. Thank you for the invitation."

"Oh, that's great, man. That's great. You'll love it. The island is just beautiful. Just magical."

My mind was whirling with logistics of my own. We'd have to drive up... Tinkler's car was probably the easiest option. But it would be a long drive and we probably couldn't do it all in one hit. And it would be very helpful to have someone spell me at the wheel. Nevada was perfectly capable of doing that, but it could be fun to enlist Clean Head. And if the island was as beautiful as Tom Pyewell claimed, she might well welcome a holiday break...

"Listen," I said, "there may actually be four of us coming..."

"No worries, my friend. The more the merrier."

We agreed dates—arrival on a Saturday morning, departure open-ended—and finished the conversation on a note of mutual cheer.

After he'd rung off I called Nevada, who was busy

scouring the charity shops of Barnes for high-fashion bargains, and she said she'd get in touch with Clean Head while I enlisted Tinkler. Tinkler took no persuading at all and when Nevada got home I asked her about Clean Head.

She showed me the text she'd received in reply to her query. Two words.

Road trip!

Clean Head insisted on driving all the way. And she drove with such jaw-dropping speed and skill that we could have done the journey in one go. But we stuck to our original plan and broke our trip with an overnight stay at an inn near Rawcliffe on the outskirts of York. This venue had allegedly been chosen because it was ideally located in terms of distance from our departure point and destination. But in fact Nevada just liked the look of their wine list.

We set off early the following morning and took the A59 to the A1 and then drove north until we turned onto the A690 and a series of small roads towards the coast. It was a very hot and very bright morning, with a searing sun high in the intense blue sky as we left the mainland for the island.

We drove down towards the beach past a sign announcing DANGEROUS TIDES and giving a list of safe crossing times. Which we were well within. Clean Head steered us down the slope towards the beach and onto the road that led in a straight line towards the island in the distance.

Although, of course, it wasn't an island at the moment, but rather a headland or peninsula, connected to the shore by a narrow neck of dry land—well, relatively dry. It gleamed around us, the sand a brilliant gold, lambent with residual water. The causeway was a black tarmac road with a white broken line along the centre, which ran absolutely straight through the centre of the spit of land, towards the rising mound of Halig Island.

The soft colours of that place, the green of trees and pink and white of house fronts and the red, blue and yellow of tiled roofs, were all turned into pastels at this distance, and the impressive half-shattered castle on top of the heaped shape gave the once and future island the look of a kingdom in a fairy tale.

The dreamlike feeling it conjured up was strengthened by our awareness that we were now effectively driving across the ocean floor. In a few hours, all this would be under water. I have to admit, the thought made me a little uneasy and I had to repress an urge to ask Clean Head to speed up.

Our tyres hummed along the damp tarmac and on either side of us we could see the pale green water of the ocean reflecting hard sheets of light as the sun broke through the clouds. The sea was much closer on our left than our right. "Now, remember," said Tinkler, squinting towards the island ahead. "No interbreeding with the locals. Not unless you want idiot children."

We ignored this observation, and numerous others, as Halig rose steadily in front of us, apparently rising out of the sea as we got nearer in a slow, steady recap of the explosive way it had first thrust itself out of the waters as a volcano millions of years ago. Nevada phoned ahead and confirmed that our B&B would be waiting for us, and also managed to get a sneak preview of the lunch menu.

"Soufflé omelette with vintage cheddar, small tomato tarts, celeriac salad and new potatoes," she reported as she rung off.

"You hear that, Tinkler?" said Clean Head. "There's a little tart waiting for you at our B&B."

"I know. My mouth's watering."

Actually, mine was too. Meanwhile Nevada was busy mentally inventorying the various wines we'd brought with us in their boxes, which were now riding comfortably behind us in the trunk of Tinkler's car—cushioned and insulated with all our other luggage packed carefully around them, to shield them from extremes of temperature, undue vibration and even—who knows—the effects of a fatal head-on collision. One has to have priorities. *At least the wine survived.* "I think the McManis," said Nevada speculatively, turning around in her seat as if she could actually see the cases locked in the trunk behind the seat. X-ray wine vision. "You know, the McManis?"

"Yes, I do," I said.

"We've got four bottles of that, so one of them is expendable, so to speak, in case it's been a bit shook up in transit and not entirely at its best."

"I'm a bit shook up," said Tinkler. "And not entirely at my best."

"You never are," said Clean Head, peering ahead through the windscreen, a bright band of sunlight on her face. She pulled down the visor and her face was suddenly in shade, her eyes protected. I noticed that our speed was creeping up almost imperceptibly since the discussion of lunch and the accompanying wine had begun.

"Yes," said Nevada, "the unctuous creaminess of the McManis should work well against the sharpness of the cheddar and the acidity of the vinaigrette."

"Unctuous creaminess," said Tinkler. "Well, I'm glad that's settled."

These and other discussions soon saw the mass of Halig rising to fill our windscreen. Clean Head's no-nonsense driving had decisively closed the distance and suddenly we were there. A fringe of sloping brown sand surrounded the irregular black rock of the island. The causeway aimed straight at a cleft in the rock and swept upwards in a kind of ramp and then levelled out in a road which ran in both directions, stretching away around the circumference of the island and gradually rising up past the fringe of sand dunes dotted with long grass into wooded slopes. I was impressed by the number of trees.

"Look to your right," said Clean Head, slowing the car. "Bullet holes."

We obediently looked out, and saw a sign like the one on the mainland warning about the danger of tides and giving safe crossing times. Except this one was, yes, pockmarked with bullet holes.

Clean Head was tut-tutting. "What is this, America?" she said. Nevada took a picture of it and then we were in motion again. Our tyres were buzzing on a new surface now, the cement of the ramp that led up from the sea bed.

It divided into a generous, angular Y-shape and Clean Head took the bend on the right. The concrete changed back into a black tarmac road and suddenly we were riding along the seafront on Halig Island. We'd arrived.

I glanced back at the narrow, low-lying isthmus of land we'd just crossed. The black line of the causeway ran straight and unwavering across the gleaming tan sand, but was the water suddenly a little closer on either side? And now it was the turn of the mainland to look hazy and dreamlike, lost in the soft distance.

"Dig the Mormon Hipster," said Tinkler. We looked out our windows to the left and, sure enough, a tall young man was standing there on the pavement, watching us go by. He had curly black hair gathered into a top knot and he was wearing a pair of faded blue denim dungarees fashionably unattached at one shoulder and equally fashionably torn at the knees. Under the dungarees he wore a khaki t-shirt, and he looked muscular and capable. But his most distinctive feature was a long and flourishing black beard, which did, indeed, somehow make him look simultaneously like a Mormon and a hipster. Tinkler had absolutely nailed him.

We all started to laugh.

Even before we began laughing, the Mormon Hipster was looking at us with what seemed like a marked, and not entirely friendly, interest. Tinkler quickly picked up on this, too, because he said, "We don't get many strangers around here." He uttered this in a vowel-stretching dim-witted yokel's voice. Clean Head reached over and punched him on the shoulder with her left hand. And none too gently, by the sound of it. She was now laughing so hard she was having difficulty steering straight.

The B&B we'd chosen was about half a mile along the seafront. The shops and pubs—there were a lot of pubs— had given way to a solidly residential district, all to our left, facing a low wall on the other side of the road and, stretching beyond that, a pebbled fringe, a sloping sandy beach and then the sea. The sea was close to the shore here and I realised we had long since left behind whatever geological feature raised the road above the water at low tide.

Clean Head pulled to a stop outside a white two-storey building, which had a cosy, cottage-like appearance, mostly thanks to the thatched roof. There were red and yellow tulips in terracotta troughs in the windows and a black wrought-iron fence in front, which presumably protected the place from attack by any particularly small tourists. There were several bike locks attached to the fence and a sign that read:

THE
B&B
B&B
BYOB

Clean Head switched off the engine, scanned the road for traffic and then, confident it was all clear, got out and walked towards the beach. Tinkler scrambled to follow her and crossed the road to join her, contemplating the peaceful vista of the sea and, in the misty distance beyond it, the land we'd come from.

Nevada was also out of the car promptly, opening the boot and checking on our precious cargo of wine. I joined her, glancing at our companions on the far side of the road. I certainly didn't begrudge Clean Head stretching her legs after the drive, but I was a little less pleased with Tinkler taking off like that. Of course, he would tag along with Clean Head at every opportunity anyway. But on this occasion it had the bonus function of getting him out of the danger zone for unloading the luggage and any other physical labour that might ensue.

Having checked to her satisfaction that our wine had survived the journey, Nevada was now up the steps and at the front door of the B&B, knocking. We waited together. She looked at me. "No one in?" I said. I felt the first faint stirring of alarm. Nevada must have read this in my expression because she put a hand on my chest and rubbed gently over my heart.

"The woman said she might have to pop out. But she'd be back in five minutes or so, and we can wait out back in the garden. She said to make ourselves at home."

"At home in the garden? Isn't that a contradiction in terms?"

"It looks like a very nice garden." Nevada turned to look at Clean Head and Tinkler over on the sea wall. "I saw photographs on her website. Anyway, let's muster the troops."

We walked across the quiet road—not a single car had passed us since we'd arrived, and this was the main seafront thoroughfare. I was beginning to get a feel for just how sleepy this place was. Peaceful might have been a good word for it, but, inexplicably, I didn't feel peaceful.

I was ill at ease and I couldn't wait to get inside the comfy-looking little house. I felt we were far too exposed out here. I looked up and down the beach that ran below the sea wall. There was no one else in sight. Out on the water, shimmering in the distance, a sailboat floated above the unstable mirage of its own reflection. A gentle breeze ruffled the water. It was the very picture of tranquillity. But I was experiencing an atavistic ripple of unease. I could feel the small hairs crawling on the back of my neck. Our little group seemed very small here on the edge of the island, looking out at the expanding vastness of the sea.

For some reason I thought about the bullet holes on the sign we'd seen.

The sailboat drifted by in the distance.

"Nobody at home?" said Clean Head, looking across the road at the house.

"Back in a minute," said Nevada confidently.

"How long are we staying here, anyway?" said Tinkler.

"Well, we were going to book for three nights, or perhaps four," said Nevada, "but the deal on a week's stay was so good I upgraded us all to that at virtually no extra charge."

"A week?" Tinkler turned to me. "I thought we were going to stay at Tom Pyewell's house. I thought he'd invited us."

"He did," I said. "But I've been trying to reach him on the phone since yesterday and I've heard nothing back. And let's not forget this is the man who promised to leave tickets for us at the festival. And failed spectacularly to do so."

"Oh," said Tinkler.

"So, just as well that someone well-organised and thoughtful booked us a week's stay at a nice little bed and breakfast," said Nevada. We all turned and gazed at the small house with its thatched roof and window boxes full of flowers. It did look nice.

"Do you really think we're going to be here for a week?" said Tinkler.

"As long as it takes to find the record."

That got his attention. He was suddenly all sharply focused eagerness. "But what if we find it on the first day? Then we've got six nights of wasted B&B booking."

"That's all right," said Nevada. "The client will just have to absorb that as part of our expenses."

"Oh, yeah," said Tinkler cheerfully. "Smart thinking."

"You do realise that you are the client, Tinkler?"

"Oh, shit. Oh, yeah." He turned to me. "Well, maybe it will take a week."

"How many of the members of Black Dog have got houses here?" said Clean Head.

"All of them," I said. "Tom Pyewell, Max and Ottoline Shcarwater, Jimmy Lynch and the late Pete Loretto."

"He was the one who was killed?" said Clean Head. Over her left shoulder I could see the sailboat. It was getting closer to shore, to us. I could almost make out the people on it.

"That's right," I said. "He was the drummer in the band."

"And his wife killed him?"

Nevada nodded. "Killed him and then committed suicide," she said.

"Depends on who you ask," said Tinkler. "There is

another theory circulating on the Internet."

"And what's that?" said Clean Head.

"That a demon in the form of a pig was responsible."

"Ah, well, the smart money's definitely on that," said Nevada. Out on the water the sailboat was moving off once more, growing tantalisingly vague again just when I'd been about to see who might be on board. Now it was becoming mere colours and shapes. The breeze stirring in off the sea strengthened and the waves smacked the shore below us with a steady rhythm that was somehow reassuring. I felt myself beginning to relax.

"Okay, so setting demonic pigs aside," said Tinkler, who was suddenly all business, "the idea is that we search the record collections of Lynch and Pyewell and the Shearwaters? With their permission, of course."

I nodded. "And I don't see why we should leave Pete Loretto off the list. Or at least, his record collection."

"You're actually planning to do that?" said Tinkler. "Go through a dead man's record collection?"

"I don't see why not. If we can locate it."

"You have absolutely no morals." He shook his head. "I love it. And I guess we won't need his permission."

"If I find the record at his place, we may need to come to some arrangement with his estate," I said.

"What estate?" said Tinkler. "Him and his wife are both dead, and they didn't have any kids. There may not be anybody to come to an arrangement with."

"We'll see," I said.

"I might get the record for nothing," said Tinkler,

doing a little jig. He turned happily to Nevada. "Dead men don't haggle."

"So I have been given to understand."

A sound took me by surprise. It was just an engine, but I had already grown so used to the quiet that it seemed oddly intrusive. The first vehicle we'd seen since we arrived was approaching in the distance. A white van, coming from the opposite direction to the way we'd arrived.

"Maybe that's our landlady now," said Clean Head.

"If so, she's abandoned her rustic theme," said Nevada. The white van had no lettering or any other form of ornamentation on it, and the windscreen was fashioned of that kind of dark, smoky glass that makes it impossible to see the occupants. It was slowing as it approached us, but then as it drew level it accelerated again and gunned its engine and vanished towards the centre of town.

"So what's the scoop on this B&B?" said Tinkler, staring wistfully across the road at our lodgings.

"Is it really called the B&B B&B?" said Clean Head.

"I know that might seem to indicate a paucity of imagination," said Nevada. "But don't forget the BYOB."

I wasn't likely to. It was the reasonable corkage—indeed the concept of corkage at a B&B at all—that had attracted Nevada in the first place. A bed and breakfast where you could bring your own bottle. Or, in our case, bottles plural.

"But what's the double B&B thing about?" said Tinkler. "Have they got a stutter?"

"No," said Nevada. "One B&B stands for the name of the owners. Bramwell and Bebbington. Or Bebbington and

Bramwell. Miss Bebbington and Ms Bramwell. She was very specific about who was Miss and who was Ms. Miss Bebbington, that is. As in *Miss Bebbington's vegetarian B&B. Reasonable corkage.*" Nevada smiled reminiscently.

"Vegetarian?" said Tinkler.

"You'll eat it and you'll like it, Tinkler. Miss Bebbington seems lovely. An absolute doll."

Tinkler frowned. "So, is this Ms Bramwell a sleeping partner, if you know what I mean?"

"I fear I'm far from certain," said Nevada. "But whatever you mean, the answer would be that she *was*. She's dead apparently."

"So you mean," said Tinkler, "that they were…" He made an odd gesture with his hands, spreading his fingers so that there was a gap between the middle digits and then interlocked his hands so the gaps met.

"Do you mean lesbians?" said Nevada.

"Ah… yes."

"And what in hell is that business with hands supposed to signify?"

"Well, um—"

"Was it supposed to signify two enthusiastic women deploying the 'scissors' sexual position to bring their glittering clits into enthusiastic proximity?"

"Yes it was," said Tinkler. Then, fondly and forlornly, "Glittering clits."

Nevada shook her head. "How does it feel to have your entire worldview informed by cheap pornography?"

"Free pornography, actually," said Tinkler. "And, since

you ask, it feels like—for once—I'm totally in sync with the youth of today."

"Is that her now?" said Clean Head. She nodded in the direction the white van had disappeared. Sure enough, a figure on a bicycle was approaching, pedalling madly. She lifted one hand from the handlebars and waved at us.

"It looks like it might well be," said Nevada. "I'll get that bottle of wine from the car."

13. NO BRAKES

The B&B only had two bedrooms with ocean views so, to avoid squabbles, Nevada and I volunteered to take one of the rooms at the back of the house instead. "This is actually a plus," said Nevada. It was; our room was larger and quieter and—crucially—cooler than those at the front, and also had the advantage of looking out over the garden, which was as pretty as promised. We opened the windows as soon as we moved our luggage into the room and took turns leaning out and breathing in the scent of roses. "Who needs sea air?" said Nevada. We unpacked our things and lay down on the bed for a few minutes. It had a big iron frame, painted a vanilla shade, and a thankfully firm mattress.

The room was light and pleasant, with William Morris wallpaper and thick, fluffy white carpet. "The cats would love that," said Nevada. She sat up on the bed and took out her phone. "Speaking of which… time to check in with the little fiends."

Finding a babysitter for the cats this time had involved

some fancy footwork on our part, because both of the usual candidates—Clean Head and Tinkler—had come along on this expedition with us. But we got lucky when it turned out that Tinkler's sister Maggie was both free and willing to move into our house for the duration of our absence.

There had been some initial teething problems, the cats regarding any stranger with considerable suspicion, but soon Maggie had settled in nicely, at least according to Nevada. She called her on the phone now and, after a brief exchange of pleasantries, got down to the nitty-gritty. "Is there any chance we could have a glimpse of the little darlings, Maggie?" said Nevada.

Maggie carried her phone to a napping Fanny, who stared up into the camera, gave an insolent, tongue-extruding yawn, and promptly rolled over and tucked herself into such a compact little bundle of striped fur that it was impossible to tell one end from another. Nevertheless, Maggie kept the phone trained on her for a generous length of time, so we could watch the stripy ball of fur gently expanding and contracting.

"At least she's still breathing," I said.

"Thank god," said Nevada.

Then Maggie went in search of Turk. Despite our house being of modest dimensions this turned out to be quite a project. Eventually a jagged shadow behind the sunlit curtains in the bedroom disclosed her presence. But as soon as Maggie poked the phone through the gap in the curtains to get a good look at her, Turk turned around and lifted her tail high, as though to deliberately expose the upside-down exclamation mark of her private parts. With this eloquent but silent parting shot of feline profanity, she then fled.

"Ah, well, they both seem well," said Maggie. We allowed that this was indeed the case, thanked her profusely and hung up.

"The advantage of having Maggie house-sit for you," said Tinkler when we joined him downstairs, "is that being so scrupulous and moral and everything she won't immediately turn your place upside down looking for your drugs and porno stash." Maggie was a devout Christian.

"We don't have a porno stash," said Nevada.

"Or a drug stash," I said.

Nevada gave me a look. "Okay, cancel that last item," I said.

"Anyway, she won't look for it."

The three of us were sitting in the breakfast room, which was a snug parlour at the front of the house containing two tables, a sideboard and various non-matching wooden chairs with cushions on them. While breakfast would be served in here, other meals—for those who booked the five-star service, as Nevada had for all of us—were served across the hallway in a dining room which was another parlour, but at the back of the house and comprising part of Miss Bebbington's living quarters.

Miss Bebbington had short silver-grey hair cut to closely fit the contours of her head, like a helmet. On her left hand she wore three big chunky silver rings, each with a roughly cut, bright gemstone in it. Red, green and amber. I wondered if the resemblance to a traffic light was deliberate.

She joined us for lunch, which was a promising sign. It's always reassuring when people are actually willing to eat what they've cooked for you. And the food was as good as it had sounded. The celeriac salad turned out to involve sliced apple, red chilli and poppy seeds. Miss Bebbington was delighted with our contribution of the McManis Viognier, though there ensued the usual dispute about the temperature white wine should be served at. Nevada solved this with the Solomonic move of providing two bottles, allowing one to be chilled in the fridge and the other decanted at room temperature. I noticed that Tinkler, the traitor, drank the chilled wine. Clean Head, however, remained true to the cause.

After a bit of post-lunch torpor during which we all retired to our rooms, we gathered again for coffee in the breakfast room and then decided to go out for a walk. Even Tinkler enthusiastically agreed to this plan, and he was a man who wouldn't walk across the room if he could help it. That was what remote controls were for.

But Clean Head was with us and there was no way he was going to miss an opportunity to lope along beside her, drinking in her magnificence.

Which, to be fair, was well worth drinking in.

It was early evening now. The heatwave that had taken the entire country by surprise this summer was also emphatically present here on the island, but the nearness of the sea softened the heat and made it more bearable. The coolness of the salt-smelling breeze coming in off the water was exquisite and the haziness of the mainland had increased, heightening the blurring of colours and general resemblance to a fairly competent impressionist canvas.

We had turned left as we came out of the B&B and strolled past a rowing club, a pub, a teashop and a series of seaside hotels that were considerably larger than Miss Bebbington's tiny establishment, but still not remotely the size of your average London hotel. There were also a lot of residential dwellings in terraces, some of them surprisingly rundown. We followed this road along until the buildings beside it ceased, ending in a disused service station with weeds springing up through cracks in its concrete forecourt. Beyond this the road itself terminated in a circular cul-de-sac of black tarmac, which allowed baffled and frustrated motorists to spin their vehicles around in a petulant fury and speed back the way they'd come. The multitude of skid marks on the tarmac indicated that more than a few had done exactly this.

Past the dead end was beach, dunes, a shelf of black rock and, rising above all of these, a thick patch of woodland. We turned around and walked back the way we'd come. Since we'd only just begun to stretch our legs we strode past Miss Bebbington's and kept on going. We were now walking back the way we'd driven in, with the sea on our left, and houses, shops and more pubs on our right.

A lot more pubs. There was the Greengage, the Red Lion, the Life Boat, the Rising Sun, the Bunch of Grapes, the Ship Inn, the Bird in Hand, the Dancing Crab and the Alexander von Humboldt all in short order.

We'd just passed the last of these when a car approached. We'd hardly seen any vehicles on our walk, and none for the last five or ten minutes, so this in itself might have singled out the car for attention. But there were plenty of other things that would have distinguished it. Like the speed of its approach and its erratic road position. It was a powder-blue hatchback descending the winding road that sloped upwards into the wooded uplands of the island.

It was coming fast and weaving wildly from side to side. So wildly that all of us backed hastily away from the road, left the pavement and moved onto the gravel apron outside the Alexander von Humboldt, where we stood, taking shelter behind some big wooden troughs full of flowers.

The pub had two parking lots—or one parking lot in two sections. One was right beside the pub, with the other and larger section across the road, towards the sea. Human nature being what it is, the parking lot nearest the pub was crowded with cars while the one on the other side of the road, a whole five or six seconds' walk away, was virtually empty.

Which was just as well, since the approaching car veered off the road and ploughed straight into it, spraying up gravel, and narrowly missing the only two other cars parked there as it did an odd manoeuvre, turning in a tight circle as if chasing its own tail and finally coming to a complete stop.

The car was now more or less facing us and the first thing I registered was that there was a strip across the top of the windscreen that read MAX. The second thing I registered was that the face staring out from under it was Max Shearwater's.

The door of the car popped open and Max clambered shakily out. He stared at us, trembling and clutching the door as though he'd collapse to the ground if he let it go. His face was as white as milk.

I was already running across the road, with Nevada and Tinkler close behind me and Clean Head slightly behind them. She was the only one of us who hadn't met Max before. Indeed, she didn't know him from Adam. But to her credit she was the first one to get her phone out, ready to ring for aid. Probably because, like me, she thought the guy must be having a heart attack.

I reached Max, who gave me a tight little nod of recognition as he caught his breath. "Are you all right?" I said.

"Yes, but only just." He was still shaking and clutching the car door.

"What on earth happened?" said Nevada.

"I was coming down the hill—do you know the hill, just past The Sea View? You know, the pub up by where the Lynches live?"

"No," I said. "We've only just got here."

"Oh, yes, of course," he nodded, his chin bobbing. His eyes were still frightened. "How stupid of me. You've only just got here." He shook his head, as if trying to clear it of irrelevancies. "I was just driving down the hill and—perhaps I was driving a little faster than I should have been, I don't know…" He gazed soulfully at us as if looking for answers. "Ottoline is always on at me about that, but she wasn't with me this time. Thank god. I mean, because of what just happened…"

I said, "What did just happen?"

"Well, all right, I admit I was going faster than I should, perhaps a little faster than I should, and it was downhill all the way, and I was picking up a fair head of steam, and the road began to curve, and some of those curves are quite sharp. Pretty damned sharp, so I began to tap the brakes, just to bring my speed down a little, just to maintain control. And there was nothing there. I mean *nothing*." He stared at us, with the expression of a man who had been utterly betrayed. "No brakes. None. They'd just gone."

"My god," said Nevada. "What did you do?"

"Well, I remembered reading something about using the gears…"

Clean Head was nodding. "Engine braking," she said.

"Yes, so I started shifting down the gears, and that did help—a little—but I was still going a hell of a lot faster than I wanted to be. And no brakes. You've no idea what it's like. You become so used to just having the ability to brake. And then, when it's gone… Christ. Sweet Jesus Christ."

He suddenly let go of the car door and hesitantly moved away from it. It was oddly like watching a baby take his first steps. Except in this case the baby was a big, elderly man. And he was starting to get very angry.

"Christ, Christ, Christ," he said, and moved back to the car door and slammed it violently shut. Then he began to walk around the car, circling it. He watched it warily as he moved, as if it were an enemy that might still do him harm. I half expected him to lunge at the car and start attacking it, Basil Fawlty style.

"My daughter Maxie has got this same car," he said. He was starting to sound calmer now. "The exact same model. I'm going to tell her to get it checked out."

"That's a good idea," said Nevada.

"Although what good that will do, I don't know. Mine was only just serviced. You really think they would have spotted something like that. That the fucking brakes didn't fucking work."

Having now assessed that there was no need to summon medical aid, Clean Head was using her phone to find the nearest garage. She walked off a short distance and came back and said, "Just leave the car here. Someone will come with a tow truck and take it away." She smiled at Max. "Don't be tempted to drive it anywhere."

"I won't be so tempted," said Max, smiling back at her. "Thank you very, very much." He held out his hand. "Max. Max Shearwater."

"Agatha DuBois-Kanes." Clean Head took his hand and shook it. Max looked around at the rest of us. "And thanks to all of you."

"We haven't done anything," said Nevada.

Max shook his head. "Oh, yes you did. I saw you running across the road." His voice grew tight with emotion and his sentences became shorter and more clipped. "Rushing to my aid. And I appreciate it. Thanks."

"The chap with the tow truck is called Gareth," said Clean Head.

Max gave rather a strange laugh and we all stared at him. "Oh," he said, "he's the dickhead who serviced it in the first place."

"Sorry," said Clean Head. "Should I try and get someone else?"

"No, don't worry. Of course it's Gareth." Max gave a chagrined smile. "Who else is there? It's a small island." He took a deep breath and looked around, as if fully taking in his surroundings for the first time. "Just let me catch my breath and then I'll ring home and get someone to pick me up. Maxie's got her car..."

Nevada nodded at the Alexander von Humboldt across the road. "Do you want to go into the pub and sit down?"

"No. No thanks. I don't feel like being amongst people at the moment if you don't mind." He gave us a thin smile. "Present company excepted, of course."

"Well, then why don't you come back to our place?" said Nevada.

"Your place?"

"The B&B where we're staying. You can sit down and take it easy and perhaps have a glass of wine while you wait to be picked up."

Max hesitated. "It's very good wine," said Clean Head. This seemed to swing it.

"That's very kind of you," he said. "I will, if you don't mind."

"It's a bit of a walk, I'm afraid," said Nevada.

"Oh, don't worry about that. I'd love a walk. In fact, I plan to walk for the rest of my life." He looked at the treacherous baby-blue car sitting there. "I never want to drive again."

Clean Head volunteered to stay with his vehicle until the tow truck arrived, and of course Tinkler volunteered to stay with her. So Nevada and I escorted Max Shearwater back along the road.

When we got to our B&B the bicycle was gone from the railings again and Miss Bebbington was out. But we had the front door key so we let ourselves in and collected a bottle of wine from our room—since it was now officially evening we'd moved onto the reds. We opened the French windows at the back of Miss Bebbington's dining room, as we'd been firmly told we were at liberty to do, and went out in the garden.

There we sat in some avocado-and-white striped canvas chairs—they'd have been right at home at the Green Ceremony—and sipped the wine and made desultory conversation while we waited for Max's ride. He was utterly exhausted, and I could hardly blame him. When a car arrived outside and a horn sounded, his face lit up. He thanked us as we went in through the French windows, shook hands with me and kissed Nevada on the cheek, then hurried out the front door.

We watched from the window in the breakfast room as he crossed the road and got into his daughter's car. It was indeed exactly the same model as his. Its colour was hard to determine in the darkness with nothing but the sulphurous glow of a nearby street lamp to go by, but it definitely wasn't baby-blue.

He turned and waved in our general direction as the car pulled away. A few minutes later Clean Head and Tinkler came back and we unpacked another bottle of the red and all went out to the garden.

"You'll never guess who Gareth the car mechanic is," said Clean Head.

"I imagine we won't," said Nevada as she opened the wine.

"The Mormon Hipster," said Tinkler.

"You're kidding."

"No. He gave Clean Head his business card."

"Well, no doubt she'll be ringing him up pronto," said Nevada, pouring the wine. "No young woman can resist a hip Mormon."

"He's not actually a Mormon," said Tinkler.

"No, really?"

"Mormons don't even have beards."

"You're the one who coined the name."

"True, true."

I sipped my wine and looked at my friends. As night arrived the sky was slowly changing from the colour of old blue jeans to that of new blue jeans. I said, "Is everyone entirely happy with what happened to Max? I mean, of course none of us are *happy* with it…"

"You mean, do we find it suspicious?" said Tinkler.

"Of course we do," said Nevada.

"His car is a Subaru Impreza 2008," said Clean Head. And the brakes on that model have a bit of a reputation. *Which?* magazine called them 'surprisingly poor'."

"I just love it that you know that," said Nevada. "But still… they shouldn't just fail completely on a hill, should they?"

"Perhaps that's the surprising bit," said Tinkler.

"On the other hand," said Nevada, "if you were going to sabotage that particular car, and you knew about its reputation, targeting the brakes would be an ideal choice."

"You have a really devious mind," said Clean Head. "I like it."

14. THE BURNT SPOT

The next morning at breakfast Tinkler was uncharacteristically full of energy. "So, when do we begin ransacking people's record collections?" he said. "And, by people, I'm referring to former members of Black Dog. So I'm using the term loosely."

"I'd rather have Tom Pyewell's introduction before we just start knocking on doors," I said. "If he doesn't turn up soon, we'll begin approaching people directly. But let's give him another day or so."

"So, what shall we do in the meantime?"

"I want to see the place where they did it," said Nevada.

"Did what?" said Clean Head.

"Burned the money."

We drove along the seafront, past the parking lot where Max's car had ground to a halt, and retraced his route up the hill until we came to the road that ran through the treeline.

At this point we turned left, whereas Max's careening car had come from the right. The thought of his brake failure made me rather apprehensive and wary, but Clean Head seemed totally in command of the situation, as ever, moving Tinkler's Volvo at a brisk and confident clip.

Miss Bebbington had given us directions, but she'd also told us that if we lost our way we could "Just ask anyone. Literally anyone." We were driving around the circumference of the island, circling around the slope of the vast volcanic cone that formed the place, heading out towards the seaward side.

Soon enough I was able to see why our landlady had been so sure we wouldn't have any trouble finding the spot. It was on a shelf of black rock, which jutted out from the main island slope, extending towards the sea in an almost cantilevered fashion. Hanging above a green pocket of forest, it was visible from miles away.

In the end we left Tinkler's car parked on the road some distance below the site. We could have driven considerably closer, but we'd all elected to walk the rest of the way up the hill to get some exercise. Well, I say 'all'. Tinkler complained vociferously. Then, as we got about halfway up the slope, he stopped moaning and started reminiscing—if you could call it that.

"You know what this reminds me of?" he said, peering ahead.

"*The Wicker Man*," said Nevada.

"That is exactly what it reminds me of. When they drag that poor bastard up the hill to burn him alive."

Clean Head grinned. "Are you scared this is all an elaborate plot so we can burn you alive, virgin boy?"

"I am not a virgin," said Tinkler. "Don't forget my interlude with Opal."

"I wish I could."

"Although, before that, I must admit it had been a long dry spell."

"We really don't want to hear about it, Tinkler."

They'd chosen the spot well. From its vantage you could see half the island spread before you, stretching outwards and down towards the pale tan fringe of beach and then the ocean. If you faced to the right the sea extended unbroken, without apparent end. To the left it was split, with the causeway cutting across it, and, in the distance, currently lost behind a haze of mist, was the mainland.

I found it oddly reassuring to know it was still there, and within reach, even if I couldn't exactly see it.

"Gorgeous," said Clean Head. Standing here at the top, we eventually stopped admiring the view—or in Tinkler's case, admiring Clean Head—and looked around for what we'd really come to see.

It turned out to be an irregular circle of white cement. Beside it was an upright pole or post, thick and rectangular and of a dark grey colour. It was so wide that it looked almost like a surreally elongated headstone. It needed to be that big so that a plaque could be fitted onto it. It was a circular blue memorial plaque with white lettering, of the kind that you see on buildings where somebody famous has once lived. Except this one read:

ON THIS SPOT
THE MEMBERS OF
BLACK DOG BURNT
ONE MILLION DOLLARS ($1,000,000)
IN THE CAUSE OF
MUSIC AND ART.

Underneath, on the grey cement of the pole, someone who was apparently both irate and well informed had written some graffiti in black.

Bollocks! Only $990,000.

Underneath the word *Bollocks*, someone else had written in red, in brackets, *(Bullshit)*. Presumably as a helpful translation, possibly by an American, of the profane British idiom to help anyone who didn't understand it. Or were they calling the whole comment into question? I suspected the former, because further down the pole, in the same red handwriting, they'd written *burnt = burned*. Which supported the American theory, and also suggested a very literal mind at work.

I turned from the pole to the large circle of white cement on the ground. It was the size of a dinner table, or at least of the dinner table we had at home. Nevada came and stood beside me. She took my hand. Her palm was still warm and damp from the long climb. "So this is where it happened?" she said.

"Evidently."

She frowned. "What are you thinking? I can see you're thinking *something*."

This comment must have sounded serious, because both Tinkler and Clean Head abandoned whatever they'd been bickering about and came over to join us. All three of them were now looking at me expectantly, as though I was supposed to pull a rabbit out of a hat.

"What's up?" said Clean Head.

I pointed at the slab of white cement on the ground. "This was supposed to be a pit."

"That's right," said Tinkler, eager to show off his erudition on the subject of all things Black Dog related. "They dug a big circular pit for the fire where they burned the money. So what?"

I nodded at the disc of cement. "So, where's the pit?"

"They've filled it in, duh."

"Yes, with cement," I said. Nevada was staring at me steadily and patiently.

"And?" said Tinkler.

"Look at this post," I said, turning to the tall grey rectangle with its plaque and graffiti. "It's cement, too."

"So what?" said Tinkler. But now he was also paying attention.

I touched the cool surface of the post. It was a dark, dirty grey. "But it's a different colour."

"Why is that significant?" said Clean Head.

Nevada was looking at the big disc of white cement at our feet. "Because it means this one is newer," she said.

"You can't be sure of that," said Tinkler. "Maybe it's just a different composition—"

"No, he's right," said Clean Head. She crouched down, sitting on her heels, and reached out to touch the disc. "In fact, this was only put down very recently."

"How can you tell?" said Tinkler, quickly squatting beside her. They made an unlikely couple sitting there like that.

"The tracks," said Clean Head quietly.

"Tracks?"

Then I noticed them. An animal had sauntered across the cement while it was still wet, leaving an insolent trail of paw prints in the surface. In fact, two animals and two trails, heading in different directions.

Nevada was looking at them now, too. "You're right," she said. "There's no dirt in the tracks." She put a finger into one of the indentations and rubbed gently, drew her finger out and inspected it. "Clean as a whistle."

"So there hasn't even been time for any dirt to accumulate in them," I said. "And given that we're in the middle of a drought they won't have been washed clean by rain."

Nevada took out her phone and began photographing the cement disc.

"What are those?" asked Tinkler. "Dog prints?"

"How appropriate," said Nevada, looking at the plaque with its celebration of Black Dog and their act of Dadaist provocation.

"Yes, *those* were made by a dog," said Clean Head. "But not those." She pointed at the second set of tracks.

"What made those, then?" said Tinkler.

We were all silent for a moment, quite possibly all thinking the same thing.

Finally it was Tinkler who said, "A pig?"

As is the way with these things, it was a lot quicker walking back to the car. And then it was downhill, too. We'd just reached the Volvo, and we were all looking forward to heading back to the B&B for some food and a shower—and, in Nevada's case, opening another one of the bottles of wine she'd so lovingly chosen—when my phone pinged to announce the arrival of a text.

My face must have betrayed my excitement when I read it, because Nevada immediately came and peered over my shoulder. "Out-fucking-standing!" she said in a delighted voice.

"What is it?" Tinkler was staring at us with big eager eyes.

"Alan at Jazz House Records. He's found a copy of the record for us." Alan was an old friend who is the UK's finest jazz dealer. But he also occasionally dealt in other genres, and he was constantly acquiring large collections. So, as a matter of course, I always notified him when I was looking for something. Even if, as in this case, it wasn't jazz by any stretch of the imagination.

"What?" said Tinkler. "*The* record?"

"Yes."

"With the flip back sleeve? And the first-pressing vinyl?"

"Yes."

"Give me, let me see," said Tinkler, reaching for the phone.

"No, get off," I said, waving him away. I was trying to text a reply and also look up an address on Google Maps, and Tinkler really wasn't helping.

"How did he find it? Is it for real? I have to know," implored Tinkler.

"He's buying a collection," said Nevada. "And among the jazz he found the record."

"Despite it being a folk album?" said Tinkler.

"Yes."

"And he's sure it's the flip back version?"

"*Yes*," said Nevada and I in disgusted unison.

Tinkler walked around in a vague little semicircle and stared blankly at Clean Head. It was a measure of his distraction that his stare was blank instead of filled with longing, adoration and/or lust. "It's too good to be true," he muttered.

"It may well be," I said. "The guy wants a lot of money for it."

"Well, just *give* it to him," said Tinkler. "I mean, just tell Alan to give it to him. And we'll pay him back."

"He doesn't have enough cash," I said.

"Oh, for fuck sake."

"And the guy is insisting on being paid in cash."

"So what do we do?" said Tinkler.

"We'll go to him. We'll stop at a bank along the way."

"But isn't his shop in Leicester?" said Clean Head, who had a soft spot for Alan.

"He's not at his shop. He's gone to the guy's house, in a place called New Herrington. He's there right now.

And…" I finally got Google Maps to behave. "It's only about an hour away."

"Then let's get going," said Tinkler, decisively opening the car door and scrambling inside. His decisiveness was less impressive than it might have been because he'd scrambled into the passenger seat and was now gazing out at us like a car-loving dog waiting to be taken for a ride.

"Wait," said Nevada, peering at her phone.

"Wait?" said Tinkler in an agonised voice.

"I just need to check the tide tables."

"Already checked them," said Clean Head, who was also looking at her phone. "We're fine. Both for going out and coming back. So long as we leave now." She wrenched the car door open and jumped into the driver's seat.

Now, *she* really did look decisive.

Nevada and I got into the back of the Volvo and slammed the doors as Clean Head gunned the engine and pulled away. I glanced back up the hill. I thought I could make out the concrete post against the sky, but then the road curved and it was gone.

15. LIKE QUICKSILVER

We drove down the hill on a winding series of switchbacks, expertly negotiated by Clean Head, descending to the now-familiar seafront high street, leading to our lodgings. And many a pub, including the one in whose car park Max Shearwater had so dramatically screeched to a halt.

But it was chiefly the B&B, and the thought of another outstanding meal, that was uppermost in my mind. We were going to miss dining with Miss Bebbington today, I realised regretfully. But time was of the essence. And we could celebrate in style once we had the record in the bag.

Instead of turning left, we turned right and were soon accelerating towards the causeway. The warning sign with the tide times was looming up ahead. "Slow down," I said.

"What?" said Tinkler.

"Why?" said Clean Head.

"Please."

Clean Head managed to make the act of slowing the car one of sullen insubordination, but I wound down the window and checked the sign. The safe crossing times were printed boldly on the gleaming surface of the immaculate metal sign, which shone painfully bright with the late afternoon sun reflecting off it. We were going to be fine. "Okay, let's go."

Clean Head grunted and hit the accelerator so hard we were jerked back in our seats. An obvious act of protest from someone who was normally the smoothest driver I'd ever encountered. "You either want to get there fast or you don't," she muttered.

Tinkler turned around in his seat and looked at me. "What was all that about?"

"Checking the tides," I said. I had the glum feeling I was going to take a lot of shit for this.

"But they already checked them. The girls. Online."

"Call me a girl again and see where it gets you," said Clean Head. But I sensed that she was hard pressed to maintain any kind of angry mood. The road ahead was clear, the day glittered around us with preternatural beauty, and we were driving at high speed on a smooth surface. She was utterly in her element.

"It never does any harm to double check," said Nevada. I felt a grateful warmth that she was backing me up. "Especially when it's a matter of life and death."

"He's just such a *worrier*," said Tinkler.

We were all lost in our own thoughts for a while, hypnotised by the eerie loveliness of our surroundings. It was like a Salvador Dali landscape, the road cutting through a slice of what was effectively seabed. Indeed, it would be under water again in a few hours. The dual nature of the road, sometimes a mundane route to the mainland, sometimes a drowned artefact, seemed singularly eerie.

I did some quick calculations. If the guy's house in New Herrington was really as close as the Internet was telling us, then providing we didn't get bogged down in protracted and tedious negotiations…

I said, "We should be able to buy the record and get back in plenty of time before the tide comes in."

"Don't forget we have to stop at the bank," said Nevada. "And draw out funds."

"I love the word *funds*," said Tinkler.

"You better," said Nevada. "They're going to be your funds."

"Oh. I'd forgotten that."

I hadn't realised there was going to be the bank complication. Evidently Nevada had laid down the law with Tinkler about carrying large wads of cash around. Despite the inconvenience of having to go to the bank, I was just as glad she had.

The car surged relentlessly forward, Clean Head urging it on, tyres purring on the eerie road, the oddly exquisite terrain stretching flat and gleaming all around us.

Tinkler turned around in his seat again and gave me a sardonic look. I could tell he was elated at the thought of the record finally being within his grasp. "Did you really think the website could have been hacked?" he said.

My thoughts were far away, back at the top of the hill on the island. On that white disc of cement.

"What?" I said.

"The website. Did you think it could have been hacked?"

The white disc of cement.

"What are you talking about?"

White cement.

"The website with the tide times on it. The one the girls—sorry, women—looked up. You must have thought it possible that it had been hacked, and altered, or something."

I was only half listening to Tinkler.

New cement.

Tinkler kept talking. "Or why else did you insist on stopping and checking the sign as we left?"

New.

"The sign…" I said.

I felt a sudden sickening lurch, deep in my stomach.

New.

"That's right," said Tinkler. "The sign with the tides. The times. The times of the tides. The tidal times. That sign."

The sign, new and gleaming and perfect.

I swallowed. Nevada was staring at me, concerned. "What?" she said.

"That sign," I said. "When we saw it yesterday it had bullet holes in it. We made a joke about it…"

"That's right." She got out her phone.

Tinkler was still staring at us over the back of the seat, but the elation had faded from his face. The Volvo slowed almost imperceptibly. "What's up?" said Clean Head, immediately sensitive to the changed mood in the car. "Is something wrong?"

Nevada held up her phone. It was a picture she'd taken of the sign. Pockmarked with bullet holes.

"Oh, Jesus," I said.

"What is it?" said Clean Head. The car was now slowing considerably as she eased off the accelerator.

"That wasn't the sign you saw just now?" said Nevada.

"No. The one I saw was brand new."

"Are you sure?" said Clean Head.

"Yes. Didn't the rest of you see it?"

"No," said Tinkler. "We were all just being impatient and thinking you were…" he trailed off.

The car coasted to a stop. Clean Head eased the hand brake on. We all looked around us.

The vast expanse of sand stretched away on all sides. Gleaming.

Did it suddenly look wet?

Clean Head said, "Maybe they replaced the sign *because* it had bullet holes in it."

"Maybe," I said.

"Oh, Jesus, oh, Christ," said Tinkler. He was looking at his phone.

"What?"

"The website with the tides on it. It's gone down."

We looked out the windows of the car. Behind us the island had shrunk to toy proportions. Ahead, the mainland was a distant smudge in the haze.

I cleared my throat. "Are we closer to the mainland or the island?"

"Hang on," said Clean Head in a taut voice. "Just

checking the satnav." She nodded her head without looking back at us. "The island. Just."

"Then we should—"

If I thought we'd been flung back in our seats before, it was nothing compared to what happened now as we were thrown *forward*. Clean Head had released the handbrake and was accelerating steeply and without hesitation—in reverse.

"Aren't you going to turn around?" said Tinkler.

"Number one," said Clean Head through clenched teeth, "that would take time. Number two, if you recall, this car of yours goes as fast in reverse as it does forward."

"Oh, yeah," said Tinkler with an odd note of pride in his voice. "The variomatic transmission. I was telling Erik about it…"

The car was now hurtling towards its top speed, its frame shaking, moving backwards. Clean Head turned around in her seat and stared, not at us, but through the back window. Her face was grim. Nevada and I instinctively moved apart, without being asked, to clear her view through the window. Clean Head's gaze was intent. She corrected the trajectory of the car with minimal movements of her hand on the steering wheel. Her shoulders rolled restlessly. "I'm going to kill my neck doing this," she said.

She turned around again, facing away from us. "You guys look out the back. Shout if you see me going off the road."

Nevada and I both scooted around in our seats so we were sitting sideways, and turned to stare out the window. "You're doing fine," I said. She was, too. The car was unerringly riding in the middle of the road despite Clean

Head facing in the opposite direction. Her left hand rose up and twitched the rear view mirror, her eyes flashing at me in reflection, dark and bright and deadly serious. "It's okay," she said. "I think I can do this using the mirrors. Just shout if you see me going way off course."

"Is there anything I can do?" said Tinkler.

Clean Head shook her head. "No," she said. Her tone of voice startled me. I was expecting her to snap at him, but instead she spoke gently, almost tenderly. "Just relax," she said. "I think we're going to be all—"

Then we heard it. A sizzling, slithering sound coming from under the car.

The sound of tyres cutting through water.

None of us said anything. We didn't need to. We were all thinking the same thing. I could actually feel the shared nature of our thoughts, as though our skulls had expanded to encompass four brains instead of just one, all focused on the same problem.

The same multi-variable equation.

The water has started to come up around the tyres.

How fast will it rise?

How fast can we go?

Can we get back to island before…

I had once seen a documentary about fire safety. The fact that stuck forever in my mind was the length of time between the first tiny flame breaking out in a house, and the entire structure being turned into a blazing inferno.

It's about thirty seconds.

This was like that.

The sound of the water around the tires dropped in pitch and became a deep, clumsy slushing. Then a laboured, muffled churning. I tried not to look out the window, but I had to.

So did everyone else.

The water was already almost halfway up the doors. And the car was slowing against the immense, lazy force of it as it rose all around us. Then suddenly Clean Head eased off the accelerator and let us drift to a complete stop. She snapped the key in the ignition and switched the engine off.

"No point killing the electrics," she said quietly.

All around us the water gleamed in the silent afternoon, smooth and endless, the flat light shining off it, like quicksilver.

"Wind the windows down," said Nevada.

"Wind them *down*?" said Tinkler.

Clean Head spoke to him in the same soft voice she'd used before. "We can't stay here," she said.

"And we can't go out through the doors," said Nevada. "The weight of the water against them is probably already too much." She began winding down the window on her side of the car, and I did the same on my side.

"Go out?" said Tinkler. But, like Clean Head, he was already winding down his window. "So, we're going out through the windows?"

As if by way of reply, Clean Head twisted around in her seat and moved lithely through the window, right arm and shoulder, followed by her head, her other arm and shoulder. Her upper body was out of sight on top of the car.

Her lean midriff disappeared out through the window as she clambered up onto the roof. We could hear her up there now. Her legs in skinny jeans disappeared through the window, the toe of one faun leather shoe just splashing into the water, which was now almost at the door handles.

"Tinkler, get out," said Nevada. Her voice was urgent. "Now." Tinkler stared at us. "Do it." He turned clumsily towards his own open window, twisting his body and attempting a sort of mirror-image replication of Clean Head's exit. But where she was lean and sinuous he was podgy and bulky. I was holding my breath—something I'd be doing a lot more of soon—because I didn't think he'd fit through. He'd get stuck. And then what were we going to do? Because, like Nevada had said, we might not be able to force the doors open against the pressure of the water.

Wait until the water flows into the car, I thought, as I tried not to watch Tinkler struggling, straining to shove his unwieldy shape through the little window. *Once the water is inside the car the pressure will equalise, and we'll be able to open the doors. We'll just wait—*

There was a little cry of triumph. Tinkler began to writhe out through the window in synchronisation with a thumping, shifting sound on the roof. I saw a twisting shadow moving across the water on the left-hand side and I realised Clean Head was reaching down from the roof to help pull him up. Tinkler's flailing legs were withdrawing through the window, giving a kick to the rear view mirror as he went, twisting it out of alignment.

The twisted mirror showed me Nevada's pale face.

She turned and looked at me. "Our turn now," she said. We stared at each other for a moment and then each began to writhe out of our respective windows. As I reached up I felt a warm hand grasp mine and saw Clean Head smiling down at me, kneeling on the roof. Tinkler was on the other side, making a hash of trying to help drag Nevada up.

I began to haul myself up. The metal of the car roof was hot enough to burn my hands. My legs were still inside the car and I bruised my right knee on the frame of the window as I dragged myself up. My left foot jerked back and punched down into the cold wet shock of the water. Nevada was on the roof of the car now and she grabbed my left arm with both her hands and pulled me fully up to join them on the roof. The left leg of my trousers was cold and heavy and wet, slopping against my leg. My shoe was full of water.

We all sat there for a moment, each at one corner of the small car's roof. The metal was hot under my buttocks, heated by the sun. The water all around us was burning with a flat, rippling white glare.

Nevada said, "We are trapped on the causeway between Halig Island and the mainland. The tides caught us." I turned and saw she was speaking into her phone and I realised she'd called the emergency services. She looked at me as she spoke, her gaze level and calm and serious. "Four of us. Yes, all adults. I think so. I hope so. In our car. We're on top of it now. No, I know. We're going to have to swim. Back to the island. It's nearer. Yes. I know. I know. I will. I understand." There was a pause. "Thank you," she said. Then she hung up. She looked at the others.

"We have to swim?" said Tinkler.

"Yes." Now it was Nevada's turn to speak to him gently. "You do swim, don't you? I mean, you know how?"

"Yes. Not for years, but yes. I suppose. I guess. Yes."

Well, thank god for that. Nevada and I could both swim. In fact, visiting the Putney Leisure Centre to use the pool there was part of our weekly routine. And Clean Head? I looked at her. She was gazing out across the water, relaxed and at ease, her body in a posture of dynamic readiness. She turned to me, looked me in the eye, and nodded without saying anything.

She had probably been the captain of her school swim team.

For a long moment everyone was silent, looking at the water all around. "Are they coming for us?" said Tinkler.

"Yes," said Nevada. "They've got boats, and a helicopter…"

"Thank god."

"But they can't get to us immediatcly. It's going to be some time. We have to start swimming."

"Can't we just stay sitting here?"

"There isn't going to be any *here* in a minute," said Nevada.

Indeed, the water had already reached the level of the open windows and now it had begun to flood into the car with a slurping gush. As we listened, the sound grew louder, the car filling in an instant with the sea churning into it from every window. I looked down and saw there was a sizzling, creamy flow of foam fringing the windows, accompanied by a chuckling of bubbles. The water inside the car was at the same level as the water outside. And it was rising fast.

The roof of the car creaked as we all shifted around on it. For a moment I felt a flare of alarm, thinking it might collapse under us. Then I realised the water would soon be high enough to support the roof, and our weight on top of it.

And then it hit me that this was all irrelevant because the water would soon be *above* the roof.

Indeed, the last of the air was already being forced out of the car with a choking, farting sound and a rush of larger bubbles, roiling the water on all sides into a thick white froth which dissipated into the calm, stony green expanse of ocean.

The roof of the car was now just a tiny island, barely raised above the level of the water all around us. And then the water began to creep in on all sides. We stood up as if all driven by the same instinct, and gathered together in the centre of the roof, a warm little cluster of life, shoulder to shoulder, back to back.

"All right," said Nevada, as if we were about to discuss which restaurant to dine at this evening. "We're going to swim back to the island. It's not too far and we should be able to manage it without any trouble. The danger is the riptides."

"Riptides," said Tinkler, like he was memorising the term for an exam he would have to take.

"They're completely unpredictable. They can catch you and carry you out to sea. But listen, this is the most important thing. If you get hit by one, *don't fight it*. If you do, you will just wear yourself out. And you will drown. So, go with it. Just stay afloat and relax and let it carry you out. Because it will eventually weaken. And it should carry you parallel with the shoreline again."

Should, I thought, but I said nothing.

"And then it will sweep you back in towards the shore. *Then* you swim. Does everyone understand?"

We all nodded. The water was encroaching on the roof now, flowing towards us in a neat, shrinking circle.

"One other thing," said Nevada. "If someone does get swept out to sea, let them go. If you try and go after them and try to save them, you'll both end up drowning. Understood?"

We all nodded again.

"All right then. Can everybody see where we're headed?"

The island was clothed in a shining haze, once more giving it the spurious look of an enchanted place—a cheap special effect in a low-budget fairy tale. "Aim for the castle in the centre as you swim," said Nevada. "That should keep you on track. Let's all try and stay together. But like I said, if someone gets swept off, just let them go."

She hesitated and looked at me. She'd suddenly run out of things to say and she looked hesitant and awkward. Almost like a child.

"Let's do it," said Clean Head. Her voice was harsh, almost a snarl. She pulled her shoes off and stuck them in the pockets of her jacket, then leapt off the roof in a neat dive, smoothly entering the water with the smallest of splashes, and began to cut through the water with a concise, powerful stroke, heading in a beeline towards the island.

The rest of us pulled off our shoes, tried to stick them in our pockets, then variously realised we couldn't. Nevada slipped hers inside her blouse. I tied my shoelaces together and hung them around my neck. Tinkler, watching me, also tried knotting his laces together, fumbled with clumsy fingers, then just gave up and threw them away. They splashed into the water and sank. There was no longer anywhere dry left on the roof of the car, so it was less a matter of entering the water now than just letting it roll in over us.

Nevertheless we all dived in, trying to imitate Clean Head in this as well, with varying degrees of noise and clumsiness. After waiting on the hot roof of the car, the shock of the cold water suddenly made the situation very real.

I braced myself and swam, rolling my head with each stroke, through the water and up into the air, taking a breath and moving steadily forward, keeping watch on the island in the distance. I had salt in my nose and in my eyes, and the cold was becoming intense. I swam as hard as I could and as fast as I could, to get my body heat up.

I was in the middle of our little group, with Tinkler on my left and Nevada on my right. Tinkler was attempting a laborious breaststroke, but within a minute or two he began to imitate the front crawl that Nevada and I were using. The three of us moved forward, roughly in line. Nevada remained fixed in the same position on my right, but Tinkler kept lagging back. He was doing a surprisingly good job though, all things considered, and I began to realise we might all get out of this alive.

Ahead of us Clean Head was just a dot in the water and a chevron of foam as she swam strongly and unwaveringly towards the island. Suddenly she rolled over, sleek as a seal, and began to do backstroke. I realised she was doing this so she could keep an eye on us.

She must have deliberately slowed down as well, because the gap between us and her began to close. Soon we were near enough for me to make out the features on her face. She gave me a white flash of smile and then rolled over again and began to resume front crawl—pulling effortlessly away from us again.

"Show-off," said Nevada at my side.

And I began to laugh, having to time it with the rolling movements of my head so I wouldn't get water in my mouth. I realised, with a surge of exhilaration, that this really wasn't so bad, swimming strongly through the vast cold water with a huge bright sun beating down on us, the people I loved all around me. It wasn't so bad. It was an ordeal and a trial and a battle. But it was one we were going to win. This island was growing perceptibly closer now. We were going to be there before you knew it. Dry land, blankets, brandy.

Ahead of us, Clean Head did another one of her swift, seal-like manoeuvres, this time streaking to her left with amazing speed and suddenness. She really was a show-off. I wondered what she was up to. Was she correcting her course? She was cutting through the water with astonishing velocity.

Then I realised her arms weren't moving. Her face was turned towards me, her eyes wide with terror. She streaked away through the water, carried off, dwindling, her figure shrinking, her face a tiny shape, a pinpoint, nothing.

Tinkler gave a tormented cry and began to clumsily lunge off in the direction Clean Head had gone. "No!" yelled Nevada. "Tinkler! Stay!" It was horribly like shouting at a dog. But it worked. He subsided, thrashing for a moment and sobbing, and then he came back in close to us, his arms cutting the water in time with his sobs.

There was no sign of Clean Head, or of the tide that had taken her. It was as if a huge hand had grabbed her underwater and just pulled her away from us. Taken her somewhere else. I heard an ugly rasping sound. It had a disturbing edge of hysteria to it, and it frightened me. When I realised it was my own breathing, I grew more frightened still.

The island was getting visibly nearer. The phony-fairy-tale shimmer had dissipated and instead its outlines were clear and sharp. The muscles in my shoulders were aching and my legs were heavy as I tried to keep kicking in a steady rhythm. The cold was now becoming intense, and worryingly numbing.

But I knew I could reach the island.

I felt it in my body, the possibility of it, the physical certainty of achieving it.

But what did it mean? To reach dry land, and walk on it, with our friend gone?

Tinkler made a loud noise. It wasn't like the sobbing from before. This wasn't despair. It was savage anger. It was an astonishingly ugly sound. I turned to look at him. His eyes were fixed on mine, and the pure fury in them was shocking, a revelation. But in a moment I couldn't see them anymore because his face was too small, too far away, as he was dragged away with preternatural speed, the riptide carrying him off.

For a moment I could still hear him yelling.

Then he too was gone.

"No," I said.

There was a sound to my right and water splashed into my face as Nevada came swimming in towards me, closing the gap between us. Her eyes were fixed on mine, lambent and ferocious.

"Don't go after him," she said.

I shook my head, hardly different from the endless rhythm of it rolling through the water.

Roll, stroke, breathe. Roll, stroke, breathe.

Nevada and me, swimming side by side.

Just the two of us now.

Tears were flooding down my face, indistinguishable from the seawater but hot where it was cold. *Don't go after him*, she'd said. But by the time I'd even thought of it, he was gone.

"You couldn't do anything," called Nevada. She had eased further away from me again.

"It's not your fault," she called. Her voice was further off still. She had increased the distance between us. Why was she doing that?

Then we looked at each other. We both realised it at the same time.

She wasn't moving away from me. I was moving away from her.

I was being carried away.

I wasn't moving; I was motionless and all the world was shifting around me. Like when you look out the window of a train and the station outside seems to lift itself up and it begins to lumber off behind you as you gather speed.

I was gathering speed.

Within a few seconds Nevada had dwindled to a tiny figure in the distance. Then she ceased to shrink. For a moment she remained the same size. Then she began getting bigger again. Her arms were chopping at the water with merciless speed. At first I wasn't sure, then I was.

She was getting nearer.

I realised with a shock, far more profound than the shock of being taken by the tide, that she was coming after me.

"Don't do it," I shouted. "Stay away."

Her small face was gouging through the water, stubborn and determined, her pale arms coming down into the water in a relentless, ceaseless rhythm. "Stay back!" I screamed.

I felt a huge, irrational fury, my pipsqueak emotions utterly dwarfed by the immense mechanism of the ocean that was carrying me away into its anonymous vastness.

But, even so—how could she ignore her own advice like this?

And she kept getting closer.

Nevada was moving with bewildering speed. How could she be swimming so fast? Then she stopped stroking, and just let herself float, and she kept on rocketing towards me and I realised she wasn't swimming at all. She was caught in the same riptide as me. She loomed closer and closer. The cold green water swept us together.

I reached out and caught her hand in my mine. I dragged her to me. We were riding the water as if we were sliding down an endless slope together.

The cold, stony green waves rose on either side of us,

and we were cradled in a trough between them.

I held her in my arms as if we were lying in bed together, in the endless bed of the ocean. Maybe that was what it was. Maybe that's how it would be. Us sleeping together, endlessly, in those limitless cold depths.

A wave slapped me in the face, as heavy as a sandbag. We were no longer in a safe, smooth trough. Waves were crashing down on us. I had water in my mouth and nose and I started to choke.

I spat, coughed, cleared my throat and nose. Beside me Nevada was doing the same.

We both began stroking furiously to stay afloat, each using just one hand because our other hands were still locked together. I knew that, whatever was coming, we weren't going to let go. I stared into her eyes, in which I saw that old familiar look of concentration, the look that said she had a goal in mind and nothing was going to make her quit. A look of primeval, immovable stubbornness.

I loved her, with every cell in my body, and I was equally furious with her.

"Why did you do it?" I shouted.

She said something, but I never heard what it was, because just then something slammed into my back with immense force, knocking the wind out of me. Then the water lifted me again, then slammed me down again. The third time I was slammed down I let go of Nevada's hand, helpless and beaten.

But it didn't matter.

I was bouncing against sand.

We'd reached the island.

I rolled over, put my hands down into wet sand, dug my fingers in, lifted my shoulders, lifted my head out of the water, and breathed. Beside me, Nevada was doing the same. A wave crashed down on top of us, slamming us to the wet sand again. Water surged into my mouth and nostrils, and I realised how silly—and how easy—it would be to get this far and still drown.

I felt Nevada's hand grip mine again and together we crawled forward out of the water, using our four legs and our two free arms, like some strange, clumsy linked creature that had just evolved enough to leave the ocean. When we were beyond the reach of the tide, on a low slope of dirty sand, we let go of one another's hands and collapsed on our backs.

I heard her harsh, sharp breathing and my own. Gradually they both slowed. Above us tattered white strips of cloud were curled in a strange formation against the hot blue sky.

I turned my head, and stared past ragged strands of my own hair, now clotted with sand, towards Nevada, who was staring back at me, her own hair pasted tight to her skull on one side and spread out on the sand like strange black seaweed on the other. We just lay there and stared at each other.

I felt a savage exultation. We'd survived. And then that mood crashed and I thought of—

"Tinkler. Agatha." Nevada whispered their names.

We rose to our feet and started walking. We didn't have the strength, but we walked anyway. I peeled off my socks and walked barefoot. Nevada's feet were already bare. We'd both lost our shoes. I looked back at the ocean, out towards where the car must be, but all I saw was a flat green expanse of water with the sun glaring off it. A gull was bobbing lazily in mid-air. It looked utterly peaceful and benign.

I shuddered, knelt down and puked my guts out. I told myself I must have swallowed seawater, but I really don't think that was it. Nevada kneeled behind me, her hands on my shoulders, until I finished heaving.

Then we resumed walking. I didn't look back towards the water again. As we walked along beside it, I kept my head turned away so I wouldn't see that vast expanse of moving green. The gull gave a mocking cry, as if noting my cowardice.

Nevada took out her phone. "It's dead of course," she said. I checked mine.

"Dead too."

"We're supposed to stick it in a bowl of... what? Dried lentils?"

"Rice, I think."

We walked past ugly black outcrops of rock, tidal pools shimmering with a rainbow slick of petrochemicals, heaps of rubbish brought in by the tide—bottles, drink cans, anonymous crushed plastic shapes. Our bare feet left neat prints in the wet sand, like a pair of carefree holiday beachcombers out for a stroll. We passed upended fishing boats, rotting charcoal-coloured hulks, and then ahead of us we saw a strange, shapeless lump lying at the margin of the water.

We hurried forward and the lump resolved itself into two soaked, intertwined figures. We began to run.

When we reached them, Clean Head looked at us and croaked, "I think your boy copped a feel. I'm going to kick his ass, as soon as I get my strength back."

She staggered to her feet and there was an anguished cry from the remaining sodden figure lying there.

"I did not cop a feel," said Tinkler.

I believed him.

Then there was a brief pause. "I wish I'd thought of it." Then another pause. "You can still kick my ass, though."

But Clean Head was some distance away, sitting on the sand. She reached into the pockets of her jacket and took out her shoes and put them on. She was the only one of us who managed to retain them.

"There's posh for you," said Nevada.

I kissed Nevada on the ankle as I eased her legs off my shoulders. I slipped out of her and she rolled over, reaching behind herself to draw me close, and we lay in the bed spooning. Warm late evening sun slanted into our room, lighting up the cream ceiling and the lemon-yellow curtains, stirring in the breeze of the half-open window. Nevada kissed my hand, then hugged it between her breasts.

"One good thing about this case," she said. "It's certainly perked up our sex life."

"So we're calling it a case now, are we?"

She murmured a reply but, like whatever she'd said to me in the riptide, it was lost forever because I was sliding headfirst down a dark chute towards sleep and oblivion.

* * *

The following morning we showered and dressed and went down to the breakfast room. Not surprisingly, we were ravenously hungry.

Tinkler and Clean Head were already there. As we walked in, Tinkler said, "What did I tell you? Look at them. They're positively glowing." He nodded at me. "You did, didn't you? You had near-death sex."

"Yes, we did," said Nevada complacently, sitting down at the table with them. "And it was great."

"You see," said Tinkler, turning to Clean Head. "I told you. Why couldn't *we* have near-death sex?"

"No way," said Clean Head, shaking her head. She reached into the basket of freshly baked croissants and chose one.

"Why not? It's a once-in-a-lifetime opportunity! Why won't you take advantage of it?"

"Because," said Nevada, evidently speaking on behalf of Clean Head, "none of us would have had a near-death experience in the first place, indeed we wouldn't be here at all, if it wasn't for your stupid obsession with your stupid ex-girlfriend."

Clean Head broke open her croissant and sniffed its steaming golden interior with approval. "Roger that," she said. She looked at me. "I don't understand how they did it. Set the trap with Alan." She took a bite of the croissant. "I mean, you were texting him, right?"

The croissant looked good; I grabbed one and so did Nevada.

When we'd got back to the B&B yesterday we'd borrowed Miss Bebbington's phone to make some calls, before using all her hot water in a series of showers and collapsing into bed. I'd rung Alan, just to confirm what we already knew—that there had never been a copy of *Wisht*—and also to make sure he was all right.

"I haven't bought any record collections for weeks," he told me. "And I've been stuck here in Vulcan House all day sorting out books and magazines. I've got a nice set of *Down Beat* if you're interested? From Gene Lees's run as editor." I told him that yes, I was interested as a matter of fact, but could I get back to him later. I didn't mention the near drowning or anything else. There didn't seem much point.

"They spoofed Alan's number," said Tinkler, helping himself to the last two croissants before they all vanished. "That's easy. So it looked like you were getting a text from him, when in fact you were getting a text from them."

"Whoever *they* are," said Nevada.

"But what about when I texted him back?" I said. "Can they spoof that, too?"

"That's not so easy," said Tinkler. "But it's doable." He shrugged. "It must be, since they did it."

"But how did they even know that you knew Alan?" said Clean Head. Then, to Tinkler, "Give me one of those croissants."

"Can we have near-death—"

"No."

"Okay." He handed over the croissant.

I said, "There are links to Alan and his shop all over my website. That would have been the easy part."

"What was the hard part?"

"Intercepting his text back to Alan," said Tinkler. "And I suppose hacking the web page for the tide times."

"And the bullet-riddled sign," said Nevada. "They must have changed that, too."

After I had called Alan on Miss Bebbington's phone, Nevada had called the emergency services to tell them that we had survived. Oddly enough this elicited not congratulations on our tenacity, grit and luck, but rather a lengthy lecture about how stupid we'd been to ignore the tide tables. As soon as Nevada had finished the call, our landlady felt obliged to deliver much the same lecture.

Never one to take criticism easily, Nevada had insisted on dragging Miss Bebbington down to the causeway to look at the sign there. The shiny new sign. I had gone along, too. I was utterly exhausted and drained, but no more so than my beloved. Now shoeless, I had slopped along in the old retired pair of rope-soled espadrilles I'd brought with us to serve as slippers.

Of course, the shiny new sign was gone and the old bullet-riddled one was back up in its place.

"You see?" said Miss Bebbington mildly, somehow managing to convey that she was accustomed to people taking way too many drugs and getting out of their heads and seeing things that weren't there. But, nevertheless, it was wrong to do that and also mess with the tide tables.

Nevada had turned to me, her face framed by the rusted

and pockmarked sign, and said, "These fuckers are nothing if not thorough."

No amount of rice was going to restore our phones. They were write-offs. "Rice-offs," said Tinkler.

More sadly, so was Tinkler's little car. Our local island motor mechanic, Gareth the Mormon Hipster, hauled the battered and dripping little vehicle back from the site of its doom once the tides withdrew again and delivered it to us with the manner of a man who'd done this sort of thing before. He gave us a look that was strangely compounded of affection, contempt and acceptance.

So did everyone else. Suddenly we felt like part of the island community. People who would have ignored us before now greeted us in the street. We'd apparently hit on the perfect way of breaking the ice. "We're the stupid mainlanders who ignored the tide tables," said Nevada. "Now everyone can look down their noses at us." It was true. Any conversation about any subject was guaranteed to work its way around to a discussion, however tangential, of how ill-advised it was to ignore the times of the tides, the tides themselves, and indeed the implacable nature of— well, nature.

We very rapidly gave up any attempt to explain that we'd been suckered into trying to travel along the causeway at the most lethal time of day. However, we did try to get in touch with the people who operated the tide table website we'd consulted, which had displayed the false information and had then gone down. They seemed to almost deliberately misunderstand what we were trying to tell them. Instead of allowing any possibility of looking into what had happened, they responded instead with some boilerplate legal language about how they were in no way responsible for anyone who misunderstood or ignored the warnings they posted about the tides. Their email also included a brief personal message about the dangers of messing with Mother Nature.

Anyway, our phones were history and so was Tinkler's poor little car. But, in fact, the most annoying loss was our shoes.

16. RELIANT ROBIN

Nevada and I were walking along one of the side streets that ran uphill from the seafront, having just visited the second-hand bookshop we'd discovered for fresh reading supplies, when a car came bouncing over the cobbles. It was a strange-looking pale green vehicle—simultaneously old-fashioned and futuristic in appearance—and it only had three wheels. I mean that it was designed to have three, not that it was missing one.

It clattered along at considerable speed and narrowly missed us as it screeched by. When I say 'narrowly missed', I actually mean we had to jump out of its path, up out of the narrow roadway and onto the still narrower footpath.

"Jesus wept," snarled Nevada.

As if as a direct result of this blasphemy, the little car came to a sudden halt just ahead of us, on a rising section of road where the cobbled surface climbed up the hill. The vehicle seemed to have died in the attempt to scale this puny rise.

We looked at each other. "I didn't know my own strength,"

said Nevada, immediately cheering up. But then there was a clashing sound of clumsily engaged gears—Clean Head would not have been impressed—and the car began to come back down the hill towards us, at first impelled by gravity and then, apparently thanks to the relevant gear finally being located, with its engine running in reverse.

We got the hell back out of the road and flattened ourselves against a shopfront—*Island Textiles, the Fairest of Fair Isle Pullovers*—but the car slowed down to a sedate pace and then braked to a rocking halt immediately opposite us.

The window on our side wound down, a surprisingly elaborate procedure, and a woman's face peered out. It was a rather elderly face, but bright-eyed and alert.

"Hello," she said. "I'm Valentyna."

It took me a moment to place the name, perhaps because I was still expecting a disappointed homicidal driver, and Nevada got there first.

"Valentyna with a 'y'," she said.

The woman nodded impatiently, as if to say *catch up*. "That's right."

It was Valentyna Lynch, wife of Jimmy the fiddler. She opened the door of the car, evidently to get a better look at us. She was wearing a baggy white dress with a pattern of tiny green shapes on it. In her hair was a plastic clip of matching design. In each case the colour seemed to have been chosen to match the shade of the car. I felt like the Green Ceremony had pursued me from the mainland.

Nevada smiled at the woman, giving every appearance of being delighted to see her.

"I have been looking everywhere for you," said Valentyna, a note of annoyance in her voice, as if we'd been deliberately giving her the runaround.

I thought this was pretty rich and, since I still wasn't best pleased about having had to leap from her path, I said, "We weren't even sure you were on the island."

She looked at me with careful attention and evidently was about to offer a full and informative response to this statement. But instead she said, "What size are you?"

Nevada gave me a look. She didn't have to say anything. I knew what she was thinking. She was wondering if this was some kind of blunt opening gambit before inviting us to join an island sexual swingers society.

I responded with the wit and acumen that such an enquiry demanded.

"What?"

Valentyna shook her head with disgusted impatience. The plastic clip waggled in her hair. It wasn't properly fastened and looked like it was about to fly off. "What size are you?"

"Size?" I said, just to vary my obtuseness.

Valentyna lowered her head and gazed down at the old rope-soled espadrilles I had on. Ideal for brief slipper duty, they were fast becoming even more grubby and frayed with full-time use as outdoor footwear.

Valentyna spoke like the slow option on a language-learning website. "What shoe size are you?"

"Oh. Nine."

Suddenly all irritation vanished from her face. She

smiled. It was the first time we'd seen it, and it was a radiant smile. It took about forty years off her. And she looked not only young and pretty, but mischievous, too. "Wonderful," she said. She wound up the window, fought briefly with the gears, and pulled away again at speed. The little green car slithered up the hill successfully this time and went over the crest, bashing its metal underbelly against the cobbles, and disappeared.

We watched it go and then Nevada looked at me. "When she was asking about your size—"

"You thought, depending on the answer, that she was about to invite me, and more hopefully us, to partake of some kind of hideous island sexual swingers society."

Now Nevada was staring at me. "Yes. That is exactly what I thought. How did you know?"

"I don't know. I just knew."

She took my hand. "That's one reason why I adore you. Because we're on the same wavelength. It's a weird wavelength. But it's the same one."

As we walked back towards the B&B, she said, "Did you say 'hopefully us'?"

"Yes, because I'd never want to be separated from you. Especially if I was inducted into a hideous island sexual swingers jamboree."

"How sweet. I'd say something about adoring you again, but we've had more than enough sentimental bilge for now."

When we got back to Miss Bebbington's we found Clean Head and Tinkler sprawled peacefully in the deckchairs in the back garden, the long grass rising around them, both engrossed in books—Clean Head was deep in *The Flight From the Enchanter* by Iris Murdoch, but she looked up as I described Valentyna's car to her. And before I'd said more than about three words, she said, "Reliant Robin. Fibreglass body. Made in Staffordshire somewhere. Tamworth. That's it. Tamworth. Widely regarded as one of the worst cars ever invented."

"I thought it looked kind of cool," I said. "In a midcentury design sort of way. Now that I think about it, I'm pretty sure I saw them around when I was a kid."

"Probably. Top speed of 85 mph."

"I bet you could make one go faster," said Tinkler from the depths of his own deckchair, where he was reading a William Gibson novel. Or, rather, was holding it open on his stomach.

"Of course I could," said Clean Head.

"He's just buttering you up," said Nevada.

"Of course he is. Speaking of design, the complete lack of drip rails is kind of interesting."

"On Tinkler?"

"On the Reliant. They got rid of them ten years before Fiat did. Those Reliants were more a motorcycle than a car. You didn't even need a licence to drive one."

"You're kidding." That made sense in the context of Valentyna's near murder of us in the thoroughfare, not to mention her epic battle with the gears.

"Nope. Interesting vehicle in all sorts of ways. Nasty tendency to flip over if you go downhill at speed and execute a sharp left turn, though."

"This one was going uphill. And it had Valentyna Lynch at the wheel."

"Jimmy's wife?" said Tinkler.

"Yes."

"Was Jimmy with her?"

"No."

"Well, he could have been," said Clean Head. "It has a surprisingly capacious interior, the Reliant Robin. There would have been plenty of room for him."

Our discussion came to an abrupt end at this point because Miss Bebbington came out through the French windows and said, "A friend here to see you." Any mystery about the friend in question was instantly banished as our landlady withdrew back inside after this announcement, to be replaced by Valentyna.

Valentyna was about to say something to—or at least in the general direction of—Nevada and myself. But then she saw Tinkler lying there with his bare feet propped up. And instead she turned to him and said, "What size are you?"

Normally Tinkler can be relied upon to furnish even the most innocent of remarks with an obscene connotation. But now, to my astonishment, he glanced at his feet and then back at Valentyna Lynch, and simply said, "Nine."

"The same as your friend."

"I was size nine first. He just copied me."

But Valentyna wasn't listening. She was smiling that lovely smile again and shaking her head in happy wonderment. "That's so perfect." She clapped her hands and looked at us. "You must come with me, immediately."

Tinkler sprung up from his chair, or at least sprung half up, and fought the rest of the way out of the canvas embrace. I looked at Nevada. "Go ahead," she said, "but I'm coming, too."

We glanced back at Clean Head as we headed for the French windows. Valentyna had already vanished inside. Clean Head had made no move to rise from her chair and had opened her book again.

"Aren't you coming with us?" said Tinkler.

"Nope."

"Why not?"

"Only four seats in the Reliant Robin," she said, and resumed reading Iris Murdoch.

We squeezed into the little car, Tinkler sitting up front and Nevada and me in the back, partly because that was our habitual seating plan when Clean Head was driving the late lamented Kind of Blue. But also because, it's shameful to admit, in case there was some kind of head-on crash, Nevada and I would be spared the brunt of it.

On the other hand, what would happen if we flipped over after going downhill at speed and executing a sharp left turn was anybody's guess.

All that talk of not needing a licence to drive this thing had inflamed my apprehension at being a passenger in Valentyna's car—already at a fair level based on what we'd witnessed of her driving in the high street earlier.

But in fact, after the traditional battle with the gear

lever had been surmounted, she proved to be not that bad. We wound upwards out of the village and through a fringe of woodland, up the sloping cone of the island. It was pleasant and leafy up here, the car bursting out of tunnels of green foliage and through sun-dappled openings, then back into cool green shade. The trees opened out on one side and the view of the sea thus presented would have been ravishing to anyone who hadn't recently been confronted with the likelihood of being underneath all that goddamned water.

At first I thought we'd left the residential part of the island behind at the seafront, but glimpses of houses set back from the woods, surrounded by trees and stone walls, and often protected by elaborate gate systems, made me realise we'd merely left the low-rent housing behind.

This was clearly where the rich folk lived.

The road took a baffling series of curves and blind turns and then we were running along what was virtually a tunnel with high hedges on either side. I began to feel a little claustrophobic just as we burst out into the open again and sped past a handsome white-walled pub with a sign reading THE SEA VIEW. I remembered Max Shearwater mentioning the name, and felt doubly grateful that Valentyna had managed to get us this far intact in her wacky car.

The Sea View's sign featured the image of a rather retro-futuristic-looking science-fiction submarine painted on it. *A drinking hole for the Jules Verne fan*, I thought, just as another literary allusion loomed into view.

An enamelled metal sign in black and white pointed

a slender arm ahead, reading TO THE LIGHTHOUSE, with a redundant arrow painted on it.

"A Virginia Woolf reference," said Nevada.

"Clean Head would feel right at home," I said.

"Only if it was a Penguin Modern Classic edition," said Nevada.

"It isn't a real lighthouse," said Valentyna from the front seat, raising her voice to make herself heard over the assorted car noises, and causing Tinkler to jump a little, snapping out of the daze he'd been in since we'd set off.

"What isn't?" he said.

"That," said our driver, giving a redundant turning signal to the empty road behind us as we veered left onto a gravelled lane that ran through an open gate set into a wooden fence painted dark green and largely overgrown with ivy. She cut the engine, applied the brakes, and we coasted to a stop in front of a very odd building indeed.

It did look like a lighthouse. For a start, it was cylindrical. And it was white, in the traditional livery of a lighthouse. And it had the same sort of conical roof you'd associate with that kind of structure. But there was no light at the top, just windows. And also it was—

"Only four stories tall," said Valentyna, getting out of the door. She stood holding the door open while Nevada clambered out of the small car. Tinkler did the same as I got out on my side. "It's a faux lighthouse." Basically, it was a turret.

"But it's absolutely lovely," said Nevada, in full charm-offensive mode.

"It is until you try and hang a sodding picture on the

sodding wall," said Valentyna, shaking the ring of keys in her hand as she looked for the one to the front door. The door was painted green and, set in the white stucco wall of the house, it replicated the colour scheme of her dress. Standing close behind her as she unlocked the door I could see that the little green shapes on her dress were stylised cartoon cats.

Ah, a kindred spirit.

"Come on in," said Valentyna, pushing the door open and kicking aside an assortment of muddy boots and empty wine bottles that blocked the immediate entrance. One of the wine bottles rolled off into a corner and I saw Nevada trying to read the label on it as it spun across the floor.

I could see what Valentyna meant about the pictures now. There was no shortage of them on the walls—mostly rather well-executed watercolours of sea scenes. But they were all hung on some kind of custom-made black iron brackets, which held them out some distance from the curve of the wall in the middle and allowed them to touch it on either side.

To the right of the front door was a tall coat rack, which at the moment seemed to be hung exclusively with long silk scarves. I recognised them as being the sort that Jimmy Lynch liked to wear, whatever the weather. Beside the coat rack was an inner door leading to a narrow staircase, which ran upwards in a curve which followed the wall. "They're up here," said our hostess, and led the way.

Windows set at regular intervals along that wall—also custom made, clearly: curved glass—provided plenty of daylight on the staircase. We trooped up after Valentyna.

Tinkler was making an extraordinary amount of commotion, slopping up the stairs in the bright orange flip-flops he was wearing. In fairness, they were the only things he'd been able to find to buy in the island shops, it not being a place overburdened with shoe stores.

Which was kind of why we were here. We came to the next floor. The staircase continued upwards but we exited through a door at this point.

We found ourselves in a snug, comfortable lounge, but not for long. I just had time to glimpse a large shelf densely packed with LPs before Valentyna led us into the next room. Tinkler pressed close to me and whispered, "Records!"

I said, "I know, I saw."

The room we'd now entered was so dim that I couldn't make anything out until Valentyna flicked a switch. Cold white electric lights in recessed ceiling sconces came on and revealed extensive custom-made shelves fashioned from dark, polished wood, following the curves of the wall, lining, and mostly concealing, its white surface.

And on the shelves… shoes.

Shoes and boots of every description.

They gleamed with the same dusty dark glow as the wood of the shelves.

"I heard about your dilemma," said Valentyna, looking at Tinkler and myself. "Losing your shoes like that. You should really be more careful and read the tide tables. You could have lost a lot more than that."

"Good lord," said Nevada softly. She was too busy inspecting the array of shoes to be annoyed by the safety lecture.

"He had a mighty collection all right," said Valentyna. I noticed the use of the past tense.

So, apparently, did Nevada. "These all belonged—belong—to your husband?"

Valentyna nodded and shrugged. "He just won't get rid of them. But what use are they to him now?" she said. It seemed a cruel statement, though true enough. Then I thought of something.

"What about his prosthetics?" I said.

"What about them?"

"I mean, doesn't he have to wear shoes on those?" I remembered those artificial legs of his we'd seen at his house on the mainland—I'd actually begun to think of it as 'the mainland' now—with their shoes attached.

Valentyna gestured at the shelves and shelves of footwear. "Most of these won't even fit on the prosthetic. Certainly none of the boot-cut ones. And anything with leather soles would be just lethal for him to shuffle around in… just lethal. Like walking on a skating rink. Especially on a marble floor. Take a couple of steps and *whoops*. Smash down he goes." She paused thoughtfully for a moment to consider this, as though perhaps it wasn't such a terrible notion after all.

Then, emerging from her reverie she said, "Anyway, he's had the same bloody shoes fitted on those prosthetics for the past fifteen years. He probably couldn't get them off if he wanted to. No. He doesn't want any of these. Not really." She locked her eyes on mine as if daring me to contradict her. "So, just help yourself."

I looked at the grubby, fraying espadrilles on my feet. "I suppose I could do with a pair or two…" A sharp nudge in my ribs from behind signalled that Nevada had higher ambitions. "Or indeed however many you can spare."

"Spare? Oh, I can spare all of them," said Valentyna happily. "I'll just go and get a bin bag." She looked at Tinkler, who had already taken a pair of square-toed, toffee-brown Chelsea boots off the shelf and was wiping the dust from them. "Two bin bags," she said, positively chuckling, and left the room.

As soon as she was gone, Nevada said, "Sorry about the jab, but let's liberate as many pairs as she'll willingly spare."

"Almost a song lyric," said Tinkler, cheerfully inspecting the prospective loot. "Indeed, many a false-rhyming lyricist would have been happy with it."

"And anything I'll never wear…" I said.

"More lyrics," said Tinkler.

I took a pair of crazily long- and narrow-toed black patent leather winkle-pickers off the shelf and held them up to Nevada by way of illustration. "Anything you'll never wear, I'll sell," she said.

"That doesn't even vaguely rhyme," said Tinkler.

"I'll flog them on the jolly old Internet," said Nevada. "There's vintage footwear classics all over the place here." She surveyed the shelves, virtually purring with anticipation.

"Okay, good thinking," I said, though I did have a little vestigial pang of guilt that we were robbing poor old Jimmy of his beloved collection. But speaking of beloved collections… "Why don't you choose for me?" I said, and headed back towards the lounge.

"Why, what are you going to do?" said Nevada.

I pointed through the doorway to the lounge and mouthed the word *vinyl*. Nevada got it instantly. "Ah, also good thinking."

Tinkler got it, too. "You're going to look through his records?"

"Keep it down to a low shout, please."

Tinkler looked from the lounge door to the shelves of free footwear all around him. "Oh, shit, now I'm conflicted," he said.

"Don't worry," I said. "If I find anything interesting, I'll tell you. I can search for both of us."

"Okay, okay."

Nevada was already briskly inspecting the shoes and making selections as I went through the door. I heard her say, "Christ, most of these are handmade."

"Handmade for the foot," said Tinkler.

Their voices became muffled and distant as I moved into the next room. I crossed to the window and looked out. There was a large garden surrounding the house, consisting of flowerbeds overgrown with big shaggy orange roses. By the garden wall was a shed and Valentyna had her head sticking in it and her sizable buttocks jutting out, her white dress tight across them as she searched for something—presumably the two bin bags she'd promised. Her search was growing quite impatient, however. For example, she flung a rusty watering can over her shoulder and sent it arcing into a rosebush behind her in a shower of orange petals.

While she was thus gainfully occupied I decided to get on with my own search.

The records were in a wooden wall unit, custom-built like the shoe shelves next door. There were about four or five hundred records there, I judged—a decent small collection. Other sections of the wall unit contained a hi-fi system and a television, both relics of an earlier age. I took a quick look at the hi-fi, rather a nice vintage Bang & Olufsen set-up with a linear tracking arm, and then I got started on the records.

I tugged a bunch of them out of the shelf, about twenty albums, pulling them far enough out so I could see and identify a sufficient portion of the cover on the first album in the bunch. Then I quickly pressed that album back in with my thumb, so the cover of the next one was revealed, and so on.

In this manner I got through the first hundred LPs quite rapidly. Then the noises in the garden stopped. I went quickly to the window and looked out. To my relief, Valentyna was still standing by the shed. Indeed, she seemed to have pulled out most of its contents, including a small platoon of gnomes who stood watching in wonderment as she got on with what was now looking like a complete rearrangement of everything that had ever resided in the shed.

Unable to entirely believe my luck, I opened the window wide to keep an ear on goings-on below, and returned to the record collection, pulling out another chunk of it and working my way quickly through the albums.

What I had found so far was, not surprisingly, a great deal of fiddle music. There were some very obvious entries, like Dave Swarbrick, a household god of British folk fiddle. But apparently Jimmy Lynch's taste—I was sure it was Jimmy's collection and not Valentyna's—ranged more widely than that. I thoroughly approved of entries such as the blues luminaries Big Bill Broonzy and Lonnie Johnson, both of whom like Jimmy played fiddle as well as guitar. Then, perhaps the best of all, was Papa John Creach, another blues master. Also represented were Clarence Gatemouth Brown and Don Sugarcane Harris and some serious jazz players like Ray Nance.

But there was no sign of anything by Jimmy Lynch himself, or indeed any member of Black Dog. Let alone the much sought-after *Wisht*.

Then I heard the sound of footsteps on the stairs. I darted to the window to double check and saw that, indeed, the gnomes were now alone outside the shed and looking like they didn't know what to do with themselves. Valentyna was coming up the stairs.

Nevada and Tinkler were still in the next room. I joined them, just in time to be standing there innocently as Valentyna Lynch joined us. She was carrying two large black plastic rubbish sacks. "Sorry I took so long," she said. "You know how it is; you start looking for something, and you have to tidy things up to find it, and then once you start tidying things up, you just…"

She ground to a halt as she looked at the shoes on the floor, and then at the shelves. Now it was her turn to have her face fall.

I realised we must have gone too far.

But she said, "Couldn't you take a few more?"

17. THE DROWNING MAN

Not content with giving us most of her husband's shoes, Valentyna also insisted on making mint tea for us. As she rattled around the kitchen choosing mugs, spoons and teapots, Nevada and Tinkler and I sat quietly and waited, or at least Nevada and I did.

Tinkler scraped back in his chair across the tile floor so he could get his legs out from under the table and extended one foot to admire his new shoe. He had chosen to wear the brown Chelsea boots right away, despite having no socks. "I love my shoes," he said, with an unaccustomed note of simple sincerity in his voice.

Valentyna was busy filling the kettle at the sink. "Good, good," she said.

Nevada looked at me. It was my turn to be polite. I looked at my own footwear, a rugged pair of hiking boots. "And these are great, too," I said obediently.

Valentyna looked around from the stove where she'd ignited a hissing blue flame and set the kettle on it. "Oh, those are a lovely pair. Great for walking. Great for rugged terrain. We hiked all over the island in those. Not both of us in the same pair, ha ha, you understand. I had my own." She went to a cupboard and took out a big jar of brown sugar. "Now you can explore the island, too," she said.

"We've already done a bit of that," said Nevada.

"Oh, yes?"

"Yes, we've been up to the—" Nevada stopped. She'd been about to say *the place where they burned the money*. But she'd abruptly realised this might be a very sore point, even after all these years.

But I decided there was nothing else for it. In any case Valentyna had turned around to look at us quizzically, the sugar jar open in one hand, as the silence began to grow and grow.

"Up to the place where they had the bonfire," I said.

"Oh, yes," said Valentyna. "Lovely views up there. You can see for miles." She began to shake out some sugar into a small bowl.

Everyone around the table relaxed. Since it didn't seem to be a sore point after all, I decided to probe a bit further.

"One thing we noticed," I said, "is that there's been a cement cap placed on the site of the fire itself."

"Oh, yes, yeah, yep."

"And we, ah, couldn't help noticing that it looked *very new*."

Valentyna gazed at me with guileless eyes.

"Oh, yes," she said. "It would do. They only put that there last week."

"Last week?"

"Yes. Yep."

"I wonder why they did that?" I said.

"Oh, health and safety. You know the sort of thing. Didn't want children falling in the hole."

"And who exactly did it?" I said.

"Who did it?"

"Who was responsible for deciding to pour the cement, after all these years?"

"Good old Jimbo," said Valentyna.

"Your husband?" said Nevada.

"That's right. I mean, in collaboration with the local council and with their permission and everything. But it was Jimmy's initiative and he insisted on paying for it."

Did he now, I thought. I said, "Have any children ever actually fallen in the hole?"

"Not to my knowledge." Valentyna was crouching in front of another cupboard, this one at floor level, struggling to extract a tray.

I said, "I wonder why there was a sudden urgency to seal it up, then?"

Valentyna straightened up, victorious in her skirmish with the contents of the cupboard and now clutching a tray with a varnished black and white photograph of Marilyn Monroe on it. "Oh, Jimmy just really wanted it out of sight. He said it was an eyesore. And he's always *hated* that place. Because it's a reminder, you see. He's still seething with rage about his share of the money being burned. You'd think if he found it so upsetting he might have raised an objection at the time. But, anyway, he didn't. So… *poof*. Up it went.

In smoke. Do you know that it would be worth about ten million dollars now? With inflation and whatnot."

I repressed the urge to ask whether she meant Jimmy's share, or the whole caboodle.

"But aren't you seething with rage, too?" said Nevada.

Valentyna shrugged. "It's only money." She set Marilyn Monroe on the table in front of us, the star's dazzling black and white smile now largely concealed by tea things. "I'll just pop out to the garden and pick the mint."

She went out the back door, leaving it open and allowing a welcome cool breeze to blow in on us. Nevada and I looked at each other.

"It's only money," she said, as soon as our hostess was out of earshot.

"Admirable attitude," I said.

"What do you think of Jimmy deciding to put a cement cap on the fire pit just before we arrived on the island?"

"I think it's a damned good way of preventing us from finding anything out after all these years," I said. "Just in case there were any traces up there of how they could have faked burning the money."

"And how do you think that could have been achieved?"

I shrugged. "I don't know. And now we never will. Because there's a big fucking cement cap sealing the whole thing off."

"I smell a rat," said Tinkler decisively, looking up from his inspection of his shoes.

"Really? Have you even been following the conversation?"

"Parts of it."

Valentyna came back in from the garden, just as the kettle on the stove began a shrill whistling. She was triumphantly gripping a bunch of bright green mint leaves. She proudly told us about this year's bumper crop, and how she was providing fresh herbs and vegetables for the local pub, as she dropped several sprigs of the mint into the teapot.

Tinkler suddenly spoke up. "There were some footprints," he said.

Valentyna glanced at him as she poured hot water over the mint. "Footprints?"

"On the cement over the fire hole," said Tinkler. "The money-fire hole."

"Not footprints," I added. "Paw prints. A dog must have walked through it when it was wet."

"And there was something else, too," said Nevada. "Some other sort of tracks."

"Oh, yes. The pig." We all waited for her to elaborate on her statement, but she didn't show any signs of doing so.

So I said, "You think it was definitely a pig?"

"Not *a* pig. *The* pig."

"When you say the pig—"

"The devil pig."

"Ah, I see."

"The pig that killed Pete and Sarita. It walked through that wet cement deliberately. To make a statement. To send a message. And it's still on the loose, up there somewhere. It's a good job you visited that place during the day." She looked at us. "I wouldn't go up there at night," she said matter-of-factly.

I was beginning to have that we're-not-in-Kansasanymore feeling you get when you're talking to an apparently normal person and then they suddenly start sharing their intensely fundamentalist religious beliefs, or reminiscing about the time they were abducted by a flying saucer and thoroughly probed. I turned around in my chair so I was looking at Valentyna more squarely.

"I thought," I said, in my most polite and reasonable voice, "that Sarita shot Pete and then herself."

Valentyna shook her head emphatically as she brought the teapot to the table. The mint smelled good, although not as good as coffee. "Sarita would never have done that," she said. "Pete might do something that horrible, but Sarita? Never."

"So you think perhaps Pete shot her, and then…?"

"I don't think he *shot* her." Valentyna sat down at the table with us, her hostess duties complete. "But I think he was responsible." She began spooning sugar into her own cup. "I think he was responsible for summoning the forces that caused this terrible thing to happen."

"Summoning the forces," I said neutrally.

She nodded. "The boys in the band were always mucking about with magic, both white and black. But Pete Loretto took it more seriously than any of the others. And he was always the darkest in his practices."

"So you think he summoned this pig…"

Valentyna finished stirring in her sugar and drew the spoon out of its tiny brown vortex and tapped it impatiently on the edge of her saucer. "He didn't *summon* the pig. They *bought* the pig. He summoned the diabolical forces that came to inhabit the pig and set in motion these wicked events." She looked up at me, her eyes surprisingly clear and rational for someone who'd just said all the stuff she'd just said.

"I really can't see any other explanation," she concluded.

I could.

When we got back to the B&B and Miss Bebbington saw the bags of shoes, she laughed.

"So, she finally did it," she said.

It turned out the reason Jimmy Lynch was still on the mainland was because he was busy seeing his girlfriend.

"Or girlfriends," said Miss Bebbington. "Plural."

"And Valentyna knows about this? I mean these? I mean them?" Nevada flashed me a look. This began to make ample sense of the carefree way she'd been disposing of her husband's worldly goods. Of course, it was true he'd probably never wear any of those shoes again, but even so…

"Oh, yes, indeed," said Miss Bebbington. "Long-standing arrangement. They go and stay in their house on the mainland, and then Valentyna comes back early and he stays on so he can see his dolly birds."

"And they're like, what… groupies?" said Nevada.

"They're exactly like that. He's been seeing them for years. It's sort of a tradition."

"They're the same ones? I mean, all these years?"

Miss Bebbington nodded. "Pretty much. Though occasionally a new one is inducted."

"Inducted? Good lord," said Nevada.

"You know, fresh blood."

"Fresh blood, ugh," said Nevada.

"So in any event, you can see why Valentyna would have plenty of reason for, uh…"

"Revenge?" suggested Nevada.

"Yes, I suppose. Revenge is not too strong a word."

"But she said she'd been wanting to get rid of all that…" Nevada chose her words carefully, "…surfeit of footwear for years."

"Oh, yes," Miss Bebbington nodded, her eyes gleaming. "And she's been looking for a means of revenge for years, too. So when she heard about your… unfortunate accident…" I could see the effort it cost her not to pause here to reiterate the standard lecture to us mainlanders about the dangers of ignoring the tide tables. But she overcame herself gamely and managed to carry on. "When she heard you'd lost your shoes, that gave her the perfect opportunity."

"Well, always happy to help," said Nevada brightly.

Miss Bebbington chuckled and then turned decisively to the kitchen. "Must get on with supper now."

Evidently gossip time was over, and we'd been dismissed. That was fine with me. I had no desire to disrupt the preparation of the evening meal, if it proved to be up to the usual standard. So we went into the back garden where we found Clean Head lying in her deckchair, asleep in the sunlight and snoring softly, with her paperback rising and falling gently on her tummy. Tinkler was upstairs, also having a nap. Possibly dreaming of his new shoes.

We sat in the garden, speaking quietly so as not to wake Clean Head.

"That's one more reason for Valentyna not to be upset about the cash being burned," I said.

"What do you mean? Oh, 'It's only money.'"

"Right. She can have that attitude because there are at least compensations as far as she's concerned. In terms of it really pissing off Jimmy. And anything that pisses her husband off is okay with her."

"So that explains her being so laid-back about the loss," said Nevada.

"Yes."

"But you know what might also explain her being so laid-back?"

"If they'd never actually burned the money but somehow managed to steal it for themselves and conceal that theft all these years from the other band members."

"Precisely," said Nevada. "I do like the way our minds run along the same lines. And how those lines tend towards high-grade duplicity and criminal chicanery."

Nevada and I had a nap and then, a few hours later, wandered down to the sitting room to eagerly await whatever culinary delights Miss Bebbington had in mind for our supper that night. Clean Head was already there, one leg hooked elegantly over the arm of the leather armchair in which she was ensconced. She put a finger into *The Flight from the Enchanter* to save her place and gave us a sardonic look.

"Don't think you're fooling anyone with this 'nap'

nonsense," she said. "You should just thank god Tinkler isn't here to take the piss out of you, and generally drag your sex life through the gutter."

"Where *is* Tinkler?" said Nevada as she sank down beside me on the big red velvet sofa.

Clean Head frowned, glanced at the paperback she was holding, looked around for a bookmark, found a postcard on the table beside her chair, stuck it in the book and set it aside. She leaned forward, her arms on her knees, and spoke in a low voice.

"He's found a girl."

Nevada gave a cackle of astonishment.

I was pretty astonished myself.

"What? When?" said Nevada.

"While you two were 'napping'." Clean Head made elaborate air quotes around this word.

"That was fast work." Nevada was now leaning forward, her arms on her own knees, in an intent echo of Clean Head's body language. She even dropped her voice to the same conspiratorial level. "What the hell happened?"

"He went out for a walk, but actually I suspect to go and moon over the wreckage of Kind of Blue."

"At the Mormon Hipster's garage."

"Yeah, there, to study the wreck and generally torment himself about the car being a write-off."

"Poor Tinkler."

"Poor nothing. He met this girl while he was out and, I know it's hard to believe, hit it off with her."

"Do you think she's some kind of *special*–" it was

Nevada's turn to make air quotes around a word "–denizen of this island?" The implication here was clearly *inbred halfwit*.

"Nope. Tourist girl. Anyway, he came haring back here to spruce himself up and then went trotting off again to meet her. Said we wouldn't be seeing him for the evening meal because he's buying her supper at a pub."

"Tinkler paying for a meal?" Nevada glanced towards the sitting-room window as though expecting to see an oddly coloured sky announcing the end of the world.

And later that night Nevada lay tautly awake beside me in bed, for all the world like a worried mother—or a worried cat owner—awaiting the little one's nocturnal return. My darling was unable to sleep until we finally heard Tinkler rattling his key in the back door of the B&B. Nevada leapt out of bed, nude and lithe, the colour of ivory in the moonlight, and shot to the window where she peered out. Her shoulders dropped and she relaxed. "Nope. He's on his own." She sauntered back from the window and checked the illuminated face of the alarm clock we'd been forced to borrow since our phones had drowned. "Hmm. Almost one o'clock... Do you think he had time to...?"

"No," I said, as she snuggled back down beside me. "And can I just say that this obsessive interest in the sex lives of others is not only unwholesome, but downright Tinkler-esque."

"You *can* say that," said Nevada, already starting to sound sleepy as she burrowed against me in the big bed. "But *may* you? That's the question."

* * *

Despite the extreme unlikelihood of having consummated his new acquaintance on such short notice, Tinkler could scarcely have been happier if he had done so. He was nothing short of jubilant when we saw him the next morning. In fact, he looked like the cat who'd got the canary. Or, in the case of Turk, the cat who'd got a full-grown magpie and somehow managed to drag it in through the cat flap, black and white wings pinioned in her jaws.

We all lingered over coffee after breakfast and listened to his account of the previous day's events. We weren't just interested, we were veritably fascinated—it was the same kind of queasy fascination as exerted by a bad road accident. Because we all knew that was what Tinkler's relationships ended up resembling.

"Her name is Alicia," he gushed. "Alicia Foxcroft."

"Foxy Foxcroft," said Nevada, and Clean Head chuckled and I got the immediate sense of a nickname that was destined to stick like a cyanoacrylate adhesive. Or, if you prefer, superglue.

"And I'm going out with her again today," announced Tinkler proudly.

"Is she blind?" said Nevada, in a voice of kind enquiry.

"No, she is not blind."

"Is she off her rocker?" said Clean Head, sipping her café au lait and studying the arts pages of the *Guardian*.

"She is not."

"Is she as ugly as home-made soap?" asked Nevada.

By way of reply, Tinkler sighed disgustedly and took out a small digital camera.

"Where the hell did you get that?" I said.

"I bought it. To tide me over until I get my new phone. I'm sorry for using the word 'tide', by the way."

"Why do you need a camera?"

"To take photographs of his car," said Clean Head without looking up from her newspaper.

"For insurance purposes?"

"Yes, that's right," said Tinkler, a little too quickly.

"So that he can preserve memories of his beloved," said Clean Head.

"Well, anyway," said Tinkler. "I also took *these* photographs." He scrolled through the camera display, then passed it to us. It showed a series of photographs of a young woman, the last few in the sequence being selfies taken with Tinkler at her side. She was pretty, in a big-eyed, impish kind of way. And those photos of her beside Tinkler revealed her to be almost pathologically petite.

"Good Christ, Tinkler," said Nevada, "you didn't buy her alcohol, did you?"

Clean Head was staring over Nevada's shoulder, the *Guardian* arts section now quite forgotten. "The islanders will be preparing pitchforks and a noose for you right now, Tinkler," she said.

"She doesn't come from the island," said Tinkler.

"So they'll be forming a posse on the mainland even as we speak."

"Why? Why will they be forming a posse?"

Nevada shook her head sadly. "You know what they do to people like you in prison, Tinkler?"

"*She's twenty-three years old.* And she's doing a master's degree in media studies."

"Do they even have a master's in media studies?" said Nevada, looking at Clean Head. "I thought those Mickey Mouse degrees had the good grace to terminate at graduate level."

Clean Head shrugged and took the camera from her. "I'm just relieved he didn't take any up-skirt shots," she said.

"She was wearing jeans," said Tinkler. Then he looked up hastily with a mortified expression. "Not that I'd do anything like that anyway. Not that I'd dream of doing anything like that. Not that I ever have dreamed of doing anything like that."

He was a reformed character, all right. I was impressed.

Tinkler took the camera back from Clean Head and said, with becoming shyness, "What are you doing tomorrow evening? Or maybe the day after?"

"Why?" said Clean Head, managing to draw the word out to a truly extraordinary length.

"Well, I was down at the garage talking to the Mormon Hipster…"

Clean Head immediately tensed up. Which was rather odd, because she wasn't a tense kind of person. "Talking to him about what?"

"Well, I was just thinking. I thought we might go to the pub."

"You were thinking we might go to the pub?"

"Yes," said Tinkler. "Me and Alicia…"

"Foxy," said Nevada and Clean Head instantly and in unison.

Tinkler nodded. "And you and the Mormon Hipster."

"What?" said Clean Head, this time setting a world land speed record for uttering a clipped and unbelieving word.

"You mean like a double date?" said Nevada, helpfully. But I recognised the signs of uncontrollable laughter rising in her.

"Uh, yes, I guess. Sort of like that," said Tinkler, eyeing Clean Head worriedly.

She leaned across the table towards him, and spoke with great precision. "I don't want a double date with the Mormon Hipster."

"Oh."

"I don't want a single date with the Mormon Hipster."

"Oh."

"I don't fancy the Mormon Hipster."

"Oh," said Tinkler for the third time. But this time he was unable to conceal his happiness at the turn of events. I realised that, for him, this had been a win-win situation. He either got a double date out of it, or confirmation that Clean Head had no interest in this other man. Sneaky Tinkler. "But would it be okay if I invited Alicia—"

"Foxy," said two voices in accord.

"To join us for supper here tonight?"

"Oh, yes," said Nevada.

"Oh, please," said Clean Head.

Tinkler turned to me, apparently to get my input. "I wouldn't miss it for the world," I said.

"You better clear it with Miss Bebbington, though," said Nevada. "An extra mouth to feed and all that."

"I already have," said Tinkler proudly. "I've already paid her, too." *Fast work*, I thought.

Tinkler rose from the table. "Well, if you don't mind…"

"Going out to meet Foxy?" said Clean Head, ostensibly engrossed in her newspaper again. Nevada sniggered.

Tinkler tried to look dignified. He composed himself, turned to go, then turned back. "Just so you know… and so you don't inadvertently say something when you first see her because you're so shocked… she has *freckles*. Just remember she was born that way and can't help it."

I said, "Nice to see you back again, old friend. I was worried there for a moment that you were gone for good."

Tinkler gave me a toothy grin and a rakish salute. The salute was new.

Alicia 'Foxy' Foxcroft turned out not to be foxy at all, at least in the sense of crafty, conniving or vulpine. Indeed, what she mostly projected was an air of wide-eyed innocence. She did have red hair though, definitely a foxy shade. But not the pale skin normally associated with redheads. In fact, she possessed a handsome and healthy-looking golden tan, which set off strikingly the darker brown of those freckles Tinkler had so thoughtfully warned us about.

All in all she was charming and pertly pretty, with a small snub-nosed face framed by a genuinely dramatic froth of red curls. She wore jean-style leggings, pink Converse sneakers and a sort of cowgirl blouse in white with large red poppies in a symmetrical pattern on the front.

Tinkler was obviously very struck with her. To me she seemed rather quiet, but then the poor thing had come to dinner with four virtual strangers who were close friends and who had known each other for years—a brave move in itself—so maybe it wasn't surprising that she didn't exactly dominate the conversation. But she did giggle a lot, signifying her appreciation and approval of what was under discussion.

What was under discussion grew increasingly eccentric as the evening progressed and supper was consumed—a vegetable moussaka with meaty mushrooms accompanied by Nevada's favourite budget red wine, the Jaboulet Parallèle 45. Rather a lot of the wine.

"They should have a music festival here," said Nevada at one point. "An arts and music festival. It could really be a big money-spinner. It's amazing they haven't got one already, but apparently they haven't."

"It could be like Burning Man," said Clean Head, nodding enthusiastically.

I suddenly felt a rippling thrill of connections being made as I realised, with an almost déjà vu-like inevitability, that the Burning Man festival had been inspired by the film *The Wicker Man* in the first place.

"We could call it Drowning Man," I said. And everybody started laughing. "We could build a large wooden effigy of a man—"

Clean Head was wiping tears of mirth from her eyes. "And carry it up onto the cliffs and throw it into the ocean!"

"They could carry it up to that place where they burned the money," said Nevada. "And throw it off from there."

We all roared with laughter.

Alicia 'Foxy' Foxcroft looked at us. She wasn't laughing, but she was smiling broadly, her big eyes sparkling, drinking it all in.

"And watch it sink into the ocean," said Tinkler happily. "What a great idea." He was apparently seeing it all right now, in glorious colour, in his somewhat drunken mind.

"It is a great idea," said Alicia politely.

"Well, they may not have any festivals here—" said Clean Head.

"*Yet*," said Tinkler.

"They may not have any festivals here yet," said Clean Head. "But they do love a party. Especially on the beach. And we're all invited to one. Tomorrow night." She looked at Alicia. "You too."

"Thank you," said Alicia.

"Whose party is it?" said Nevada.

Clean Head suddenly looked thoughtful. Or as thoughtful as a young woman could after drinking that much wine. "Ours, I suppose."

"Ours?"

"Well, I helped to arrange it. It's for us." She turned to Tinkler. "And especially you."

"Me?" Tinkler was astonished. So, for that matter, was I.

"For you and Kind of Blue." Clean Head poured herself another glass of wine and inspected it carefully, perhaps because she didn't want to meet the soulful gaze emanating from Tinkler's big brown astonished eyes. "I know how much that car meant to you." She sipped her wine then chanced a glance at him. "So we arranged a Viking funeral for it."

"A Viking funeral?" I said.

"What a great idea," said Tinkler, his voice thick with emotion.

"Who is 'we'?" said Nevada, always one to keep her eye on the ball.

"Me and Gareth, the Mormon Hipster," said Clean Head. "Apparently he's the man to go to if you want to arrange a Viking funeral around here. Or any kind of beach party."

"Kind of Blue is a car?" said Alicia.

"That's right," said Tinkler, tearing his gaze away from Clean Head.

"What happened to it that it died and needs a funeral? Was it in a wreck or something?"

No one else seemed in a hurry to recall this particular event, so I said, "We got caught out on the causeway with the tide coming in, and we had to abandon it."

Alicia's wide eyes grew even wider. "But those tides are really dangerous. You could have really got into trouble." She looked around the table at us. "You should always check on the times of the tides. They have a sign up with them posted on it. And you can look them up online."

"Really?" said Nevada. "We'll have to try and remember that next time."

18. VIKING FUNERAL

"It's a full moon, too," said Nevada the following night. She was leaning out the window of our room, craning her head up to the sky. "Perfect party conditions," she announced, coming back in.

We'd been instructed to wait until dark before going along the beach to the site of the festivities, and, it being summer, that meant we had to wait until nearly ten o'clock. At first I'd thought that such a late start would have rendered us weary before we even set off, but, in fact, there'd been a growing sense of excitement throughout the day, and now both of us were eager and ready to go.

We collected Clean Head and stepped out into the mild summer night, with the sound of the sea shrugging and throwing itself against the sand in the darkness nearby.

We were going to meet up with Tinkler and Alicia when we got there. They'd spent the day together, doing what exactly we didn't know, although it had been the subject of much speculation between Clean Head and Nevada. "Not having sex, anyhow," said Clean Head. "I think we can be fairly certain about that."

When we'd asked where the party was, we'd been told in classic Halig Island fashion that we'd be fine because we couldn't miss it. This proved to be correct because as soon as we emerged from Miss Bebbington's B&B we became part of a steady stream of people who were walking purposefully along the seafront high street, clearly with some set destination in mind. It reminded me of coming out of a Tube station on the way to a gig and falling in with all the other people who were heading to the same venue.

There was already a large crowd gathered on the beach. It seemed like the entire population had turned out to say farewell to Kind of Blue. "Impressive," I said.

Clean Head nodded. "Looks like the Mormon Hipster did his bit."

We walked across the beach, among the throngs of people. They were mostly, but by no means all, young, and in everyone's hand there seemed to be the white shape of a drinking cup, the glint of a can or the glowing tip of what might be, in the best-case scenario, a cigarette.

A general party mood was abroad, and conversation was loud and excited. In the sky above us a mass of cloud shifted and the full moon suddenly poured cold whiteness down on the scene. Some people applauded as though this was a particularly clever stage effect. Others took out their phones and began to take pictures, puny little flashes going off, drowned by the immense light coming down from the heavens.

"Look there," said Nevada.

In front of us was a familiar shape. The shadowed contours of Kind of Blue itself. Moonlight gleamed on its windscreen, with a black frond of seaweed caught under one wiper blade, stretching up raggedly across the glass like a thick crack. We went over to the car and peered at it.

It was very strange, and strangely moving to see it like this. Although the car was nominally the focal point of all this activity, we seemed to be the only three people on the beach taking any real interest in it. Poor old Kind of Blue.

The windows were still open, as we'd left them when we'd scrambled out and climbed onto the roof. I put my head inside and then pulled it out again quickly. There was a powerful odour of mould in the car. I put my hand on the roof, where we'd stood a few days ago before taking the plunge. I had the ridiculous feeling that I was comforting a great, fatally wounded beast. And that it needed comforting.

Nevada put her own hand on my shoulder.

I turned to her and saw that both she and Clean Head were looking at me with serious expressions. The moonlight sheared my vision in bright white, angular patterns so that I could hardly see them, and I realised that—ludicrously and shamefully—my eyes had filled with tears.

"Come on," called a very familiar voice. Tinkler came trotting out of the crowd and gestured excitedly at us. "Quick! You're going to miss it."

We turned and hurried after him, leaving Kind of Blue behind in the dark. I hastily wiped my eyes. Crying over a car seemed more silly than ever, not least because Tinkler sounded perfectly happy, and it was his car.

We followed him down to the water where the crowd had formed a rough semicircle. At the very edge of the water were four young men in wetsuits, two of them wearing only the wetsuit bottoms so as to reveal their sculpted and ripped torsos. "Don't look, Agatha," said Nevada. "You'll go blind."

"It will be worth it," said Clean Head.

On the ground by the aquatic posers was a miniature raft, made of tree branches lashed together. In the centre of it was a pile of kindling like a large, untidy nest. And in that nest rested a couple of pale rectangles of metal, with black numbers on them.

Tinkler came and stood beside me.

I said, "Are those the—"

"The licence plates from Kind of Blue, yes," said Tinkler softly. Maybe he wasn't as happy as I'd first thought. He sounded moved. Alicia Foxcroft came over and stood with us as we watched.

The four young men in the wetsuits were now handed burning torches. With their other hands, and a little awkwardly, they picked up the raft, putting the corners of it on their shoulders like pallbearers. Then they walked out into the waves and dropped the raft so it floated between them.

Lowering their torches onto it they ignited the kindling around the licence plates. This must have been soaked in accelerant, because it caught fire quickly and dramatically, burning blue then a hot orange.

The men shoved the burning raft out and it floated a little distance from them, then caught the swell of a wave and slipped smoothly away as we watched. Nevada took my hand. We stared out at the little flame on the waves as it moved off into the night, a hot gleam in the darkness, which shrank and shrank and then finally winked out, whether simply with distance or the extinguishing crash of a wave, we'd never know.

I turned to see that Tinkler had his arm around Alicia's waist. I noticed now that she had a professional-looking sound-recording device hung by a strap over her shoulder and was holding an equally professional-looking microphone with a furry wind-baffler on it. It looked like the fat tail of a frightened cat. What was all that about?

"Viking funeral, eh?" said Tinkler.

"Yes, very nice," I said.

"It was the least Kind of Blue deserved."

"Yes, it was." It had only been a stupid car, but we'd had a lot of adventures in that stupid car. I nodded at Alicia, who had moved off with her recording equipment. "What's going on there?"

"Oh, Alicia thought we should record this event for posterity. So a friend of hers has got a camera and is filming it, and Alicia is recording the sound."

"Shouldn't both of them be together, then?" I said. "So that the sound and film match up?"

"She's recording a wild track." He shook his head in fond wonder. "A wild track."

"Do you even know what a wild track is, Tinkler?"

"No, but she's such a smart woman and I'm such a lucky man."

The raft-launchers had now waded back onto shore, still carrying their burning torches. They used them to light big piles of kindling sitting on the sand. Each sprang to life, throwing light and surging shadows across the sand.

Beach bonfires.

Someone turned on a music system somewhere in the darkness and it began to boom out. Suddenly we were in the middle of a proper beach party. The bonfires were throwing off heat and slender curls of smoke rose towards the full moon. There were whoops from the revellers and people surged all around us.

Bottles were being passed around and cans of beer were everywhere in evidence. Not to mention the joints glowing in the dark, and vaporisers and hash pipes. The smell of weed soon obliterated the smell of wood smoke.

From back in the direction we'd come there was suddenly an intoxicating pulse of bongo drums. We followed this rhythm up the beach, towards Kind of Blue again, like children drawn to the Pied Drummer of Halig. In contrast to the rest of the music, these drums were real and being played live. And whoever was playing them actually knew what they were doing.

To my surprise, this turned out to be the Mormon Hipster himself, sitting cross-legged on a red and black checked blanket on the sand beside the car. A girl was dancing on the roof of Kind of Blue, her sinuous body writhing in time to the bongo beat. She was wearing a leopard-print bikini and had a lean, muscled torso. A tattoo of a snake went writhing up her body, from her right ankle to her left ear. The whispering head of the snake was revealed intermittently as she threw her long mane of blonde hair around.

"It's the Shearwater daughter," I said, raising my voice to make myself heard over the music and, now, the approving cries of the crowd.

Clean Head nodded. "It was supposed to be me."

"What?"

"Yes. The Mormon Hipster invited me to do the bikini dance on the car and I said no." She shook her head. "I'm beginning to regret it now. At least I can actually *dance*."

After the car-top dance routine ended, we wandered through the partying crowd. It was noisy and chaotic, shadows twisting in the firelight, people dancing and music booming, and I was soon separated from both Nevada and Clean Head. I just turned around and they were gone.

I wasn't surprised. They seemed to be mounting a full-scale surveillance campaign on Tinkler and Alicia Foxcroft, shadowing their every move. And apparently this reconnaissance had led them away from me.

Eventually I found myself standing beside the Mormon Hipster, his duties as bongo drummer now discharged. We stood elbow to elbow and watched the festivities, smiling. It was quite a night.

I leaned towards him and shouted over the music, "Thank you."

He shrugged modestly. "For what?"

"For sorting the car."

He shot me a surprised look. "What has Agatha told you?" He was staring at me worriedly now.

"Nothing," I said, and shrugged. "Should she have told me something?"

"No, no, no… no." He peered at me. "What did you mean about the car, then?"

"All this," I said, indicating the beach party which was in full swing around us. "I was just saying thanks for arranging this and giving a nice farewell to Tinkler's car."

"Oh, that." He looked relieved. "You're welcome." I wanted to ask him what he'd thought I meant, but this would clearly be a non-starter. So we just stood in silence—well, in the midst of the riotous noise of the party, but unspeaking—until he looked up at the full moon and gave a little shiver.

"I wonder if the pig will turn up," he said.

For a moment I thought he meant that a hog roast was in the offing. But then he said, "It was a full moon on that night, too."

"What night?"

"When it killed Pete and Sarita Loretto." The drummer and his wife.

"When what killed them?"

He shot me a *keep up* look. "The pig."

"You think a pig killed them?" I'd already had versions of this from Valentyna Lynch and Tinkler, but I wanted to hear the Mormon Hipster take on it.

"*The* pig. The demon pig."

I sighed and took a deep breath. On second thoughts, could I even muster the energy for this discussion? It was a bit like forcing myself to make real coffee. There was an intrinsic value in an effort directed towards a worthwhile end. Like denying the existence of murderous demon pigs.

"But they were shot," I said, "weren't they?"

"Right."

"She shot him and then shot herself."

"Yup." He nodded. I was glad there wasn't going to be an argument about whether a pig could operate a gun with its trotters.

"So how does the pig come into it?" I said.

"It *caused* it. It caused the whole situation."

"By…"

"By just being there," said Gareth. He was seeming a lot more Mormon and a lot less hipster as we delved deeper into his intriguing belief system.

On the other hand, you couldn't really argue with his position… If the pig hadn't been there, had not been involved at all, then there never would have been a gun in the equation and the shooting could never have happened. The idea, as I understood it, had been to kill the pig and then set about butchering it. In the wonderful rural manner. Poor pig.

He looked at me. "They say he's going to come back."

"The pig?"

"No. Pete Loretto."

"Come back from…"

"The dead."

"Oh."

"You know he was practising black magic."

"So I understand."

"They say that's what the pig is all about."

"Do they?" I said, far from clear what he was getting at but by no means eager for clarification. But I got it anyway.

"They say it's his spirit returning," said Gareth. "In the form of the demon pig."

"Hang on," I said. "You said it was the demon pig that killed him. How can he return in the form of the demon pig if it was the demon pig that was responsible for his death in the first place? This *is* the same demon pig we're talking about? There is just one?"

Gareth was staring at me and I realised I might have gone too far. But what the hell. In for a penny, in for a pound.

"Well?" I said.

He looked me up and down. "I can see you're a sceptic."

"You've got that right."

We both shifted around now, so instead of standing side by side in companionable discussion, we were half facing each other in pugnacious confrontation. I could sense things escalating, but to be honest I didn't feel like backing down. The Mormon Hipster's chin was lifting aggressively.

"You think you mainlanders know it all, do you?"

"Nope. But we do know that demon pigs are a heap of horse shit—sorry, pig shit."

Gareth rocked back and lifted his arms with his elbows tucked close to his side and I wondered, for the first time since the days of the schoolyard, if I was going to get involved in a fistfight.

But then a tall figure stepped out of the darkness and clapped hands on our shoulders. "Well, lads. How's it going?"

It was Tom Pyewell, and I was preposterously pleased to see him, considering that he hadn't returned any of my calls. In fairness, though, I hadn't recently possessed a phone on which he could have returned them.

"I've been looking all over for you," he said, leaning over and shouting in my ear. The music had suddenly risen again, making conversation problematical. "Why the hell didn't you call me?"

I tried to make a reply and then, all things considered, just gave up and shrugged.

"I said you could come and stay at my place," yelled Tom. "I'm going to be offended, if you're not careful!" He gave me a gleaming grin to show that he was joking.

Gareth broke in on our conversation, seizing Pyewell companionably by the arm. "Great to see you, Tom. Catch you later." He gave me a nasty look and walked away.

"Catch you later, Gareth," Tom called after him. The music dropped to manageable levels again as he turned to look at me. His gaze was sardonic and speculative. "What was all that about? You seem to have really annoyed our Gareth."

"We were discussing the demon pig that is alleged to be haunting these parts."

"Oh. And you don't think there is one?"

"Well, I did say 'alleged'," I said.

"Did he explain about Pete Loretto?"

"If by explain you mean make some vague comments about being mixed up with the dark arts, then yes, he did."

"Well, Pete really did believe in those dark arts."

"So I understand."

Tom Pyewell looked at me, the light of the bonfires reflected in his eyes. "Don't you think that belief can summon such things into existence?"

"Not in the way that you mean. Or that Gareth means."

"Do you know *The Crucible*, the play by Arthur Miller?"

I repressed the urge to say, *Oh,* that *Crucible*. "Yes."

"Do you remember the scene where the girl believes she sees this demonic thing flying around the room, and then all the other girls begin to see it, too?"

"Yes, but that girl you're talking about doesn't really see anything. She's deliberately misleading the others because she knows they're susceptible."

"Hmm, fascinating. I'd love to talk to you more about your interpretation of that." He slapped me on the shoulder. "But there's someone I have to find…" He peered around at the tumult of the beach party and I thought, *Good luck*. He glanced at me. "You don't mind if I…"

"No. Not at all," I said. "I'll catch you later." He nodded and smiled and moved off.

For a moment I was alone and peacefully at a standstill. And then there was suddenly an enormous roar of approval from the crowd and I turned to see what might have occasioned it. It had come from the direction of Kind of Blue and I headed that way through the crowd.

In the distance, in the firelight, I could make out a figure dancing on the roof of the car. But even at this remove I could tell it wasn't Maxine Shearwater again. In fact, it looked like someone I knew…

I pressed through the throng of onlookers and soon I

could see that it was indeed Clean Head. At first I thought she'd stripped down to her bra and knickers, but then as I got nearer I saw she was wearing a proper bikini, an elegant black and white domino creation.

Someone had a beatbox pounding out 'Dance to the Music' by Sly and the Family Stone and Clean Head was really throwing herself into it, her entire body shimmering to the pulse of the song, lithe and elastic and twisting around the beat. She was right. She was a far better dancer than Maxine Shearwater.

And the crowd thought so, too. They were clapping their hands in time to the song and shouting ecstatically, whistling and cheering, every face turned up to gaze at Clean Head, blissful, rapturous and entranced.

Except for one. Maxine Shearwater stood there watching with a look of stony hostility. *This is how a real professional does it, Maxine*, I thought. *Watch and learn.*

Sly and the Family Stone segued into 'Superstition' by Stevie Wonder. Who had chosen these tracks? Clean Head herself? They were perfect. The beat of this one was slower, and even more funky—if that was possible—and Clean Head was writhing and clapping her hands and the entire crowd was swaying and clapping along with her.

Except for Maxine, who had turned away and was slipping off.

I felt a hand on my shoulder and turned to see Nevada smiling at me. "Where have you been?"

"Arguing about demon pigs."

She kissed me with her wine-tasting mouth and clung

to me as we watched Clean Head. As the song came to an end Clean Head stopped dancing and began to lower herself off the car roof. There were moans of disappointment and imploring cries from the crowd but she just grinned and shook her head and jumped to the ground, where she was instantly surrounded by a circle of admirers, male and female, who were eagerly offering her every alcohol- and cannabis-delivery system ever invented.

Nevada turned and grinned at me. "What did you think of our girl?"

"Very impressive."

"Wasn't she just?"

"I'd rather have seen you up there, though."

Nevada took my arm. "That was the correct answer," she said.

"By the way, did she go all the way back to the B&B and change into that bikini?"

"Oh, yes, a class act all the way, our Clean Head. Poor Tinkler, though."

"Why poor Tinkler? Did he miss the show?"

"Oh, no, he was over there. Watched the whole thing. But he had to pretend he wasn't in the least interested. Because he's with his new *girlfriend*." She didn't actually put air quotes around the word, but I could see the effort it cost her.

"Ah, there you are," said Tom Pyewell, stepping out of the shadows again. He grinned at me, and then Nevada. "You must be Nevada Warren?" *Full marks for remembering the name*, I thought.

"Yes," said Nevada, taking his extended hand. "And

you are... Tom Pyewell?" Full marks for accurate guessing.

"Yes indeed," he said, shaking Nevada's hand perhaps a little longer than strictly necessary.

"Did you find your friend?" I said.

He looked at me and shook his head. "No, but I'm sure she's knocking about somewhere."

"Now, Mr Pyewell..." said Nevada.

"Tom. Yes?"

"There was a vicious rumour that you'd invited us to stay at your house."

Pyewell laughed. "I did, I did. I'm not quite sure what went wrong."

"Well, not to worry. We're staying at a lovely little B&B. With our friends."

"Still," said Tom Pyewell, "I'm sorry about the hassle."

"No hassle."

"Perhaps by way of compensation I can buy you all dinner?"

"You can certainly try," said Nevada.

He chuckled. "What about tomorrow night at the Alexander von Humboldt?"

"That's the pub on the seafront?"

"It's definitely one of them. And the food there's not bad at all."

"Well, now you're playing our song," said Nevada.

"Speaking of songs..." said a new voice. We all turned around to see that we'd been joined by none other than Max Shearwater. Indeed, the entire Shearwater clan. His daughter Maxine was standing behind him, still dressed in her leopard-print bikini and now looking bored as only a beautiful and posh young woman can. Meanwhile a considerably older woman, Max's age, stood at his side. In her face I could see echoes of Maxine's bone structure.

"You must be Ottoline," I said, taking the plunge. She gave me a somewhat snaggle-toothed grin. The imperfection was somehow charming, and I found myself thinking she must have been a stunner when she was young. She was a bit on the plus size now, and wearing the sort of loose flowing dress that provided ample camouflage. This particular one was white with a pattern of jagged black lines, which looked African. As did the very large and very angular ebony earrings she wore. She managed to carry this ensemble off, though. She had a considerable volume of silver hair, which seemed unacquainted with a comb in recent years, but again this looked good on her. As did the large spectacles with purple frames through which she peered at me.

"Guilty as charged," she said, grabbing my hand in both of hers and giving it the sort of firm and energetic shake you apply to a can of spray paint before desecrating a monument.

"And this is our daughter, Maxie," said Max. He extended his right hand in a patriarchal gesture in the general direction of his serpent-tattooed offspring. In his other hand he was clutching a CD, the silver disc catching and flashing reflections from the distant beach fire.

"Yes, we've bumped into each other before," I said, nodding at the daughter.

Maxine Shearwater showed the first flicker of interest—or, at least, awareness of our existence. She narrowed her eyes a little and studied me as though estimating my exact position for calling in an airstrike. "Really?"

"Yes, at the Green Ceremony."

"Oh? Really? I don't recall."

"Sadly," said Nevada, "we had to be content with just admiring you from afar."

Oh, well, I thought. *The gloves are off now.*

Tom Pyewell suddenly draped his arms over Nevada's shoulders and mine. "These are the good folk this party is in aid of," he said.

"Really?" said Maxine doubtfully. "I thought it was in aid of a car."

"It's their car," said Tom. "It was destroyed when they got caught out by the tides."

"Oh, you poor things. How utterly gutting," said Maxine, smiling at us. "You really should pay attention to the tide tables, though. You might have got yourselves hurt."

I could see Nevada formulating a response to this, and apparently so could the Shearwater Daughter, because at this point she simply turned and walked away.

Ottoline was frowning with concern. "Good god. You really must be more careful. Those tides are lethal. There are warning signs with the safe times to travel. And there's a website. Please check before you drive next time."

Luckily Tom Pyewell changed the subject at this point. "What was that you were saying, Max?" He indicated the CD that Max Shearwater was still clutching. "About a song?"

Max looked at the CD in his hand with surprise and a little alarm, as if he'd just discovered a sinister growth. "Oh, what? Ah, yes." He turned and gave me a toothy grin. His dentition was more regular than that of his missus, but even in this uncertain light, a tad yellow-looking. But then they both hailed from an earlier age when you didn't need good teeth to be rich or famous. Or even beautiful. "This is a little gift for you."

He handed me the disc, and I realised it was a CD-R actually, home recorded, with a title handwritten in Sharpie across the non-playing surface: *Reveries in Rhythm*, followed by a long string of numbers. "I would have brought you a copy on vinyl, but it hasn't been pressed on vinyl yet. When it is I shall make sure you get a copy. Hot off the press. Or rather the stamper."

At least he knew his vinyl terminology. But then he'd worked in the music business back in the days when vinyl had been the only game in town. "Do let me know what you think of the music. I put my number on it." His number? Of course, the string of digits scribbled on the CD were a phone number. He gave me a shy smile and I suddenly realised that he was nervous about how I might react to his music. It was strangely touching.

Ottoline took his arm and they turned away and set off determinedly, marching across the sand into the darkness. Just before they were out of sight, Max turned and shouted, "Great party." Then they were gone.

"Here's my number, too." Tom Pyewell handed me a business card. "My private number. The direct line."

That would have been helpful to have a few weeks ago, I thought. But I forced down my irritation and thanked him.

"So we're having dinner tomorrow?" he said.

"You do realise there's four of us?" said Nevada.

"No worries. Absolutely no worries."

"Hang on," I said. Something had suddenly occurred to me. I saw Alicia 'Foxy' Foxcroft standing over by the nearest bonfire, pointing her microphone towards the flames, presumably to record their crackling for posterity. Standing in attendance, and watching her dotingly, was Tinkler. "Jesus, there might even be five of us." Stranger things had happened.

"No worries. The more the merrier."

19. TEAM MEETING

Clean Head was in her running gear when she joined us the next morning.

She'd just done her post-breakfast route along the seafront and, as she sat down, she checked her wristband, which monitored the number of steps she'd run, or her heart rate, or some damned thing. Tinkler endeared himself to everyone present by not staring at her abbreviated outfit—grey shorts with pink stripes, grey top hardly more than a sports bra—as she perched on the end of the bench, gradually catching her breath. Out on the water, the early sun was burning off the haze. I tried to resist the notion that it looked like something Turner might have painted, but in the end I just gave in. The air smelled so strongly of brine it almost stung my nostrils. I breathed in deeply anyway. Up above us gulls screeched generalised criticism.

"So, team meeting," said Clean Head, clasping her hands together and placing her elbows on her knees.

"Correct," said Nevada.

"Why didn't we just get together and sit down and talk at the B&B?" asked Tinkler.

"Why do you think?" Nevada turned and gave him an expectant look.

"Well, that's what I'm asking."

"But why do you think?"

Tinkler sighed. He was now clasping his hands together in imitation, though probably unconscious, of Clean Head. "Because we don't trust Miss Bebbington, or because the place might be bugged, or because we're clinically paranoid, or because the Great Lord Satan might be listening in the next room with a stethoscope pressed to the wall..."

"Or all of the above," said Nevada. "Though it's not that we *don't* trust Miss Bebbington, it's just that we *can't*. Or rather, we can't afford to. We can't afford to trust anyone."

"See my earlier remark about clinically paranoid."

"I preferred your earlier remark about Satan with the stethoscope," said Clean Head. "Does it have to be especially adapted to fit over his horns?"

"Or into his pointy ears," said Tinkler, starting to chortle.

"The reason we are here," said Nevada firmly, treading on any possibility of levity or laughter, "is that someone tried to kill us."

That shut everyone up.

"Does anyone disagree with that assessment?" said Nevada. "Does anyone think luring us out onto that road when the tide was coming in was just a harmless jape?"

Silence.

"Right," said Nevada. "That party last night was a lot

of fun. But seeing poor old Kind of Blue brought the whole incident back to me. Not that it needed much bringing back. And what we have to realise is that instead of holding a Viking funeral for a car, someone might have been holding a non-Viking funeral for all of us." She looked around to see if anyone disagreed with the logic of this. No one did.

"So, we need to work out who did that to us. Who tried to kill us. Right?"

"Right," said all of us.

"So let's look at what we know about the person, or persons responsible. As far as I can see, we can discern two things about them. They knew how to hack the website where we checked the tide tables. And they were able to switch the sign." We all turned and looked down the road to where it dipped and joined the causeway, where our merry undersea adventure had begun on that memorable day.

"They didn't just hack the website," said Tinkler. "They also did something to your phone," he turned to me. "Remember how you exchanged texts with Alan at Jazz House Records? Well, like I said at the time, spoofing his number on an incoming text would have been straightforward enough. But intercepting your text back to him would have been rather more tricky. I've been thinking about how they might have done it. And I've concluded the most likely way was simply to take over your phone."

"Take it over?" said Nevada. I could see that she was mortified on my behalf.

Tinkler nodded. "And not just his. Probably all our phones, just to be on the safe side."

We all looked at each other. "Wouldn't they need physical access to the phones to do that?" said Clean Head.

"Nope. They just need to introduce malware or a virus."

"Don't we have to be naïve and click on a link?" said Nevada.

"Not necessarily. There are myriad ways of doing it."

"Myriad," repeated Clean Head. "Nice."

"It literally means ten thousand," said Tinkler proudly. "Anyway." He began counting on his fingers. "They can be airborne, via Bluetooth. They can insert malware into legitimate online ads. They can repackage and infect apps. The phone's operating system can have inherent vulnerabilities. The Wi-Fi network can be insecure." Tinkler had now run out of fingers. He was well short of ten thousand, but it was still a worryingly long list. He looked at me. "Or they might even have been able to install the malware with that initial spoofed text, the one that appeared to be from Alan."

"In other words," said Nevada, "we're talking about someone who is computer savvy."

"Or has a credit card," said Tinkler.

"What is that supposed to mean?"

"He means anybody can buy this stuff," said Clean Head. "All you need is a method of payment and access to the dark web."

"Actually bitcoin would be better," said Tinkler. "Let's say, rather than a credit card, anybody who has bitcoin."

"And who has access to bitcoin?"

"Anybody with a credit card."

Nevada sighed. "Am I alone in finding the whole notion of the dark web dispiriting? I don't suppose it's full of cat videos?"

"Only very dark cat videos," said Tinkler.

"Okay," said Nevada. "So that's what happened to our old phones. Let's assume that whatever sinister software was introduced to them died with them." She unzipped her shoulder bag and took out a white padded envelope the size of a hardback book. "There should be no such problems with these." Inside the envelope were four identical Nokia phones. "Thanks to Tinkler for paying for them."

"Always a pleasure," said Tinkler.

"They're basic models, but they'll do until the insurance coughs up and we get proper replacements. They'll more than do." She handed the phones out. "I've programmed each of them with the other three numbers, so at least we are now back in contact with each other. I've also added Miss Bebbington's number at the B&B."

We all pocketed the phones, except Clean Head, who didn't have any pockets.

"So much for the attack on our phones," I said. "That leaves us with the sign." I pointed down the road towards the causeway. "Somebody physically went down there and switched it just in time for us to drive past it."

"How would they know when to do that?" said Clean Head, then she snapped her fingers and answered her own question. "When they sent the text that was allegedly from Alan. And you replied to it. All their timing was based on that."

Nevada looked at Tinkler. "How long would it take

them to hack the tide table website? Could they do it as soon as they sent the text?"

"They wouldn't have to," said Tinkler. "They would pre-hack it. Have it all set up and ready to go, so that as soon as they sent a signal the real web pages were replaced with their fake ones. They could just prepare it beforehand and, at the required moment, put it into action."

Clean Head was staring along the beach now, towards the road to the mainland. "Could anyone have witnessed them replacing the sign that day?"

I shook my head. "I don't see how. Nevada and I took a walk along there and had a careful look. There's no CCTV cameras anywhere in the area, and the sign is placed in a dip well below what is street level up here, so it's effectively concealed from the sight of any casual passers-by."

"What about when they were coming and going?" said Clean Head. "Wouldn't they have had to walk along the road up here when they were on their way there?"

"With a great big fucking fake sign under their arm," said Tinkler. "Possibly wrapped in brown paper so as not to look suspicious."

"On their way there, or their way back," said Clean Head.

"With the sign again," said Tinkler. "Having removed it after it had done its sinister job. I'm really warming to this brown-paper theory."

"Anyway," said Clean Head, "it might be worth asking in the shops along the seafront."

I nodded. "We thought of that."

"We also thought," said Nevada, "that if someone

wanted to do it undetected the best way would be to get off the road some distance away and approach along the beach. There'd be no problem doing that, at low tide, and they'd be out of sight all the way, coming and going."

It was Clean Head's turn to sigh. "You reckon they thought of that?"

"I reckon they thought of everything," said Nevada. We were all silent for a moment. The more I considered it, the more chilling her statement seemed.

"What about traffic along the causeway itself?" said Clean Head. "I mean people driving to and from the mainland. Someone messing with that sign would have been highly visible to anyone on the causeway."

"Unfortunately," I said, "there wouldn't have been anyone."

Clean Head looked at me, then nodded. "Of course. They did this just when the tide was coming in. So there wouldn't be any traffic out there."

"That's right," I said. "Everyone was too smart to be on that road at that time of day. Except for us."

"The bastards thought of everything," said Clean Head.

"Let's look at this from another angle," I said. "Who could have done it? Got a new sign made like that. And, more importantly, who would have *wanted* to do it?"

"Occam's razor," said Tinkler. "Let's go at this from first principles."

"Somebody wants to get rid of us," said Nevada. "Why? My guess is because we somehow represent a danger to them."

"*Me?*" said Tinkler. "I don't represent a danger to

anyone." He paused for a moment. "Except possibly myself."

"Clearly we all represent a danger," said Nevada. "Even Tinkler. But why?"

"My money is on the money," I said.

"The money they burned?" said Clean Head. "The million pounds?"

"Million dollars," said Tinkler.

"Whatever, it's still a lot of money."

"Enough to kill for," said Nevada.

Tinkler leaned forward from where he was sitting on the bench so he could look at me. "What are you thinking? That they didn't really burn the money at all?"

I nodded. "And that's the sort of information that someone might be willing to kill over. To stop it becoming public knowledge."

"Well, who's the likely candidate?" said Clean Head.

"Hmm." Tinkler was doing his thoughtful look. "Well, supposedly burning the money was the entire band's idea. A collective Black Dog decision. But after it was burned…"

"Or apparently burned," said Nevada.

"After it was *apparently* burned, and they started getting a lot of grief from people—the sort of people who didn't have a million dollars to burn, which come to think of it is almost everyone—some of the band members started to distance themselves from the decision. Suddenly it wasn't *their* idea."

"So, whose idea was it?" said Clean Head.

"The two leaders of the band," I said. "Who were, and I suppose still are, Tom Pyewell and Max Shearwater.

They're certainly the two dominant personalities."

"And both of them claimed to be the one who originally came up with the idea," said Tinkler. "Which is their relationship in a nutshell. They were always fighting over taking the credit, over who was the *one*. The big dog in Black Dog. The difference is, after the money was burned—or not burned—and the shit hit the fan, and the band started coming in for a lot of criticism, Tom Pyewell also began to distance himself from the decision."

"But not Max Shearwater?" said Clean Head.

"No," said Tinkler. "He's shown no remorse. He still thinks it was a *great* idea. Meanwhile, the others—well, except for Pyewell, who's tried to rise above it—the others have all got more and more pissed off because everybody in the world thinks they're dicks for burning a million dollars and because... well, they're also pissed off because they burned a million dollars."

"Which they could have had to spend," said Clean Head.

"Yes, on drugs and clothes and cars and other essentials of the folk-rock lifestyle," said Tinkler. "Like guitar picks. Imagine their regret. Imagine the number of guitar picks that could have purchased."

"But never Pyewell or Shearwater?" said Nevada.

"Well, Pyewell basically adapts his attitude to whoever he's talking to. If they think burning the money was a great idea, he makes out like it was indeed a great idea. If they think it was insanely stupid, he goes along with that. But he always makes it clear that he's above any messy disputes about the matter. He's on a higher plane. A higher plane where he agrees with whoever spoke last."

"But not Max Shearwater."

"No," said Tinkler. "Max never shows any regrets, no matter who he's talking to. At least he's always been consistent. He was the original trickster in the band. In some ways he genuinely is the most committed artist."

"He ought to be committed," said Nevada. "To a suitable institution."

Tinkler nodded. "Many might agree with you. But you sort of have to admire his chutzpah. The money really seemed to mean nothing to him. He was the lord of misrule. To him, burning it was a pure Dadaist gesture."

"Or not burning it," I said.

"Now I'm trying to work out if being a Dadaist trickster makes him more or less likely to have stolen it," said Clean Head. "That's what we're talking about, right? Pretending to burn the money but actually stealing it instead."

"Right," said Nevada. "That's exactly what we have to do. We have to work out who was most likely to have stolen the money."

"Well…" said Tinkler. "Of all of them, Shearwater was the only one who was independently wealthy. His family was rich."

"Which is *why* the money meant nothing to him," said Nevada.

Tinkler shrugged. "It's certainly why the others were so pissed off with him when they sobered up afterwards and realised what they'd done. And that there was no way of getting the money back, since it had gone up in smoke."

"Or into someone's pocket."

"They were pissed off with him because he was the only one who didn't feel the pain," said Clean Head. "About the money being gone."

"Right."

"Personally," said Nevada, "I've known a few rich people, and seen them up close." She glanced at me and I knew she was thinking of a certain Mr Hibiki. He'd once been her employer. I'd been in his house on a memorable visit to Nagasaki Prefecture. It had been a very nice house. "And there was never one of those bastards," said Nevada, "who wasn't keen to pick up a little extra cash on the side."

"So we can't rule Max Shearwater out," said Clean Head. "What about the others?"

"Tom Pyewell is suspiciously well off," I said.

"But he's the one who has had the best, or at least the most lucrative, solo career post Black Dog," said Tinkler.

"Yes," I said. "Mostly in Japan, though, right?" Thinking about Mr Hibiki's house in Omura had reminded me of this aspect of the Black Dog saga. I'd believed that Pyewell was all washed up after the band split. And indeed he'd made a bid for mainstream success and fallen flat on his face. But further research revealed that was only the initial part of the Tom Pyewell story—before, inexplicably, his popularity had taken off in Japan.

"Ah, true."

"If you wanted to launder a million dollars stolen from your bandmates," I said, "wouldn't that be an ideal set-up? A career that takes place on the other side of the world."

"Or an alleged career," said Tinkler, warming to this theory.

"What about Jimmy Lynch?" said Nevada. "After all, he was the one who filled in the fire pit with cement, so we couldn't inspect where the money was burned."

I nodded. Indeed I'd forgotten all about Jimmy and his sudden eagerness for health and safety. "That's right. Good point."

"And it's that action which, as much as anything else, has got us thinking that burning the money must be what someone doesn't want us looking into." Nevada was looking at me. "Sorry, was that even a sentence?"

It was clear enough to me. "No, you're right. Very true. Good old Jimmy Lynch."

"But who else is there?" said Clean Head. "In the band?"

"Ottoline Shearwater," said Tinkler. "Max's wife. She played bass."

"And Pete Loretto," I said. "The drummer. He was the one who was murdered."

"Oh, yeah."

"By his wife, or by a demon in the shape of a pig. Depending on who you talk to."

"How could I have forgotten?" said Clean Head.

"Well, either way, he's off the list," said Nevada. "It could have been any one of the others who stole the money and don't want us to find out about it."

"There's another possibility," I said. Everyone looked at me. "It could be more than one of them, working in concert. In fact, it could be *all* of them."

"You mean they all faked it?" said Clean Head.

"Pretended to burn the money but instead divided it up among themselves?"

"It's possible," said Nevada.

"But why do that? Why bother to pretend to burn the money in the first place? Why not just keep it?"

I said, "Because whatever else you can say about that bonfire, it certainly brought them more than a million dollars' worth of publicity."

"And these weren't chaps who were averse to having their names in the newspapers," said Nevada.

"But would that even be worth it?" said Clean Head. "I mean, a million dollars split... what? Five ways?"

"A million dollars in the late 1960s," said Nevada. "What would that be worth in today's money?"

"I don't know," said Tinkler. "Not exactly. But maybe, like Valentyna Lynch said, around ten million in modern currency."

"That still sounds like a lot of dollars to go around."

"That's another thing that bothers me," I said. "Dollars. Why dollars? Why not burn pounds? It would have been so much easier."

"What are you thinking?" said Nevada.

"That rather than do some kind of switch when you're burning the money, wouldn't it be much easier to do the switch earlier on? The earlier the better."

"You mean when the currency was exchanged?" Nevada was frowning and nodding. "And then... what? You burn counterfeit money?"

"Maybe."

"And counterfeit US dollars might more easily pass

muster than counterfeit English pounds, since you're doing this in England?"

"Maybe."

"But wait a minute," said Clean Head. "If they pulled the switch long before they burned the money, why would anyone want to pour cement in the fire pit to stop us inspecting it?"

That silenced us all for a moment.

"And there is one other possibility," said Nevada. We all looked at her. "It could be someone who isn't in the band. Someone we don't even know about."

That silenced us for quite a while.

"I wonder what Miss Bebbington is making for lunch?" said Tinkler.

20. ALEXANDER VON HUMBOLDT

When we turned up for dinner with Tom Pyewell we immediately knew that Maxine Shearwater was at the pub, because her car was parked outside. It was identical to Max Shearwater's, right down to the sticker with the name MAX on the inside of the windscreen above the driver's seat. The only difference was, instead of baby blue, this one was painted shocking pink.

It was similar enough to look very strange and somewhat ominous standing there, virtually where her dad's Subaru had ended up after its eventful and brake-less downhill excursion.

"Isn't that cute?" Nevada inspected the vehicle disdainfully. "His and hers cars."

"And further evidence of daddy-daughter creepiness," I said.

"Did you know," said Clean Head, "that until World War One pink was the colour for little boys, and blue was for little girls?"

"Yes," said Nevada, who would never concede being ignorant of any aspect of fashion.

"No," I said. "That's fascinating."

Inside, the pub was crowded, indeed heaving, in a sort of polite and amiable way. The first people we recognised were Maxine and her mother, sitting on tall, stylish chrome and black leather stools at the bar. They were looking rather stylish themselves. Ottoline was wearing another capacious dress, but this one was black with distorted white star shapes, like a negative image of the one she'd worn the night before. Her purple specs were the same but now she was wearing a green turban, which somehow managed to look more elegant than ridiculous, though it was a close thing.

It was the Shearwater Daughter, however, who was the real cynosure. She was wearing black high heels, black stockings, and a wine-red dress slashed to below the waist at the back to reveal a considerable portion of her snake tattoo. Her extensive blonde hair was tied in a long braid that hung curving and twisting down across her back to provide an interesting contrast with the contours of the snake—a double helix, perhaps—in a way that was anything but uncontrived.

I noticed the two of them had chosen to sit at the one spot where the mirror behind the bar opposite them wasn't blocked by bottles, and thus allowed an unimpeded view of their own reflections. Narcissists 'R' Us.

Thanks to the mirror they could see us as soon as we stepped into the pub and, to my astonishment, they both spun around on their stools with big warm smiles of greeting and waved to us—the ambient noise in the pub making any called greeting merely theoretical.

This was all very nice, and indeed quite convincing. But then Maxine caught sight of Clean Head and, just for a moment, couldn't stop a look of unadulterated hatred appearing on her face. *Ah yes*, I thought. *The great Car Rooftop Bikini Dance-Off.* At least young Maxine was smart enough to know when she'd been beaten. She managed to plaster the smile back on her face pretty quick. But even so, as we walked past them, I half expected her to reach out and swat Clean Head on the shoulder, the way one of our little monsters would do when she caught her sister coming through the cat flap.

But we made it past the bar unmolested and into the dining area. This consisted of bare wooden floors and walls made of reclaimed timber, some of it with fragments of the original signage still legible on it. The room had apparently been added to the pub as an extension or afterthought. It was lower than the main structure and had a vast skylight extending across it, allowing for ample natural illumination.

The rectangular tables were all made of glass, or perhaps some transparent acrylic, so you could see the curling black iron legs that supported them underneath. At the widest one of these tables, right at the back of the room, sat Tom Pyewell and a much younger woman dressed in a gold and blue sari. Indeed, she looked like she'd just come fresh from a musical number in a Bollywood movie. Whether she was actually Indian or not was a good question, though. Her skin tone was approximately that of a very white woman who'd just caught a bit of sun. She was sitting intimately close to Pyewell, but was currently busy on her phone in the modern manner.

Pyewell spotted us and enthusiastically beckoned us over. There was already a bottle of wine open on the table, and that was a good sign. And it was red, which was even better, because Miss Bebbington had warned us against the white wines at the Alexander von Humboldt. "The red list is fine, but for some reason the whites are all ghastly."

We sat down at the big glass table with the happy couple and Tom introduced his companion as Lakshmi.

Lakshmi deigned to briefly set her phone aside, and looked at us during the introductions without apparent interest—except for Alicia Foxcroft. I thought there was a flicker of recognition on her face when she saw Foxy. But then it was gone, and the next moment Lakshmi was back on her phone, texting attentively.

Our waiter introduced himself—also in the modern manner—and menus were distributed. I glanced at mine and saw that it looked promising. Nevada, naturally, set hers aside and asked for the wine list. We all made small talk. Lakshmi had a strong Northern accent and I gleaned that she was from Bolton. None of which, of course, ruled out the possibility of a rich, varied and authentic Indian heritage. I still had my doubts, though. She excused herself to go to the loo, her phone remaining clutched firmly in her hand.

As soon as she was gone I asked Tom, "Is she actually Indian to any degree?"

"Never quite got to the bottom of that. Doesn't do to ask too many questions." He grinned at us.

"So, what does Lakshmi do?" said Nevada.

"What does she *do*?" Tom Pyewell made a great show of puzzlement. "Oh, you mean for a living." It was impressive the way he managed to convey that his initial interpretation of the enquiry had been something relating to his girlfriend's ability to act out whole swathes of the Kama Sutra for his gratification, all this without actually saying anything explicitly. "She's a software consultant."

"Oh, really?"

"Yes, you know. Computers. The Internet. All the stuff that I don't know anything about. Which is just as well, because I don't know anything about it. Anyway, she's been helping me out. Streaming services. My website. The Black Dog website. Digital marketing of our music. All that malarkey."

"How did you meet?" said Nevada. A question that always seemed to interest women. Though this time it interested me, too. "Presumably not online."

"No." He laughed. "Not online. Definitely not online."

"So… how *did* you meet?"

"Card in a newsagent's window," he said. Now we all laughed. But judging by the blank way he looked at us, which I don't think was put on this time, maybe we shouldn't have. Luckily Lakshmi came back at that point, weaving her way sinuously back around the table as though she was about to launch into a snaky dance number scored by A. R. Rahman, and sat beside Tom. She snuggled up to him. At least I thought she was snuggling up.

But then I realised she was whispering furiously in his ear. He was nodding and smiling suavely and apparently listening with full attention. After a spell of this, during which she could have read him most of the contents of a small dictionary, perhaps an English–Hindustani dictionary, he turned to us and said, "If you don't mind, we just have to pop outside for a moment. Please go ahead and order your food, all of you."

"What about you?" I said.

"We've already ordered. You guys go ahead. We'll be back in just a tick."

"And wine?" said Nevada in her most innocent voice. "Should we order wine, as well?"

"Oh, yes, of course, please do. Whatever you like. As I say, back in a tick." He and Lakshmi extricated themselves from behind the table and headed towards the door of the pub, moving rather rapidly, especially considering that she had resumed whispering in his ear. Or perhaps shouting, as they were now contending with the ambient noise in the loudest section of the bar. Tom Pyewell turned his head towards Maxine and Ottoline Shearwater as he walked past and smiled and nodded.

They smiled dazzling, mother-and-daughter smiles back at him, then returned to their conversation. They were as thick as thieves.

A moment later, Tom Pyewell and Lakshmi were through the door and out into the evening.

I turned to Alicia. "Do you know her?"

"Who?" she said, eyes wide with apparent innocence.

"Lakshmi. I thought she recognised you when we arrived."

"Oh, yes. I know what you mean. And I thought I

recognised her. But I'm not sure from where." She smiled a guileless smile at me, and I decided I wasn't going to get any further with this line of enquiry. I picked up the menu.

"I think they're having an argument," said Clean Head, nodding her head in the general direction of our departed host and his girlfriend.

"Your relationship spidey-sense is tingling," said Tinkler. Alicia giggled.

Clean Head nodded haughtily. "You're right. It is."

"Does anybody know what they want to order?" I said, setting the menu aside. Nevada was still busy studying the wine list as though it might contain the secret to eternal life. Which indeed it might, if you added up all the hopeful column inches devoted to the beneficial effects of wine consumption.

"The salmon," said Nevada decisively, which was particularly impressive since she hadn't even looked up from the wine list. I'd spotted this myself. Alaskan salmon fillets on a bed of charred fennel and wild rice. "And a light, fruity red will go very nicely with it. I've spotted an absolutely devastating pinot noir that they've got. What is everyone else having in the way of food?"

"I'm thinking of the salmon too," said Clean Head. "I feel a bit guilty. It's like we're pigging out on seafood just because we're not at Miss Bebbington's and it's our chance not to be vegetarian. But what the hell. This is an island. We are by the sea."

"And the fish very nearly ate *us*," said Tinkler. "And fair is fair."

That killed the conversation for a moment. But only for

a moment. "Salmon fillets is fish, isn't it?" said Alicia. "I think I'll have white wine with my fish."

"Of course," said Nevada, in a tone of voice which of itself could have chilled white wine. "Is there any white wine in particular you'd like?"

"A chardonnay I think, please."

"A chardonnay, right." Nevada's voice had dropped a few degrees lower. But she raised an eyebrow and summoned the waiter and we ordered. The wine came before the food and the waiter poured a glass of the pinot noir for Nevada to try. She sipped it thoughtfully and then nodded a happy nod. The waiter tried to pour her a glass of the chardonnay, too, but Nevada passed it straight to Alicia, who took a decorous sip and announced, "Delicious."

Then Alicia excused herself and headed for the loo. The door had hardly swung shut behind the poor girl when Clean Head and Nevada got started.

"Delicious!" they exclaimed in unison.

"Delicious Alicia," said Nevada, and Clean Head laughed and clapped her hands.

"Delicious Alicia."

"I thought she was Foxy Foxcroft," said Tinkler.

"We may need to vary our mockery," said Clean Head.

"Which shouldn't be difficult," said Nevada. "'Salmon fillets is fish, isn't it?'"

"Oh, now that's just cruel," said Clean Head. "Funny… but cruel."

"Okay, that wasn't her finest moment," said Tinkler. "But she's a very intelligent woman."

"Of course she is," said Clean Head. "But my relationship spidey-sense is telling me you're not going to get your leg over."

"Perhaps I have already," said Tinkler.

"Have you?"

"No."

Nevada picked up Alicia's bottle of chardonnay and studied it, then poured a homeopathic quantity into a clean glass, sniffed it suspiciously, and finally tasted it. She set the glass aside expressionlessly.

"How is it?"

"More oak than Sherwood Forest. Miss Bebbington was evidently correct about the white wines here."

Alicia came back to the table and then Tom Pyewell and Lakshmi came back inside just as the food arrived, which was a relief since on past form I thought he might have just taken off and left us stuck with the bill. He hadn't been lying about them having ordered earlier, either. Their meals came with ours. Tom had chosen steak and chips, which seemed disappointingly unpretentious for him, while Lakshmi was more on form. She had gone for herring coated with some brilliant vermilion spice. It looked very dramatic on its bed of white rice surrounded by various green vegetables. She'd also ordered an assortment of ancillary curry dishes, perhaps all to shore up the Indian impression she seemed so intent on making. I'd pretty much decided by now that she was a complete fraud and about as Hindu as I was, though to be honest this was largely based on the dislike I had taken to her because of her being constantly on the phone while in company. She did set it down now, though, for a brief interval, as she set to work on her food.

"That looks good, Lakshmi," I said. And it did.

"You are what you eat," she said, as though she'd personally just coined the phrase.

Tom Pyewell leaned over towards me. "Have you had a chance, by any chance, to listen to that CD old Maxie gave you? You remember? On the beach last night?"

I did remember, and as a matter of fact we had. And it was startlingly good. I said as much now. The tracks consisted of recordings of ordinary people speaking about their lives. All old men, with pronounced regional accents—a fisherman reminiscing about working on the water, a retired milkman discussing his rounds, a baker detailing his daily routine, starting very early every morning as he lit the ovens.

In summary it sounds like a recipe for boredom and disaster, but it was actually impressive, and deeply moving. Because these ordinary voices of ordinary people were accompanied by a soulful fiddle, playing quietly but clearly underneath their reminiscences. Jimmy Lynch's fiddle, I was sure. And every contour, rhythm and inflection of their speech was brilliantly echoed by his lilting, lyrical playing.

"This is really good," I'd said to Nevada when I listened to it. Indeed, it was; goosebump-inducingly good.

"Have *you* heard it?" I asked Pyewell now.

He nodded, sawing away at his rather rare steak, and then impaling first a pink chunk of it and then a fat golden chip on his fork. "Yes. He made damned sure of that. No avoiding listening to Max's new project."

"Isn't it great?" I said.

He chewed thoughtfully and at length, and then said, "I suppose. But it's just Jimmy Lynch playing the fiddle."

"And the voices," I said.

"Sure, and the vox pop, those people speaking. Those old geezers. But that's all you've got. Old men talking, and Jimmy playing his fiddle. Just those two components. And Max uses one as a sound-bed for the other. And that's it. That's all it is. Jimmy's fiddle and the old buggers talking."

"That's the beauty of it," I said.

"*Beauty?*" he said, and he looked at me in a way that made me glad I hadn't used the word *genius*, which I almost did. "It's just the fiddle and the voices. It's just Jimmy and the old farts. It's all them. It's *just* them. What did Shearwater do?" I noticed it was suddenly Shearwater now, not Max or Maxie. "Where is his contribution?"

"He had the idea," I said.

There was a long pause. Tom Pyewell looked at me carefully. "Ah, well now," he said. I'd begun to think he was a little drunk, or perhaps more than a little. "Isn't that interesting?" he announced to the table at large.

"Isn't what interesting?" said Nevada. Lakshmi looked up briefly from her phone and then returned to its screen.

"That's exactly what good old Max would say," said Pyewell. We were back to Max again. He clasped me firmly on the forearm and squeezed it warmly. "It's the *idea* that matters," he said. He seemed genuinely affectionate now, as if congratulating me on my perceptiveness. But a moment ago he'd seemed angry, both with me and Max Shearwater. I wondered if it had anything to do with Shearwater remaining true to his own eccentric path, never deviating, never compromising, and still retaining the ability to surprise, and to come up with the occasional genuine work of art, even after all these years.

Whereas our host had tried to go commercial and sell out, and had largely been unsuccessful even at that.

Could this be grounds for hostility, I thought. What were the odds?

But now Tom Pyewell looked up and smiled a big smile and said, "Oh, look, there's the man himself."

Jimmy Lynch had just come in through the door of the pub. He was wearing his customary faded jeans, this time with a shirt with a granddad collar with thin blue and white stripes. And, also as usual, he was wearing a long silk scarf, this one with thicker blue and white stripes on it, which hung down past his waist. He cut a distinctive figure with his frizzy greying hair and somewhat haggard, smiling face and no one would have been surprised to learn he was a musician.

He walked with that slightly hesitant, stiff-legged gait that I now regarded with astonished admiration, since I knew how difficult it must be for him to achieve. Jimmy saw the Shearwater mother and daughter at the bar and went over to them and said something and they all laughed, and then he looked up and caught sight of us and began to amble towards us with that slow, deliberate stride. He was still a good distance from the table when Tom Pyewell began to shout good-natured greetings at him.

"Jimmy, you debauched miscreant, why don't you come over and join us?"

"What do you think I'm trying to do, you little shite?" Both men laughed and Lakshmi looked up briefly from her phone to see what was happening. Then Jimmy reached our table and stood in front of it, leaning on the glass surface with both palms firmly planted flat on it, smiling at each of us in turn. "This must be Lakshmi," he said.

"Yes, it must be," said Tom unhelpfully. Lakshmi for her part just smiled her trademark mysterious smile. But she'd put her phone away. A rare honour being accorded to Mr Lynch.

"This lot I know," said Jimmy, looking at our party. "Except you." He smiled a big smile at Clean Head. "And you." A slightly smaller smile for Alicia.

"This is Agatha," said Nevada.

"And this is Foxy," said Clean Head.

"Alicia," said Tinkler, firmly.

"I don't mind Foxy," said Alicia.

"Well, hello, Agatha. And hello, Alicia who doesn't mind being Foxy." Jimmy was smiling and crinkling his face agreeably and apparently exerting every sinew to be charming. Then he turned to Tom. "Let me buy you a drink. Let me buy you all a drink." He picked up the bottle of pinot noir from the table, now sadly empty, and said, "Another one of these?"

"Yes, very much, please," said Nevada. "That would be lovely."

But Jimmy Lynch was now feeling at the pockets of his

jeans. "Oh, don't tell me," he said. "Don't bloody tell me. Christ, don't tell me. I've only gone and left my flipping wallet in my jacket at home."

"Doesn't matter," said Tom Pyewell, shaking his head.

"In my jacket, hanging on the coat rack in the hall at the house." I remembered seeing that coat rack, adorned with scarves.

"Absolutely doesn't matter, old son."

"I only left the house without taking the bloody wallet out of the bloody jacket."

"Just sit down and join us, Jimmy," said Tom. "We'll have that bottle of wine and you can help us drink it."

"Well, all right," said Jimmy. "That's very…" He suddenly fell silent. He was staring at the table.

Or rather, staring *through* it.

He was looking through the glass table at the floor. Or rather, at my shoes.

Or rather, *his* shoes.

He looked up at me, eyes gone blank. Then he looked at Tinkler. Then down at Tinkler's shoes. Tinkler was wearing the toffee-coloured Chelsea boots, of which he was already inordinately proud. And if there had been any possible ambiguity about the source of my hiking boots, there was absolutely none about Tinkler's footwear.

This time when Jimmy's eyes came up, they were rapidly filling with rage.

Apparently he didn't have any trouble at all putting two and two together. Because he then yelled, "The fucking bitch!"

The pub suddenly fell silent. Everyone was staring at us.

Jimmy didn't seem to notice, or to be bothered. "I'll murder her!" he announced. He turned away from the table, stalked back through the crowd at the bar, ignoring Maxine Shearwater and her mother, and slammed out through the pub door.

We all looked at each other. People were varying degrees of aghast, except Lakshmi, who was absorbed in texting on her phone again.

21. THE SEA VIEW

After supper we ordered a taxi and when it turned up outside the pub Nevada and I said our goodbyes and hurried off. We were heading up to the Lynch house to see if we could repair the damage we'd done.

We actually did consider going back to the B&B first and picking up the bags of shoes, so we could return them as a peace offering. But we decided this would be too time-consuming, too cumbersome, and besides, on some level, I knew Nevada was still hoping we might end up keeping them.

Clean Head didn't come with us because she'd had nothing to do with the great shoe heist, and Tinkler didn't come with us because he was a coward. "He might forcibly remove my shoes, and then where would I be?" he'd said. "Shoeless."

"This is all my fault," said Nevada as the taxi cruised through the summer evening. "You would have only taken one or two pairs of shoes if it hadn't been for me."

"One or two pairs of shoes would still have been enough to set him off. You saw the way he reacted when he saw what

Tinkler and I were wearing. That was two pairs of shoes. And it was enough. He probably doesn't even suspect about all the others."

"My god. Do you think? Then it really will be all my fault. I'm a uniquely appalling person."

"No. If we'd found that Jimmy had the flip back copy of *Wisht* in his record collection the other day, I would have let Valentyna sell it out from under him without a moment's hesitation. In fact, I would have let her give it to me for nothing, just out of spite on her part."

"No, you wouldn't."

"No, okay," I said, "I would have insisted on giving her some money for it and getting a receipt from her, to make the sale official, and make damned sure he couldn't get it back from us."

Nevada studied my face for a moment, then she leaned against me. "Thank you. You made me feel better." We sat in the taxi in a peaceful silence that gradually became a tense silence as we got nearer to Jimmy and Valentyna's house.

"Wait a minute," said Nevada, leaning forward suddenly. "Stop here, please," she told the driver.

We were just passing the pub with the submarine on its sign, The Sea View, and I saw what Nevada had spotted. Jimmy Lynch's yellow Saab, parked in the car park outside the pub, at a rather novel angle. My heart lifted. It seemed he'd never got home. Instead he'd apparently lingered here to drown his sorrows.

We paid off the taxi and hurried towards The Sea View, pausing to quickly look into the Saab. It had the hand controls. Definitely Jimmy's vehicle. "I didn't think there could be two bright yellow ones like that," said Nevada. "But always best to check…"

We went through the front door of the pub and I was immediately struck by the utter contrast with the Alexander von Humboldt. It was pleasantly quiet and peaceful in here. An old man and a young man were playing darts; a skinny yellow dog was thirstily lapping water from a big brown ceramic bowl in the corner; a young couple in a booth were staring raptly at the screens of their phones, school of Lakshmi; a bald man in a white shirt and a paisley bow tie was busy wiping glasses behind the bar—and Jimmy Lynch was sitting alone at a table, staring wistfully across at the enthusiastically drinking dog as if he wished he could get down on all fours and join him.

Instead, though, he would just have to make do with the assortment of bottles on the table in front of him. These constituted an impressive collection. As we got closer I saw they were all bottles of cider of various kinds. Not just apple cider, by any means. Among the other ones that immediately called attention to themselves were strawberry, blueberry, lime, watermelon and various blends thereof. And they were all empty. Jimmy might have been conducting a thorough review for an article in a weekend magazine.

He'd evidently found some means of paying for booze after all. Or he had a line of credit hereabouts.

Jimmy looked up at us as we approached him. For a moment his eyes were blank, and then he recognised us. The strangest thing was, he smiled. A hesitant but quite sincere little smile. It seemed there were times when any company was better than being on your own, and this was apparently one such time. "Well this is a coincidence," he said.

"Not a bit of it," said Nevada, sitting down firmly opposite him with me at her side. It was a small round table made of dark wood, which was a welcome relief after the transparent treachery of the one at the Alexander von Humboldt. But even if this one had been made of glass it was so completely covered with Jimmy's empty cider bottles that he wouldn't have been able to see my footwear with any clarity. "We're here to apologise," said Nevada.

"What for?" said Jimmy. He picked up a bottle and tried to sip from it, but it was empty. He picked up another one; same problem.

"For the shoes I'm wearing," I said. "And the shoes my friend is wearing."

"So where's your friend? Didn't he fancy coming along to apologise, too?"

"He feared your wrath," said Nevada, and Jimmy chuckled, and I began to relax. My other half's famous charm might make everything all right, after all.

"No need for apologies," said Jimmy. "Not from anyone." *He's certainly changed his tune*, I thought. "And no need for you to come all the way up here." I could tell he was pleased that we'd made the effort, though.

"You did sound a tiny bit cross," said Nevada, "back at the old Admiral von Humboldt."

"Admiral!" Jimmy chuckled. "That's a better name. Poncey, pretentious boozer, isn't it?"

"Their white wines are certainly their Achilles heel," said Nevada. Jimmy beamed at her. She was going to have him eating out of her hand soon. Possibly salted peanuts or pork scratchings.

"Now, this is a proper boozer," he said, his hand sweeping around to take in the pub in its entirety— the darts players were chalking up a score, the dog had enthusiastically splashed half the contents of its bowl on the dark wooden floor, the barman was replacing a bottle of whisky hanging upside down on a dispenser behind the bar, and the young couple in their booth were wrapped in what would have been a passionate embrace if they hadn't been staring over each other's shoulders at the screens of their respective phones.

The barman's activity seemed to remind Jimmy of something. He began to search among his own bottles on the table, looking for one that still had something in it. He picked each one up and then set it down again, like a chess master handling pieces and considering every possible move.

"Let us buy you a drink," I said. Nevada gave me an approving glance.

"Nah." Jimmy waved a dismissive hand in my direction, not looking my way, still concentrating on his search for the elusive bottle that still had some cider in it. He wasn't going to find it. "No need, you don't owe me anything. You don't have to apologise. It's not your fault. I wasn't angry at you. It wasn't your fault. It was her fault."

"But we don't want you to be angry at Valentyna, either," said Nevada in her most peaceable and reasonable tone. She was also using her big eyes on him in a manner which, if he'd just look up from his cider-bottle chess game, would surely have clinched the deal.

"Ah, I'm not. I'm not angry at her. What does it matter? It doesn't matter. It's just one of those things. Shit happens. It is what it is." He paused, apparently trying to think of another cliché to match the calibre of the previous three, failed to do so, and abruptly rose. "What are you drinking?" he said.

"No, let us get this round," said Nevada.

"No, it's my shout."

"I'll argue with you about it on the way to the bar," I said, and he chuckled. I walked with him to the bar and noticed that despite the impressive amount of alcohol he'd downed he was still steady on his—artificial—legs. The barman smiled and nodded at us.

"These are friends of mine, Desmond," said Jimmy. "They can have anything they want. What do you want, mate? What does your missus want?"

"A look at the wine list, I imagine. It's a risky business ordering anything for her that she hasn't approved first." Jimmy laughed and pounded me on the back. I tried not to flinch. Those oak-tree arms had made themselves felt. "I like a man who knows when he's beaten," he said. Desmond handed us the wine list and I took it back to our table. By the time Nevada had scrutinised it, made her decision and I'd returned to the bar, Desmond and Jimmy were deep in conversation. Jimmy looked up at me.

"They do nice food here, you know," he said. "Isn't that right, Desmond?"

"We try, we try."

"Better than that show-offy crap at the von Humboldt. The *Admiral* von Humboldt!" He shouted this to Nevada, who responded with a dazzling smile.

"I couldn't possibly comment," said Desmond, also smiling.

"Their use of fresh herbs here is particularly awesome," said Jimmy. "Do you know why?"

"Because you grow them in your own garden?" I said.

"Ah, Valentyna told you, did she? And the vegetables. She's the one who grows them, mate, she's the one who does all the work in the garden. And not just in the garden. She's the one who does all the work of every sort. And don't I know it? And I'm a lucky man. Lucky to have her. Don't I just know it?" To my astonishment, his voice was thickening and tears were glinting in his eyes.

"That's right," said Desmond, cutting off this monologue. He was apparently no more eager than I was to listen to a drunken and lachrymose paean to the joys of marriage from a man who'd suddenly and rather arbitrarily decided that his wife was a jewel beyond compare. "In fact, Sarah—that's our girl—she's up there collecting a basket of veggies and herbs right now," said Desmond. He glanced at the clock on the wall. "She should have been back ages ago. Honestly, that girl."

"Oh, it will be Valentyna's fault," said Jimmy. "She'll have started nattering and poor Sarah won't be able to escape. Or get a word in edgewise. She can talk the hind legs off a donkey, my missus. Never listens, but oh my god, how she can talk."

Now it was my turn to interrupt a monologue, though one that was rapidly heading in a less happy direction. "Well, *my* missus has chosen some wine," I said. Desmond the barman shot me a grateful look. I ordered two glasses of Hedonist Shiraz and Jimmy managed to find a cider based on a combination of exotic fruits that he hadn't already sampled. I tried to pay but he would have none of it.

"I've got my wallet with me this time," he said, taking it out of his pocket and waving it in my face as if I'd recently and repeatedly questioned its existence. It was a battered fat brown leather wallet with many odd pieces of paper sticking out of it, like bookmarks from a book.

So he must have gone home after all, before coming here for his adventures in the world of cider.

When he set the wallet on the bar and opened it I saw that they were assorted supermarket coupons offering an exciting range of discounts. Jimmy carefully extracted a payment card and handed it to Desmond.

After he'd paid, Jimmy insisted on carrying all three of our drinks back to the table. Which he did with a surprising degree of success, not spilling a drop. Once again I was impressed by the steadiness of a man who had so many legitimate excuses to be stumbling about the place. He set one of the glasses of wine down in front of Nevada with a flourish. "Thank you," she said. "How lovely."

"You chose it, love."

"Ah, but you paid for it, and that's always the most ticklish part of the transaction."

Jimmy laughed and sank down happily in his chair. He lifted his bottle in a toast and clinked it against our wine glasses. We sipped the Hedonist, which didn't surprise me by being fabulous. Both because Nevada had selected it and because it was an old favourite. I made a mental note . not to let Jimmy order a bottle of it, though, because it featured a rather charming picture of a pig on the label and I didn't want it triggering another fucking discussion about hogs from hell.

A cool breeze blew into the pub and I turned to see that the young couple were on their way out the door. No doubt to find a quiet, secluded spot where no one would disturb their further inspection of their phones. Or maybe they'd buck the odds and actually have sex. I hoped so. The door swung shut, but only for a moment. It opened again and another couple came in. These two were older. In their twenties, or perhaps even their early thirties.

The man had short cropped tobacco-coloured hair and a lean, pockmarked face. He wore a business suit but no tie and his collar was unbuttoned. The woman was plump and pretty, though her face had a severe intensity to it. She was also wearing a business suit.

I felt my stomach go cold.

They came all the way into the pub and looked carefully around. They saw us and immediately came over to our table. Jimmy hadn't seen them yet, and he was chatting happily. But Nevada saw the way I'd been looking and turned and she saw them, too. Her face changed.

The man and the woman stood beside the table, slightly

behind Jimmy and on either side of him. "Mr Lynch?" said the woman. "Mr James Lynch?"

Jimmy hitched around in his chair and looked up at her happily. "Jimmy, love. Call me Jimmy. The queue for autographs starts over there." He indicated some indeterminate, faraway spot. He didn't seem to realise that everything had changed. Even the air in the pub seemed to have changed. The two darts players were staring at us. The thirsty yellow dog was staring at us alertly. Behind the bar Desmond was staring at us. But then his phone buzzed and he looked at that, instead.

"Mr Lynch," said the woman. "Will you come with us, please?"

Jimmy was still happy, but now he was also baffled. He raised his bottle and waved it around a bit. "Come with you? No thanks. Come with you where? But no thanks. I'm quite happy here."

"Mr Lynch, I'm DS Ruth Montague and this is DS Benjamin Riley. Will you come with us now, please?"

"You're the *police*?" said Jimmy. He sounded appalled, as if some terrible trick had been played on him. "You want me to come with you? To the police station?"

"Would you come with us now, Mr Lynch."

"No. No way. No fucking way." Jimmy looked at us. It was the look of a drowning man who wanted to be pulled out of the water.

"Mr Lynch, I am arresting you on suspicion of murder. You do not have to say anything, but it may harm your defence if you do not mention when questioned something which you later rely on in court. Anything you do say may be given in evidence."

"Murder?" said Jimmy. He suddenly rose to his feet as if the national anthem had started playing, and he was a committed patriot. "Murder?"

The cops looked at us as they led him out, but Jimmy didn't look at us again.

As soon as they were gone Desmond came out from behind the bar. He was still holding his phone, and he was trembling. "The bastard," he said. "The bastard killed his wife. My girl found her, lying there on the kitchen floor. His wife's dead. The bastard killed her."

22. DECKCHAIRS IN THE DARK

I walked out into the dark garden behind Miss Bebbington's B&B. It was very late, and the whole town, the whole island, was indistinctly spread out around me in silence. In the distance I thought I heard the soft repetitive sound of the sea, but I wasn't even sure about that.

There was no sound of traffic, no voices, no music. No lone dog barking. Everyone was long since in bed and asleep. But behind me, in the little house, lights were burning at the windows and worried faces were peering out. Tinkler, Clean Head and Miss Bebbington herself.

Nevada was sitting alone in the garden, sprawled in a low deckchair, sitting in the dark and staring up at the night. She didn't look at me as I sat down in the chair next to hers.

"I know what you're thinking," I said.

"Of course you do. Because you're thinking the same thing. Everybody's thinking the same thing. Because it's true. He killed her. And it's entirely my fault."

"Maybe," I said. Out of the corner of my eye I saw

her pale face turn towards me in the darkness.

"Maybe?" she said.

I leaned over so I could look at her, or look at the blur in the darkness that indicated her. "I've been thinking about it."

"So have I. About nothing else."

"Then you'll have asked yourself the same questions," I said.

"Like what?"

"Like how could he have gone home, killed her, and then got back to that pub where we found him in time to drink all those fucking bottles of cider. You saw how many there were. He'd settled in for a serious session there."

"He had time to go home and get his wallet, though, didn't he?" said Nevada. "He didn't have that at the Alexander von Humboldt." I noticed she'd got the name of the pub right. "But he had it with him when you went up to the bar together in The Sea View, though, correct?"

I peered towards her in the darkness. "Yes, but I'd imagine murdering your spouse takes a little more time than just popping back in to the old homestead to retrieve your wallet."

"Are you sure about that? I imagine it could happen pretty quickly."

"Well," I said, "personally I can't imagine it happening between those two without a great deal of shouting going on first."

There was silence from the deckchair beside me. I sensed that I was beginning to make progress.

"All of which takes time. And then the act itself. She was

strangled, right?" Desmond, the barman at The Sea View, had filled us in on the grisly details, just as his daughter in turn had filled him in. She'd found Valentyna lying on the kitchen floor with one of Jimmy's scarves knotted around her neck. Desmond had been furious, and deeply shaken at the thought of his teenage girl having witnessed the aftermath of this horror. But that didn't stop him hungrily telling us every detail of it. Come to think of it, it hadn't stopped her telling him, either.

"And strangling someone wouldn't be as quick as you might think," I said.

"Oh, I don't think it would be quick at all. Not at all."

"And then there's the aftermath. What does he do? Kill her and immediately think, right, that's done. Now let's pop to the pub? I don't think so. I think there would be some considerable time staring at the body and thinking about what he'd just done."

"Before he pops to the pub."

"Before he pops to the pub, right."

"I still think it was doable," said Nevada. "In the time elapsed."

"And then there was the way he reacted," I said. "The way Jimmy reacted when the police came into the pub. He wasn't at all bothered at first. He had no idea who they were, and when they identified themselves he pretty much told them to piss off. And then, when they did tell him why they were there, he seemed genuinely shocked."

"He did, didn't he?" said Nevada, slowly and thoughtfully.

"He looked like a man who'd been struck by a lightning bolt. And I simply don't think he's that good an actor."

I heard Nevada stir in her chair and I saw the pale blur of her face shift as she turned to look at me.

"Neither do I," she said.

I sensed something, and I reached out my hand towards her in the darkness and found her hand reaching out to me. I took it.

"And then there's the small matter of him announcing that's he's going to murder his wife, loudly and clearly, and in front of dozens of witnesses. Before immediately going home and—guess what?—murdering his wife. And what was the murder weapon?"

"One of his trademark scarves," said Nevada softly.

We lay there in the dark, side by side in our chairs, holding hands and talking about murder.

"Right," I said. "Why not just post the whole thing on Facebook, if you're going to be so obvious about it? I mean, I suppose it could happen that way, and people do give themselves away by being clumsy and obvious like that, but…"

"But?"

"But the whole thing smells wrong to me. The whole thing stinks. You remember how you said these fuckers, whoever they are, are nothing if not thorough? Well, this has all the hallmarks of one of their little projects. I think for some reason they want Jimmy out of the way."

"And Valentyna. She's out of the way, too, now… poor Valentyna." There was a soft, rhythmic sound, which somehow merged with the gentle sound of the sea in the distance.

Nevada was crying.

A shadow rose up as she got out of the chair and got onto mine with me, the firm warm weight of her curled on top of me, her tears falling cold on the side of my neck.

23. HONEY TRAP

Not surprisingly, we slept late the next morning. Finally Nevada got up and went downstairs and, after an unconscionably long interval, came back with cups of coffee and got back into bed with me.

"Something is definitely going on between Gareth and Clean Head," she announced.

"The Mormon Hipster?"

"Yes. She keeps making excuses to slip off. And when she does, she ends up seeing him. Sort of accidentally on purpose. I've been keeping tabs."

"You don't think they're having an affair, do you?"

Nevada snorted. "You heard her. He's not her type. Besides, if she was, she'd tell me."

"Are you sure? Maybe she's ashamed of his beard."

"And besides, I understand the Mormon Hipster is busy seeing Lakshmi."

I said, "Tom Pyewell's girlfriend Lakshmi?" It was a stupid question. Could there be two?

"Well, ex-girlfriend. Apparently that's why they split up."

"Wait," I said. "They split up? Tom and Lakshmi?"

Nevada nodded. "That's what all the business was in the pub, all the weirdness that Clean Head picked up on. And going out to have a private conversation on the beach and so forth."

I shook my head. "Tom was pretty calm, though, wasn't he? It didn't seem like they were having a serious argument." Of course, it hadn't seemed like they were head over heels in love, either.

"They weren't having a serious argument. They just were splitting up. Apparently it's been on the cards for a long time. And Lakshmi and Gareth have been seeing each other for a while."

"What, while she was still with—"

"Tom Pyewell, oh, yes."

"Well," I said, "it explains why she was on the phone all the time, anyway."

"Oh, no, I thinks she's probably just like that. Shallow, self-absorbed and phone-addicted. Don't let her off the hook so easily."

"But why him—I mean why Gareth?" Admittedly Tom Pyewell was vastly older than her. But balanced against that was his wealth, fame and—I suppose some people would call it—charisma. All of which I would have expected to weigh heavily with someone as shallow as Lakshmi. Or at least as shallow as I'd rather arbitrarily decided she must be. But still, if she was going to choose someone to leave him for, "Why the Mormon Hipster?"

Nevada shrugged. "Small island. Limited choice, I guess. Maybe they met when he mended her brakes. Or, knowing Gareth's standard of workmanship, failed to mend them."

"By the way," I said, "how do you suddenly know all this stuff?"

"Miss Bebbington. She runs a first-rate bed and breakfast and is also a clearing house for all the finest local gossip."

Of course, the real gossip this morning was nothing to do with Tom Pyewell and his love triangle. It was all to do with Jimmy Lynch and his strangled spouse. But we studiously avoided discussing that.

When we went down to the breakfast room we found Clean Head standing at the window, staring out. Joining her and looking over her shoulder we saw that the pavement outside, which was normally deserted or at best featured a sporadic few pedestrians, now had a steady flow of people walking purposefully towards the centre of town.

It was highly reminiscent of the night of Kind of Blue's funeral. "Is there another party?" I said.

Clean Head turned and gazed at us. She did not look happy.

"What's the matter?" said Nevada.

"You better brace yourself," said Clean Head.

"Christ. What?"

"Stinky Stanmer. He's just arrived on the island. *With a camera crew*."

To simultaneously feel horror and relief is quite an odd sensation, but that is what I experienced now. Certainly the presence of Stinky, indeed just the prospect of it, suddenly threatened to poison the whole experience of Halig Island. Which, despite us having nearly died on its causeway, was turning out to be a very pleasant one. But even so… "When I saw your face," I said, "I thought it must be something much worse."

"It is," said Clean Head. She went and sat at the table and we joined her.

"Well, what is it?" said Nevada. "Spit it out, girl."

"Ah, well, it turns out that Alicia…"

"Oh, no," said Nevada.

"Oh, shit," I said.

"She's something to do with Stinky?"

Clean Head nodded.

In a horrible way, it all made sense now. Tinkler suddenly and uncharacteristically picking up an attractive young woman with recording equipment, her wanting the two of them to spend every minute together…

"She's working for him," said Clean Head.

"Foxy Foxcroft is working for Stinky?" said Nevada. She sounded as unhappy as I felt, and as Clean Head looked.

"Yes. She's apparently the sound recordist on his film crew. And also a researcher."

"A researcher," said Nevada. She looked at me. "And she was researching what?"

"Stinky is here to make a documentary about Black Dog, about burning the money and all that."

"Gosh, I wonder where he got that idea," said Nevada.

"So Alicia came here early with her friend, the one who

was doing the filming at the beach party. So they could do some groundwork before Stinky arrived."

"And part of that groundwork was getting close to us," I said. "Finding out what we were up to, and what we knew."

"That's right."

"You know," I said, "I never did actually see the friend who was doing the filming that night. The camera person."

"Well, you can see her now," said Clean Head.

"What?"

Clean Head got up and went back to the window, and we followed her. "There she is." Clean Head indicated a tall young woman with short dark brown hair sitting on the sea wall across the street. She wore a sleeveless yellow T-shirt, raggedly cut-off denim shorts and Doc Marten boots. The T-shirt had black lettering, which read WAKE ME UP WHEN IT'S QUITTING TIME. She was seemingly engrossed in looking at her phone.

"How long has she been sitting there?" said Nevada.

"Ever since Stinky made landfall on the island. She's apparently keeping an eye on us."

We went and sat back down at the table. I felt distinctly uneasy now that I knew we were being watched. It was all I could do not to spring back up and go to the window and make sure that the camera person was still sitting in the same place. And hadn't, for example, crossed the road while putting on a ski mask and taking out a gun.

I told myself not to be ridiculous. Stinky and his entourage were annoying, but not dangerous. Still, it took a pronounced effort to remain in my chair.

"So Alicia was really a honey trap for Tinkler?" said Nevada.

"So it seems," said Clean Head.

"Did he actually get any honey?"

"This is Tinkler we're talking about here. Of course not. Oh, shit, here he is now." Clean Head was staring towards the window where the top of Tinkler's head was visible as he came in through the gate. A moment later the front door opened and closed, there were footsteps in the hall and Tinkler came into the breakfast room.

We all must have been staring at him, because he said, "Come on, it's not as bad as all that."

"Tinkler, I am so sorry," said Nevada.

"Me too," said Clean Head.

"Me too," I said.

Tinkler sagged into a chair at the table with us and sighed. "I've been out there... trying to avoid Stinky. And trying to talk to Alicia." I winced at the thought of this. "Avoiding Stinky was the easy part," he said. "He's engulfed in people, would you believe it? Standing there on the seafront, holding court. Adoring fans all around him. *Adoring*. The limited gene pool of these island types is really beginning to show itself."

"Did you talk to Alicia?" said Nevada gently.

"Oh, yes. Oh, yeah." Tinkler fell silent, frowning, his eyes cast down. Finally he looked up at us. "She was just pumping me for information, all that time, you know. And the rest of you. She wanted to know what we were up to. That's what it was all about."

"She's a vile little hag," said Nevada succinctly.

Tinkler shook his head sadly. "No. No, she's not. She was just doing her job."

"For Stinky Stanmer!"

A ghost of a smile appeared on Tinkler's face. "But while she was getting information out of me, she didn't realise I was also getting information out of her." He leaned close to me and lowered his voice, conspiratorially. "It turns out that Stinky isn't just here to make a documentary. He's also looking for a copy of *Wisht*. The flip back version, of course. He wants to buy it and add it to his collection. You know, like a trophy."

"Hmm," said Nevada. "I wonder where he got the notion that he might find a copy here?"

Tinkler waved his hands in the air in a helpless gesture. "It was me, of course. With my big mouth. I told Alicia all about it."

"Don't worry, Tinkler," I said. "Once we came here it was inevitable Stinky would follow. He obviously scents a documentary on the subject of Black Dog, and he won a BAFTA by following us once before." That had been his programme about Valerian, which was entirely based on our research and our ideas. Needless to say, we'd received no credit. "But since then it's been all downhill for him…"

"Because the little shit has never had an original notion," said Nevada.

"So here he is," I said. "Shadowing us again, hoping to get lucky. And once he arrived on the island it was only a matter of time before he found out that we were looking for the record. Assuming he didn't know already. So don't blame yourself."

Tinkler gave me a grateful look. "But you know what we have to do now?" he said.

"Of course," I said. "We have to beat Stinky to the punch."

An hour later I made a pot of coffee and we sat in the breakfast room sipping it, holding a council of war. I said, "We came here to look for *Wisht* because there were four band members who had record collections where we might find it."

"Four?" said Clean Head.

"Including the dead one," said Nevada.

"Pete Loretto," said Tinkler. "The drummer. Why is it that the drummer is the least surprising one to end up dead?"

"So far," I said, "we've managed to look through just one of these record collections—Jimmy Lynch's." As terrible as it sounds, one of the many emotions I felt on learning that Valentyna was dead was a guilty sense of relief that I'd already checked Jimmy's LPs. Because I wouldn't be able to get to them now, since the house was a crime scene.

This in turn had got me thinking.

"Obviously," I said, "what we need to do is look through the other record collections as soon as possible."

"Before the other members of the band get killed?" said Clean Head.

That led to a protracted silence.

"Actually," I said, "that hadn't occurred to me." What *had* occurred to me was that the other crime scene, at the

Lorettos' house, must have ceased to be a police priority, or the focus of any activity… I didn't mention this yet, though.

"So we need to get in touch with Max Shearwater and Tom Pyewell as quickly as possible," said Tinkler, looking at me. "Or is that what you've been doing?"

"That is exactly what I've been doing," I said. Remarkably, I actually had working phone numbers for both of them and I'd called them up before this little meeting. To my amazement, in each case I'd managed to reach them on my first attempt.

Initially, though, they'd both reacted with identical wariness, for identical reasons. They'd thought that I was calling to discuss Jimmy Lynch's arrest, and his wife's murder. When they learned I had something else entirely in mind, they'd both relaxed.

I'd played it somewhat differently with each of them.

I told Tom Pyewell that we wanted to take up his kind offer of coming to stay at his house. His response had been enthusiastic. "I've split up with Lakshmi," he confided. I didn't tell him I already knew this, thanks to the efficacy of the island grapevine. "So there's plenty of room at the house. Even more than there was before. You guys can use the swimming pool. And Nevada can explore the wine cellar. I had stuff put down there years ago, and I've forgotten what I've got."

I told him that sounded fantastic, which it did. But we wanted to pay him a preliminary visit today and look for the record. Business before pleasure, so to speak. This seemed to make sense to him, and he'd agreed, saying we could turn up at any time.

With Max Shearwater I'd begun by praising the CD he'd made for me. In this I was simply telling him the truth, so it was easy. And I obviously sounded convincing because Max had been delighted. If he'd been a cat, he would have purred.

Then I asked him if we could drop by at his house and have a look for *Wisht*. I was hoping that we might be able to do this today, after visiting Tom Pyewell, but Max had said today was impossible. So we agreed to do it tomorrow.

I didn't like waiting. There was so much that could go wrong now that Stinky was in the equation. So, since truth had worked so well with him earlier, I decided to come clean.

I sipped my coffee and looked at the serious faces of my friends around the table. "I explained to Max that Stinky Stanmer was on the island, and I said that he might make an approach to try and buy the record before we did."

"What did he say to that?" asked Nevada.

"He said he'd tell Stinky to take a running jump."

"A man after my own heart," said Clean Head.

"So he's not a big Stanmer fan?" said Nevada.

I shook my head. "Particularly since it seems that his daughter Maxine is dating Stinky."

"You're kidding," said Nevada in chorus with Clean Head.

"Dating may be overstating it. But they've hooked up a few times, and Maxine's mum and dad aren't too delighted about it."

"Smart people," said Nevada.

"And Tom Pyewell?" said Tinkler, rather admirably keeping his eye on the ball for once.

"He's expecting us any time."

Clean Head half rose from her chair. "Let's go, then."

"Not me," I said.

Clean Head and Tinkler looked at me. "What do you mean?"

"The rest of you go, but I'm not coming with you."

"What the hell—" said Tinkler.

"Why not?" said Clean Head.

I nodded towards the window. "I take it we're still under observation?"

Nevada went over and looked out and nodded. "Yes, the giantess is still on stakeout," she said.

I leaned forward, looking across the table at the others. "If I go with you, Stinky will hear about it. And I don't trust him not to turn up at Tom Pyewell's and make an attempt to buy the record himself. And I don't trust Tom Pyewell not to sell it to him."

"So what are we going to do?" said Tinkler.

"You guys go up there without me. Nevada will go through Tom's record collection. With your help, of course, Tinkler. If the LP is there, you'll find it."

Nevada came back and sat beside me, nodding. "Both because he's a sexist moron and incapable of lateral thinking, it will never occur to Stinky that we're going to look for the record without *him*." She kissed me on the cheek.

"Okay," said Tinkler, looking at me doubtfully. "So, you're just going to stay here?"

"Not exactly," I said.

24. PORKY AND PERKY

After the others set off for Tom Pyewell's house, I went into the kitchen and joined Miss Bebbington.

She smiled at me and said, "How's the stomach?"

Just to cement the story that I wasn't going anywhere, we'd got Tinkler to text Alicia saying that I'd been laid low with food poisoning and was spending the day in bed. The pretext for contacting her—the text pretext—was that Tinkler was concerned about Alicia, because she'd also ordered the salmon at the Alexander von Humboldt last night.

I felt a bit bad lying about the pub's food—which had been excellent. But not as bad as I would have felt pretending that one of Miss Bebbington's meals had given me food poisoning. Come to think of it, I doubt we would have dared to say that; we would have had to come up with a different story.

Anyway, Alicia now believed I was out of action and no doubt Stinky would immediately be operating on exactly the same information.

I'd decided to come clean and explain all this to Miss Bebbington. Letting her in on our plan proved to be a smart move, because it turned out that she loved a good conspiracy. And she didn't love Stinky Stanmer. "Sometimes his programme comes on when I'm listening to the radio while I'm cooking and I have to turn it off right away, even though my fingers are covered with flour or something. He's just so obnoxious and smarmy."

I allowed that these were two very good adjectives for Stinky.

I also needed Miss Bebbington's help in showing me how to get to the house where Pete and Sarita Loretto had lived. Farmhouse, as it turned out. It would be about half an hour's walk from the B&B. Maybe forty minutes because a lot of it was uphill. The best part was that I could begin my journey by climbing over the back wall of Miss Bebbington's garden.

This meant that Stinky's camera person, whom Nevada had rather cruelly called the 'giantess', and who was still stubbornly staked out outside the B&B, wouldn't be aware of my departure.

"You won't have any trouble climbing the wall," said Miss Bebbington. "I do it all the time, to get to my vegetable patch. I just use the stepladder. She nodded towards the window that overlooked the garden at the rear of the house. "I've got it out of the shed and set it up for you."

Sure enough, standing against the back wall was a sturdy-looking aluminium stepladder, glinting rather invitingly in the afternoon sunlight.

"Now," she said, "I'm going to have a little snooze if there's nothing else I can do to help? I've finished drawing the map and I've put it with the key. And I've left the computer on. Switch off the monitor when you're finished."

I said I would, and that I had everything I needed, and wished her a pleasant nap.

"Remember to stay hydrated and stick to bland fare like rice and bananas," she said, and went out chuckling wickedly. She just loved the food-poisoning cover story, not least because it reflected badly on the Alexander von Humboldt's cuisine.

I picked up the map, folded it, and put it in my pocket along with the key. Then I made myself a coffee and went and sat down at the computer, which had a surprisingly large LED monitor since Miss Bebbington liked to have a number of different recipes open on it at once. It was officially the kitchen computer, or KITCHEN KOMPUTER, as a hand-lettered sign on the top of the screen declared.

I forgave Miss Bebbington for that.

There were no recipes open on the big screen at the moment. Instead there was a browser page displaying the blog that had belonged to the late Pete and Sarita Loretto. I had originally wanted to look at this just because it was plentifully illustrated with photos of their house and the area around it. But I soon discovered that it actually made for riveting reading.

The Lorettos had started blogging in earnest when they decided, as part of their rural self-sufficiency, to go in for pig rearing. This had begun as a cheerful adventure for them and Sarita had documented it in a series of engagingly written posts especially devoted to the saga, starting with the day they had bought two little chaps.

The young pigs had been virtually treated as domestic pets. An enclosure with a trough had been built for them in the Lorettos' extensive garden, but they wandered freely and at will, and often spent time in the house. One pig was considerably larger and they'd called him Porky. The smaller, more energetic one was dubbed Perky. But then as they grew, they sort of reversed. Perky had swiftly caught up with his friend and had become rather porky. Meanwhile, Porky had grown steadily more active and become rather perky.

The adventures and misadventures of this duo were recorded by Sarita in lively detail and with considerable affection and abundant photographs. The pigs were intelligent and friendly creatures. Surprisingly intelligent. And also surprisingly friendly, given the ultimate nature of their relationship with the Lorettos.

But they couldn't be expected to have any inkling of that, or of their eventual fate. And Sarita did her best to put it from her own mind as she lovingly chronicled life with two pigs.

However, that eventual fate loomed ever closer, with Porky scheduled as the first to go. And the inevitable day came when Pete Loretto and his wife had to take him to the pig killer on the mainland.

Here the blog took a distinctly dark turn, giving a graphic account of the nightmare journey across the causeway as they left the island, with Porky increasingly distraught in the back of their car.

At least, I thought, *they didn't end up underwater.*

But things didn't improve much when they got to the pig killer, who was a sort of environmentally conscious, back-to-the-land hippy type who operated a small independent abattoir. Unfortunately, it turned out that what he *couldn't* operate was the grossly misnamed 'humane killer'. This was a bolt gun that was supposed to be held to poor Porky's head to usher him out of this world instantly and painlessly.

It did anything but. Repeated attempts to apply it led to blood, screams and intense suffering. And not just on the part of the pitiable pig. The account of how they finally killed Porky, using knives and blunt instruments, was unbearable. At least, *I* couldn't bear it, and I skipped whole chunks of the text, content just to absorb the general thrust of what happened.

Sarita Loretto, however, recorded every detail unsparingly, including the hideous dismemberment of Porky when he was finally, thankfully dead. And turned into meat.

Not surprisingly, she was utterly traumatised by the whole incident, and she stopped writing the blog for a while. It was left to her husband to do a 'guest post' about the first meal when Porky's remains were served up. Pete Loretto wrote rhapsodic descriptions of the mouth-watering smell of the roast in the oven, the moist golden pork that emerged, the perfection of the crackling, etc.

There were photos of the meal—which, it has to be said, looked pretty good—and of the people who had attended. The Lorettos had invited a bunch of friends around to join them. The smiling faces around the table included

Jimmy Lynch and Valentyna, and Tom Pyewell and—I was surprised to see—Lakshmi. I was even more surprised to see Gareth the garage mechanic there.

But the most striking person in the photograph was Sarita Loretto. In contrast to the happy grins of the others, she looked pale, drawn, positively stricken. A spectre at the feast.

Troubled and disgusted, she refused to take even a mouthful of the meat, as she explained the following day, when she began to post sentimental reminiscences about the late Porky. The website briefly began to look like a condolence book for someone who had died. But it quickly segued into radical vegetarian and then radical vegan pronouncements.

These were very different in tone from her earlier jolly writings. But if they were a bit doctrinaire and humourless, I couldn't really blame her. And she argued the case for veganism with passion and clarity.

Her husband continued to offer the occasional guest post and for a while their two blogs ran in parallel, although there was really no contest between the two. Pete posted only very sporadically, and the content of their posts was separated by more than ideology. Pete's writing was stilted and seldom more than a string of banal clichés.

Things really began to get tense when Sarita started writing about the surviving pig, Perky.

Perky was heartbroken at the sudden and inexplicable loss of his lifelong friend. Sarita wrote about this in a way that broke the reader's heart, too. But at least Perky earned a temporary reprieve, as both the Lorettos had

Porky's last hours hellishly fresh in their memories, and had agreed that they never wanted to go through that particular nightmare again.

Nevertheless, Pete Loretto soon began to write, with a horrible forced jolliness, about the approaching date of Perky's dispatch and transformation into pork for the larder. Pete put a heavy-handed emphasis on the humane—that word again—approach he'd use this time.

It dawned on me that he was addressing these comments as much to Sarita as to any supposed audience out there on the Internet. In fact, I was willing to bet that by now this was the only way the couple were communicating with each other.

Pete's lumbering attempts at humour also concerned the heatwave that even then had been going on for weeks. Evidently Pete and Sarita were suffering in a farmhouse that had been built purely for comfort in cold weather. I reflected that the rising temperature could only have added to the rising marital tensions.

Pete Loretto tried to patch things up between them by buying a very expensive and elaborate air conditioning unit—but it hadn't worked. Either as a cue for a reconciliation, or indeed as an air conditioner. And his efforts to strike a light-hearted tone became increasingly strained as he related his attempts, and his continued failure, to get the complicated apparatus to operate properly.

The only one who'd been surviving the heat in some degree of comfort was Perky himself. Sarita had set aside a corner of their garden for him, digging up the lawn and hosing down the exposed earth to create a mud hole, where Perky wallowed ecstatically. There were some wonderful photos of the grateful porker liberally covered in mud. He actually seemed to be smiling.

Accompanying these, Sarita gave a lucid account of temperature regulation in *Sus scrofa domesticus*—the expression 'sweating like a pig' is nonsense, because pigs don't have sweat glands. Their only cooling mechanism is to coat themselves in something like mud. Although most pigs live in such terrible conditions that good clean mud is never an option.

As the heatwave continued, to the increasing discomfort of everyone except Perky, cracks definitely began to show in the marriage. And the two streams of posts diverged wildly in content.

Sarita's had settled back into a humorous and affectionate—even loving—diary recording details of Perky's life. The pig had by now got over the loss of Porky and had bonded more deeply than ever with Sarita.

Perky also began to feature again in Pete's writings. Indeed, they were both now concerned with the fate of the pig, but they had dramatically different ideas about how they should proceed...

Sarita obviously wanted Perky to remain alive. Indefinitely, or at least until fate finally took a hand. As, she pointed out, that it would eventually, in the fullness of time, for everyone. Death would in due course come calling for all concerned... including her.

And of course her husband.

I felt a distinct chill on reading this.

Meanwhile, said husband was still jauntily planning Perky's demise, although he wanted it to be different this time. For a start, it must take place at home without the trauma of travel. So Pete Loretto would do the killing and subsequent 'dressing' of the carcass himself, and for this purpose he'd ordered a set of specialist knives. Crucially, he also vowed to make the dispatch of poor Perky less of a bloody disaster this time.

To that end, he hinted, he would go about securing something more reliable than the hideous bolt gun that the idiot hippy had wielded.

Nothing more was actually said about this particular initiative on the blog, which wasn't surprising. Because, as the police had later established, what Pete Loretto had done was to source a highly illegal handgun from somewhere. No doubt the Internet had been involved.

Finally the fateful night arrived. It was supposed to be a fateful morning, but postponements and feet-dragging meant that it was suitably dark, and still swelteringly hot, by the time the ugly business commenced.

Perhaps surprisingly, Sarita was determined to attend the event. But she felt she had to be there, to provide moral support for Perky. "I can't let him die alone," she declared in her final post… in which she also let slip that even at this late stage she was determined that Perky shouldn't die at all.

She was resolute that she'd talk her husband out of his course of action.

At that point, the blog ended.

And there were two different versions of what happened next.

In one Sarita had indeed passionately tried to sway Pete to spare Perky, he had stubbornly refused, they had argued, and fought over the gun. And Sarita had got hold of it and either deliberately or accidentally shot Pete dead. Then, overcome with remorse, she'd shot herself.

This was the story subsequently endorsed by the police.

The other account was largely similar, except with the important difference that Sarita had been swayed by the influence of a demonic spirit that had possessed the pig. With some variants claiming that the demon pig had come into being as a consequence of Pete Loretto's dabbling in black magic.

Both versions agreed that Perky, a.k.a. the demon pig, had fled the scene during or after the shooting and was now at large somewhere in the wilds of the island, hiding in the considerable band of forest that clad its slopes. He was either scared and on the run or waiting with malevolent patience to do some more demonic stuff, according to your preference.

I switched off the monitor, finished my coffee and washed the mug in the sink. Then, checking that I had the map and the key in my pocket, I went out the French windows and crossed the garden, smugly reflecting that there was no way anyone waiting in the street could see what was going on back here.

I climbed the stepladder and just as I was about to step over the garden wall I glanced back towards the house. I saw

Miss Bebbington was awake and standing at her bedroom window. She smiled at me and waved with one hand. With the other she was holding her phone to her ear.

I waved back and went over the wall.

25. FARMHOUSE

On the other side of the garden wall was a wooden ladder, which seemed to be permanently stationed there. I climbed down it and found myself in an area of several acres covered with a patchwork of allotments—small gardens allocated to the island dwellers to grow fruit, vegetables or flowers. Over the years Miss Bebbington had bought up a number of plots from her neighbours and now had extensive space for what she called her vegetable patch immediately on the other side of her wall. Hence the well-established stepladder routine.

I walked among the allotments with the sun shining down on me, bringing out first the intense scent of a dense green mass of tomato vines that I brushed past, and then the perfume of a tall, unruly patch of lavender I skimmed my hand through. I breathed these in deeply and happily. It was a beautiful day, a wonderful day for a walk, and the pleasure was only intensified by knowledge that we were hoodwinking Stinky Stanmer, good and proper.

On the far side of the allotments was a gate in the centre

of the brick wall. It was a crude wooden affair with a Yale lock high on the right-hand side. I inserted the key Miss Bebbington had given to me, opened it, stepped through and made sure it clicked locked behind me. I didn't want to be responsible for any vegetable theft.

After I'd been walking for about thirty minutes, moving steadily uphill, I came to a place where the trees became sparse and then ceased. In front of me was a field bounded by a barbed wire fence. I consulted my map, oriented myself, then climbed carefully over the fence and struck off to my left. Moving in this direction I came to an irregular and ancient-looking stone wall, and felt a little pang of excitement.

I'd reached the Lorettos' farm.

It wasn't a working farm anymore, not since being purchased by the drummer in his years of affluence. I climbed the wall and found myself in what was effectively a very large and somewhat neglected garden. Of course, there'd been no one to look after it of late, but it showed signs of having begun to be neglected long before that.

There were fruit trees, which provided some much needed patches of shade. But mostly it was grass. What had once been lawn was overgrown and painfully dry and yellow. Over to one side I saw a large blotch of brownish earth standing out raw among the grass and I realised with a start that this must have been the site of the pig's mud bath. Nearby was a trough, in an area enclosed by a sagging and partially collapsed wire fence.

The Lorettos' house was wide and rambling, only one storey, made of rough grey stone spotted with yellow lichen.

It looked ancient, until you saw the windows, which were modern and double-glazed. The roof was red shingles and the guttering was painted an odd shade of yellow, perhaps to match the lichen.

The front of the house was ringed by dense beds of poppies, which looked to have been deliberately planted, and then gone exuberantly wild and spread. They looked rather lovely. Somewhere I heard the buzzing of bees. The wind fluttered through the fruit trees with a sound like rain where there was no rain, and hadn't been for weeks.

The whole place was sunny, breezy and peaceful.

And the white and blue police tape twisting in the wind provided an attractive contrast to the red mass of poppies.

I had been quite prepared to smash a window to get into the house, although the double-glazing would have made that problematical. But luckily the front door opened readily when I turned the handle. Maybe locking up after themselves hadn't been the top priority of the local constabulary.

It was hot and airless in the house, and smelled stale, with an indeterminate but spicy and slightly unpleasant scent pervading the place. I was tempted to leave the front door wide open and let a fresh breeze blow through, but on the whole I thought that was inadvisable.

I stood and looked around.

What hadn't come across in the blog I'd read, but had come across in conversations with just about everybody I'd spoken to, was Pete Loretto's fixation with the occult.

And this didn't waste any time in making itself evident. I was in a hallway with a wooden floor painted black and rough whitewashed walls. Opposite the front door was a bookcase of dark wood built into the wall but jutting out just enough to provide a narrow lip of shelf at the top.

Sitting on this shelf were framed photographs of irregular size and shape. They were all black and white pictures of the faces of men. A couple I recognised right away. Aleister Crowley, well-known sorcerer and charlatan. And John Blacklock, less well known and basically a low-budget version of Crowley. I'd learned about him when I'd been involved in the search for a record by Valerian. I took a step closer and inspected the photos.

A careful study of the other men in the pictures told me nothing, though judging by the wacky headwear of a couple of them, they were also in the black magic racket.

I lowered my gaze and examined the books in the bookcase itself. They were a mixture of hardbacks and paperbacks, pristine copies and beaten-up volumes that were falling apart. There was a large selection by Arthur Machen, with titles like *The House of Souls*, *The Great God Pan* and *Tales of Horror and the Supernatural*. There was also a substantial number of anthologies—*In the Dead of Night*, *I Can't Sleep at Night*, *My Blood Ran Cold*, *Weird Shadows from Beyond*—which contained stories by an assortment of authors, including Machen.

To the left of the bookcase was a small alcove in the wall at just over waist height. In it were three black candles—*Of course, black candles*, I thought—half burned, in antique silver holders, and what looked like the bones of a bird, resting on a square of purple cloth. They hadn't got that decorating tip from the IKEA catalogue.

I looked away from the bookcase and turned to my right, and froze.

There was a doorway in the whitewashed wall, but that wasn't what I was looking at. Hanging on the wall beside the doorway was a large photo behind glass in an ebony frame. It was square, about two feet high. And it was the image from *Wisht*.

But whereas the album cover had been tinted in a range of unreal and trippy colours, this was a luminous and brooding black and white. Clearly it wasn't some kind of reproduction of the cover, but had been made from the original negative. Which suggested that it had been created in the darkroom personally by a man who had once tried to kill me. I noticed a squiggle of handwriting in blue ink in the lower right-hand corner and moved closer to read it. Yes, it was Nic Vardy's signature.

A signed original of a classic album cover. This would normally have spurred me to covetous thoughts, but now I just wanted to get the hell away from the thing as soon as possible.

I could see my own reflection in the glass, the shock showing clearly on my face.

I turned away and went through the door, entering a dining room dominated by a large oval antique table made of a reddish wood. The room was silent and warm and musty. The walls were painted a kind of Wedgwood blue and hanging on them were framed prints, small but immensely detailed watercolour illustrations of mushrooms and toadstools. They looked like they were pages carefully cut from a book.

To my left was a grandfather clock, taller than I was and standing in a shadowed corner just inside the door. It seemed to be made of the same wood as the table.

As I walked past it, the silent clock suddenly started ticking...

Obviously the vibration of my footsteps had caused something in the mechanism to shift and brought it back to life.

But this sudden reawakening didn't exactly have a beneficial effect on my nerves.

Nor did the rambling, chaotic floor plan of the house, which meant I found it impossible to work out where I was in relation to anywhere else, and that I had no idea what room I'd wander into next.

As it happened, the room I wandered into next was the late Pete Loretto's home studio, which was equipped with an impressive drum kit and a large selection of unusual percussion instruments. But no records.

From here I passed through another door, this one oddly low, so I had to duck to avoid banging my head on the rough-hewn rustic lintel beam. It seemed I had entered an older section of the farmhouse. And one in which the windows were either the originals or had been added at considerable expense. Because instead of being double-glazed and modern, they were made of stained glass in roughly diamond-shaped panes edged with strips of black lead, and looked very old indeed. They glowed with candied colours—red, blue and yellow—but didn't allow much in the way of useful light in. And the slightly crude look of them, which should have impressed me with how traditional and handmade they were, actually seemed peculiarly ugly and unappealing.

This room didn't have any obvious function. It was painted black and was small and very oddly shaped—a hexagon. The two sides of the hexagon on my right had the windows in them, forming a gently V-shaped niche, which had a green leather bench running across it. An assortment of silverware had been left spread out on the bench, on a black cloth.

The side of the room opposite the doorway through which I had entered had a further door in it, which led uninvitingly into shadows. I could hear the distinct ticking of the grandfather clock back in one of the rooms behind me, measured and patient and resonant.

The two sides of the hexagon to my left were fitted with black wooden shelves, which ran from floor to ceiling except for central gaps in which hung two matching brass mirrors. They were circular and were topped with oddly unpleasant-looking birds—eagles, judging by their beaks and talons. The mirrors reflected the colours of the stained glass—red, blue and yellow lozenges with the sunlight behind them, boiled sweets from the days when no one worried about using poisonous food colouring.

The shelves were covered with small white shapes, difficult to make out in the dimness of the room. I stepped closer to see what they were, and then rather regretted I had.

Skulls of small animals. The first one I saw looked like it had belonged to a weasel. I didn't bother examining the others closely.

In the centre of the room was a hexagonal table, surfaced with green leather. From where I stood it was largely concealed by a high-backed antique chair made of black wood, upholstered with the same green leather. I felt no desire at all to sit in that chair and take a load off my feet.

I had the odd certainty that this was Pete Loretto's inner sanctum. I turned away from the wall of weasel skulls and looked at the cutlery spread out on the bench.

And then I saw it wasn't cutlery. It was heavy-duty knives and cleavers. I suddenly realised it was the set of pig butchery blades that Pete Loretto had blogged about so proudly. They looked brutal and lethal.

I turned away from them. I had now moved further into the room and I could suddenly see what was on the table.

An old, wrinkled and dog-eared manila folder lay there. On its discoloured brown cover, written in spidery, angular black handwriting, were the words *How to Return*.

I looked at it for a long time.

I was remembering what Gareth, the Mormon Hipster, had said the night of our farewell to Kind of Blue. About Pete Loretto working on ways to come back from beyond the grave.

Despite myself I felt a shudder of disquiet.

I looked around at the animal skulls, all of which suddenly appeared to be watching me with their sightless eyes. Then I looked back at the folder.

How to Return.

Just because it was nonsense didn't mean that *he* hadn't believed it...

The hair at the back of my neck writhed and stood up. I stepped around the table and got out of the room quickly through the door opposite. I was now in a windowless and shadowy corridor with dim light at either end. It was hot and smelled of dust and it was very quiet. I could hear my heart thumping in my chest. I hurried down the corridor, away from Pete Loretto's sanctum.

Then I stopped.

I stood there for a long time, breathing in the darkness.

Then I forced myself to turn around and go back.

I'm not sure if it was bravado or curiosity that drove me, but I think it was mostly that I didn't want to be the guy who was ruled by fear.

I came back into the hexagonal room. I looked at the hexagonal table and the folder lying on it.

How to Return.

I circled the table as though it was a pond of icy water and I was trying to nerve myself up to plunge in. I was breathing very rapidly and my heart was pounding at a ludicrous speed. I forced myself to stop walking.

I found it remarkably difficult to reach down for the folder and open it.

But that is what I did, albeit with shaking hands.

As you might imagine, I stared at the contents of the folder for quite a long time.

Inside was a leaflet neatly printed in black ink on white paper. It read:

HOW TO RETURN

We want you to be happy with your Frigloo™ Air Conditioning Unit, but if you are not 100% satisfied after installation according to these instructions, please call Customer Services on the number below within one month of purchase. Or log into the Frigloo website using your unique customer number and we will provide you with your returns authorisation number. Please fill in the 'Returns form' slip below and include this with the unit you are returning.

Your satisfaction is our goal!

In retrospect, finding the air conditioner leaflet was the best thing that could have happened to me. Because its ironic reminder of how suggestible we all are came at exactly the right moment.

It left me smarting at allowing myself even the hint of the possibility of believing any of that crap, and thus feeling even the most tiny, exploratory tremor of fear.

In other words, I was at my most angry and sceptical. Which was very lucky, considering what would happen soon.

I walked down a short rope-matted hallway and into the kitchen. The windows in here were sealed with folding wooden shutters, which had warped and didn't quite fit, so thin brilliant slices of daylight fell across the room at odd and irregular intervals.

But they provided me with enough illumination to make my way through the darkened kitchen without actually falling over any of the angular and potentially painful rustic wooden chairs, and reach the sink, which was a vast white rectangle with elaborate antique brass taps and a long, swivelling spout that extended over it.

I considered which of the two sunflower-shaped taps was more likely to be cold water—the one on the left, I guessed, even on Halig Island, and I reached out and twisted it.

Or tried to. It didn't want to budge.

I leaned forward and began to work on it with both hands, keenly mindful of the situation-comedy possibility of it coming off in my hand with a jetting arc of water spouting from it in the joyful commencement of a full-scale kitchen flood.

But that didn't happen. The tap eventually shuddered and squeaked and rotated and water spilled thankfully from the spout.

I let it run for a long time. I held my hands under it. At first it felt warm and, although this might have been my imagination, a bit gritty. Then eventually it was cold and clear and I put my open mouth under the thin stream and drank. Doing so required bending my head at an odd angle and, as I did this, I saw something across the room.

There, in a narrow ribbon of white light, was the damp dark gleam of an eye.

I paused, closing my mouth, letting the water flow across my face. I told myself it was just something that *looked* like an eye. Or possibly the eye on an ornament—a stuffed animal head that had been taken down from the wall and placed in a corner...

Then the eye closed lazily and opened again.

A vast portion of the darkness in the corner of the kitchen raised up slightly and began to move. It was about the size of the coffee table in our sitting room in London. A coffee table big enough to comfortably accommodate two cats, numerous books and even the odd compact disc. So... big.

The shadowy bulk of the pig moved across the kitchen towards me. Its eyes were relentlessly focused on mine, first in light, then shadow, and then light again, pitiless and inhuman. I remembered the stories of the demon pig and I felt a tremendous rising wave of panic in me.

And then I remembered the Frigloo air conditioning leaflet.

And the panic abated a little.

The pig had paused, turning its head away from me. It was probing for something on the floor, invisible in the shadows. There was a small grinding, screeching sound, and the pig resumed its approach, but with its head bent down. I realised that it was pushing something with its snout.

It came towards me, grunting, nosing the object across the floor. I saw that it was a large water bowl, of the kind you might have for a big dog.

And it had the word *Perky* printed on it.

It was, of course, bone dry.

The pig pushed the empty bowl across the tiles, quietly screeching as it came, until it touched my toes. Then the pig backed away and looked up at me with its disconcertingly soulful eyes.

I got it.

The tap was still running, so I lifted the bowl into the sink and filled it with water. Then I set it down carefully and stood back. Perky came forward and began to drink with such obvious enthusiasm and relief that I began to feel thirsty again myself. The bowl was empty in a few seconds and the pig raised his face to look at me. I refilled it and, while he was drinking, stuck my own head back under the tap. Then I kept filling the bowl for him until, finally, he emptied it one last time and then shoved it aside with his snout.

Then Perky lumbered forward a little closer to me and set his chin down across my feet, the way one of my cats might. He lay there happily, his ears twitching slightly. His head was heavy, but the weight of it on my feet was oddly comforting. I looked down at him and wondered if a pig perhaps really was like a big cat.

To test this theory I reached down and scratched him behind the ear.

He didn't purr, but he did give a long, contented sigh. I rubbed him behind the ear until my arm got tired and my back began to ache, and then I straightened up. Perky gave me a 'fair enough' look and lifted his head off my feet, then set it back down on the floor and continued to lie there. On this hot day I imagine the cold tiles felt good against his skin, what with not having any sweat glands.

When scratching behind his ear I noticed that he was wearing a collar. It was made of greyish pink plastic, much the same colour as Perky himself, which is why I hadn't spotted it straight away. It didn't look particularly comfortable, and in fact appeared to be digging into his flesh. I decided to take it off him at the earliest opportunity.

But right now I walked gingerly around him, making sure I didn't step on his tail in the darkness, and went to the door that led out into the garden.

The door had a large dog-hatch in it, easily big enough to have allowed access for Perky. Of course, that is what it had been designed for. I wondered if he had come in because he'd heard me in the house.

I held the door open and turned around to look at the kitchen with the daylight flooding into it. Perky gazed up at me from his spot on the floor.

The poor pig had been running and hiding all over the entire island, but finally he'd come home.

I went outside and Perky followed me with such speed that it suggested he was thirsty for company as well as water. I found an old rattan chair on a blue and red brick patio, which was mostly overgrown with weeds, and I sat down in the sagging chair and the pig eased his bulk down on the warm, weed-grown bricks in a patch of sunlight beside me. His ears twitched and he looked up at me speculatively as I took out my phone and made a call. He kept watching me for a while after I put the phone away, then finally seemed to make up his mind about something, and relaxed and went to sleep.

That was the way Nevada found us an hour later. By then I'd gone back into the house and made a final search for Pete Loretto's record collection, and I'd found it. A hundred or so LPs on a shelf in what looked like it had once been a spare bedroom but had now suffered the fate of spare bedrooms everywhere, being given over to storing random junk. The records were an uninspiring lot—largely disco, if you can believe it.

I was more relieved than ever that I hadn't had to actually break into the house. Going to prison for disco records would have been the last straw.

After I'd made sure that these were the only LPs in the house I'd accepted defeat and selected a paperback from the bookcase by the front door and gone out to read with my faithful pig at my side.

I was gainfully engrossed in a Fritz Leiber story when Perky stirred and lifted his head. Then I heard the sound of a vehicle pulling up, and doors opening and closing. A moment later Nevada came around the corner of the house. When she saw us, her face lit up.

"You've found a friend," she said.

She tried the ear-scratching thing, which the pig seemed to like—even better coming from Nevada than me—and then, when she heard about the incident with the water, she went into the kitchen and came out with the drinking bowl filled to the brim. She set it down beside Perky and he raised his head and gave it a token slurp or two. But it was obvious he was just being polite, which charmed Nevada all the more.

I showed her the plastic collar I had cut off his neck with a pair of kitchen scissors. It had turned out it wasn't just a collar. It had some kind of technology attached to it. "It looks like a supersized Fitbit," said Nevada. "But I don't suppose it is."

"My best guess is that it's some kind of GPS device," I said.

"Like an ankle tag on an offender?"

"Or a LoJack device on a car."

Nevada took the grubby collar and examined it. "Do you think someone could track Perky using this?"

"Not anymore," I said.

Nevada smiled. "So Perky is a free man at last. Or rather, a free pig."

Then we had the challenge of coaxing the free pig into the back of the van Nevada had arrived in. Luckily Ms Bramwell had brought a ramp along.

When I heard about Ms Bramwell I realised that today had seen one bona fide return from the dead after all.

She was the other 'B' in the B&B B&B. We'd thought she was deceased because Miss Bebbington was in the habit of speaking of her very emphatically in the past tense. But it turned out this was the result of a rather messy break-up rather than any actual demise. Ms Bramwell, a slender fiftyish woman, now lived on a farm of her own on the other side of the island. A rather unique farm in that the animals on it weren't called upon to die, any more than she had been.

They provided contributions in the form of eggs or milk, or were simply pets. "A vegetarian farm," said Nevada. "When I rang Miss Bebbington and asked for advice about what to do with Perky, she immediately offered to get in touch with Ms Bramwell. Apparently they hadn't been on speaking terms, but they immediately set aside their differences when they discovered the fate of an animal was at stake." Nevada smiled happily. "Now that they're back in touch, I'm thinking romance might reignite."

We were chatting as we walked back to Miss Bebbington's together, having seen Perky safely on his way to his new home, and we'd just reached the gate to the allotments. I took out the key and let us in. With evening coming on, the smell of fresh growing things in the place had become quite wonderful. We walked through it, hand in hand, as Nevada told me how the visit to Tom Pyewell's had been a bust both vinyl- and wine-wise.

"He had a lot of bottles in his cellar, but it was all very expensive and rather dull. Bordeaux and Burgundy. Nothing from the Rhône. As for the LP, Tinkler and I carefully scrutinised every record in the place, but there was no copy of *Wisht* with a flap back. Don't bother correcting me."

"I wouldn't dream of it," I said. "But that means we're almost out of places to look."

"So, one way or another, we'll be going home soon."

"Yes."

"I'll rather miss this island," said Nevada. "They've only tried to kill us here once."

That was about to change.

26. ESTABLISHING SHOTS

Nevada went to take a shower and I settled down to continue reading my Fritz Leiber story—yes, I'd stolen a book from a dead man's house, but I rationalised this as fair payment for pig rescue—when the doorbell rang.

Miss Bebbington was out, as we'd discovered on our return. Nevada was in the shower. So I went to answer it.

While you could look out the window in the breakfast room and see people coming in through the garden gate, once they had approached a little more closely to the front door it was impossible to see them from any window in the house.

If you wanted to know who was out there, you had to open the door.

I assumed it was Tinkler having forgotten his key, or perhaps Miss Bebbington herself, ditto. So I didn't hesitate. I opened the door wide.

And a figure came muscling in, brushing past me in a peremptory fashion. It was a man with a hoodie pulled down low over his face and both hands jammed deep in his pockets. Presumably for anonymity. In which case he should have chosen a hoodie that wasn't a bright raspberry shade of pink.

He also wore frayed, stained blue jeans and honey-coloured Timberland boots with flopping laces and a backpack with a skateboard logo on it.

All this I absorbed in that first surprised moment as this newcomer bulled his way past me in the narrow hallway. Only when he was halfway along the corridor did he turn back towards me, allowing me to see his face. Indeed, he pulled the hood of his hoodie fully down so there was no chance of me *not* seeing his face.

Stinky Stanmer.

His mousy hair was now dyed a blatantly phony peroxide blond, but the original shade was still prominently on display because, astonishingly, Stinky had grown a full beard. A very full beard. It was the sort of beard that Gareth sported. But not as successful as Gareth's.

Because this beard made Stinky look not like a Mormon Hipster but rather a rabbi engaged in a disastrous attempt to transform himself into a surfer dude. Amidst the beard and above it, the thick fishy lips and the preternaturally bulging eyes were unchanged. Now more than ever, Stinky was no one's idea of a prepossessing physical specimen.

Yet, fame being what it is, he was apparently dating Maxine Shearwater.

Stinky's beard shifted and those fish lips opened to reveal expensively white and even teeth in what was presumably supposed to be a smile. "Well met, wanderer!" he said, and moved his left arm in a strangely stiff circular gesture of greeting, as if he were holding an invisible rag with which he was wiping an invisible window.

"Stinky…" I said.

"Hello, mate," said Stinky. "You feeling better? After the food poisoning?"

In the shock of seeing Stinky I had completely forgotten about the food-poisoning ruse. Suddenly I was at a loss for words as my mind whirled with alternatives. Should I fake stomach cramps, bending over and moaning? Or just alter my facial expression to one of pained, pale strain? The latter would be easy enough, given to whom I was talking.

But any need to shore up my cover story vanished because Stinky instantly forgot about my food poisoning, in fact forgot he'd even asked me the question as he moved briskly on to his favourite subject. Stinky Stanmer.

"We're here on the island filming a documentary."

"So I understand."

"About Black Dog. You know, the band."

"Yes, Stinky, I know who they are. In fact, I believe this entire enterprise is based on an original idea by yours truly."

"Well, you do have the best ideas, bruv." Stinky did the thing again that was meant to be a smile and stepped closer to me and clouted me lightly on the elbow. I think this was supposed to be a comradely slap on the shoulder, but he hadn't quite mastered it yet. "You just lack *follow through*," he said, and chuckled. "So that's what we're doing, me and my team. My film crew. We're here following through. We shot some preliminary footage today and it looks great, great.

You know, establishing shots and so forth. Local colour. And my researchers—they came here a few days early—"

"I know. One of them vamped Tinkler so she could find out what we were up to."

"Vamped! I love your turn of phrase, mate. Love your turn of phrase. That would be Alicia, our sound recordist. You know what? She and Sydney—"

"Is Sydney the giantess?"

"Giantess? Ha ha ha. Well, yes, she is a bit on the tall side. But I like a tall girl. There's more of her to love, if you know what I mean. She's our camera operator."

"She's been hanging around outside," I said. "Right there outside in the street. Just across the road from us. All day."

"She's scouting locations, bruv. Scouting locations. Busy girl. Very talented. She and Alicia got some *great footage* the other night. Of that beach barbecue. Your beach barbecue. For your mate Tinkler's car. I mean, barbecuing a car! You're mad, you lot. I heard about what happened, by the way." Stinky suddenly put on his serious expression. It was not a pretty sight. "You've got to be careful, mate. You could have all got drowned. They could be fishing you out. That road to the island is dangerous, bruv. It's under water several hours a day. But there's a website with the times, and a sign down there. You've really got to check it before you go driving along there, mate. You could have died. So next time, check the times."

I opened my mouth, getting ready to say all sorts of things. But it was just too much effort, and Stinky wasn't interested in listening anyway, so I just said, "Good advice."

"The best vice is good advice," said Stinky, and barked with laughter. "We're the advice squad. The good advice squad. No charge. Not for old friends. Free of charge. So, anyway, what were we saying? Oh, the filming. Yeah, it's going great, bruv. And you know what we're going to film tomorrow?"

"Your colonoscopy, perhaps?"

"Ha ha ha. Already been done, mate. Already been done. But not by me. Jonathan Ross, mate. No, we're going to Pete Loretto's house."

That shut me up, very effectively. Perhaps Stinky took my silence for incomprehension, because he said, "He was the drummer with Black Dog."

"Yes," I said, my mind racing. But mostly I was preoccupied with an intense sense of relief that I'd got there before Stinky and his team. By the skin of my teeth.

"...a creepy deserted farmhouse," Stinky was saying. "Still a crime scene, officially. But we asked permission to film there and it turns out, you know what? One of the local cops is a fan. A Stinky Stanmer fan. So, no problem. Permission to film. Or at least, they're going to turn a blind eye. The cops. Justice is blind! So we're going to film there tomorrow. At the murder house. You know about the murder, do you?"

"I heard about it."

"Well, you should read about it, bruv. Jesus, what a story. Crime of passion. How his wife turned vegetarian and she shot him because he wouldn't turn vegetarian. That's the gist of it, anyway. Not the details. The details are fascinating. You should read about it. On their blog."

"You read the Lorettos' blog?"

"Well, one of my researchers read it for me. Quite a story, though, eh?" He looked at me with his bulging eyes. "It's as if you killed and cooked one of your cats and Nirvana got really upset about it. And then you wanted to kill and cook the *other* one and—"

"All right, Stinky," I said. "I get the picture."

It was Stinky who didn't get the picture. If 'Nirvana' found any jokers messing with our cats, they wouldn't be long for this world. The jokers, that is. And just then, as if she was sensing that someone had taken her name in vain, I heard the bathroom door upstairs open.

Stinky didn't notice because he'd suddenly unslung his rucksack from his shoulder and was busy unzipping it. "Got something I've got to show you, mate. Something you must see."

As he delved inside Nevada appeared at the top of the stairs and called down, "Who are you talking to, love?"

"You'll never guess, darling," I said.

"What cheer!" yelled Stinky.

There was silence from the top of the stairs for a moment, and then, "Oh, Christ. Stinky."

Nevada came halfway down the stairs and looked at us. She was just wrapped in a towel. Normally Stinky wouldn't have been able to conceal his delight about this, but at the moment he was entirely preoccupied with ransacking his rucksack.

I said, "Stinky was just telling me that he and his camera

crew are going to Pete Loretto's farmhouse tomorrow. To film."

"Oh, Christ," said Nevada again, then immediately put her hand to her mouth as if concerned that she'd said too much. But Stinky, of course, hadn't noticed.

"That's right," he said cheerfully, still digging around in his rucksack. "Tomorrow. First thing. But never mind that. Look at this." He proudly brought out an elegant-looking bag made of heavy, glossy pink paper with black lettering on it. It was the sort of bag you'd be given to hold your purchases at an expensive shop. In this case the name of the shop, there on the shocking-pink bag, was Faddish Fetish. "It's a present," said Stinky.

"For us?" I said. "You shouldn't have."

"Ha ha ha. Not only shouldn't I have, I didn't. No, it's not for you, mate. It's for Maxie. You know, Maxine Shearwater. Max Shearwater's daughter. She's a lovely girl, lovely."

"Yes, I know, we—"

"I just loved that footage of her dancing on the car roof. You know, at your beach barbecue. She really went for it, didn't she? I call her Maximum Maxine. Because she really goes for it. Have you seen her tattoo? Oh, my. Anyway, this is for her. A present. From London."

Despite herself, curiosity drew Nevada down the stairs. She joined us in the small hallway as Stinky opened the bag and lovingly unwrapped the pink tissue paper inside, to reveal what took me a few seconds to realise was a bikini.

A microscopic bikini made of PVC.

It had strong black outlines at its edges but otherwise was completely transparent.

"I'm going to restage Maximum Maxine dancing on the car roof, and I'm going to have her wear this."

"Have you asked her if she wants to?" said Nevada.

"She hasn't seen it yet."

"I'm not sure she ever *will* be able to see it," said Nevada. "It's completely see-through. It's virtually invisible."

"I know! It will really show off her snake tattoo nicely."

"Yes, I'm sure that's why you bought it," I said.

"You should love it, mate. It's made of vinyl!" He held the transparent bikini aloft and grinned his toothy, bearded grin at us. "Just think of the low-angle shot."

"We are," said Nevada.

I said, "Isn't it time you were going, Stinky?"

Of course, it wasn't as simple as that, but we did eventually prevail upon Stinky to put his fetish bikini back in its bag and go.

When the door finally closed behind him, Nevada turned to me and said, "You only just got to the Lorettos before he did."

"I know."

"We've got to get to Max Shearwater before he does."

"We will," I said. "It's all booked. First thing tomorrow."

27. THE STATUE GARDEN

The following morning, immediately after breakfast, we got a taxi to Max Shearwater's house. We didn't worry about any cloak-and-dagger manoeuvres this time because we assumed Stinky would be busy at the Loretto farmhouse and, in any case, Sydney the Giantess was no longer stationed outside the B&B keeping an eye on our comings and goings.

Nevada and Tinkler and I all set off together, but Clean Head apparently had business locally and said she might join us at Max's later.

"By 'business locally' she means she's seeing Gareth again," said Nevada.

"Do you think she's having an affair with him?" said Tinkler.

"Almost certainly."

"Are you just saying that to torment me?"

"Yes."

The taxi took us up from the seafront along a route that

had become familiar. Indeed, unpleasantly familiar, since it took us past The Sea View where we'd witnessed Jimmy's arrest, and then the Lynch house, where we'd been among the last people to see Valentyna alive. We all fell silent as we passed it.

As it happened, we didn't have far to go from there to Max Shearwater's place. If we could have driven straight up the slope, we would have been there in a minute or two—indeed, we probably could have walked it that quickly—but the taxi had to laboriously wind its slow way uphill around some rather unusual terrain.

It appeared that in some distant epoch, part of Halig's volcanic cone had collapsed into the sea, creating an inlet from which a jagged series of giant perpendicular stone pillars rose straight upwards, instead of the usual gentle slope of the island. The Shearwater house was situated on a broad ledge at the top of one of these outcrops of rock. It was a dramatic location, made even more dramatic by having the house extend beyond the ledge, out into the empty air high above the ocean.

The house itself was a piece of modernist architecture like a stack of glass-sided concrete boxes of different sizes, with one end of the bottommost and largest box simply jutting out over the edge, supported by nothing.

Of course, what it was supported by was the rigid structure of the rest of the house, which I guessed must include some reinforcing columns in the basement. But it looked crazily suicidal, as if the whole thing might just topple into the waiting waves far down below. I suppose that was the point.

As the taxi took the final curve in the ascending road and we got our first glimpse of the place, Nevada said, "Wow."

And Tinkler said, "Living here wouldn't make me nervous at all."

"It's bloody mad," murmured our taxi driver, which was pretty much the extent of his conversation since we'd left Miss Bebbington's.

Nevada looked over at me. "Does it remind you of something?"

I nodded. "The spot where they burned the money." That too had jutted out from the slope of the island, extending over the sea. But it had been a natural formation, accidental. This was anything but.

"Do you think it's deliberate?" said Nevada. "I mean, the resemblance?"

"You bet."

We paid off our loquacious taxi driver and walked the short distance from the road to the house. The Shearwaters had quite a slab of property here, and a rather idyllic location, surrounded by forest at the back and facing the ocean at the front. Instead of any kind of wall or fence, privacy was provided by a dense belt of pine trees, which thinned out and simply became part of the adjoining woods at the boundary of their property. Access was through a gap in the pines, where a driveway covered with grey and white pebbles ran up from the road towards the house.

At least, I thought it was a driveway. But as we walked up it we discovered that the pebbles widened and spread out so that they surrounded the entire house. There was plenty of greenery, though, too. Low Japanese-looking trees and shrubs in beds were dotted among the pebbles. And sculptures.

These were large stone or metal statues of modern design dispersed throughout the garden. Most of them were of abstract but recognisably human figures. Some were simply giant heads, reminiscent of Modigliani or traditional African design.

"They look like Henry Moore," said Nevada.

"Or the cover of *The Division Bell*," said Tinkler. "That's a Pink Floyd album, by the way."

There were a few rather more elaborate installations, too. These looked like failed attempts to build robots out of junkyard spare parts. Several seemed designed to have at least some limited form of clockwork motion, although they were all peacefully stationary at the moment. They reminded me of the work of Bruce Lacey.

Studying these, we almost walked straight past Ottoline Shearwater, who was kneeling on a cushion in front of one of the beds of greenery, busy with a hand trowel and a bag of plant food. "Hi," she called, smiling and waving at us. "Max is waiting for you up at the house."

We came to a big circular slab of concrete on which was parked the pale blue Subaru, but not the pink one. Evidently Maxine was not in residence at the moment.

On the other side of this Max was indeed waiting for us, dressed in immaculate white trousers, bright orange Crocs, and a kind of long-sleeved African kaftan in a purple batik pattern. Oh, well; he was at home.

Max grinned, shook hands with me and Tinkler, kissed Nevada and then proceeded to give us a guided tour of the premises, of which he was obviously enormously proud. The highlight of our tour was the section of the house that extended out over the sea. Most of this was, naturally enough, given over to a living room, which had stunning ocean views. Absolutely nothing obstructed these views because the house was cantilevered so this part of it stuck out from the cliff. The seaward end of the room was all floor-to-ceiling windows. On the left they terminated against an inner wall that separated this room from the bedrooms, which had a similar layout and view.

On the right there were windows stretching all the way back to the rear wall of the sitting room. For the first four or five metres these looked out onto empty space, towards the further band of cliffs. But then the house rejoined solid ground and the garden stretched away, with its expanse of pebbles and beds of shrubs and various sculptures, bounded by a wall at the cliff edge to prevent careless art lovers from plummeting to their doom.

The rear of the sitting room was long and high and white with a fireplace in the middle of it, set in a surround of natural stone. There were paintings hung along the wall on either side of the hearth.

Max next showed us the bedrooms, briefly, and then, at the far end of this cantilevered wing of the house, a narrow utility room, hardly wider than a corridor.

After our experiences at Erik Make Loud's, I thought Tinkler and I would never want to step into a room containing laundry appliances again. But this was different, and rather fascinating. At the far end, the seaward end, there was a sort of hinged circular steel hatch set in the concrete floor. Max delightedly flipped it open for us and suddenly a cold breeze was pouring in and we were looking down, down, down at the green and white tumult of waves moving on the surface of the ocean far below.

"Like in a medieval castle," said Nevada.

"Yes, except here it's not a toilet." Max shut the hatch again and the wind ceased. "We just use it for any organic waste from the kitchen or the garden that doesn't go in the composter. Just whoosh, straight into the ocean. Back into the great cycle to feed the marine life."

"Did you have it in here when Maxine was little?" said Nevada. I knew what she was thinking. The hatch was much too small for a grown-up to fall through, but a child…

Max grinned. "We had a padlock on it in those days. But she's a big girl now. And we haven't got any pets who might come to grief."

"Better watch out for midget visitors, though," said Tinkler.

Max and I went off to see the real objective of our visit—his record collection. We left Nevada and Tinkler in the kitchen with coffee and pastries. It was a point of honour for me to go through the vinyl on my own this time, since I'd abnegated my duties yesterday and delegated the two of them to search Tom Pyewell's.

Max's records were in a games room on the ground

floor. It was windowless, with soft grey carpet and grey walls. There was a pool table in the centre and the walls were lined with white storage units especially designed for vinyl. Max turned the lights on. "A few years ago Maxie earned some pocket money by sorting my record collection into alphabetical order for me." He shook his head. "Or at least, Maxie's idea of alphabetical order. So, good luck. If…" He smiled and paused. "Let's think positive about this. *When* you find the record, just come to my office and we'll discuss terms." He gestured to a doorway down the hall, and left me alone.

I turned to the records. I recognised the shelving they were stored in as coming from everyone's favourite Scandinavian flat-pack furniture emporium. And it was a sizable collection, requiring such storage solutions. There were ten units, each five shelves high. Doing a quick estimate, that meant about two and a half thousand records. They'd better be in some kind of sequence or I was going to be here all day.

It only took a few seconds to realise what Max had meant about his daughter's idea of alphabetical order. The LPs were alphabetical, all right, but by title. So, nothing under *B* for Black Dog. Instead I looked under *S*, and found *Scarlet Ceremony*, their second album, in what was clearly an early or first pressing. At this point I started to get interested, indeed excited. This confirmed that Max actually did have some records by his old group in this collection. It also confirmed that his daughter was a complete ditz, because there were several hundred classical records in the

S section, just because they all had *Symphony* in their titles.

I moved quickly to the last of the shelving units, looking for *W*. At the very end of the bottom shelf in the last unit I found *White Ceremony*, the first Black Dog album. I could have howled like a dog myself in frustration. Maxine may have had nutty ideas about what constituted a title, but within her own system she was scrupulous about maintaining alphabetical order. If *Wisht* was here, it should have been the next record along, to the right of *White Ceremony*. But there was nothing there. The collection simply ended at this point.

Then I took another look at the section of blank wall beside the shelving unit. It had thin vertical lines in it, running from floor to ceiling. And, looking closer, I saw a pair of indentations at waist level. With a warm flow of recognition I realised that this was a wall closet.

I put my fingers in one of the indentations and tugged. The section of wall hinged open, folding into slim, tall doors on smoothly oiled rollers. I pulled the other section open, but already my sense of triumph was draining away.

In front of me was what appeared to be a flat green expanse of wall with a thin white line painted down the middle. And a narrow band of netting hanging across it.

Netting…

I realised this was a ping-pong table. Or rather, a flat sheet of fibreboard which when placed on top of the pool table, would turn it into a ping-pong table. I found the edge of the board and moved it aside, and suddenly I was looking into a closet with one last white storage unit standing in it. Most of the shelves of the unit were piled with board games, but the top one was full of records. I moved to it and checked the first record on the left-hand side.

My heart sank. The LP was *Work Song* by Nat Adderley. A great jazz album, but too far along in the alphabet. We'd gone from *White Ceremony* to *Work Song* with no *Wisht* in between.

So that was that.

Game over.

How appropriate for the games room.

But then something occurred to me. The LPs on this shelf were jammed in very tightly together. I could understand the impulse to get the rest of the record collection neatly into this last shelf and not have an untidy few stragglers spilling over into the one below.

So, maybe…

I tried to pull a few records off the shelf. It wasn't easy because they were squeezed so tight. Patiently I worked half a dozen or so free from the centre of the mass and eased them from the shelf. This suddenly created a more reasonable fit—indeed, I imagined I could hear the poor compressed records sighing with relief—and it also gave me room to operate.

I slid *Work Song* off the shelf…

And there it was. Jammed in on the left of the Adderley album, it had slipped forward as the shelf had been relentlessly packed, until its spine had ceased to be visible.

Wisht.

It was the flip back cover. I took the record out of the sleeve. It was in perfect condition—and it was the original pressing, with the narrow track between two wide ones on Side 2.

We'd done it.

I carried the record back down the corridor, feeling strangely weightless. I couldn't wait to see Tinkler's face when he saw it. I knocked on the door of Max's office. "Come in," he called. I opened the door. It was heavy and thick and swung on an impressively smooth and noiseless mechanism. It was the door of a recording studio.

Max was sitting at a desk behind a computer. It was cold in the room, the consequence of some aggressive air conditioning, and he had a blanket with a Native American pattern on it draped over him. He was looking at a Mac with two huge screens, the kind used for video or audio editing. He turned and gazed at me blankly for a moment, as if trying to place me, then comprehension dawned. I wondered if this was a florid affectation, or if he had indeed been so deeply engaged in his work that he'd forgotten I was around.

"I've got it," I said, holding up the record.

"Great. Bring it over here. Let's have a look."

I walked over to the desk, and came around beside where he was. As I did so, I could suddenly see what was on the wall behind the desk. Hanging there, the way someone else might have a Route 66 road sign or an old enamelled metal plaque advertising Coca-Cola, there was a very familiar sign.

It was the one with a warning about tidal times. The one without any bullet holes in it. The one with the wrong times. The one that had almost got us killed.

I looked at Max Shearwater. He was smiling at me, a quiet little smile. I realised I'd been supposed to notice the sign on the wall.

That was why he'd told me to come into his office.

He shrugged off the blanket that had been concealing his hands. Those hands were wearing purple latex gloves and were holding what at first looked like a stubby length of thin piping.

But, in fact, it was a sawn-off shotgun.

Max pointed the shotgun at me with one hand and pressed a key on his computer with the other. "All done now, dear," he said.

"We're ready in here, darling," said Ottoline's voice from the computer.

Max took the record from me and set it down on his desk. It seemed amazingly irrelevant all of a sudden. Then he walked me down the corridor at gunpoint to the living room.

There was something odd about the room; something had changed about it. Then I saw what it was. On the white rear wall, with the fireplace in the middle, all the paintings on one side had been removed. To the left of the fireplace the wall was still covered with them. But to the right, it was just blank white wall. And the furniture that had been here— some armchairs and a Navajo rug—had been removed, too. The floor was bare.

Nevada and Tinkler were standing on the bare patch of floor, their backs to the bare wall. On a chair some distance from them, Ottoline was sitting pointing a gun at them. It was a sawn-off shotgun, just like Max's. His and hers weaponry.

"I suppose you're wondering why we've asked you here," said Max, and both he and Ottoline laughed. He gestured with his shotgun, indicating that I should go over and join Nevada and Tinkler. I did so, and the three of us stood there as if posing for a photo, perhaps in a police line-up.

"You really have no one to blame but yourselves," he said. He pulled up a chair and sat down beside Ottoline. Behind them was a table with one of her sculptures on it—a bust of a misshapen head. It seemed to form a grotesque family trio with the two Shearwaters on either side of it.

"If only you hadn't gone to Erik Make Loud's that day," said Max. "You never would have been mixed up in any of this. And poor Stanley wouldn't have got so confused and bungled everything."

I had to think for a moment who poor Stanley was. Stanley Strangford, the would-be assassin with the red and green ski masks.

"He just wasn't prepared to have so many people to kill," said Max.

"You knew what he was going to do?" said Nevada. Her voice was carefully toneless but underneath it I sensed a growing rage. She didn't like people pointing guns at us.

Ottoline must have detected it too, because she said, "Just so you understand the situation fully. These are shotguns, which have been rendered highly illegal by having their barrels cut down. What that means is, if they're fired, the pellets disperse over a very wide area. That is why we have moved the furniture away from that whole section of the room. Because that whole section of the room is what you might think of as the blast area. Anything in the vicinity will be utterly shredded if we fire these weapons. So if you try anything, say for example trying to take these guns away from us, you will all be killed instantly. Sorry, darling, what were you saying?"

This last was directed at Max, who looked at us and said, in a tone of mild annoyance, "I didn't just *know* what Stanley was going to do, I *got* him to do it. I went to quite a lot of trouble preparing him for that particular task, and it was all wasted."

"You groomed him," I said.

Max chuckled. "That's right! I groomed him online. In the modern fashion—and they say you can't teach an old dog new tricks." Ottoline chuckled at this. "But, essentially," he said, "I used the same techniques as I did with Berit."

Berit Barsness. The Loopy Groupie. "You got her to kill Norrie, your manager?" I said.

"Yes, I did. Although in her case the campaign was a little more elaborate. The dog howling outside her window, and so on." He gave a nostalgic sigh. "I had a lot of fun putting those tapes together."

"Why all the killing, Max?" said Nevada.

Max shrugged. "Why do you think? Money, I'm afraid."

"The money you were supposed to have burned."

"Of course. What else?"

"What really happened to it, Max?"

"Well, it was all very unfortunate. You see, just at that

time my family had run into financial difficulties. So I needed a big cash injection. So I decided the chaps in the band should all chip in and help me out." He smiled at us. "After all, none of them would have had their careers if not for me. I was the leader of the band. I was the brains of the outfit. If you looked at it coolly and objectively, they owed me the money. But of course I wasn't crazy enough to think *they'd* see it that way. So if they were going to make a contribution, they'd have to do so without knowing it. That's why I came up with the wheeze to burn a million dollars. Note dollars not pounds. Initially I thought I'd be able to pull the old switcheroo when we did the currency exchange. Swapping real pounds sterling for fake or counterfeit dollars. But I soon realised that would never pass muster. For the stunt to work at all we would have to invite the press to witness it, and they'd be bound to want to examine the money before it went in the fire. So I came up with another way of pulling off the trick."

"How?" I said.

"Ottoline was already doing her sculptures by then, and she helped me. We built a heatproof ceramic chamber and put it in the middle of the fire pit. It had some metal components, to allow us to seal it when it was full, but it was chiefly ceramic. It had real flames all around it, but the chamber itself was completely secure. The money would go in there when I was apparently tossing it into the flames and instead of it burning up it was perfectly safe. I was standing directly over the chamber, the only angle from which you could see it. From every other angle all you could see was the flames. Of course I had to burn a bit of the real stuff, to make sure some genuine half-destroyed banknotes were carried away on the wind to create the illusion. After the bonfire, we just left our stash there. For weeks, because we didn't want anybody to see us digging around in the ashes. But eventually we went back, Ottoline and I, and we uncovered our lovely ceramic chamber with all the money inside, safe and sound. We took the loot and I removed the chamber itself, of course."

"And threw it in the ocean?" I said.

"God no." Max sounded genuinely shocked. "How could we do that to a beautiful mechanism that had functioned so loyally? We incorporated it into one of the sculptures outside. Anyway, all the evidence was gone. But when I learned you were coming to the island I suddenly felt insecure. And it's not like me to feel insecure. I suddenly wondered if there might be something I'd missed. Something you might find in the fire pit, even after all these years."

"So you got Jimmy Lynch to campaign to have it filled with cement," said Nevada.

"Yes, I could always twist Jimmy around my little finger. By the time I was finished with him, he was convinced it was his own idea. The only thing I had to do was pay for it. Or rather, pass him the money under the table so *he* could pay for it. Very tight is old Jimmy. Poor old Jimmy."

"You killed Jimmy's wife, didn't you?" I said.

"Ah, now," said Max. He seemed very eager to talk, which was good. Because the longer he talked the more chance we had of finding a way out of this. "That was sort of a combination of long-term project and spur-of-the-moment inspiration."

"The long-term project being to get rid of everyone else in the band," said Nevada.

"Well, I suppose you could put it like that," said Max. "Our manager Norrie came very close to working out what we did with the money, so he had to go. Then, for years and years, everything was fine. But then we got careless. One night we were reminiscing about the money and the fire, Ottoline and I, and Maxine overheard us. So then she knew. Of course she never told anyone, but..."

"It's such a burden on the poor thing," said Ottoline.

"Exactly," said Max. "One day she might inadvertently let something slip. And in this age of social media, the cat will truly be out of the bag. So we decided to take pre-emptive action."

"And kill the rest of the band," said Nevada.

Max shrugged. "We're the only ones with a child. So when the others die, their claims on the money will die with them. It's like a long-term art project I've been working at, on and off, for years. When Stanley Strangford was ready, I unleashed him on Tom at Erik Make Loud's house. That didn't work out, no matter. There'd be other opportunities. Meanwhile, my project with Pete had come to fruition."

"That was very satisfactory," said Ottoline.

"*Very* satisfactory," said Max.

"And then the other night," said Ottoline, "I'm in the Alexander von Humboldt with Maxine and Jimmy starts shouting about wanting to murder his wife. *In front of witnesses*."

Max and Ottoline glanced at each other and began to giggle helplessly. But they both returned their gaze to us, and the guns didn't waver.

"So I texted Max," said Ottoline. "And told him what happened."

I said, "Did your daughter know what you were doing?"

That stopped the giggling. Max and Ottoline now wore identical scandalised expressions. "Of course not," said Max.

"She knows about the money, but not about anything else," said Ottoline.

"Anyway," said Max, "as soon as I got Ottoline's text I began thinking at a million miles per second. I prepared a little special something, and then I literally ran down the hill. I got to Jimmy and Valentyna's house in about two minutes flat, and I went straight in through the front door without knocking. And the first thing I saw was that coat stand with all the scarves on it. My eye just went straight to it. I think my mind must have already been working out the possibilities all the time I was on my way there, ever since the text, and on some level I had already decided that a scarf was the way to go."

"Of course," said Ottoline. "Subconscious deliberation. It's the most powerful part of the creative process."

Max nodded. "So I grabbed a scarf off the rack without even pausing and I called out for Valentyna, I gave a merry little yell, and she replied from the kitchen. And I scooted along to her. She was surprised, but not all that surprised, to see me. She was accustomed to me dropping round, and it certainly wasn't out of character for me to come through the front door without knocking." He chuckled heartily. "It was almost as if my past behaviour had been a preparation for that day, that moment."

"The subconscious again," said Ottoline, nodding vigorously.

"So I trotted into the kitchen, looking all cheerful, and Valentyna smiled when she saw me. She was sitting there at the kitchen table with her sleeves rolled up and a big bowl in front of her, shelling peas. My good mood was infectious. She even smiled when she saw me holding Jimmy's scarf. And she laughed—she actually laughed—when I threw it around her neck. Giggled, actually. Girlish giggle. But then she saw I was wearing gloves." Max looked at the purple latex gloves on his hands. "Just like these ones. And in that second, in that instant, something changed in her eyes. I suppose maybe she saw something in *my* eyes. Because she began to resist. To fight back. But it was too late, of course. I already had the scarf around her throat and I started to pull it good and tight. She wasted a lot of time trying to get it off her and I just kept tugging it tighter and tighter and I dragged her off her chair and down onto the floor and then I really began to tighten it. She was struggling like hell, but I had her and I wasn't going to let her go."

"Did you have an erection?" said Ottoline, apparently in a spirit of detached inquiry.

"A huge one," said Max Shearwater.

"You old lecher," said Ottoline, and they both laughed.

At that moment I felt a terrible sense of sadness and loss. Not for Valentyna specifically, although she was part of it, but for everyone and everything. It was as though the bottom had dropped out of the world.

I had met some very bad people and had known them to do very bad things. But there was something about these two that just seemed to call everything into question. The fact that they could exist, and behave the way they did, seemed to devalue the very quality of the world.

I couldn't stand to look at them anymore, so I turned my head away, and stared towards the window.

It was the window on my right, the garden window.

Clean Head was standing outside.

28. GARDEROBE

Clean Head stood there among the statues in the garden, just on the other side of the window.

Our eyes met. She gave me a tense nod. She understood what was happening and she was on the case. A hot surge of relief broke in my chest.

Nevada was unaware of what I'd seen, but I felt Tinkler stir at my side. Suddenly there was something very different about him. Maybe it was his breathing. He must have spotted Clean Head, too.

Then, horribly, Ottoline must have also sensed something, because she began to turn towards the window.

And the instant she started to do so, Tinkler let out an anguished cry and fell to his knees. All eyes in the room turned towards him. Mine too, though an instant later than the others, because first I took in the sight of Clean Head running from the window and disappearing around the corner.

Only then did I turn to Tinkler.

He was grovelling on the floor. "Please," he begged.

"Please just let us go. Don't tell us any more. We won't tell anyone what you've said. Just let us go."

It was, I have to admit, a great performance. In particular I admired his voice, which was little more than a rusty croak. And he had completely covered Clean Head's escape. *Quick thinking, Tinkler.*

"Now, you know we can't do that," said Max Shearwater, shaking his head in a gesture of reprimand, as if to a naughty child. "We can't let you go. But what we most certainly can do is make the process much less unpleasant for you."

"What process is that?" said Nevada.

"You know what process," said Max patiently.

"Killing us, you mean," said Nevada coldly. "And how the fuck do you propose to make that 'less unpleasant'?"

"We have a supply of very pure heroin, and we shall administer a small injection to each of you."

"Starting with the girl, I think," said Ottoline. "She strikes me as the troublemaker in the bunch."

That will never happen, I thought. *I'll never let that happen. They'll have to kill me first. I will go for them and they'll have to shoot me with the...*

Then I realised the true nature of their threat about the shotgun. If any of us tried anything, the blast would kill all three of us.

"Good idea," said Max. "We can start with her." Then he looked at me, and it was horribly as if he'd read my mind. Or maybe he'd just read the expression on my face. "But we know you love her," he said.

The words were unimaginably unpleasant. It was true,

but hearing this man say it was like having worms crawl around inside my head, exploring every contour of my skull. My most private places.

"We know how much it will hurt for you to see her go," he said gently. "So we'll make sure we do you next. There won't be any delay. You won't have time to suffer."

"Do both of them at the same time," said Ottoline.

Max's face lit up. "That's a wondrous idea," he said. "Utterly brilliant, my darling."

"Do them simultaneously. Then neither of them has to go through watching the other die first."

Nevada and I looked at each other. Looking into her eyes was like looking into a furnace, with the rage and hatred for these people burning in them.

"Utterly inspired, my love. And we shall record it. On video."

"Of course we shall." They too were gazing into each other's eyes. I looked at Nevada. We were both thinking the same thing. *Should we jump them now?* Then we both looked at the shotguns and knew there was no chance.

Max saw us looking at the guns, and perhaps again he followed our chain of thought. "That would be a horrible way to go," he said. "It would be quick I suppose, but it would also be unimaginably agonising. Why would you do that when you could go out the other way? A simple, painless injection. I don't know if you've ever taken heroin, but if not, you're in for a treat."

His voice took on a crooning, wheedling quality. "It will be the most luxuriant physical pleasure you will ever have experienced. You will literally dissolve, evaporating blissfully into the universe. What a way to go!" He whistled and laughed. "I almost wish I was joining you," he said, and then he laughed some more and Ottoline joined in. Their heads were close together, happy conspirators, and the sculpted head on the table behind them seemed to be leaning forward and listening, perhaps even nodding with approval.

"So it's a heroin overdose," said Nevada. "Then what?" I had to admire her aplomb, even now.

Max Shearwater spread his hands in a gesture of helpless mystification. "Who knows?" he said. "Who knows? But you will find out. You and your beloved." He nodded at me. "The two of you—and your friend." He lifted his chin to include Tinkler in the discussion. I suspect Tinkler would have been very happy to be left out of it. "You will all be setting off on a journey together into the final great enigma. Now, I'm not what you'd call conventionally religious, but even I believe that something—"

"No," said Nevada, shaking her head in disgust. "I don't mean that. I have remarkably little interest in your surmises about the afterlife. I meant, how do you propose to explain our disappearance? We have friends and family and they know where we are. They even know we were coming to see you—"

"If you mean your friend with the shaved head, we already have a plan in place—" My heart leapt at the mention of Clean Head. Could they be aware of her out in the garden? My body suddenly crawled with warm sweat. Of course they couldn't. They wouldn't be sitting here casually chatting with us if they knew about Clean Head.

"No, I don't mean her," said Nevada tersely. "If you do anything to her, you're just compounding your problem. You'll have four disappearances to explain instead of one. All of us have friends, family, connections…"

Cats, I thought, with stupendous irrelevance. But I imagined the furry little fools waiting at home for us, waiting forever… And the thought wrung my heart the way nothing else had yet. Perhaps because it was small enough to get in under my guard. It made the whole thing real to me in a way it hadn't been until now. My heart began to slam in my chest with such force that I could feel my blood in my toes and fingertips. My body wanted me to escape from this, prolong our survival, avoid the brutal, idiotic ending that was rushing towards us.

But how?

"There's no way," said Nevada. "There's no way all of us can just disappear. If you kill us, that will be the end of you both. You will be found out and you'll both go to prison for the rest of your lives. How will you like that? Maybe you can turn your cells into installations. Man in cell. Woman in cell. A final work of art. But a pretty fucking boring one."

"There's no way you can all disappear?" said Max Shearwater. He smiled and looked at Ottoline. "Do you want to tell them, dear, or shall I?"

"You tell them. This is your project, after all."

Max rubbed his nose and smiled at us. "You've actually prepared the perfect method for us."

"To be fair," said Ottoline, "it wasn't really them, darling. It was you. It was all you."

"Was it? I suppose it was, if you think about it. I suppose I did, we did, when we lured you out onto the causeway just when the tide was coming in."

"You would have saved us all a lot of bother if you'd just let it happen to you then," said Ottoline. She sounded genuinely pissed off.

"Just stayed out there and drowned, you mean?" said Nevada. She was smiling at them. I hoped I would never have occasion to have her smile like that at me.

"But what have you gained by not staying out there and drowning? By coming back? What have you really gained?" Ottoline shook her head with disgust. "A few shitty little pitiful days."

"Don't get angry, love," said Max.

"I'm not getting angry, it's just such a *nuisance*."

"But it sets the scene so superlatively well for us now."

"Yes, I suppose it does," conceded Ottoline sulkily.

Max looked at us. "That little episode has made you famous on our island. Famous as the mainlanders who don't know how to read the tide tables."

"You're going to do that *again*?" said Nevada.

"Well, we're going to process you here, and dispose of your remains in such a way that no one will ever find them. But yes, we're going to use that as the explanation. We're going to make everyone believe that you drove out on the causeway at the wrong time again."

"Drove out? Drove out in what? Our car has been totalled, Einstein," said Nevada.

"Oh, that's no problem," said Max good-humouredly.

"We'll just rent one for you online. Using your phones and your credit cards. Get it dropped off here. No problem. We'll see that it ends up in the ocean in the right spot. I'm afraid you'll lose your deposit, though!" He chuckled. "So it will be just like last time. Except this time you did drown. And your bodies will never be found. There will be a big search for them, but they will never be found."

"Because we will have cremated you in my kiln," said Ottoline. "And scattered the remains into the sea. Through the garderobe in the utility room."

"I showed that to them earlier, dear," said Max, as if this mattered.

"No one will believe it," said Tinkler.

"Why not?"

"No one will believe we're stupid enough to make the same mistake twice." But his voice wavered and I knew he was thinking what I was thinking. That is exactly what they'd believe.

"On the contrary. Far from making anyone think *that*, your little fiasco previously will have convinced them you're arrogant, careless mainlanders who are absolutely just the sort of people who would make such a mistake. The sort of people with no respect for the lethal majesty of nature."

I saw Ottoline stirring impatiently now, looking at her watch. "Actually, darling…" she said.

I could see she was eager to get on with the 'project'. We had to stall them, to give Clean Head time to arrive with the cavalry.

So I quickly said, "Why did you frame Jimmy for murder instead of killing him?"

Max opened his mouth to reply—always eager for a natter, was Max Shearwater—but at that moment the doorbell rang.

Ottoline and Max exchanged a quick, worried glance. Obviously they weren't expecting anyone. My heart swelled with joy. Clean Head had got here with the cops really quickly.

"I'll go," said Max. He hurried out. Ottoline shifted her chair just a smidgen, to face us more squarely, adjusting her shotgun and aiming it carefully. Not that it mattered with that thing. The misshapen bust stared at us over her shoulder, as if supplementing her wary vigilance.

There were voices in the hallway. Max's and somebody else's. A male voice. At any moment I expected to hear the shock and surprise from Max as he was clapped in handcuffs. But the voices remained casual and grew closer.

Max came back into the room with Stinky Stanmer.

Stinky smiled at us and said, "I knew they were here because I saw Clean Head outside."

"Clean Head?" said Max. He had a companionable arm over Stinky's shoulder.

"You know, the mixed-race girl."

"Oh, yes, of course. Agatha. Such a striking young lady." Max released Stinky and took a step back. "Where exactly did you say you saw her?"

"Outside. In your garden."

"Thank you. You have been very helpful indeed, Mr Stanmer. Now please join your friends."

This was the point where Stinky saw the gun that Max

was holding. He turned to us, aghast, and then also saw the gun Ottoline was holding.

"Over here, Mr Stanmer," said Ottoline. And Stinky obeyed, coming to stand beside me. Meanwhile, Max hurried out.

"What have you fucking done?" I hissed at Stinky. "You told him Clean Head is out there?"

"I didn't know," he said. "I didn't know about any of this. I just came here looking for the record." Tears filled his eyes. "Why are you always getting me into these situations?"

"You're supposed to be filming at the fucking Lorettos'."

"There was a problem with police permission. My friend in the police…" Suddenly the tears stopped welling in Stinky's eyes. He turned to Ottoline. "My friend in the police knows I'm coming here. I told him I was coming here."

"No, you didn't," said Ottoline, with massive confidence.

At my side, Stinky began to tremble. Full points to him for trying to lie. Though of course lying was what Stinky did best.

This time he just hadn't been able to sell it, that was all.

There was the sound of a door opening and closing and a moment later Max came back in with Clean Head at gunpoint. To her credit, she didn't look frightened. Just disgusted. "I found her hiding behind *Homage to Brâncuşi*," said Max.

He prodded Clean Head and she came over and joined us. The gang was all here.

Max sat down again and looked at me. "Now, what was your question?"

"About *framing* Jimmy," said Ottoline. She pronounced the word with contempt.

Max shook his head. "That wasn't the plan. The plan was to have him commit suicide." He frowned as if I'd made some critical remark in response to this. "I know, I know. It was the same scenario as with Pete and Sarita Loretto. Murder and suicide. That was its chief flaw. Repetition. A true artist doesn't repeat himself. I'm ashamed I even tried."

"No, darling," said Ottoline fiercely. "It wasn't the same. With Pete and Sarita she killed him and then committed suicide. With Jimmy and Valentyna it would have been the other way around—husband kills wife and then himself. It wasn't repetition. It was a brilliant variation on a theme."

"Thank you, darling," he said, and suddenly took her hand, her non-shotgun hand, in his own non-shotgun hand. They briefly glanced into each other's eyes. Heart-warming evidence of a long and happy marriage. If only they weren't a couple of serial killers.

I said, "How the hell did you propose to make Jimmy commit suicide?" It was a valid question—the powerfully muscled Jimmy could have snapped Shearwater in half—but my main objective was just to keep the mad motherfucker talking and prolong our own existence.

"Oh, I'd prepared a hot shot. A syringe containing an overdose of heroin, mixed with some other fun ingredients."

Ottoline stroked his hand. "You thought of all that so quickly, darling."

"Inspiration, darling."

"But how were you going to get the heroin into him?" I said. Again with the notion of him being snapped in half. It was a very attractive notion.

Max's eyes blazed. "Ah, now that was going to be the fun and exciting bit. The improvisation. I wasn't sure precisely how I'd do it. But in all honesty I think it would have been pretty easy. My favourite scenario was to pretend I'd just happened to drop by, share in his horror and astonishment at the murder of Valentyna, lying there dead in the kitchen, and simply offer him the heroin by way of comfort for a grieving husband. Knowing Jimmy he would have gone for it like a seal after a fish. Avoiding dealing with unpleasant reality was always his top priority. And when they found him lying there dead in the vicinity of his murdered wife, I think it would have gone down a treat." He sighed. "But it was not to be, because that girl turned up on her bicycle. The bloody girl from the bloody pub. To collect the bloody herbs and bloody vegetables for their bloody kitchen."

"That stupid little slag," said Ottoline, the loyal helpmeet.

"I thought I heard something outside—luckily," said Max. "So I crept to the kitchen window and peeked out. And there she was in the garden, helping herself. Then I turned around and looked at the kitchen table, the bowl that Valentyna had been filling with fresh peas. It was *huge*. She couldn't possibly have been planning to use all those herself. It dawned on me that when the girl was finished in the garden, she'd be coming in here. And at that moment, what do I hear but the sound of a car. It's only bloody Jimmy. I hear him come in and start bellowing to Valentyna, shouting obscenities about his shoes. Then he slams the front door, and drives away again."

This would have been Jimmy retrieving his wallet from

the coat hanging in the hallway and storming off to go for a drink at The Sea View, where Nevada and I had found him later that evening.

Max shrugged. "So, that was that. Jimmy had come and gone, and it was only a matter of time before the girl came in and found Valentyna. So I just slipped away quietly." He paused and sighed wistfully. "All a bit of a mess, I fear. But then that's the risk you run with improvised works of art."

Then he smiled at Stinky and said, "This one is going rather well, though. Plenty of room for five in a Land Rover." He looked at Ottoline. "Mr Stanmer drove up here in his Land Rover."

"Very handy," said Ottoline. "We won't have the bother of renting a car for them now." She checked her watch. "We'll have to move soon to catch the tides, though."

"What will your daughter think?" said Nevada.

"Maxine will never know about any of it," said Max, sounding a little exasperated, explaining the obvious to a dull pupil. "Like I said, she found out about the money but she never knew about any of the killings, and she never will."

I realised why Nevada had started this line of questioning.

Because, standing there in the living room doorway, was Maxine Shearwater. And she'd heard everything.

Her presence was explained by the bag she was carrying. It was a stylish pink paper confection with the logo of Faddish Fetish on it. This was the same bag from which Stinky had so proudly produced the transparent bikini, except now additionally written on it in large letters in surprisingly bold yet girlish handwriting were the words "Fuck off Stinky".

A welcome phrase, and one indeed which, if we'd had a coat of arms—perhaps featuring two cats, rampant—would have been our family motto.

Maxine stared at her parents. Her parents stared at her. Then she turned and fled.

"Maxie!" said her father in an agonised voice. He lurched to his feet, looked at the gun in his hand, and hastily set it down on the chair. Then he ran out the door after her, moving with astonishing speed for a man that big.

As he disappeared through the door, Ottoline turned to watch him go.

Nevada was a blur of motion.

She reached the table with the bust on it, scooped it up and swung it two-handed at Ottoline just as she was turning back to look at her. The bust must have been hollow, because it rang with a low, throaty note as it connected with Ottoline's skull, like an exotic percussion instrument.

Despite being hollow, it was still clearly plenty heavy because Ottoline gave a grunt at the moment of impact, her eyes rolled up in their sockets and she slid to the floor in a boneless mass.

"How's that for being a troublemaker?" said Nevada, looking down at the unconscious woman at her feet. She threw the bust across the room, into the far corner, where surprisingly it shattered. Then Nevada bent forward and plucked the shotgun from Ottoline's limp fingers. She picked up the other one from Max's chair, and hurried out of the room, a sawn-off shotgun in either hand.

She came back a moment later, no longer carrying the guns.

"What did you do with them?" said Clean Head.

"I dropped them down the garderobe. Now they're in the sea, feeding the great cycle of nature."

"Don't you think we might need them?" said Stinky tremulously.

"Pull the trigger on one of those things and you kill half the island," said Nevada succinctly. "Come on, let's go."

I made everyone wait while I went into Max's office to get the flip back copy of *Wisht*. I wasn't going to let us go through all this and come out of it empty-handed. When I got back to the living room Nevada and Clean Head were busy trussing up the still-unconscious Ottoline, using bathroom towels. They tied her arms behind her back and bound her legs at the ankles. Even when she woke up, she wouldn't be going anywhere.

Outside the house, the only car in the circular parking area was Stinky's. The Land Rover that Shearwater had been so keen to use in his staging of our deaths at sea.

"No Subarus," said Tinkler. "Pink or blue."

I said, "So Maxine took off in hers and Max went after her in his?"

"It looks like it," said Tinkler.

"Well, let's get the fuck out of here before he comes back."

Clean Head nodded. "I suppose we need to go anyway," she said. "Before the police arrive."

"The police?" said Tinkler. "The police are coming?"

"Yes."

"Why?" I said. "Or perhaps I mean, how?"

Clean Head gave me a slightly disdainful look. "I called them as soon as I saw you guys were being held at gunpoint. Why wouldn't I?" She sounded genuinely annoyed, bless her.

Now she said, "Where are the keys, Stinky?"

"Keys?"

"For your vehicle."

"Oh." Stinky dug them out and handed them over to her without protest. Clean Head pressed the fob and the Land Rover came to life. We all piled into it and she drove us away from the house jutting over the sea.

At speed.

29. TWO RECORDINGS

Getting out of there fast had seemed like not just the smart, but the only thing to do.

However, we weren't even back at our B&B before doubts began to besiege me. Should we have stayed and waited for the police to arrive? But, given the current state of their overstretched resources, it could be a while before anyone turned up, even for an emergency call. And in that time, who knew what deviltry the returning Max might have cooked up for us?

Nevada had got rid of the two guns we knew about, but there could have been all sorts of other deadly surprises in store.

On the other hand, now that those guns were gone, there was no physical evidence we could use against the Shearwaters...

I tried to force these worries from my mind and listen to Clean Head. As she drove, she was telling us what had happened since we'd left her this morning. "I went down to see Gareth at his garage and I took Perky's collar with me."

She glanced over her shoulder at me. "I was thinking about your theory that it was some kind of LoJack tracker and I wondered if he could identify it. But while I was down there Foxy Foxcroft came sniffing around. I think she fancies Gareth. Sorry, Tinkler."

"Hey," said Tinkler fervently. "I'm just glad to be alive."

I think he was also glad that it wasn't Clean Head who fancied Gareth.

"Anyway, it turns out it isn't a tracking device at all. It's a *recording* device."

"Recording?" I said. "Audio recording?"

"Yep. A state-of-the-art, long-life audio recorder. Foxy Alicia spotted it right away, what with being a trained sound engineer and all."

And Alicia had also showed Clean Head how to play it back and listen to it. "I was sitting there at Miss Bebbington's with earphones on and sipping a cup of tea. I wished it had been something stronger. I needed it."

It was our turn to listen to the device when we arrived back at the B&B. It began with a helpful introduction by Max Shearwater. As soon as I heard that voice I had to stop listening. It had only recently been telling me, in its mellow and measured tones, how he was going to kill me and everyone I cared about.

"Too soon?" said Clean Head, as I pulled the earphones off.

I nodded. She looked at Nevada. "Do you want a go?"

Nevada shook her head. "I'm with him."

We were sitting out in Miss Bebbington's garden, and had been since we'd got back.

We'd been enormously relieved when, living up to her reputation as being the island's leading nexus for gossip, Miss Bebbington had reported to us that the Shearwaters' house was 'crawling with cops'. No one knew quite what was going on, but there were still police arriving from the mainland, some in a helicopter.

Well, that was that.

Even so, I found that I didn't want to be inside just at the moment. It seemed too easy to be trapped if you were inside. Outdoors there were plenty of directions in which one could flee. I was hoping this feeling would pass away before bedtime, otherwise I was going to be sleeping wrapped in a blanket under the stars.

The others seemed to feel much the same, and Miss Bebbington brought our supper out to us and we ate al fresco and then worked our way through a couple of bottles of the good wine that Nevada had brought with us. "The *best* wine," she said. "No point scrimping or hoarding when one has just been reminded of one's mortality."

"Can one have a bit more wine in one's glass?" said Tinkler.

It was dark by now, and perhaps not surprisingly the wine had gone instantly to my head. The way a sledgehammer might—albeit an extremely smooth, biodynamic red sledgehammer from the Rhône region.

A fat silver moon was playing hard to get behind a bank of clouds, occasionally revealing itself and then coyly disappearing again. The night smelled fresh and clean and a cool breeze was flowing in from the sea. I was just debating whether I had the energy to go inside and get myself a sweater, or if I could trick my beloved into getting it for me, when Miss Bebbington came out of the French windows. She was outlined against the lights of the lounge, but even in silhouette there was something about her posture that put me on full alert.

"What is it?" I said.

The tone of my voice cut through the happy chatter of my friends and they all fell silent. Miss Bebbington cleared her throat.

"Max Shearwater is dead," she said. "And so is Ottoline."

It had taken what seemed to me an unconscionable time for the police to turn up at Max Shearwater's house. I suppose I was being particularly unforgiving because I was thinking that a delay like that might have led to us all being killed by the Shearwaters. Or, at the very least, having to listen to a load more of their pretentious bullshit.

But my first reaction on learning that Shearwater was gone, oddly, was a sudden desire to listen to that recording device after all. The one that had been fastened onto Perky.

I guess I could endure hearing his voice now that I knew he was dead, and that my loved ones and I were safe.

So I put the headphones on and lay back in one of the deckchairs and stared up at the night sky, the smell of warm canvas close and comforting. Nevada poured a brimming glass of the Chapoutier and brought it to me, then went back and sat on the grass with the others. The murmur of their conversation provided a faintly audible background to the recording—what I suppose Max would have called a sound-bed.

"Introduction to a new audio project," said Max Shearwater's voice in my ear. "To follow the life of a pig from its birth to its final destiny as the meat on our table. Note to self. End on sound of sizzling bacon but mix back to squealing of newborn piglet as used at the beginning. Adjust waveforms to make the two sounds blend seamlessly and move back and forth from one to the other in an almost oceanic way… the rising and falling of the waves—Ha! The rising and falling of the wave*forms*—until the listener is unable to tell if he is hearing the beginning of the pig's journey or the very ending."

There then ensued, sure enough, the squealing of newborn piglets. And much else besides. So, like Clean Head before me, I skipped ahead.

To the lethal night.

Max Shearwater had always been on the lookout for wacky audio projects. So when the Lorettos had obtained their pair of piglets, he'd dreamed up this one. And with the couple's permission he fitted a recording device to one of the piglets, on an adjustable collar that could be loosened and expanded as the pig grew.

The problem was, Max could never remember which one of the two pigs he'd chosen. The similarity of names didn't help. Nor did the fact that, as they grew, Perky had become porky and Porky had become perky.

So when Pete and Sarita returned from their nightmare odyssey taking Porky to the hippy pig killer, they'd been subject to a visit by a somewhat panic-stricken Max Shearwater, who demanded to know why they hadn't been answering their phones, and if they'd remembered to salvage the recording device from the abattoir.

He'd got short shrift from the traumatised Sarita, who merely told him, "It's fine," then went upstairs to bed.

It was left to Pete to provide an enlarged explanation, along the lines of, "It's fine because it's the *other* pig who is wearing it, you moron, the one who hasn't been killed yet."

We know this because Sarita began using the recording collar as a kind of informal audio diary.

Which is also how we know that, when Pete was trying to find a way to make the dispatch of poor Perky less of a bloody disaster, and looking for something more reliable than the hippy fool's hideous 'humane killer', it was Max Shearwater who suggested he obtain a proper gun. An automatic pistol. Indeed, Max sourced it for him. Just as he had done for the Loopy Groupie.

Because Max had suddenly seen an opportunity.

A chance to get rid of the Lorettos, as part of his continuing project to protect the money he'd stolen.

So he made sure he and Ottoline turned up, unexpected and uninvited, at the special fenced-in section of the Lorettos' garden on the night scheduled for Perky's killing. For moral support, they declared.

This was also the reason that Sarita was there. Although

in her case she wanted to provide moral support for Perky. "I couldn't let him die alone," she'd said in her final post… where she also let slip that even at this late stage she was determined that Perky shouldn't die at all. She was resolute that she'd talk Pete out of his course of action.

This blog was an essential part of Max Shearwater's plan. Because he could shoot Pete with the pistol and, with Ottoline's help, then shoot Sarita, making it look like she'd killed herself after murdering her husband. To save Perky the pig.

All of this should have worked. And it did indeed work, for a while. The police believed what they found at the staged crime scene.

And it might have continued to work.

Except for two things.

Perky, panicked by the shots, escaped. Surging through the fence as though it wasn't there.

And Perky was still wearing the recording device, which had recorded everything…

Max: We're not going to shoot you. Relax. Relax. We just want you to hold the gun.
Ottoline: We just want your fingerprints on the gun.
Sarita: Why?
Max: Never mind, darling. There.
Ottoline: Good girl.
Max: Perfect.
(Gunshot.)
(Battering noises.)

Max: What the fuck is that?

Ottoline: The pig. Trying to smash through the fence.

Max: Well, make him stop.

Ottoline: Don't worry. He can't break through it.

Max: I'm not worried. I just want him to stop.

Ottoline: How do you propose that I make that happen?

Max: Shoot him, just shoot him—

Ottoline: I'm not going to shoot a *pig*.

Max: No, shit, don't you realise—

Ottoline: What?

Max: I forgot—

Ottoline: What?

Max: He's still wearing the recorder.

Ottoline: But it's not on, is it?

Max: Of course it's fucking on. It's on all the time.

Ottoline: Why didn't you switch it off?

Max: I told you, I forgot!

(The battering noises build to a crescendo.)

Max: Shoot him! Give me the gun! Here, give it to me—

Ottoline: No, I'll—

(A crashing sound.)

Ottoline: (Growing distant.) Christ! He got through!

Max: (Fading in the distance.) Stop him.

Ottoline: (Angry and loud, so still audible.) How?

Max: (Shouting, but just barely audible.) Come back, you fucking pig.

(Their voices fade in the distance as Perky flees.)

* * *

No wonder Max Shearwater hadn't wanted anybody to hear this thing.

So he'd set about making sure people would steer clear of the pig—not that poor Perky had any great reason to trust people or approach them, but even if he did he was likely to find that Max's negative PR had got there first. *Stay away from the devil pig. It brings death with it.*

Arguably he'd done a sufficiently good job to make anyone think twice—I'd even thought twice myself, and had been willing to perceive this peaceful, friendly creature as something frightening. But on Halig Island, with its oddball inclination to mysticism, and where Sarita and Pete Loretto had been well known and well liked, it proved particularly effective.

But in the end, for Perky at least, there had been a happy ending.

Not so for Max and Ottoline. The story that was spreading was that they'd both committed suicide. But Max being Max, he couldn't just depart this world quietly. So instead of leaving a note, he'd filmed a farewell message.

And then released it on the Internet, of course.

He'd gone to some trouble to stage the affair, with contrived lighting and a carefully chosen camera angle. He was sitting on a sofa in their living room overlooking the sea. Indeed, he changed the angle of it so the windows and the sea view were visible in the background.

Nice composition, Max.

He had the body of his wife, face covered decorously with what looked like a pillowcase, lying on the sofa at his side. Max gazed directly into the camera and spoke solemnly and evenly, that sonorous voice giving its last performance.

He started by saying that his daughter Maxine knew absolutely nothing about his crimes. Then he went on to list those crimes. The murder of Norrie Nelson and the suicide of Berit Barsness, both at his instigation. The attempted murder of Tom Pyewell 'and others'—we didn't even get a name check—by Stanley Strangford, at his instigation. The murder of Pete and Sarita Loretto, actually by his hand. Ditto the murder of Valentyna Lynch.

He didn't say anything about stealing the money from the band. It seemed clear to me he was hoping that this would be forgotten in the whirl of events and Maxine would be able to retain all the fruits of that particular crime.

I noticed that he didn't implicate Ottoline directly in any of the killings. But maybe he thought her lying dead there beside him was comment enough. Personally I rather doubted that she'd actually killed herself. She just didn't seem the type. I was more inclined to the view that Max had helped her on her way, possibly while she was still somewhat groggy from the clout Nevada had given her.

I also noticed that his attempt to murder me and my friends in his house didn't feature anywhere in his final confession. But then an artist doesn't like to dwell on his failures.

On the other hand, he went out of his way to make it clear that Jimmy Lynch was innocent and absolutely blameless, an action which, coming from anyone else, I might have described as decent.

When he finally shut up, Max proceeded to administer

to himself an overdose of heroin, the same method he'd used on Ottoline and had intended to use on us. Luckily, the version of the clip I saw was one that cut off before the actual moment of death.

I suppose watching this thing should have made me sad. But to be honest I only felt a scorching contempt.

For all his worshipping of originality, Max Shearwater had basically pursued the same bloody pattern of murder and suicide every time he wanted to make his life more comfortable. He'd even used, or tried to use, the husband/wife murder/suicide four consecutive times, if you included his and Ottoline's final bow.

Call me vicious, call me vengeful, I like to think that this awful fact dawned on him, with all its irrefutable proof of his ultimate mediocrity, just as he put the needle in his arm and pushed the plunger. And thereby entirely spoiled his blissful evaporation into the universe.

I felt no pity for him.

The one I did feel sorry for was Maxine Shearwater. I'd never liked her, but you'd need a heart of stone not to be moved by what happened to the poor girl. Her parents may have been homicidal lunatics, but they'd been her parents, and by their own admission had been careful to hide from her any evidence of their more hideous transgressions.

And she'd not only lost both of them, she'd had to endure the hellish firestorm of publicity that ensued. I wouldn't have wished that on anyone.

And there was one other thing...

As I understand it, when Max Shearwater rushed out

of the house after his daughter that day, he found her. And spoke to her. And then he went back home, and killed his wife and himself.

What exactly did Maxine say to him that sent him home to do that?

Whatever it was, I was glad it wasn't a burden I was carrying.

30. KIND OF RED

The next day we all felt pretty low, as you might imagine.

But Clean Head said she had something that would cheer us up.

So we trooped down with her along the seafront and up a side road to Gareth's place of business. The man himself was standing outside, by the closed door of the garage, with a big smile on his bearded face.

He was genuinely pleased to see us, and not just Clean Head and Nevada. His truculence to me, so marked at the Viking funeral, seemed entirely gone. Perhaps Clean Head had told him about the near-death experience all of us had just been through and he was cutting me some slack. Or maybe she'd told him about the saga of Perky, the strictly non-demonic pig, and he was doing some hasty Mormon Hipster backpedalling.

Anyway, he smiled that big welcoming smile and rolled open the doors of his garage.

Inside was a car, which was not surprising.

What *was* surprising was that it was a Volvo DAF. Just like Tinkler's old one. Except this one was red. A rather odd shade of red.

Kind of red…

So this was what all the conspiratorial business between Clean Head and Gareth had been about.

As we stared at the little red car in stunned silence, Clean Head said, "We found one pretty quickly, the right model and year and everything, but it needed some work, so it took a little while before we could spring it on you." She looked at Tinkler. "It's even got some of your old car's parts in it. So it contains some of Kind of Blue's DNA."

"What a sweet gesture!" said Nevada. There were tears in her eyes. And mine, too. Also Tinkler, of course. And possibly even in the eyes of our hip Mormon friend.

Not so Clean Head. She merely grinned. "I just like to have access to a car I can drive really fast backwards." She threw the keys to Tinkler, who for once in his life managed to catch something in mid-air.

"And you have to pay for it all, of course, Tinkler," said Clean Head.

"But of course."

It may not be entirely surprising that we checked the tide tables about twenty-seven times before we drove back across the causeway to the mainland. Luckily we were able to set off very early the next day, and then do the entire drive back to London in one hit.

Well, I say 'we'. It was Clean Head who drove all the way.

It was late evening, with the sky just darkening to night, when she dropped us off in front of the Abbey, then set off to Putney to drop Tinkler and collect her taxi.

Nevada and I walked the last tiny distance towards our house with our bags. There was a little cry from the darkness and Fanny emerged from the patch of lavender beside the electrical junction box on the corner of our estate. She fell in beside us, making a running commentary in her squeaky voice, as if offering a list of complaints about how she'd been looked after while we were away.

As we approached our house there was a rustling in the dark jungle of foliage opposite and Turk came streaking out, dodged in front of us, dropped low and squeezed under the gate before we could open it, running to the door of our house where she turned and began, like Fanny, a long and complicated monologue.

"Now, girls," said Nevada, taking out her keys, "I'm sure Auntie Maggie can't have treated you *that* badly."

Fanny immediately gave a high-pitched squeak and Turk simultaneously emitted a loud and sour yowl, as if by way of firm contradiction. Nevada laughed and opened the door and we all went inside.

Human nature being the ghoulish thing it is, the sensational death of the Shearwaters and the gruesome revelations of their murder spree led to a huge surge of new interest in Black Dog and their music.

This meant that Tinkler's copy of *Wisht*, which in the end we'd got for nothing—if by nothing one means at the risk of very nearly losing all our lives—was suddenly worth a solid, blue chip fortune. Right up there with an original vinyl pressing of Prince's *Black Album*.

And with renewed sales of the Black Dog back catalogue, money flooded in to the surviving members of the band, Tom Pyewell and the widowed but now exonerated Jimmy Lynch. And also, and most especially, Maxine Shearwater. Since her father had been the main writer in the band, she also received the fat bonus of composer royalties.

So suddenly she was richer than ever.

Any enmity I'd felt towards Maxie had vanished when I saw the legacy she'd been landed with.

Also, she had saved all our lives.

But I came to positively admire her for what happened next. She dropped a financial bomb on herself by volunteering the information that her father had swindled the other members of the band out of a fortune when he had pretended to burn the cash and absconded with it. And she went on to announce that she wanted to pay back the money and was already in negotiations with Tom and Jimmy, and the Lorettos' estate about coming to a settlement.

Max Shearwater's trick with the money had been fraud, which is a crime. But when Max died, the crime died with him. And so did any possibility of criminal action against his next of kin, which was Maxine. However, Maxine was still exposed to civil action for any fraud her father had committed.

So a cynic might have said that coming clean and settling was just good business—heading off any lawsuits and striking a more advantageous deal. Plus it was a smart PR move, both pre-emptive and good publicity.

But I didn't think it was like that at all.

I'd often wondered—as I'm sure everyone was supposed to—about Maxine's tattoo. What exactly the snake was whispering in her ear.

Maybe he just told her to do the right thing.

EPILOGUE

One morning I was in the kitchen summoning the moral strength to make some real coffee when I heard a noise which at first I thought was Turk cursing at the big fat grey squirrel who sometimes invaded our back garden. It sounded very similar—vehement, impassioned, wordless and threatening major mayhem if circumstances were only slightly different.

But it wasn't Turk, it was Nevada.

I went to see what was wrong.

She handed her phone to me without a word. On the screen was a tweet announcing a major new music festival, to take place next summer on Halig Island.

Called Drowning Man.

And under the auspices of Stinky Stanmer, of course.

Tickets available now.

I started making some wordless cursing sounds myself.

AUTHOR'S NOTE

Once upon a time there was a band who really did burn a million dollars. A million pounds, in fact. But that band was The KLF—Bill Drummond and Jimmy Cauty. And they burned the money on the island of Jura.

I hope they won't mind me playing a variation on their theme.

As for Halig Island, you won't find it on any maps because it is entirely my creation. However, readers may have noticed its resemblance in some respects to the real Holy Island—Lindisfarne. I was inspired by Lindisfarne, but I didn't want to be constrained by that real island's location, geology, terrain, inhabitants or—most especially—its tide tables.

AC

ACKNOWLEDGEMENTS

My thanks to my old friend Gordon Larkin, who advised me on the British folk scene of the 1960s and gave me a reading list. To Alan Ross at Jazz House Records for keeping the vinyl flowing, and graciously consenting to a cameo in this book. To Miranda Jewess, my editor, for volunteering to work on this book even while she was on maternity leave. To Nick Landau at Titan for his support of the series. To Lydia Gittins, my fine publicist. To my agent John Berlyne for having my back. To Joanna Harwood, my hard working and fab new editor at Titan. To Lars Pearson and Christa Dickson, for their unfailing patience in helping me to source records from America. To Bill McBryde and Smudgy for providing me with both a rare old Art Pepper LP and a rare new friendship. My warmest thanks to the wonderful Thomas Wörtche, a fellow jazz lover, and Nicole Herrschmann, adroit press agent, both at Suhrkamp Verlag, and Susanna Mende, my splendid German translator. And to Joe Kraemer for writing the theme music for the Vinyl Detective LP — coming to a record store near you soon!

ABOUT THE AUTHOR

Andrew Cartmel is a novelist and screenwriter. He is the author of the Vinyl Detective series, which was hailed as "marvellously inventive and endlessly fascinating" by *Publishers Weekly*. His work for television includes commissions for *Midsomer Murders* and *Torchwood*, and a legendary stint as script editor on *Doctor Who*. He has also written plays for the London Fringe, toured as a stand-up comedian, and is currently co-writing a series of comics with Ben Aaronovitch based on the bestselling *Rivers of London* books. He lives in London with too much vinyl and just enough cats.

THE RUN-OUT GROOVE

A VINYL DETECTIVE NOVEL

ANDREW CARTMEL

His first adventure consisted of the search for a rare record; his second begins with the *discovery* of one. When a mint copy of the final album by Valerian—England's great lost rock band of the 1960s—surfaces in a charity shop, all hell breaks loose. Finding this record triggers a chain of events culminating in our hero learning the true fate of the singer Valerian, who died under equivocal circumstances just after— or was it just before?—the abduction of her two-year-old son.

Along the way, the Vinyl Detective finds himself marked for death, at the wrong end of a shotgun, and unknowingly dosed with LSD as a prelude to being burned alive. And then there's the grave robbing…

"Like an old 45rpm record, this book crackles with brilliance." **David Quantick**

"This tale of crime, cats and rock & roll unfolds with an authentic sense of the music scene then and now – and a mystery that will keep you guessing."
Stephen Gallagher

VICTORY DISC

A VINYL DETECTIVE NOVEL

ANDREW CARTMEL

This time the search for a rare record ensnares our hero in a mystery with its roots stretching back to the Second World War. Three young RAF airmen played in a legendary band called the Flare Path Orchestra. When a precious 78rpm record of their music turns up in the most unexpected place the Vinyl Detective finds himself hired to track down the rest of their highly sought-after recordings.

But, as he does so, he finds that the battles of the war aren't over yet—and can still prove lethal. While fighting for his life, our hero unearths dark secrets of treason and murder, and puts right a tragic miscarriage of justice. If all this sounds simple, it's only because we haven't mentioned drive-by shootings, murderous neo-Nazis, or that body in the beer barrel.

"An enthralling mystery with a wonderful gallery of grotesques." **Ben Aaronovitch**

"One of the most innovative concepts in crime fiction for many years. Once you are hooked into the world of the Vinyl Detective it is very difficult to leave."
Nev Fountain

TITANBOOKS.COM

For more fantastic fiction, author events, competitions,
limited editions and more

Visit our website
titanbooks.com

Like us on Facebook
facebook.com/titanbooks

Follow us on Twitter
@TitanBooks

Email us
readerfeedback@titanemail.com